MONTECITO

MONTECITO

For Pam and Cedric, with thanks for your kind friendship, Louise

LOUISE **S**CHWARTZ

MILL CITY PRESS

Mill City Press, Inc.
2301 Lucien Way #415
Maitland, FL 32751
407.339.4217
www.millcitypress.net

Printed in the United States of America.

ISBN-13: 978-1-54564-526-0

For Alan and Peter with Love

CHAPTER 1

January 1962

When I returned to Montecito I was racing to pull my husband back from the dead. I only knew to go get him and take him away, to where he wanted to be. He? He would not be there, only pieces of him. I promised I would scatter his ashes on his farm. In my body I knew I could not have Harry back. He was absent forever, never to talk to him, to hold him.

Driven out of London past the brick row houses, the green fields to the check-in counter, rubber floors, the clouds and blue air, flying home a widow, I saw nothing, believed nothing. Landed in Los Angeles, I sped past the landscape of my youth; the San Fernando Valley, the grade onto the Camarillo Plain and out to the coast.

Blind from tears and the reflection of the low sun the Pacific Ocean I drove the highway along the coast. The tide was high, white waves crashed across the pavement, a path eked out along the face of the highlands. I held tighter not to slide, could not let go to roll up the window. Splashed, I expected to be swept out to sea.

Up the steep hill of the Rincon, to the rows of lemon trees at Carpinteria and to Montecito, a village of gardens, home of my grandmother, place of my husband's death. When I was a child I was glad to arrive through the tall trees. Now I felt I would never be happy again. These gardens were no longer safe.

Montecito was my mother's hometown. She left as soon as she could, the village in the hills beside Santa Barbara. My grandmother Claudia Dunwoody lived in the house that my great-grandmother built in the warmth of California, she to escape Chicago, its winter. Its restrictions.

I loved the house, a solid grand place, big enough to get lost in. I used to pretend I was a princess. Will myself to be beautiful. Was there space there for me now in my room, to fight the chaos, recover. I was scared everywhere, even here I realized as I rang the bell. What would be the new reality in this old house? Would I still feel alone?

My grandmother greeted me with a hug, pressed cheeks. Her face was softer. She stood back and looked at me, without asking the questions in her eyes. Flowers from her garden filled the entry room and scented it with rose. "You've come back."

"My Emma?" She hugged me again. "You're in your rooms on the third floor. Still the nursery." We put my bags on the elevator and walked up the winding stairs. I counted the steps from habit. Could I be that girl again?

"Remember I taught you to count on these stairs? You held my hand." Now she held the handrail and leaned on the carved mahogany.

"I still count."

"I'm taking the elevator too much these days. Let me hold your hand." She kept hold of the rail. "I hoped your children would be here to stay in the nursery."

"Harry and I didn't know we had to hurry."

"Emma, I'm so sorry. You look fine. Pale, London will do that. How are you?" I heard her pity. "It is so terrible."

"That it is." I took her arm as we walked down the hall to the nursery suite. The warm blue room reminded me of who I was before the on-rushing torrent of emptiness filled my life where grief should be.

"Emma, darling?" Claudia sat in the armchair. "They say someone found him on the railroad tracks, near the Miramar." She hid her face in her hands, would not look at me. "Murder?"

I could not lean on her now, she would fall. She looked old and sad. I was young and sadder. I put my bags on the embroidered straps of the luggage racks out of the deep closet. My clothes, shoes, designed to fit in, for me to disappear, to stay alive to do what I had to do. I was in a hurry to go back to Europe.

"Will you stay?"

"I'm sorry Gran. I have to leave in a few days."

She looked up at me.

"I have to take his ashes back." Burn him, collect him and take him back to France.

"I'll let you get settled."

All I wanted to do was hold him. I knew if I started crying I would not stop. I sat at the wood drop-down cupboard – my old desk – and opened the drawers to find notes from my youth. When I stayed with my grandmother I wrote letters to my mother there and filled in a diary of daily thoughts.

"The police called. A detective's number is on the desk. Not my friend."

"How did the police know to call you, when they found him?"

"Adelino's nephew is a detective, Manuel Garcia. My gardener's sister's son. When the police found Harry, Manuel called me."

"I have to go to the police. For paperwork. And go to the mortuary."

"Why you?"

"It's my job. Wife." I had been so proud to use that word. If I saw his body would I realize what was true?

"Will we have a service?" my grandmother asked. "I can call All Saints'."

"Did he have friends here?"

I wanted to fall to the floor, wail with my hands on my face. I looked at her and wanted him. His laugh was stilled. His body was in a box, his face, his chest, his arms. Why did I think I could stand for it? I opened the window into the rain. "No memorial. They did that in New York."

"How was that?"

"I was not invited. Friends told me."

She was shocked, hand over mouth. She stood and patted my hair. "So unkind. You rest, dear. Dinner is at 7." Her hand was strong on my shoulder, comfort meant to be bracing. I could not rise.

"Forgive me I won't come down for dinner. Too tired"

Asleep until morning, I rolled over to a darkened room and slept past noon. I called the police number from the card, horrified. I needed to stay alive to do what I promised to do.

Claudia drove me into Santa Barbara to the Police Station. I did not see the day, the sea, the courthouse. I was burning with anger and grief, scenery no distraction.

Detective Martin, elderly, straight-backed, dyed black hair sat behind his desk. "Your husband was found next to the railroad tracks by a man walking his dog. We identified him through his clothes. Labels–"

I choked and he paused. He looked at his hands, not at me. I still did not cry. My Harry in the dirt, like war dead. Alone, in his fine clothes.

"The shoes," he said, reaching for the file. Did he smirk? He looked at the papers. "Lobb. They had him on file in London. Then Detective Garcia knew your family."

He looked at me with the first apparent curiosity. Who I was married to was my business. How my husband ended up dead on this force's watch was one more question for his in-basket, I thought then. But why did this Garcia know us? I did not say.

"Where were you four days ago?" he asked.

"Is that when it happened?" What was I doing when he left his body, left my Earth and me here alone. Was I walking the London streets?

"I was in London."

"Were you separated?" We were apart more often. Harry said it was temporary, our careers needed building.

"No. I had work in London so Harry came to Santa Barbara without me to consult with a client." And now he was dead. I came too late.

"Did your husband wear rings?"

"On his little finger, left hand," I answered. "Why?"

"His fingers were gone. Possible robbery motive."

No fingers? I gasped. "Someone cut off his fingers?" Finally my eyes cried long tears and I let them fall, shaking.

"Don't know. We'll stop now. Please sign this. If you think of anything let me know." He put a paper in front of me.

"After you sign, you take charge of the remains. Hader Mortuary has the body. They'll release him to you."

Release him, like the doves flying from a furled net. Rise, his soul a carrier pigeon, without any message from me. We were still angry but I kissed him goodbye before he went out to the car for the airport. I knew his lips that last once more.

I found my grandmother on a bench at the courthouse lawn, a stack of pink pastry boxes beside her, a scarf over her head. She felt like my guardian; she would stay with me now and forever, strong or weakening, she was with me.

"Finished? What next?"

"That's the question."

"You can stop with me, Emma. Rest, before you take on the future." My grandmother, who seemed to me so old that I did not picture her with a future, might take me in and share her present with me.

I only knew the past. I had to go to France, to hide my grief from that California sun and rain.

The mortuary was up the main street in Santa Barbara. My grandmother waited outside the small room. Harry lay on a shiny wood table in a borrowed box. He wanted to become ashes. I wanted to see him first. Open casket, he was there, his eyes closed, make-up on, he did look like wax. I couldn't believe it, my husband, wax, his warm smooth skin. Aghast, I touched his forehead and felt a cold that told me he was gone from this box. There was no reason to look for him there. I knew the deep cold of my husband's head from cooking dead meat. I knelt so I did not have to see him not there. What was I to do? Harry's hands were in his pockets.

I left Santa Barbara to keep my promise to my husband that I would scatter his ashes in the orchard of his beloved Perigord farm. First step, I flew down the coast to Los Angeles, over land curving with the sea, roads small through the mountains, a tanker lacing the water. Glad to be leaving. I hated Montecito for taking Harry. I felt betrayed. And afraid. If I came back to Montecito it would be to find my husband's fingers.

CHAPTER 2

I flew the box over, direct to Paris, in my old carry-on. Burnt up, he was there at my feet. I never said goodbye. I stared at the world like the enemy. In Montecito I was pulled out of time, yanked into the West that took my Harry. Sun when it should be night. Now I returned to my body's time. Going home, to see who was still there. I felt Harry would be.

I drove out to the Perigord country, daring trucks to kill me. I didn't stay in the chateau he bought before we were married. I couldn't test the rooms of my husband's house for the new reality. Was I still there? Harry proposed to me there, I think because I loved it all too. I loved to open the house, push out the shutters, fold them back, fling sheets off the furniture, and fold them with him in the sun and the dancing motes, clip boughs for the vases, start the fire in the kitchen.

After the long drive from Paris I checked into the hotel in the medieval town near our farm. The routine comforted me. My passport, signatures. No one in a hotel knows where changes have come, a hotel always changes and my world shattering was another regular day for the little stuffy place on the river.

I carried him in the best fishing bag I could find in his closet in the Paris flat. I walked along the river out past the town in the light of the early winter twilight, looking for a fishing hole, for a promising eddy, pretending I would stop to fish. I ate alone, ashes above me in the room.

Awake, I lay crying through the blue night into the grey morning, the box in the window, as if his ashes could smell the Perigord dawn. On the terrace for coffee, wrapped for warmth, the box in the bag on the cold metal table, I stared at the muddy river water, the sun rising pink, the ducks and their wake. Alone again. I could feel inklings of my new world. I stood to leave, francs on the table. Those glimpses into the depths made me flee from eyeing myself in the future. With the detachment of a mad woman I walked the cobblestones to my car and contemplated the tragedy, the mystery of my husband's death. Murder, so unfair. So violent. What does his spirit do?

I drove through the fern forests and up the alley of big trees, their strong branches bare, arching over the dirt road that led to Harry's chateau. When I parked I sat and looked at my hands, my rings on the wheel as the thick mist of the French winter countryside drifted toward me.

I loved my rings, like pets. Harry gave me a gold band and a sapphire and diamond ring for our marriage. The colors, the facets of light, took me in, comforted me. I saw into them and escaped. I saw Harry in my life. Delusion. I had only his precious gifts. I would watch my fingers age around them. Pass them on? Not to Harry's children. Were cold jewels all I was to have left of him?

Harry left me the house in France, his chateau, a very big house, not with towers. French windows onto a park, shutters closed for the winter and his absence. No longer always cold and drafty–Harry put in heaters,

9

and plumbing. None of the old French furniture was left as the Revolutionaries burned most of it and the family took the rest when they sold to Harry. Harry furnished his chateau like an American country home–comfortable, and indestructible. Except for the leaking roof.

The park was his joy. There I would scatter him, ashes in the cherry trees. Where there would be blossoms, there I was to leave him forever. Until the wind came, rain, bugs. I shuddered. Harry chose for me, the idea of ashes instead of a slab of ground or a drawer with a plaque. We had hoped not to think of these choices until we were very old with little else to think about. But Harry let me know this much.

We stayed in France all summer unless he was working, with visitors in August, many meals.

Harry had escaped his world. His family was wealthy, and he used his brains, his art and his drive to transcend them and their vision of his life and their plans for him. He was architect first, then friend and host. Generous host, though he had the rich man's affectation of penury. Were we a pair because I could pay my own airfare and buy for the house in the Perigord? Our Dutch-treat life seemed natural to me. When we were just friends I paid my share, and I continued after we married.

Now I think Harry married me to stop his family from asking him when he would marry.

The dogs; the tenants would keep them. The dogs came to greet me at the car, curious, looking for more. They walked with me, ranged and looked for Harry. So did I. Around a tree, down a path.

Harry loved those black dogs as much as he loved me. More, I joked to myself, when they were out and I alone. Harry communicated with them, with kisses and secret talks by the fire and on long jaunts across the French countryside. They'd all come back muddy and tired to dinner with me, cooked by the tenant's wife. Local pate, stews and confit, tarts and local cheeses, mixed for the dogs. As I saw the weight go on, I insisted on joining Harry and his dogs on a few walks. He talked to the running dogs with whistles. We walked for miles, to explore and to deserve our meals.

As I walked into the formal garden, the dogs roamed ahead in the patterns, black movement between the green. I remembered our wedding. Floating through the geometry of hedges. A civil service before the mayor in the village and, at a party for his friends at the chateau, a surprise ceremony under a woven lily bower with an American minister from Paris. Harry chose my dress, invited the designer and all his friends for a summer party and surprised our guests with the wedding in the garden. He paraded me before them, happy and proud. I was in a dream.

When he called his parents—father and step-mother—on our wedding day, he was bragging. They seemed shocked. Not because they weren't invited and hadn't met me, though they hadn't. "We didn't think Harry would marry. Well I never did, Lloyd," his stepmother handed over the phone. Mr. Chase got on the line, "Congratulations, Emma, Let me talk to the sneaky bastard."

"We should not have called at cocktail hour," was all Harry said after he hung up, hugged me and pulled me out to the dance floor, train trailing, flowers falling—all in love.

How he would have hated that I was the only one walking him through the chambers of his garden in the wet grass to the orchard. I should have thrown a party, used one of his ideas–one of his transporting fantasies for a send-off he deserved. I asked our friends. But Harry was gone, why should they come? For me and the ashes? I forgave the Europeans their world-weariness and self-concern. The Californians, movie people, they were busy, too far away. The New Yorkers probably couldn't decide if the weekend would be amusing, what to pack. His parents stayed away. They disapproved, they wanted him under stone in the frozen ground in their town.

Determined to be an elegant widow wading through the grass, I wore my Hermes jodpers that he talked me into buying when we were first married, loose as they had never been when he was alive. Lobb boots, we ordered ours together in London. He died in his. I stumbled. A damp morning like that, he would have worn his green rubber boots. I heard him say 'galoshes' with his rolling American tongue. I wished for him, his arm around me under the fairy umbrellas of the flowering plums, not to be alone in bare branches and wind. My promised errand. Would I walk out of there again? I felt I could unhinge and fly off the world, disappear. How would I spend the rest of my life if each moment could be my last?

At the side of the hill I threw out a rug, sat with the dogs, opened the box and waited for him to fly out, catch the wind and leave. What a grizzly, lonely job. Awkward, shaking out a dead fire, few ashes for such a big blaze as was my husband. His body that I claimed in life, these small remnants, I poured into the winter orchard, the garden he created, asleep. I talked to him, refusing to believe these grey specks were him, but talking none the less. Widow things. You can't leave me like this. What will I do without you? Will I never see you again? What happened?

I rubbed the dogs for goodbye, crying. "I'll return soon to fix the roof. Yours too."

"Thank you Madame. We have to use many pots in both houses." They stood at attention with the dogs swirling around them.

I drove away and did not look back.

Back at the hotel in the medieval town I ordered dinner on the little river, too much wine, a slab of foie gras, duck, chocolate cake, and picked at the food. Would I eat and sleep alone forever? I felt like the world was new and very far away. My life had exploded. I was set loose, adrift. Now I had to schedule for myself only, choose and find a life. I needed to find a way to want something –to earn money, to find out about Harry's death.

Oblivious to the trucks, heedless of the plateaus and mountains, I drove back the next day to Paris. Dirty stone bridges of aching loveliness over the brown Seine, rusty metal fences along the bridges where women in spike heels, pointed toes, full skirts, coats with lapels and gloves crossed the Pont Neuf. Trucks parked and men unloaded boxes like half coffins. Flower vendors sat in coats and scarves, leaves everywhere. Unpainted follies in the park. Stone walls, stone steps to the entry, metal open elevator up to our apartment and a view across Paris to the church steeples. I had thought Paris was my home. Now it was too grey, too foreign.

Alone in our apartment, I gave in, crying, screaming, rending my brow, pacing until I lost the energy for noise and curled into myself, like an erupted volcano, surrounded by my own grey lifelessness, alone in desolation.

The next day the telephone called me out of my stupor. "C'est Pierre a l'aparail. Mon amie, you're in Paris. Come here. I'll meet you outside." I knew Pierre before Harry. He was married. He said he loved me and stroked my cheek. He told me to find a husband and stopped taking me for long lunches and more. A tall Huguenot, he did not want to hurt me and backed away as he saw me want him more. He told me that he would never divorce. He had ideas for projects for me, so I would have a future. A gentleman, he knew he could provide me with none.

His excitement and insistence jolted me from my sorrowful stupor. "Put on your coat and scarf and take the Metro to the Musee. Meet me now."

I obeyed, walked to the Metro, passed under the art deco arch to go underground. The train, leather seats, glass and wood, rattled me to my stop.

Pierre met me on the street and kissed my cheeks hello. He punched in the code and led me through the courtyard and up the winding stairs.

"Tell me more?" I was curious at his excitement.

"Wait." The door was tall and carved with garlands.

"We have found treasures from California, from Santa Barbara. Your home isn't it?"

Was it?

"We found them in the caverns of the Museum of Man. Ignored. Lost." Pierre rejoined his associates at the wooden boxes, packed with hay.

His team unwrapped baskets of originality and order so finely done, some caulked with burnt tar, baskets meant for the fire or for carrying water I know now. Then when I knew so much less I saw only lovely designs, shell inlay, quill outline. Feathers. How could they keep their color when their creature was so long dead?

They were boxes of tools, riches of a civilization I was to intersect on the bluffs and the beaches of Montecito. The town of my husband's murder.

A young woman with a plain crush on Pierre came over: "Where are the journals? Where is the research?"

"Keep looking."

"What will happen to them?" I asked him.

"They'll be catalogued and stored again. One day we will have the space to show them." He was still so handsome and French. And married.

So was I, widowed counts as married, just lost. "Who was the collector?"

"de Cessac, an acquisitive French explorer in 1850. I remembered it is your hometown. Aren't they remarkable?" He held my back with the flat of his big hand. I felt safe

"Your husband died?" he asked me as he walked me out, my arm in the crook of his elbow.

"Murdered."

"Good God!" He dropped my arm. "By who? Why? You will find out when you go back?"

How did he know I would go back? "Will I?"

"Look into De Cessac when you return to Santa Barbara. We found his boxes but no journals." He pressed his cheeks hard against mine as we left each other.

I felt lucky and cursed to have been in the room with the boxes full of the past. Was it Pierre who propelled me into my future?

Brasserie Lipp on Sunday afternoon, the white aproned waiter led me up the stairs to a small table with a view. I was glad to be exiled to the first floor. From there I planned to see the elegant man who recommended Harry for his job in Montecito. What did he know? We had met at dinner parties, but I could not call him and expect him to remember me. My plan was to run into him.

Knees under the white cloth, I could see down to M. de Vlamnick, in tweed for a weekend on the Left Bank. Chic Parisians in forest green and brown stopped at his table to say bonjour. For a few men he stood and bowed, a kind of salute. For a few women he stood, lifted their hand and mock kissed the back.

This small man with a strong nose was a Paris friend of Harry's. He was not at our wedding, nor at the weekends that followed.

I passed his table and stopped, as if I'd just seen him. "M. de Vlamnick, it is Emma Chase."

"Of course." He stood and took my hand to faux-kiss. "It is a pleasure to meet you." He dropped my hand slowly.

"Thank you. Monsieur," How did I say it? "I need to ask you about my husband's client in Santa Barbara."

"Montecito. Of course. I may offer you dinner tomorrow night? La Closerie des Lilas?"

"Thank you, yes."

"We can talk then."

He had reserved a table on the glass covered patio of the restaurant. Nervous, determined, I was early. I studied the metal jointed supports for the awning until he arrived, hat wet, shoes polished.

Starting with champagne, a toast and eye contact with his very brown irises over the bubbles, he ordered our dinner. We spoke of mutual acquaintances, the weather for gardening, my plans for Harry's property. He owned a farm near-by I learned. He did not mention murder, nor did I.

"Tell me who is the man Harry worked for in California? "

"Walter Skeffington?" He looked far off, then back at me. "I've known him for years. Art collector. Among other things." He sipped his wine. "He needed an architect for a museum. But not for his art, I heard."

"Harry said it was to be a library. How do you know Mr. Skeffington?"

"From the South. San Tropez. The Skeff I knew had many interests. We were young together. We were friends in the old days. He had a house in Antibes. We don't see each other much anymore, but I knew he would appreciate Harry." Said without the H. And a smile. "Why do you ask me about Skeff?"

"He was my husband's –Harry's last client. Harry was there." Couldn't he see?

He leaned over the table to me, looked me in the eyes, his eyes intent, and said "Do not think you can solve Harry's murder. It will only make you unhappy, more unhappy."

Who was he to say this to me? How dare he? I turned my fork over – finished with this dinner. "How do you know?"

"I know many things." He motioned to the aproned man with the pad. "You'll never find out. Things like that just happen there."

I choked swallowing. "In Montecito?"

"Yes."

"Everywhere I suppose," I said to take his focus off me, off my forming the idea to go back to Montecito to follow Harry's last steps.

"How did you know Harry?"

"Before you came. From the club." He smiled. I was afraid of his smile. "Join me for an after dinner drink? I'll take you to our club."

I had not intruded in Harry's life from before we were married and I thought I knew him. I assumed I had a lifetime of him to learn more.

"I will join you," I said, feeling the challenge.

I rode with M. de Vlamnick to the club. His driver who parked on the sidewalk waited in the car. I felt safe as an anthropologist, an archeologist, just visiting. I followed de Vlamnick on the path where Harry led me. Into darkness and cruelty, beauty and art. One culture I had seen unpacked that morning, then I was headed into another.

We walked down steps into a bar in a cave club under arched stone walls. In the dim light, tables surrounded a square dais, lit by spotlights. On it were naked women and a whip. The only sound was the whip and flesh. I winced and wanted to plug my ears. It was not loud. Seated I could hear de Vlamnick murmur over whip sounds then sultry screams. He faced the light. His eyes watched the show, not me, then me. He was curious.

"Why did you bring me here?" I asked.

"To open your eyes."

"Harry came here?"

"Often." He looked to see my reaction.

"When did you see Harry last?"

"Here before he left for California, in passing." He drank his champagne. "This fall, Harry missed some times. To be out there – California? I guess he needs the work– you Americans like work." He looked up as a handsome man came over and joined us. This young man drank a shot of whiskey like a cowboy, looking around then into the eyes of M. de Vlamnick and over to me. It was time for me to leave, his eyes told me. I was afraid to be there, my first reasonable fear following Harry's path.

"What will you do next?"

I lied with no answer and looked at him to say I would not tell him.

The show started again. This time the whips wrapped around a couple copulating, necks arched back.

"A fall to remember." The young man laughed. De Vlamnick continued. "Prefect Papon made it easy for us. We would drag the CIV camps for men. For boys. And use them until they died," he whispered to me. The young man squirmed. With pleasure.

"CIV Camps?" I avoided the real question. Used? Died?

"Centre Identification de Vincennes– just a name. Papon's police rounded up Algerians, all who looked Algerian, into detention. Our opportunity, like '58. We came to like Algerian boys. Too much dark meat perhaps.

You don't want to know, do you?"

"I must go."

"Finish your wine." I toasted back with a fearless look into his eyes. I did not know enough to be afraid. Now I do. Who was this man I met with Harry at the motor races? Surely he must have spoken in metaphor. I was still a sheltered thinker with no imagination of such a world. I thought I was protected by my innocence. Now I quail at the horror.

It was soon dawn. I walked on cobblestones, bricks and stairs, by stone walls, big posters for jazz. Cars parked, streets empty, lights off. Leaves everywhere, men in blue with cord brooms sweeping water and leaves down to the gutters. In the bird market I passed an eagle, brown, too big, head pressed against its cage.

Home to a kitchen of propane burners, wood cabinets nailed to the wall, shelf with a rod for hangers for Harry's suits in the back bedroom. Silver radiator, long mirrors on the armoire doors, Herald Examiners from the news kiosk, American news on the tables.

I packed up, gave the key to the concierge and flew to New York and direct to Los Angeles. On my way back to Santa Barbara, to Montecito.

Had my eyes been opened? Who was this man I loved and married? I was angry at him, for dying and for hiding, for being more than he showed me, more than I knew. Would I find him in Montecito?

CHAPTER 3

I arrived in daylight and looked around me. Los Angeles, flat city next to the sea, was a stranger to me. The streets were shiny and wet, the skies broken open to blue, between storms,–one over Catalina Island and one over the northern mountains.

I rented a car that smelled of American cigarettes, a car as big as a room in Paris. It drove like the cars I was used to being driven in, like a boat with slow reactions, big and heavy with no power steering. Adjusting the mirror I started for Montecito. I wound along Sepulveda Boulevard beside bulldozers on bare land, a new highway through the pass. The San Fernando Valley was horse farms with picket fences between lines of citrus groves out to the oak-dotted hills of the Malibu mountains. It had rained and the landscape was in intense green, waking up, green, not yet sliding.

This was the ride of my vacations, visits to my grandmother, sometimes for school. To a part of me Montecito was home. I wanted it to be my home – to deserve the beauty. Then Harry took me away and gave me more.

In the next valley in the eucalyptus trees of the movie zoo I saw the long necks of giraffes and the humped backs of elephants. I could pretend to be on vacation, my grandmother waiting.

21

Immersed in the presence and absence of the past with no idea of a future, I coasted down the Conejo Grade, no brakes, so faster and faster in the heavy car on to the farm fields and to the ocean at Ventura. I took the Pacific Coast Highway along the water to Montecito.

I was back to chase Harry's ghost. I wanted to grab it, keep it with me as I left for my new life. Harry died here, I thought as I left the highway and curved up to my grandmother's. Murdered in Montecito. I would not forgive the town. But I was here, with no place else to go, with no other purpose.

I drove over the gravel and parked beside the hedge. A maid met me at the door with a basket of wet lemons and oranges and pointed the way. My grandmother was in her library.

"The US has declared an embargo on Cuba." Claudia turned away from the radio to meet me with a real smile. I kissed her cheek and she patted my shoulder. "The Pope excommunicated Castro last month."

"Why?" We talked about politics, the outside world, not the personal. Better this than questions, concern. Still beautiful, softer along the chin, I loved her with a child's love. What could I tell her? I was suddenly very tired and wanted to sit.

"I suppose it's because Castro's Communist. No matter. He's better than that Batista. I'll ring for tea." She did, pressing the floor beside her chair with her toe. Soon the maid was there carrying silver service and cookies.

"I'll pour, Graciella. Emma, you'll stay a few more days this time? I can show you the gardens." Claudia Dunwoody, my mother's mother, watched me as she poured through a silver salver. She thought it proper that I had come back to the gardens of my youth. Maybe she thought I could be young again, spend my days walking and dreaming on the paths. Rediscover my way. She didn't see the hole in my soul, filling with hatred. Those dreams had come true, then were stolen from me. I came as the enemy to spy on the town that killed my husband.

"You rest tomorrow. Richard will return your car. The barn is full, I could never sell an old car. I retire them like horses. The trip wasn't too bad? You saw friends over there?"

None. I shook my head. Oh god, what was I to do? To stop the swirling.

"Was it better that way?" Maybe it was. "Tell me darling, are you all right?"

"It's like icy water. It hurts so much and then you go numb."

Claudia asked "Do you need money dear?"

I knew she did not have much cash, just the little bit her mother left that was doled out by men in Chicago.

"Not right away. I have to figure it out."

"Well, you can stay here, for a little while." She drank her tea and nibbled on a cookie. "I'll have to put the dogs down before I die. They'll have no life without me. Unless you want to move back, live here? But you don't want to do that."

Was I welcome here, in my only home? Claudia did not want me to stay, I could feel it.

"You've escaped. Stay away darling."

"Don't you like it here?"

"I love it. But I haven't been very productive in my quiet life. You're adventurous – you can do it for both of us. Don't get stuck here by the beauty."

So she did not want me to move in with her, become her companion in her old age. I had to get a job. Sell things? The house and farm in France? The mirror collection, men's bespoke suits?

I had to fix the roof to sell the house in France. Could I bear to sell it? I longed to go to the big rooms, find Harry in the corners, in the armoire we swore to each other we one day would climb into and through the door. He did not keep his promise. He went through the door here, under these trees, on the ocean. Where did I find that door? What would it avail me to find it? Was there anything on the other side for me?

I was still so startled to be left alone.

"Where else to go" I asked myself out loud.

"Back to France?"

"Yes. I think the house is mine. The trust is gone, back to his family, so the apartment will go.

"I need to stay here Gran, for a pause from everything that is out there."

"Of course Emma. There is plenty of room" She saw the despair in my seriousness.

"If I can, I need to find work, save money –"

"Do you have friends to call while you're here?" Claudia asked.

I was still thrown by a time limit on my visit. "I'll think."

"Friends will make you feel better."

"I'll be better if I find out what happened." Did I really think so? Why? I needed a purpose. "To start with the basics – Harry was here to design a museum in the hills for Walter Skeffington."

"Skeff?"

"You know him?'"

"I did. He has lived here forever, like me– Another cookie?" she held up the plate.

"Tell me more– I want to see him."

"I will, darling. He's an old man around town. You'll meet him." Claudia was ready to move on, tea over. "A detective called while you were gone. His number is on your desk." Gran stood. "Emma, be a dear, come to dinner with me?"

"OK? Where?" Did I have to dress, talk to people?

"They're giving me a plate at the Valley Club. I could use your moral support."

"A plate?"

"A trophy. Please." She acted embarrassed but she was watchful, light for my sake. Her husband had died young. Didn't she know her mirth could not reach me?

I wished I could have been the young girl I once was, come to visit the West with dreams of the future ahead.

"I know you're tired. Mr. Skeffington may be there –"

"I'll go dress." She took my arm as we walked out of the windowed room in the rain.

I stripped in my high bedroom and watched the Santa Cruz Island mountains that floated above the sea like the world was folded. With the trees taller I couldn't see if there was surf at the beach. We listened for the waves when I was a girl and, by the sound, and by the view from this floor checked the size of the break. Maria and me, one friend I could call.

Home again, naked for the shower, I stood under the water and thought of what had brought me here this time. Not my mother dropping me off. This was my life. My recent life was a wandering one. My husband the architect, when he moved to a project site, I visited. We vacationed on schedule with sport: the shoot, the hunt, fishing, riding, sailing, skiing. Harry helped me be loved and I helped him be organized, made his life smooth. Packing and unpacking, I was along like a good suitcase, useful, portable. As Harry designed the mansions and gardens, private pleasure parks, I read books from neglected libraries and found work organizing them.

Harry left for California and I went to Claridges. I felt he had another woman and had lost interest in me. My grandmother called me in London to say Harry was found murdered in Santa Barbara. I followed him, too late. And now I was alone again.

Before the allee of big eucalyptus trees was a long driveway to the golf club that was more East Coast than the East Coast, with its china bug-eyed dogs, its leather padded fire bumpers. We arrived late and went straight to the table of my grandmother's golfing buddies, cheerful and robust, still the young friends of their youth. Full of dread, I sat with my grandmother and looked for Mr. Skeffington.

My grandmother, tall and thin in her tweed suit, sat with her hands folded as the program started. She was not happy. One of her goals in life was to avoid being the center of attention. She was more than reserved, she was anti-social, except for golf. She would barely speak. I checked the crowd, couples in their seventies, some in matching blazers, telling one another who we were. At a table of younger golfers, laughing, drinks raised for a toast was an animated handsome man who whispered to an overdressed pretty woman. Across from him was a man, my age, young for that crowd but looking eclipsed, almost middle aged, dark blonde hair cut short, face serious. The laughing man was blonder and tan.

Gran leaned over to me. "I'm tempted to split this popstand." I knew she could flee. She had me with her to anchor her there in the center of that noisy room.

She stared at me, focusing, willing me to take her away. Then her friend on the other side began a conversation.

My boredom quickly became misery. I tried to keep tears from my eyes, despair from my face. The serious man at the loud table looked like some strange fate had stuck him there and he was plotting his escape. He looked familiar, probably a type, I thought, happy boy who grows up to be a lawyer, had not yet let his body go but his cheer was dribbling away.

The man at the podium called Gran up for the trophy. She ignored everybody as she walked to the front. She said a firm thank you to her partners and to the greens keepers, took the silver plate and began a slow trip through her friends in the room.

I excused myself and fled outside onto the patio overlooking the golf course that was cut out of old citrus orchards; now lawns and greens between old oaks. Thick stars lit the night scented by eucalyptus. The sea's dampness on the wind chilled me before I wanted to go back inside.

I didn't know what life I would have without Harry. The people in that overly cozy room had golf as a constant. What would be mine? It had been my marriage, the warm spoon body and arm hung over me at night. An owl dropped from a tree, feet out.

How would I live? I was panicked. I had no schedule, no appointments for tomorrow, no one who cared about me, so I how could I trust that the next day would come. It was entirely floating, waiting to be realized.

Could I really search for the murderer? Return the call from a private detective in Los Angeles? Call the policeman friend of my grandmother? What did I know? I knew the name of Harry's last client. Walter Skeffington.

I felt I was as alone out on that patio as I was in life. I started to walk. It was dark except for the Milky Way. I almost fell.

"Watch out for that branch" a man said. I swear he tripped me, caught me and set me back on my feet. "Gregory Lowell here. Good thing I was here to catch you."

"You tripped me!"

"No."

"I stumbled?" What a thing to say. I minded that he had tripped me and lied about it. Not enough to say it. Well trained. He was handsome enough I guessed he assumed I would not make a scene.

"You're visiting, Mrs. Chase?" How did he know my name?

"Here with my grandmother." That's all I cared to share.

"I'll walk you back. I know where the path is."

I heard the high yips of coyotes.

"You're afraid." Greg put his arm around me.

"No." I moved out of his arms. Who was this presumptuous man?

Every story has a start. This was Greg, the laughing man from inside. I felt a beginning. I should have known I was entering this tale in the middle, late.

With the smooth steps of an athlete, he stayed by my side. "I've been waiting to meet you. You golf?"

So that was why he'd pounced. "No." I had been playing bad golf since I was a child. But I had no wish to be polite nor to regain touch with the world.

We came back to the light of the patio. Younger than me, tall, very tan in grey flannels and blue blazer, he held out his soft hand. He stared at me as if he recognized me and knew a secret of mine. His eyes flashed from some interesting place with a liveliness that wasn't humor, but was attractive.

"I know who you are," he said. "You're Emma Chase. Are you a merry widow or a black widow?"

What did he ask? Widow, a word I had not accepted.

"You don't know it yet but you have great power. I can see it." People talked like that here? Gregory Lowell did.

"As beautiful as your grandmother. I know her too," he said. "She's a good golfer." He looked inside the window. He didn't seem to expect me to say anything, and kept talking as if glad I had no responses. "Better than I am. She and my father. That generation have the concentration for it."

"Is that it?"

"And the time to play. I have to join my party. I'll know how to find you," he said, leaving, back into the dark.

Through the window my grandmother was next to our table looking for me. I went back in.

"Congratulations, Gran."

"All that time on the greens, I should be this good." Gran collected her alligator bag, ready to join me in a quick exit.

As we walked to the lower blacktop lot in the darkness of the Montecito night, I saw a man in the oak trees and was reminded.

"A man came up to me tonight," I didn't want to think that was weird, or worth commenting on, but I was curious. "Gregory Lowell. He said he knew you."

"I knew his uncle and his father. When we were children. Montecito was small then."

"When?"

"In the Twenties. When we came out on the train, with our mothers to escape the Chicago winter. They were the Lowell brothers, also from Chicago."

"Brothers?"

"Charles and George Lowell. That man's father and uncle. Their mother was a social friend of my mother. We were put together a lot."

"Do you know Greg?"

"No. George, his father, was not my favorite. The son seems too handsome to me. I've heard stories." More than that she did not tell me then.

Why didn't I ask? I felt these people meant nothing to me.

"Was Mr. Skeffington there?"

"No. Sorry. Will you drive Emma? Let's put the top down. I want to watch the stars."

Claudia rested her head on the seat and the stars of the Milky Way in the navy blue flashed by in the trees. Greg Lowell, he knew who I was. Was the town that small? Was I the talk of the Valley Club? That world seemed too far from murder to have my story known.

Home again, high on the third floor I pressed my forehead on the cold window listening to the crickets, feeling my childhood lost and my self gone. I reclaimed my grief and forgot the physical pull I felt from the too handsome Greg Lowell. I stared at the familiar yet always strange face in the mirror, my feet cold in the tiled bathroom. Checking in, my regard searching in that face to see who was there. Those eyes, that I only sometimes noticed were blue, and I had looked at each other for years- in mirrors, windows, water. I used to look for where I came from, then who I was. Now I looked for someone to be there, for a sign that I knew how to go on. The end of love, the end of a life together.

Then you're just done for: a water balloon, turning somersaults, leaking water; dough unkneading itself into a raggedy strip.

I washed and lay on the cool sheets until the weariness of the night dragged me under.

CHAPTER 4

On the balcony in my slip at dawn, longing for sleep, my body didn't believe it was supposed to wake. Rain again, pouring down thick, I was soaked and freezing, but I stayed there hanging on to the branch of a live oak tree that arched up as tall as the house. Down the long hill the Pacific Ocean under the storm clouds was invisible. A gardener walked onto the lawn from a side path, under a wet hat.

Where was the sun? There had been hard rain for days. Everything was new green and almost visibly growing. I went back inside, dripping.

The bell rang on the old black phone, my grandmother calling from the breakfast room. "Coming soon darling? I have tea and coffee. Eggs for you?"

"Morning Gran. I'll be there."

I wanted to sleep all day, get back into bed and stay under the blankets for weeks, until I forgot or my life changed. And stay up all night so I wouldn't dream. I didn't want to have to show up for a regular breakfast.

Skirt and sweater, loafers and a scarf, I was dressed and on the stairs before my eyes cleared.

Claudia, her hair combed back into a loose chignon, sat in her robe in the breakfast room. The newspaper was read, and refolded at my place. I kissed her soft cheek and sat beside her, took the wood handled silver pot and poured coffee. From the long meals of my childhood I knew the pale yellow silk wallpaper, the mountains, pagodas, ladies trailing patterned cloth, men riding horses, willows over rivers, fish jumping, storks flying. I felt the sensation I had in that room when I was a child–that I traveled among those adventurers on the walls. The color seeped into the air so it seemed to wave across my arms and out the windows to where I longed to go. I was one of those adventurers, born to it, I was not a sleeper, an avoider.

Fury at the thought that a person took Harry from me, that a person hurt him so much. Was he dead before they mutilated him?

I willed myself, for my grandmother''s sake, to keep the peace, to settle next to her, to accept the regularity of toast from a silver rack, to find comfort in the beautiful room and the morning sun. My grandmother watched me butter and salt my bread the French way. "Ah, the French influence. Cuba is scaring me. I don't have friends there anymore. I'm out of touch."

I needed to read the paper. Cuba?

"What do you do today, dear?" Claudia was clear: I needed a schedule. And breakfast, for every day. She was probably right. So I didn't fly off the earth, lost, so I didn't run too hard into a danger I couldn't contemplate. She was setting the rules, to check up on me before she left for her day of golf, garden, or charity work.

"Maybe nothing, really nothing. I'll walk in the garden. I haven't been down yet." Maybe I was going to the police station to hound the detectives. "I'll unpack. Settle in for my visit."

She would not let me stay, especially if I told her that I was determined to find Harry's murderer. In truth, I wanted a reason to live, and the guilty one. I needed to

33

find the last traces, his last trails. Could I find Harry's ghost there, catch him to stay with me, for his company? Neither answer was acceptable to my grandmother.

"Maybe call the private detective," I added.

"I suppose you must?" Claudia had a careful world with its own inhabitants and I assumed private detectives were not a part of it. My grandmother was a calm beauty who you felt did you a favor by letting you look at her. When I was a child being with her made the time seem better, like being with Harry as an adult.

"I'm curious. Detective Martin is your friend at the police? "

"Martin?" Claudia's mouth showed her distaste.

"You know him?" So police were part of her life.

"He has been around a long time."

"Is that a good thing? He's in charge."

"Of what?" Claudia asked.

"Harry's murder case."

"They're sure it was murder?"

"What else?"

"Suicide?" Blame the victim. I sighed. She didn't know the gruesome details. Harry couldn't have done that to himself.

"Isn't that worse, Gran? Sadder."

"But then we know, that means there's not a murderer among us."

"Someone took Harry's fingers."

"Oh no. So it really was murder." She looked at me me shocked. Of course. "Adelino's nephew, Detective Garcia. Try to get him to help."

Why did she have an opinion of murder detectives? She recovered by gazing on me fondly. She meant to be kind.

"You're glad to be back?"

"I think so. I miss France. The country." I didn't know if Paris would ever be the same to me. I knew there was an underbelly to Paris, but now I'd seen it, felt it, the dirty city on top was only grey and dank.

"Have you heard from Harry's family?"

Father, stepmother and half brothers I'd met once when they came to the Perigord for a short visit. "They threw their grenades and withdrew."

"What?" She looked confused, beginning to anger, pink cheeks.

"His family blames me. To them I was Montecito. I lured him here and let him die. Alone. I failed them and him."

"That's ridiculous." Gran was sharp. It just made me sad. I blamed myself too. "What did they say?"

"His father won't speak to me. His stepmother told me not to come to the memorial in Manhattan."

"For heaven's sake, why be so cruel?"

"She said I had no right to walk as his widow. We married without the family. I would only cause gossip and upset his father." Gran shook her head, angry.

"They lose too much by losing you," Gran said. "Tragedies echo."

"You can hear it?" I asked, thinking it was some terrible song.

"They do," she answered. "My husband, your grandfather who never knew you, died young, here, in a polo match. His family never forgave me."

"Harry was murdered," I said.

"There's not a big difference. My husband, a horse, yours a man – the killer is eventually irrelevant."

Maybe to her. I poured myself more coffee, I watched the milk swirl around itself. Revenge, to get me going, make me live to learn what happened.

"I'm in the garden today. I have to get ready for my mason's inspection. Adelino. He comes tomorrow. He built our walls. Adelino is Detective Garcia's uncle." Gran said. "It is our yearly ritual. I'll ask him."

We ate in silence then. Orange juice and toast. Eggs scrambled for me. The cook brought them from the kitchen.

"Tell me about Walter Skeffington," I asked.

"We were good friends." My grandmother sounded like a girl, sad. "Maybe I could call him for you."

"I tried. I've left messages with his house man. He's out of town."

"Does he owe Harry money?"

"I don't know."

"Dear, he was fair always. Funny thing to be so strong in a boy, a sense of fairness. He'll give you whatever he owes."

That's not why I wanted to meet him. I thought he could have killed Harry. That I did not say.

"How was he your friend?"

"From our winters here. Months together. Days across the plains on the train from Chicago, then here. We had adventures, discussions. So young. We were great friends really. Now I haven't seen him for years. Harry was here to design a library for him?" She paused to watch a bird in the rain. She looked sad again. "He's probably forgotten me."

"What happened?"

"The old secret is that he's inclined toward men not women. That didn't matter when we were children, of course. Later it did. Then there were rumors."

"Rumors?"

"Of bad behavior. Briefly. He left town and when he came back he wasn't seen or heard from. Except on

36

museum boards. He waved to me, bowed, smiled at our aging. And I'd smile back, feeling the folds of skin, the tightening expressions. The acceptance of disappointment. But that's too much on age for you. Don't worry about that. Or me, dear. Take care of yourself. Get out of this place. I wish I could loan you for the roof."

Would time take this widow's pain, this loss of all possibility? Something would and must enfold. Action happened even if I didn't move. I could find a way forward, in the search for what killed the life of possibilities I had with Harry.

I stood and gave her a kiss. "May I borrow a car?" I asked.

"Of course. Keys are in the drawer in the mud room. They should all start. Check the tires." She wanted to ask me more, but she didn't. It wasn't done in our family. I took pity on her.

"I think I'll call my friend Maria Ortega. Then I may go for a sail." I finished my coffee. Since I was a girl I had called Maria first thing on coming to town. She was my escape from my family.

"The caterer?"

"A surfing buddy."

"You have a surfing buddy?" said like a cold dip into the vernacular. "Here?"

"You've met her. You knew her mother, Bernarda Ortega," I knew Maria's tiny mother as the arranger for all the Montecito ladies. She told them who to hire and she helped with parties for Gran when I was a girl.

"Oh yes, Bernarda." Claudia didn't say 'the Mexican'. She probably didn't think it either, though I thought she did at the time. I was sure my grandmother was a snob, proud of her family, still more of Chicago than of California and the West. "Her Maria was your friend? She runs her mother's business. Now it's a catering company. Everybody uses them, the new people and the old," Claudia said, reminding me she had a long life, still current in this town. "I hear she works for Walter Skeffington."

Then I thought of it. "She might have met Harry?"

"I don't know. Did he tell you?"

"Harry didn't say who he met. I didn't ask him– " Of course.

Gran's maid came in to say the telephone was for me. When I came back I answered Claudia's unspoken question.

"The private detective. He wants to meet me."

"Here?" She was about to forbid it.

"In Los Angeles. I'd rather not meet him around here."

"Is that safe?" She sounded frightened.

"We'll meet in a restaurant. It should be all right." Harry's murder had not yet scared me off all life. I felt unassailable in my grief.

"A private detective? Whose?" she asked.

"He said Harry's parents hired him. To talk to me for them, I guess." I read what I saw in her face. "To harass me for all I know."

"What's wrong with them?"

"They never liked me."

"For heaven's sake, why not?"

"They thought I was after his money."

"That's ridiculous." Gran looked at me sharply, as if I was a fool to marry anyone with parents like that.

She stood and walked around the room, straightening paintings. She was enraged as if her failings had let me meet people who could think badly of me. Dismayed at her failure to protect me, to set me up in my own cosseted life. "You were in England. You loved your husband. Do they think you killed him?" Claudia was not a small talker.

"I could have hired someone to kill him." What a susceptible bunch we were, willing to consider possibilities from crime novels.

"They think our police can't handle it?"

"They don't think there's anything real out here."

"Their son thought so," she said. "Manuel Garcia must be your detective. Nephew of my mason, cousin of my head gardener." My grandmother spoke as if that familiarity was a character recommendation, a decisive one. "He will find out."

"Why him?"

Claudia was finished and looked at me to accompany her through the dining room into our day. "Manuel knows this town. And he's young."

Maria was not home. I left a message with a brother who remembered me. I drove to the harbor along the beach and pictured myself here, same scene, but on vacation, a stranger, no cares, no woes, cheered by the blue sky and sea, not oblivious or taunted with the glimpses of full lives. I rented a boat and sailed. I looked for whales and dolphin. I watched the pelican dive. The loneliness hit me full force. I had no friends. My grandmother, a study in reserved decorum, was my only family and she wanted me gone. I had an aching void where my love life used to be. Alone, feeling the separation of each from each, of all from me.

CHAPTER 5

I borrowed one of Gran's cars and sped down to the city, outrunning the rain to keep my date with the private detective, agreeing only to coffee in Los Angeles. The landscape was still wild – mountain ranges surrounding valleys. The valleys had not yet filled up with houses and oleander bushes and cars. The land rolled bare, green except for oaks, cows and, closer in to the city, horses and fences.

Du Pars coffee shop in Studio City was his choice. He sat in a booth, coffee half gone and stood to show himself to me. Tweed sport jacket, khakis, full head of thin hair, hand in his pocket. He shook my hand reluctantly. "Miles. Kurt Miles. Mrs. Chase?"

"Yes." I was disappointed that he looked like a middle manager.

"I've been asked to look into your husband's death."

"Oh yes?" After the old waitress poured my coffee I asked, "Who asked?"

"Your in-laws," he answered, without saying their name.

"I'm surprised they care." He just looked at me.

"We should have met in Montecito. I come up all the time-"

I didn't want him near my home. I wanted to be somewhere I could get up and leave him and his questions and disappear onto the highways.

"Will they find his killer?" I asked.

"Maybe." He took out a notebook. "Where did you go to school?"

"Smith." He did not seem the type to know what that school was. No follow up question. What house were you in? Did you like a women's college?

"Did you meet your husband there?" I shook my head, unwilling to say more.

"How long were you married?"

"Four years." Friends for two before that. I thought my own thoughts as I answered the questions I was so used to answering at dinner parties.

He paused to drink coffee, looking at my eyes. I would not let them tear up. "Did your husband have a social life in Montecito?"

"I don't know."

"You don't?" He looked at his notebook. "Any enemies?"

Did Harry have any enemies? Not that I knew of.

"Obviously," I said. "But I don't know who."

I motioned for a coffee refill from the waitress in a pastel skirt with a white kerchief in her hair. She looked hard at the man with me.

"Why was your husband in Santa Barbara?"

"To work." I didn't tell him Harry had come to town to design for Mr. Skeffington. "Have you found anything?" I asked him.

"Me tell you? You don't pay my bills." He looked down at his notebook again as if there were something written there.

"Do you know any of your late husband's friends in Santa Barbara?" he asked.

"No."

"What about names of acquaintances in Santa Barbara?"

"No." I was thinking it out for myself. Harry always knew people when he went somewhere to work. There were probably friends of friends in town. There always are.

"No names?" He asked as if he was compiling a list to contact.

"No."

"Do you think your husband had a lover?"

"No."

"Lovers?" Accent on the plural.

"No." I was angry.

"Do you think he was homosexual?"

"No." Harry with a man–a new horrible thought. How could I have never considered it before? I remembered his penis, warm, hard, and refused to picture it with a man.

He pocketed his book. "We'll let your in-laws pay for the coffee."

I acted calm but I left confused and drove over the canyon crying. I buried the homosexual question. Why make myself miserable by thinking of losing him to both sexes?

To make something of the trip to Los Angeles I drove over the mountain from the San Fernando Valley to an appointment at Elizabeth Ardens in Beverly Hills. There to have my hair cut and washed by someone else, to pretend to pull myself together. I sobbed as I drove the curves to the other side, the ocean side of the range.

The smiling Negro man in the back lot took my car and I walked in through Delman's proper shoes. Upstairs I gave up my clothes and sat in a pink robe in a pink room with a long mirror and ladies in chairs. Grooming. Also widows I decided. Curly hair, women with straight hair having permanents, in that suspended bubble of privilege accepted as due, not even questioned, nor least, recognized.

"Did you hear about –?" I did not listen. I was from out of town, buffered from their rumors.

Good God, Was that my mother? Under a space age dryer, whole head in the oven, eyes closed, I recognized the bracelets and the chin from under the metal hood.

"Oh, darling, I was going to call," she said when she saw me. Why did I always want to believe her? I saw her older, in little ways she could not see or she would fight them I was sure. "Are you feeling better? How are you and Mother getting along? Santa Barbara too boring yet? She must be glad to have you there. I'm on my way to Hawaii with Richard – Richard Two I call him."

She looked at me as if I might have forgotten Richard One and went back under the dryer. That husband came into my bedroom. I woke and looked at him and he tucked me in, tight. He came in another night. I pretended to be asleep. He put his hands between my early breasts and squeezed. I stayed asleep.

When I told my mother I wanted a lock, she said to ask her husband. The next time I woke up as he reached under my nightgown. He smiled. "Go back to sleep Emma."

I walked to the village hardware store and bought a brass lock and a screwdriver that traveled with me to the next stepfathers.

I told my mother after she left him about that Richard who rattled the door for weeks. She said "You get used to it. I had an uncle. Not a real uncle, a friend of my father's. He stepped in when my father died. Mother didn't know."

"Didn't you tell her?" Claudia would have done something to help her daughter.

"I knew the rules – he told me, fatherly advice from a – You can't talk about it or you'll be sent out of the family. I learned that kind of childhood is the price we pay. For all this." She wiggled her jeweled fingers for me to see.

"I locked them out," I told her.

"No wonder Richard was so pissed. I think he gave me sleeping pills on purpose."

I screwed the lock onto every bedroom door thereafter. And made sure I was not alone with the stepfathers. I escaped by going to school. My mother left lives by marrying, divorcing and remarrying, one man after another. I couldn't name them between Richards.

"Are you seeing Lucette? We'll stop on our way back and call. Love you darling." I went to be shampooed and she was gone again.

The hurt of losing her all my life felt small now that Harry who had saved me from that loneliness was so lost.

CHAPTER 6

I tried to remember happy times with my mother as I drove up the coast through muddy farm fields, Ventura, a Mission town, and onto the water. Off the highway at Sheffield, I drove around Montecito on the curving roads under the trees. It was late dusk when I parked in the garage and dark as I tripped down the gravel road to my grandmother's house. The lamps in the entry were on, casting yellow light on the black and white tiles. On the other side of the house the sky above the oak trees looked navy blue. Claudia called from upstairs.

"Meet you for a drink, in the living room?"

"I'll change first."

"I have a favor to ask."

I took a shower and cried in the water. I noticed for the first time in two months I was tired by other than my grief. I didn't remember until I stood dripping on the pink tiles that Claudia was going to ask me a favor. To go out again? I needed to stay home. I wanted to sleep, not to think, about Harry, about my mother, about the police. I missed my dogs. Each thought crowded out another misery.

Drying off, in a flash I thought that if Claudia needed me she was less likely to ask me to leave her house. Would I have to move?

Claudia rang on the house's intercom, the heavy black telephone between the nursery beds. "Dear, will you take me to a meeting I can't avoid. I know it's a favor to ask – you can drop me off. Skeffington might be there. "

I had to meet him. I was willing to hope that once I did I would know, as if this man had the key to my future. I fortified myself with a chocolate bar and dressed in cashmere, tweed, dark heels and one of the brooches Gran had given me. Life wasn't going to hold still because my body ached to go beyond the grave. I wanted to find him, I wanted his love again.

"Are you all right, dear? Successful trip?" Dressed for dinner, Claudia waited with the sherry in the living room where the wood paneling was such a blue green that I felt like I entered an aquarium. This was to become our ritual for the work day. Conversation with a drink before dinner in that aqueous room. Creating a link with all the others pausing in their day. Anywhere I was I knew just where my mother was at cocktail hour; somewhere in gold hoop earrings, bracelets, Joy behind the ears, tinkling her ice.

"Gran, I saw Mother in Los Angeles. At Elizabeth Ardens."

"Evie? Here?"

"Almost. She said she'd call on her way back through. She's going to Hawaii, sounds like a new man."

"That's not a surprise. She could have written."

"Maybe we'll be invited to the wedding."

"How does she get so many men to marry her?"

"I was lucky to find one." So lucky, then not.

"Me too," she said.

I slipped off my shoes and ruffled my toes on the zebra rug, like I did when I was a girl and thought the

hide sad. Now I knew this zebra of my great-grandmother would have been dead of old age. It was an old
friend, captured to live on with us.

"Gran, I'll take you. Can you find Walter
Skeffington? "

"Skeff? " She didn't intend to answer, just to ask
back. "I can ask. But why is it so important to you?"

"He saw Harry last. He spent time with him."

"One more for me. You're driving, right?" Claudia
said as she poured her sherry. "We have to watch out
for alcohol. It runs away with our family."

I could still picture my mother at the bar, up to greet
someone at a clubby restaurant, talking too loud to the
bartender, rude to the other patrons.

"Nothing's worse than a drunk snob. Except a mean
one," Gran said. "We have both in our family."

I was surprised she spoke to me about family.
We never talked about our family, just let it swirl on
around us, communicating by accountants, managers,
Christmas card. She and I clung to each other. That's
how I felt. We sipped our drinks with our dress pumps
off and our feet folded under us.

Claudia's daughter dumped me in Santa Barbara
whenever she was after a new man. Last I knew my
mother was married to number five, a retired bank pres-
ident. She golfed to fill the time before drinks hour and
dinner. When I was a girl, railing on about my mother,
broken hearted and angry, Gran could only sit beside
me and talk about how I must rethink it. I would learn
by respecting my mother. When I stopped complaining
we stopped discussing her.

"You know I love your mother. It was difficult for
her growing up here. I imagine she's happier now,"
Claudia said.

I didn't think so.

I finished my dry sherry. Too good. "Can you ask Adelino about his nephew?" Changing detectives sounded like a hope. Movement felt like progress, though toward what resolution I did not know. No resolution would bring my Harry back. Justice was not possible, only vengance.

"I see him in a few days, dear. "

"Gran, you saw Harry. Did he tell you what he was doing? "

"He talked a little about the library project, and he said he might take on another, a garden. He was touring my garden with a professional eye." I looked out the window and saw Harry out there, the fog and rain droplets disturbed by his passing and still resonating. A garden was a small project for Harry.

"Would this Skeffington have murdered Harry?" I asked my grandmother. The numbness of grief had emboldened me. What did I have to lose?

"Skeff? Hardly."

We walked to the car, brought down from the garage. "If he's at this meeting I'll tell him you're here."

I left my Gran at a house with a big porch and drove up to the Mission through city blocks of Victorian mansions. When I picked her up she told me Mr. Skeffington was not there. He was in Europe. No progress. The rains had stopped for the night so I fell asleep to the muffled sound of waves through my open windows.

At breakfast Claudia said "How about you take me sailing on my father's boat?"

"You kept it?"

"I had the keel redone, recaulked. Take me out, Junior Sailor.

"OK." I looked out the bay windows to hard grey rain.

"We'll watch for a break in the weather–" Claudia finished her toast and put things in order to rise.

"Tell me more about the boat –"

"You'll see. My father, your great-grandfather sailed it alone until he died. She's beautiful. Very plain. He had it built in Maine and we brought it out on the train."

The next day broke clear so we bundled up in sweaters and macs and went to the old boat, lovely in its slip, the lines stiff from no use.

Santa Barbara and its neighboring villages of Goleta, Montecito and Carpinteria are protected by the Channel Islands. Santa Cruz Island blocks the storm swells so the waves arrive along the coast at Ledbetter's, at Miramar Cove, at Carpinteria Beach, well-formed in orderly lines.

The swells surged under me, the wood boat flotsam that I steadied on a course, the tiller pulling my arm.

My grandmother wanted to talk as we sailed out toward the islands. "Montecito is orchards and dairy farms torn out for gardens, for golf clubs. You can spot the houses by the trees, they circle the houses. And see them –the rows planted along driveways straight down to the beach. We'd drive down with rugs and silver and servants to play on the beach while our mothers had tea. I look for my past, imagine it still to be there. I can see the traces."

I could not see my childhood paths, only confusion. Only questions. What did Harry do with that horrible man in Paris? What were the connections? Who was I, the wife, to be in Montecito to figure them out? Was this the world with the answers? Not my world. My tragedy, my one story – that was all I needed to know now from this settlement in the lap of mountains at the shore of the great Pacific Ocean.

We sailed with the swell far enough out to sea that the town was lost in the green, except the towers of the Mission and seminary, so small, so insignificant along the wall of the tall blue mountains. The familiar peaks disappeared in front of the bigger mountains behind.

The water splashed the deck as I came about. We were bundled up and warm enough dry.

"I remember Montecito because it's going so fast, if I don't keep it in mind where will it be? The outline of places, the bones still visible, still real to me. The tracks of the adventures of my youth, the plots of our elders come true. Gardens planted, tended and producing from the order of their beginnings."

"My life is only change," I said. "You know."

We got wet from an errant swell. "What about you. Where do you go next? Buy a house somewhere? A house of your own, a garden, that means projects. A future."

"You're ready to abandon me?" I wrong sided a swell and we lurched over. I wanted to be cruel, I couldn't help it. What was her vision of life? "I can't buy a house, Gran. Harry left me no money, not his family's, and we had none saved. I have to work." How do I start?

"Could there be a job in Santa Barbara?" Would she let me live with her? My work on Harry's affairs was my secret plan. I believed his ghost would be there at the answer. And I owed it to him.

"Don't ask me about a job," Gran smiled at her joke. "I wouldn't know, would I? We volunteer." Her scarf tied tight around her head, she looked like Grace Kelly, laughing at her cluelessness.

Another shock was to be poor, after feeling so rich. With Harry alive we had years of good work, well paid, ahead of us. Now I had no money coming in, and only some in the bank, not enough to keep the farm in the Perigord. And, I worried, not enough to live. What were my skills?

"I was beginning to have work cataloging family treasures, organizing archives. But since Harry died—"

People disappeared into the silence when Harry died. All of our friends vanished.

CHAPTER 7

The next morning as I slept late Gran knocked on the door to tell me the call was mine. I was dreaming about the orchard in the Perigord. Was the chateau mine now? I knew I shouldn't trust it to come to me without a battle.

The private detective was on the telephone. He wouldn't know about the French farm. He only knew the questions my in-laws asked and the leads they invented.

Watching me, that was probably his job.

"Kurt here. Do something for me Emma."

First name basis. He didn't bother to bargain before he demanded.

"I'm here."

"Your husband had a locker at the ice plant. Salisuepedes Street. The guy who runs the place will only give the key to you or your in-laws. We need to know what's in the locker."

"O.K." I'd go down. Why a freezer drawer in a locker plant? Bulbs for a garden, I guessed. His landscapes began and finished his buildings. And Gran said he was working on a new garden.

What could my in-laws want? They wouldn't come this way even for their curiosity. Their vision of California was as skewed as their view of Harry.

I parked on broken asphalt by the train tracks. In the locker plant I told the man behind the white adding machine who I was and he looked at my passport, then at my face, curious why no driver's license. "Your husband's key is number 58. On the board, there." He motioned with his head. "Take a coat and I'll let you in."

Off a row of hooks I took a thin army green parka with leaking stuffing. The ruddy man pulled the long chrome handle to open the door. He led me into the steamy cold and pointed down to the end of a row of white drawers to the number 50's. "What are they for?" I asked.

"Customers keep meat – hunters, we have lockers full of deer meat, boar. Ranchers' daughters with fresh beef. We don't ask. We rent the lockers and provide access."

"And coats," I said longing for a fur.

I turned the little black key and pulled open the white metal drawer. I thought I would leave flesh on the drawer, with no gloves. Claustrophobia seeped with the cold into my bones, fears that I would get stuck in there where I could see my breath and my eyelashes were sticky.

Inside were manila envelopes. I grabbed them wanting to flee the cold, too cold to think of anything but getting out of that bare bulb lit frozen room.

My guide opened the door and I followed with the envelopes. I was too cold to be curious yet.

Out in the warmth, I put the shiny coat back on its hook with the others, next time I would try the wool one. "I'd like to keep the box. The rent is due?"

"Yes, Mrs. Chase. It's monthly, your husband paid for two months and they're up next week." He was looking in a big ledger book filled with little pencil markings. He'd already seen the envelopes.

Harry had just rented the box, just before he died. For meat? No, for a garden, for bulbs and seeds that needed to be frozen. Why were there none in the drawer? The bulbs must have been on order.

"My husband was an architect and garden designer, he had to have a place to keep seeds frozen." I didn't need to explain. I was telling myself a plausible story. "Do you have some place I can look through these and put them back?"

"Sorry. No. Mostly people take things out of here and eat them. We're open til 5."

"Thanks." I gave him the key and took the envelopes. I sat in the car, put them next to me. I wanted to leave them there. Afraid of what was in those envelopes, I opened one – photographs. I could tell by the shine. I didn't look to see what they were of. Another held design plans, pencil drawn, another, his writing. I guess I was looking for a bomb, and I thought I didn't find one.

The bomb was there, ticking, a nail bomb, designed to kill and maim, to pierce like Saint Stephen, arrows of information to impale the guilty, the close.

In Gran's garden I opened the envelopes brought into the damp day from the deep freeze. I sat beside a fragrant hedge to catch the sun before it disappeared into the broken rain clouds.

First I found what I expected to see–sketches for site plans. Water. A pond? Preliminary designs. Whose project? If the sketches I found in the first envelope were all Harry had done for Skeffington's job I'd say he was just at the beginning and was distracted from the serious work. His artistic doodles made me cry again.

He left a pencil list of stone quarries, architectural fragments, with addresses in New York and Los Angeles; items to order and their suppliers I guessed. I recognized some. I'd go back to that group.

In the next envelope was a topographical map of trails in steep country with red pen circles. Photographs of vegetation, like a garden so overgrown it had disappeared.

A letter to Harry on an embossed card: "Call it a chapel. A ceremonial structure. Our collection is for private use. As you will see. Phone me when you are free." No signature.

Harry had hidden it. Why no note from him – no organizing document, no explanation.

In the next envelope were photographs: a large photograph of a man standing on the top level of tiered seats, an amphitheater, rimmed by a low stone wall, set in boulders and brush. Then a black and white photograph of the grass amphitheater at my grandmother's. It was behind me in the hedges, the outdoor theater famous to me and in the family for Isadora Duncan's dancing there. I didn't know the photo, a snapshot of my grandmother's garden from the past when the trees were smaller and the terraced stone walls that were the structure for the grass seats more obvious.

The next photograph was of an entrance to a cave or a garden grotto and a pool. A pond.

Claudia startled me as she sat next to me, in a straw hat, dirty gardening gloves in her pocket, her face happier in the garden. The love there reminded me our young closeness, our old friendship. I dropped the packets onto my lap.

She untied her hat so the ribbons floated over her shoulders.

"Gran, when did you see Harry last–?"

"The last time I saw him he came for dinner, four days before they called m..."

"After me." At least we kissed goodbye – from politeness and superstition – can't have the last time be the one time you don't kiss. And who knows what dangers lurk. I started to cry.

"Harry called me to check in. I asked him for dinner so he could give me your news. It was just the two of us. " I was jealous. She put her arm around me. "I am always glad to see him. He is a good humored man. A great and unusual quality."

I missed that most when I was away from Harry. Now gone forever was his good cheer. He was funny and he really loved me. My eyes glazed as I imagined I could escape my fate.

"He came early to see the garden." She took my arm at the elbow as she must have taken his, out for a stroll in the garden with my lost genius of space and landscape.

"Oh I could have been there." I couldn't blame her that I wasn't. Why didn't Harry ask me to join him? I had a place to stay.

"We talked about the garden. The original design, changes I've made. My plans. I wish I had asked for more suggestions." We both sighed. She put her arm around me. "He had a garden on his mind."

I wiped the tears off my cheeks. "Whose?"

"I don't know. One here I think. He asked about the herb garden. He was going to come back and take photos. At the amphitheater."

"I found an old photo of the amphitheater."

"Let's go see it," she said.

Carrying the envelopes under my arm, I followed her through the maze of hedges to a trail in a grove of evergreen trees set in delicate ivy. Wildflowers bordered our path and the lilies were waist high and wet. I bent down to smell a white lily on a tall stalk, water drops were caught in the green center and pink spots radiated out the petals.

Through an arch in a hedge we walked into the amphitheater. "I keep it up," Claudia said. "The masonry. The terraces were brown for the years I couldn't water. Harry came here just after the rains started so he saw it spring green."

We walked down the dark soppy grass terraces to the stage, a lawn with columns and a row of cypress trees behind it.

I took Claudia's pace, four steps to a terrace, and stood beside her in the center and, momentarily out of my new misery, looked back up the wonderful space.

"The walls are only as old as I am, you know," Gran said. "Seventy so years. A little younger. I watched them being built." She stared at the rocks which still balanced mortarless on each other.

I could see Harry taking the terraces in his full strides, pacing, visualizing the audience, the show. Wishing himself once again an actor.

Why was this place in Harry's portfolio, his secret files? What had he left me in the deep freeze? Did he mean me to see it? He didn't tell me about the locker but that wasn't unusual. If I was not along on a job, I heard nothing of details.

"Is this a photograph of here?" She leaned on the wall that made the stage. I stood beside her and pulled the photograph out of the envelope without looking at those below it. I had to open the rest alone.

She stared at it, pointed to the person in the back on the top level. The hedges were smaller than the figure, the walls clear and the sky blank of trees to the mountains.

"That's me," she said, and I saw.

Gran held the picture, her blue eyes only pretending to look at it, then gave it back.

"Did you give it to Harry? " I asked.

"No. That photo isn't mine." She went over to the first terrace and sat, legs dangling over the stone wall.

"In the picture the hedges haven't grown up," I said, never one to ask a question.

"It must be Skeff's photo."

"Skeff's?"

"I'm a girl in that photo."

"Mr. Skeffington?" I prompted her. Gran did not respond well to questions.

Her eyes looked for something in mine, as if, if she found what she looked for she would tell me what else was the story. Did she find it?

"We were two mother-less children. His mother was dead. Mine was shopping." She didn't laugh, for me, another motherless one. "We were friends as children, that doesn't always last.

"I'm not surprised Skeff found Harry. He always had great taste." She smiled.

"Why would he give Harry this photo?"

"I heard Skeff built an amphitheater at his new house in the mountains." New since he was a boy she meant. "Maybe Harry was building one somewhere else?"

"There's another photo. " I held out the photo of the man at the top of an amphitheater in the boulders and she looked at it in my hands without touching it.

Chapter 7

"Skeff," Claudia said. "He did it. Looks like Adelino helped with the walls."

She kissed me and stood. "Do you want to come meet Adelino? Today's the day we walk the place. You can have a real tour."

I shifted the envelopes, they were heavy with my duty and expectations. "I can't come now, Gran."

"You're all right?" Claudia looked at me with unspoken questions. The fragrance was strong. In the pittisporum bordered bower I was breathing deep, feeling for life around me, afraid of my being alone. What could harm me in the envelopes?

"No, I'll stay here for a while. Meet him another day? You'll ask him about his nephew?"

"Of course, dear." She kissed my cheek.

I had to get back into that envelope. Gran turned the corner and I sat in the front row and took out the next photograph – a black and white of a cave entrance that looked like a darker shadow in oak and boulder shadows. An arm reached out. I couldn't tell where it was. The vegetation was like the mountains behind Montecito but that could be anywhere in Southern California.

The next photo was of a garden folly, a roughly sculpted grotto beside a pool, with lily pads and a person floating, a woman who would have looked like a Pre-Raphaelite Ophelia if she hadn't been face down and naked. I figured she was a model.

Still I rushed out of that place, trying to forget what I was meant to discover.

The brick path became dirt and curved into bigger trees, oaks with drooping giant arms. Ahead Gran and Adelino in a big brimmed hat walked along the tall wall that bordered the estate. I slowed and breathed to calm myself. They didn't hear me at first.

59

On that day in Montecito those very old walkers were the real inhabitants, the younger of us, ghosts of a future yet to be imagined.

The old man in the straw hat stopped. Claudia passed him and felt the rounded stones of the wall. She grabbed rocks higher up and pushed her toes in between them until she found sure footholds and climbed to the top of the wall. I wished I could take a photo of her, her stomach against the rocks looking over the wall.

Adelino came over to me. He had a broken nose that was pressed flat against his face, his eyes were dark, his cheeks long. His face was sun, wind and age weathered. He stooped, only a bit, and walked carefully. His smile was big, his hair thick and dark.

Claudia heard me and turned. She smiled from far away. I was nervous at her look, I didn't want Claudia to leave me.

She called down. "This is our Escape Route. Adelino showed me. I used it to escape my house." Claudia reached for the right rocks with the toes of her shoes and scaled back down. I felt like a mother must feel, watching her child act on its own, dangerously.

"The 'Escape Route'?" I asked Gran back on the ground. She looked at Adelino.

The old man looked me and at his hands. "When we circle land with a wall we build a hidden route. The spaces in the rocks are there, for escape."

"Do you use them?"

"Rarely. At times we have to get in to care for something, something that mustn't be walled off. And people need to escape at times."

"Who knows about the escape routes?" The wall disappeared into high hedges.

"Only the builders of the wall, and those they tell. Usually no one else. We might have told the little mistress of the house, with so much to escape at home." He looked at Gran like an old friend. "Senora Claudia's granddaughter?" he asked looking at my face. I could feel the young eyes of this old man looking for someone he knew.

"Yes."

"It gave us sadness, your husband's death."

"Yes, me too." I didn't want to be forgotten in the grief and mystery around me. I wanted to ask him questions. Where were the walls I saw in the photographs? Was his nephew on my husband's case?

"Detective Garcia, my sister's son, can help."

"I want to talk to him."

"I'll tell him. He will call you."

The envelopes told some story. Not for the private detective. For the nephew. I had to share the photo of the floating woman. Let someone else decide if it was staged or evidence.

Harry kept secrets from me, I knew. But a whole project? Why no mention when we spoke on the phone? Harry asked questions about the dogs, the gardens, my health. He didn't say he was renting a frozen locker and risking his life.

CHAPTER 8

Younger, more handsome than I expected, Detective Garcia stood, shook my hand then sat with his big hands crossed on the desk. He started immediately on business. We were not friends.

"I called your grandmother at the first mention of this case. You came to town and left? You were in France?"

"I took my husband's ashes to his, our, place there. Minus the fingers."

"Yes, the fingers."

"Why?"

He looked at his own thick fingers. "That's the question. One of them."

Were Adelino and my grandmother right about this Santa Barbara cop? Was it his reputation, his family connections or his qualifications? This man looked the part. Would he find my husband's killer?

"Do I know you?" I asked because he looked so familiar.

"We've not met." He wasn't going to make it clearer to me. Only when I told my grandmother of the strange familiarity of this police detective, did I learn that he had been an actor, portrayer of bad guys in Westerns when he was younger and Mexicans were always banditos.

"You wanted to see me?" he said, asking why I was there with his eyes.

"I found a photo in my husband's locker. I want to show you." I took the manila envelope out of my bag. He watched my hands as I took out the picture of the floating woman. "It's of a woman in water. I'd have thought it a model, if Harry weren't dead," I said.

"May I have that photo?"

I handed it over gladly. As if he could take it all off my hands. He looked at it with an unchanging face. Then he took out a magnifying glass on a bone handle and studied the woman floating naked on her stomach.

"Tell me again how and where you found it?" I told him about the private detective's call and the locker in the ice plant.

"Who hired this investigator?"

"My in-laws, Harry's parents."

"How do you know?"

"He said so." What a fool. I just believed him.

"What else did you find in the locker plant. On Salsipuedes?"

"Yes. I found Harry's lists. A few sketches, designs, for a garden. A map with the end of a trail circled. Photos of a garden and a cave."

"I need to see everything, please," he said in his strangely courteous manner. When his eyes looked into mine I wanted to obey him, to stay with him.

"I want to keep Harry's work."

"You can't. All the contents of the envelope are evidence and may be able to help us."

Could I make a copy of everything? "I don't have the rest with me."

"You need to show me everything, Mrs. Chase. You don't mean to give them to the private-"

"No."

"He told you about this locker?" Garcia's intercom rang and he ignored it. His eyes did not leave mine. "How did the so-called investigator find out about it?"

"Harry? His parents?" That was unlikely I knew as I suggested it. "Don't detectives just learn things from a central information site?" He didn't smile at my banter.

"Bring the whole envelope by as soon as you can. If the private eye, this Miles, calls again, refer him to me. Don't bother to find out who really hired him."

"Why?"

"That's our job."

I hoped Miles didn't call.

"What should I tell him, if he does call?"

"Nothing, Mrs. Chase. We'll meet again soon." Garcia stood and his second handshake was warmer, his hand taking mine into its folds and mounds. I felt safer, less alone.

At home I took photographs of everything – the photos and Harry's notes. I confess my cowardice. I had been afraid to look at them again. But I knew I must, to find what was left of my husband. His fingers. His story.

The photograph of the floating woman at the grotto scared me. My mind searched for reasons. Maybe Harry was planning a Pre-Raphaelite mural and the woman in the pool was to model Ophelia. But she was naked.

If she were dead, and Harry had that photograph it meant that he was around death before death came into his life and took him too. Why was I talking about an abstract: Death, as if it were a spirit and not the murderer, a person. Maybe someone wanted that picture hidden and killed Harry for it. He had kept it hidden. I gave it to the cops. To the right cop, Garcia, whose family knew my family.

CHAPTER 9

Outside on my balcony, a wavy reflection in the glass doors, pale face, eyes deep, hair wet, I looked young, the lines barely showed in that Montecito glass. I knew what the mirror said. I had aged beyond my beauty. I had not escaped, my life turned from the stuff of international gossip to tragedy.

I needed a friend. Maria? I could wait no longer to recover myself enough to find her. Time to call again.

In the summers we spent together I grew taller, her face came to match her waist and hips for beauty. We rode the waves and ignored the boys who took off in front of us. An unlikely pair, a contrast in shape, color and style, I was long, blonde and gawky and looked away from anyone who looked at me. Compact, brown and sure, Maria dared them to stare. When I launched into the outside world of college, my marriage, I lost touch with her. At first I called her from the distant places on her birthday and she tried to find me on mine. Did Maria still paddle out? Or were we too old to surf? Twenty-seven.

I wondered if Maria still lived at home or did even good Catholic girls move out one day. Maria told me how every morning for her mother she dressed the Baby Jesus doll, the robes sewn by her family for generations, the outfit dictated by the feast days of the week. Maria seemed content in her family's Catholicism, and kept secret her life that could jar her mother's beliefs, separate as the clothes for a different saint, statues in another yard. I called Maria's mother's number.

On the phone Mrs. Ortega thought me a client and she gave me Maria's business exchange. I didn't reintroduce myself. She had always ignored me. Too young to be a customer, not one of hers to be a friend.

Maria was surprised, sounded pleased I was in town. "Mi amiga! I must see you!"

"Ah Maria, you're there. I called a few days ago..."

"No one told me! What brings you back to Santa Barbara?"

"It's a long story. I'm at my grandmother's. Meet at the beach?" I said. We both knew that meant Miramar.

"Think you're still up to a high tide walk?" She laughed. "Too many years of high heels?"

I'd been missing my friend Maria, just her voice reminded me of myself, who I was before. As girls we took high tide walks. The technique was to leap from rock to rock when we could see them, when the wave was out, gathering to crash again. Then we'd stop and wait in the wave until we could see again, get drenched in our clothes.

"Sunset is low tide. I checked. Not so sure of my footing these days." She was the more adventurous. She had a family, a religion, a culture to rebel against, a base to make her strong in her pushing away. Mine was so much less firm.

"I'll leave my meeting at the Biltmore. I thought you were gone forever -" she said, her voice low again.

"So did I. I'd have come back anyway."

After a day with a book in my grandmother's garden, I drove to the beach and parked along the lane. I walked down in the wind where the road dropped to the beach, a blacktop street to the sand and the waves. I sat there on the edge and watched the cove. Maria's deep laugh made me look back to see her walk down. That laugh had kept me in the water, paddling, cold, with her in the Pacific waiting for waves, cove waves that broke at the point and rolled on in a sliding fall of white curl. "Mi amiga. So good to see you!" I stood beside her, still taller, and she hugged me. I scanned her face for signs of age. None yet, just more of her, a deeper beauty. Darker, bigger eyes, her dark hair pulled back tight, her brows arched, cheeks shaped by her thinness. What changes did she see in me? What did I really see in her?

"You're a beauty, my friend." I kissed her cheeks, influenced by my time in France. "Do you still surf?" I didn't know what else to ask. It had been so long. We started walking down the beach toward the motel and the next point. We both carried our shoes.

"I'm too busy to surf. Too much work. I work, I work. I employ more cousins than my mother did." She smiled for the old days we knew. "I spend more time in Montecito than my mother ever did. New people from Pasadena like to have parties and need their houses fixed." She used to complain to me in the water that while her mother worked for some rich family in Montecito she was left to surf Miramar when she wanted to surf in town –Hendry's, Ledbetter. Her mother did not want her in the surf at all. Few girls surfed. I was glad to have a friend and to be in the water, cold as it was.

We walked on the hard, wet sand toward Fernald's, the other small point of the cove. If we were Italians we would have held hands, two old friends dodging sea weed. Pelicans glided over the water along the beach, wings tipping over swells. They dove for fish in the cove. There were so many birds. A few years later the pelicans almost disappeared, eggs too soft to hatch.

"The fish must be in." Maria turned back to watch a big bird plummet, twirling, into the ocean. "What about you? Any time for surf?"

"No surfing. Some swimming." I scooped brown pancakes of wet sand with my feet. I forgot about the years between these beaches, our separate lives. "Could I start again?"

"Why not? " We stopped in front of the Miramar Hotel, now with no guests on the beach, just the life-guard doing push ups in a red speedo under the board-walk. Maria leaned back on her elbows where the sand was soft and I sat cross-legged and braided strands of sea grass. The sun went beneath a cloud and colored the water and the day with orange pink.

"My grandmother says you're a big success."

"I'm a caterer, for parties, verdad, the same as my mother. Hiring the help, organizing," she said, digging her heels in the sand. "To tell you all, I have a beau. He wants me to keep us a secret. I suppose I should be careful. But I can't leave him. Not yet, for some reason. And you?" I couldn't help her. I was stuck too, with a dead man and a crime.

"I've been a wife. To an architect. We travelled–New York, Europe. He came out here." I looked away from the sea for a star in the blue grey sky behind the mountains. Gone, my sweet Harry. "Did you meet him, my husband?"

"Did I not? This is still a small town, " she said.

"Harry Chase."

"Oh God, " Maria's face froze and fell. She sat up and stared at me. Her eyes teared, red-rimmed. "You poor darling." She reached to hold my arm.

"He was murdered," I told her, though I saw she must have known. "Here."

"I heard about it."

"Harry Chase, I wish you could tell me what he did here, what was going on."

"If I'd known he was your husband -" Pelicans crashed one after the other into the sea, twisting, beak down. "I would have found him."

"Saved him." I was kidding. She winced. We stood. Her pain was extreme. I assumed it was for me but even then I hesitated, paranoid, feeling her new edge, her hand in her deep pockets, a manicure, a ruby ring. "Sent your brothers to save him." Her macho brothers who drove her crazy when we were young. "They must be family men by now."

"Nieces and nephews work for me now."

We walked back separated by the tide line of pink and brown kelp, shells, and tar.

What could have saved Harry? I asked that question over and over. Somewhere I thought if I found out what happened I could do what I had failed to do and he would be back. I felt I had no clue of finding my new self without him, and I had only his mystery to lead me into the future.

The tide was coming up. We ran between the rocks when the water pulled out and waited as the cold water covered our feet and the path between them. We sat on the blacktop, brushed the sand off our feet and put back on our shoes. A girl on a horse passed us, holding it back as its hoofs clattered off the road and onto the narrow sand between rocks.

"What was he like?" Maria asked.

"My Harry? Smart. Handsome, not too. Friendly. People liked him. He was funny. Cheap. The only thing he gave me was my engagement ring." I sighed though it did not matter. "Clients planned projects to bring him to town. He was here to work on a library for Walter Skeffington."

"Skeff? I work for him."

"You know his library project?"

"Cierto."

"My husband designed it."

I nodded, chilled in the evening sea air. "What did you hear?" From Maria I could learn something about this fragrant town that swallowed him up. If I knew more about his job, the world and the people, could I find hidden in it the murderer's hand? And Harry's hand. I kept reminding myself of the grotesque to make the queasy pain in my belly and heart stop. I could not bear the thought so I made the words the reality, not the act of taking his fingers nor the absence.

"I heard they found him. Where?"

"On the railroad tracks. Here."

"Jesus, Mary, Joseph."

"Down near the water tower." The water tower seemed romantic before, a small tank on high crossed struts in a meadow set against a pink sky, a moon and Venus. It made me dream.

"Have you walked down?" Maria was brave.

"No. I'm afraid."

"Come with me." We stepped from board to board between the iron rails. The police tape was tied to a big screw on the rail under the water tower.

"No blood," Maria said.

"What about?" I pointed to splotches of dark on the wood slat. The gravel was turned over, almost fresh.

"Oil." I knew she was saying that so I didn't see Harry's blood spilled on the ground.

"Maybe."

She looked uneasy. My bare misery made her uncomfortable. I was a stranger, not the girl who knew only a girl's questions. I had hoped we could ignore that present, because our past was so strong, but my grief was aggressive. It could not hide.

"I don't know anything about Harry's life here," I told her. "I don't even know where his things are."

"Try the Miramar. Skeff puts out of town people up there."

"Will Mr. Skeffington know who killed Harry?"

"No. Not likely."

"Do you?" I asked her, desperate.

"God, no."

Did I just accuse her?

"Will you stay in town?" she asked. "Finish his job?"

"I'm not an architect," I said.

"You're leaving soon?" She looked at her big ruby.

"I have to persuade my grandmother to let me stay."

"Then what?"

I stopped myself from telling her about my need to find the murderer. How much did she know that she could have told me if I had answered truthfully about my plans? If I had asked her questions she could answer.

"I have to earn money. There is a big bad roof in France."

"What will you do?"

"If I can stay with Gran I'll look for a job. Can I work for you?"

"Of course dear heart you can. We'll have to warn your grandmother. She'll flip if she sees you taking coats in a French maid's uniform."

"Yes she will. What's up besides work?" I asked.

"A beau," Maria answered. She looked up to the mountains, a high blue wall against the sea.

"A secret?" I asked to know if I could keep probing. Then I could still stop myself. I am sorry I did.

"Yes, a secret."

"Does he make you happy?"

"It's not as simple as that. I'll tell you when I can."

The sun set and we watched for a green flash in the dark orange along the water. We pretended to leave our lives aside for the moment.

We had both parked on the lane beside the railroad track and said goodbye at our cars.

CHAPTER 10

Harry had a room at the Miramar– the distracted man at the front desk gave me the number. Cars rolled by on the highway, separated by hedges. "His possessions are with the bellman. Grover, he's on his bicycle."

As I walked into the grounds, past empty tennis courts, Grover found me – a very black man, smiling on a red bicycle with a basket of red metal. On the platform behind him above the fat rear wheel was a suitcase, Harry's suitcase. "I'll put it in your car for you."

"Is that all?"

"No. Just a start."

"Will you show me his room? Please. 205."

"On the boardwalk. We cleaned it out. The rest of his things are in the garage. Let me put this bag away first and I'll show you around."

"May I wait here? It's the silver Porche in front." I gave him my key and sat on a bench facing the lawn with the sea beyond it. Harry's last home. I could hear the waves.

Grover was back quickly. "I'll take you to the storage–"

"First may we go to his room?"

Grover walked his bicycle beside me and kept a companionable silence. The birds were loud, land birds and gulls.

After we crossed the railroad tracks I could see the waves, grey on this grey day, the sky and the water the same color, fading into each other at the invisible horizon.

Grover left his bike and led me onto the wood boardwalk on pilings over the sand. He looked up so I did to a balcony in a square blue roofed building, the sliding glass doors closed, blue plastic windbreaks at the sides.

"Is his room taken?"

"Not sure. You'll have to ask at the front desk. I can show it to you." He propped his bike by the red kickstand and walked up the open stairs to a row of back doors. He knocked and unlocked 205.

"It's all cleaned up."

Was it a mess? Was Harry killed there?

"Did you know my husband?"

"Oh yes. Moved him in. A true gentleman. You look around, then I'll show you his things."

Through the room was the ocean, tide out, wet grey sand and foam of waves beyond it. All along the view of the cove waves broke on the beach where Maria and I walked and surfed. Loud in this room. I could see Harry there, drown in noise, his mind working.

"There's something I need to do. I'll be back." Grover left me there.

I dragged a rubber and metal chair to the wood balcony and sat in the breeze. The salty air like seafood was beyond the scent of mildew in the room with the blue carpet, to match the roofs. I watched the birds wade, poke their beaks into the wet brown sand. Sandpipers skittered away from the waves' wash.

I could have sat there and waited for Harry as he worked. Walked on the beach. Ate at the Somerset, danced. Hamburgers on Old Coast Highway, a beach town life instead of death. He did not ask me to come with him. Did I need to know why?

Grover stood at the door. I felt him there and left the view. I opened a drawer of a bureau to a Bible, then left with him. Grover kept my pace as we walked back across the tracks to the old white garage under an oak tree.

"We have trunks for visitors who don't. Not many do these days. Your husband has a trunk. We moved him in with a golf cart." Grover slid open the wood door to a room of trunks and bags that smelled dusty and mildewed at the same time. I saw Harry's trunk on the top of a close pile. *clothes*

"Mr. Grover, can you take this trunk to my car?" I wanted to take Harry's room for the night and look into his trunk there. But that seemed crazy and meant two moves. Better to use my grandmother's stable garage.

"You can drive your car to here. I'll call someone to help us and I'll lead you back down."

I followed Grover on his bike behind a modern building of rooms on a pool, past an old railroad car to the garage. Two men lifted the monogrammed trunk into my car. It fit length-wise with the trunk open. I had no one to take it out. I would have to retire the car and look into Harry's last life in the stable.

"May I leave the car here? Take a walk on the beach?"

"Sure, missy. I'm very sorry for your loss."

"Thank you. Thank you for keeping his stuff."

The railroad tracks were up a rise, empty longitudinal space between trees. Up the track was the water tower. I was crying. What a stupid purpose. How hopeless. I walked across the plank boardwalk and down the steps to the beach.

Once again I had something to open, something left to me to explore. I wanted my husband, not a scavenger hunt.

I stopped at the reception in the low white, blue-roofed building and asked if I could take that room for a few days and for how much. I felt I could afford the luxury of Harry's ocean front room to sort his stuff, rather than a dark stable with no hay, only cars.

The clerk called Grover on his walkie talkie. "It's a trunk."

Did I have to tell Garcia? I parked behind the ocean front buildings next to the train tracks. Grover and a young man carried the trunk to the room. I needed to see what was in it, but I did not open it. Soon it was dark outside. From the balcony the stars were thick and bright, deep fields of pricks of light. The sea was dark but for the star shine, rolling silently. I went home. Once I knew what was there I'd call Garcia.

At dawn the next day I drove back to my room in the seaside motel and opened the trunk. Objects wrapped in newspaper were lain above a layer of envelopes. Did I want to know?

First I took a walk at the low tide around Fernald Point to the jetties and cliffs. The beach became rocky over night, the sand gone. When the waves washed in, the rocks tumbled over my feet. It hurt.

A long kelp stipe was stranded, its holdfast of waxy lines woven full of animals: crabs, starfish, snails, hermit crabs, baby sea urchin and octupi. A shiny brown tree torn from the kelp bed, the underwater forest that floated off the point of the cove. I never wanted to swim in it, afraid of tangling in its waving tentacles. The animals moved to shelter in the bulk of the holdfast. . I washed the sand off my feet at the faucet at the bottom of the stairs to the boardwalk and went up to my room. Harry's room.

What was I going to find in there? Would I move Harry back in? His brushes and shirts and underwear were in his suitcase with me. I heard the waves louder, tide coming in, and the train scared me as it rumbled by, a long freight train. I wanted Garcia to be with me as I looked. The Miramar was a modern motel – I dialed 9 and Garcia's number from his card in my purse and reached him at his desk. How many cases did he have?

"I've found Harry's suitcase and a trunk at the Miramar."

"Where are they now?"

"Still here at the motel. I've rented his room – He wasn't killed here was he?"

"No. I'd like to meet you there. But I can't. Let me know what you find. Take pictures. Grover packed him up? Everything will be there."

Alone, I opened the top and unwrapped an owl, feathers still colors of life, eyes open wide; two masks of feather and bead and shell; long necklaces of shell and seeds and rawhide; a hand mirror. And envelopes as file folders. That's how Harry worked.

I could take them unopened to Garcia. Make a date to open them together. No. Maybe Maria would help? I hadn't told her about the locker plant envelopes. Was I keeping secrets from Maria? Was she, from me? Pelicans cruised the cove in staggered formation.

On the folded paper in the envelopes I saw Harry used the shapes – of the owl and its patterns; of the masks and their curves and he fashioned spaces. The drawings were early stages of a one roomed something. Plus designs for rock walls and a wrought iron gate.

His leatherwork notebooks, sketches of the landscape, schemes, and a journal I'd never seen. Red leather, his initials embossed in gold.

I had to get out of that dank room. Even with the doors open it felt like fungus lurked. I put the objects back in the trunk, kept out the journal and notebooks and called the front desk. I skipped another walk on the beach and drove to my grandmother's, the secrets in her car trunk.

CHAPTER 11

My Gran, Claudia Dunwoody, and her big house in
Montecito – I needed them again. At least while I
settled Harry's estate. Only this trunk, all that was left
to me? The rings. I had no power, no say, no part of him
except the house in France and this horrible mystery

In the nursery I found my baby toy, my cat girl. I
took her from the drawer and said hello to myself, my
caresses ruffled and wore her. She knew me when I was
just starting out in life. I found her ears, satin, and left
my thumb there to rub.

How did I feel, to find my baby self and admit this
was as far as I had come? I felt better for rubbing the
ears, the soothing of an infant, a child become me. The
thread eyes were gone. Pink thread whiskers survived.
Her ears were flattened, the satin inside protected and
smooth. My grandmother had kept this toy, this old
friend of mine, all these years. What else might I find?

I stood on my balcony in the clear cold between
storms and started Harry's journal. He made a note
everyday – walked the site at Mr. Skeffington's and
described it, the contours, the colors, the smells. A
dinner party at Skeff's: Harry met Maria, labor liaison
for the project, 'a firecracker, Can she deliver?' He did
not tell me he met my old friend, nor did she.

'The gardens, the green places designed to enhance the view of the blue skies, the blue ocean, the blue islands. Planted at the foot of the mountains wide and high behind the town, at the edge of the impenetrable forest where the Chumash hid when they learned about Mission life. Grizzlies stalked these hills, cougars ranged fifty miles. Then came farms, orchards, then gardens. Now tall trees frame and fountains reflect the mountains' peaks. The branches have grown huge to shelter the birds and divide the sky.

I need Montecito, the gardens, dark, starlit or sunny with shadows, free to play in, to find the edge, the confusion and the rapture that can combine to such excitement in this place.'

I wanted to stop. Crows gathered in the tree next to me. I went inside to the room that smelled of lavander and wood and my childhood.

Harry wrote 'I feel home in this subtle landscape. I could be happy here.' With me? When was he going to mention me? Or tell me.

'Call to Emma' I found finally.

'Call de V's friend. Local scion. Dinner proposed. See Bl Jrnl.'

Next day after the entry about another Skeffington's meeting: 'Casa de Sevilla. Abalone. See Bl Jrnl.'

Everyday he was meeting with Skeff, conflicts were resolved. 'Good idea about entry; Listened; Accepted my plan.' No me, few feelings, except about the place. A business journal. He noted beach walks, changes in the sand level, the surf. And referred to the Bl Jrnl.

He began to make some entries in code. The evenings had the mysterious notation. And more references to the other journal. Hiding?

I knew I should take it all to Garcia. First I read it. I emptied the trunk. There was no black journal.

Inside under a blanket on the day bed I heard it begin to rain. I needed to find something to do besides chase my dead husband. And I had to keep reading. Sleep, why couldn't I sleep instead?

What did Harry's dots and lines say? Another journal? Did he have to hide? How hard it must have been to hide so much. Hide from me, from almost everyone who loves you. What does that do to you?

'L saw this journal. Boring he says.'

'Cave. Spirit guide.' What was he learning here without me?

'Lowell project...? Bear lair, shaped like an owl?' Lowell– the name I knew.

'Have I found my place?' Harry wrote on the last day.

My grandmother called for me and I left the red leather journal open on my desk. Was it a black journal I needed to look for? Or a Blood Journal?

In the kitchen in the telephone book under the black phone were Lowells: Gregory Lowell on Sycamore Canyon, Michael Lowell on East Valley. My grandmother knew the Lowells. I was not yet bold enough to call them. Call and tell Greg Lowell he tripped me at the Valley Club? Tell him I read his family name in my murdered husband's journal? I needed an introduction.

Drinks with Gran, in the civilized world of the cleared oak forest, sherry from a silver tray. The waves that broke on Fernald, Miramar, Hammonds and Butterfly Beach were loud enough to hear in the house on the long lawn at the border of the deep mountains. I sipped my Portuguese sherry momentarily away from that afternoon and its discoveries,

"Gran, Harry stayed at the Miramar –"

"Really? I offered him your room."

"Maria told me that's where Mr. Skeffington puts people. I still haven't heard from him," I complained in some wonder and anger. "He owes me that, contact."

"Skeff spends the winter in Europe," Claudia said. "I don't think he is trying to avoid you."

"When did he leave? After Harry died?"

"I don't know dear. I just hear about him these days. Ask Garcia."

The next day, still sunny and cold, with rain forecast, Detective Garcia agreed to meet me at El Paseo.

Those days I didn't wear make-up. To see Detective Garcia I put on mascara so my eyelashes showed, and lipstick, a discontinued pink. My face was a stranger to me in that silvering mirror circled by blue tiles. How could I be pinked by the sun through the clouds of those rainy days?

This detective, who was he? Local movie actor returned to town to be a policeman. Why? To preserve order?

My grandmother came with me to El Paseo, she to shop and protect, me to show the detective Harry's journal. I wanted his help deciphering it. El Paseo was in downtown Santa Barbara, a Spanish marketplace built in the 1920's. We walked in the picket gate onto a garden path. The wooden shed in the garden was the jewelers'. "He has diabetes," my grandmother told me with sorrow in her voice. "He'll go blind."

The red tiled hall with walls and ceilings of curved adobe was like the tube of a white wave lit by hanging metal and glass stars. Claudia came out behind me into the central Plaza and motioned to a furniture store. "I like their things. I'll have a look. Meet me at the book-store." She had said in the car as we drove along the

water and up State Street that she would leave me and
Manuel Garcia to talk. "No. I'll stay. I want to say hello
to Adelino's nephew." She and I sat at a cold metal
table, my bag on my lap, Claudia watching me, her
hands crossed in front of her, in gloves. "Adelino is a
dear friend."

Detective Garcia came from the tunnel and Claudia
stood. He took her hand and held it. "Manuel, you're
taking good care–"

"Yes, cierto."

She patted his shoulder and glanced her good-bye
to me. She put her purse under her arm and walked to
the Scandinavian store with painted furniture.

"Going riding?" Detective Garcia looked at my blue
jeans and boots. He seemed more friendly as if Claudia
had broken some barrier between us.

"I'd like to."

"You're a horsewoman?" He sat down heavily.

"I'm not a serious rider. Always a bit afraid."

"Sensible. You have something to show me
Mrs. Chase?"

"I found Harry's journal from his time here, I read
it and figured–"

"Where do you have it?"

"Here in my bag."

"Keep it there. Walk with me back to the station and
give it to me there. I'll tell your grandmother you'll be
a few minutes."

I looked around and saw two old ladies having tea
and a business man reading the paper. Garcia came back
and stood before me, ready to help me up, to block for
me. I wanted to stand closer to him, almost fell into him
for the strength. But there was something that scared

me away from being familiar, a clear border I could not cross.

We walked out the side garden and up Santa Barbara Street past the Moorish courthouse. We passed the bakery and the pink florist shop on the side street and crossed to the beige flat roofed station. Once in his office he had me put the journal on his desk.

"Well. Was this from the Miramar? What else did you find?"

"A stuffed owl, a woven mat, an abalone and seed necklace –I like to think it was for me." Why did I tell him? I wanted to tell him everything so he could save me.

"Is it all still in the trunk?"

"Yes."

"In your car?"

I nodded.

"You will give me the trunk. You are reading the journal?"

"At first it makes sense then Harry starts to use symbols, and refer out to another journal I can not find."

"What date do the symbols start?"

"Toward the end." I was crying again. "The 'Black' journal I didn't find, he passes the personal off to it."

"Names of people he met?"

"Yes. Mr. Skeffington mostly."

"Local man. An art collector."

"That I've heard. Harry was here to design a museum for him."

"What other names did you see?"

"Builders, masons. Maria Ortega, my friend actually. And Lowell."

"Greg or Scott Lowell?"

"I don't know. Who are they? "

"Cousins. Greg is a man about town here. Scott lives in San Francisco."

Why didn't I ask about the whole family? "I may have met Greg."

"Where?"

"At the Valley Club with my grandmother." I wanted Garcia to know it was proper. Not at a bar. He made me want to live up to an idea of a lady. Not be a barfly like my mother.

"He lives in Montecito. Runs in your circles."

Did I have circles?

"The Lowells are an old Montecito family," he said to clarify, but it didn't. "Ask your grandmother."

I had to meet Greg Lowell again. Could Maria help? Though I still wondered that she didn't tell me she met Harry. I hoped Greg Lowell was easier to find than Mr. Skeffington.

"You'll leave the journal?"

"You promise you'll give it back?"

"We'll do the paperwork, then I'll come with you." He opened a wood drawer for a pad of forms and took a pen from a cup. "It was good to see your grandmother. She and my uncle are friends from a long time back." Detective Garcia's thick moustache followed the line of his mouth. When he smiled the glossy moustache smiled. It suited him, accentuated his face as did his dark eyebrows and hair. I was staring. A movie star. "What did you think Mrs. Chase? In your read of the journal?"

"It was clear until the end. Harry's ideas. Descriptions of Skeffington's site. Their meetings. His comments, open, general. I believe any secret is in what he calls 'the 'Bl Jrnl'." I spelled it out. "At the end, you'll see, he begins to use symbols."

85

"Where is this Black Journal?" Garcia was filling out the form, the pen small in his long strong hands.

"I don't know. Would Grover have taken it?"

"No. But he might know who did. He keeps a close eye. I'll look." He handed me a paper and looked into my eyes and the brown of his eyes was like beautiful lit wood. Then he looked away quickly and stood. "I'll walk you to El Paseo and your car. Your grandmother may be worried." He motioned me through the door first. "We'll drive back with the trunk."

CHAPTER 12

Claudia pushed back wisps of white hair, in a chignon until cocktail hour. Rain clouds formed together in the sky. February had begun. My visit home was a week old. We had finished breakfast. I now had my own silver pot of coffee beside my place.

"Your mother called, from San Francisco on her way East. She sends her love."

"Ah. Does she ever come here?" We crossed the entry to the stairs up to our rooms and our preparations for the day.

"No. I suppose if I asked... You're my only visitor and we have to scoot you on your way."

"Why Gran? I have nowhere else to go."

"Surely not?"

"Where?"

"Paris?"

Paris: the killing, that man's smile as he told me, infected the grey stones for me. The bridges, young men trapped and thrown into the Seine – how to walk there now? I could not make myself live in Paris.

"I can't work there, Gran." Tell her about M. de Vlamnic and the massacres of Algerians? "Gran, I could tell you horrible things about Paris." She saw the pain in my eyes. Another, a questioner, might have asked me what happened.

"New York?"

"I don't have any ties there. I can't afford the rent, Gran. Not yet. And our" – I could not yet call it mine– "house in France needs a roof. I need a job."

"And you need to stay here?"

"Please Gran."

"OK, I can do that. But we have to watch out for you, that you not get stuck here."

Like Harry. His ghost ripped from him, from me, and set loose here.

"Sarah Hoar at the Natural History Museum. She may know about a job." Claudia stood. She was still tall and straight. "See you at dinner?" She kissed me on the head and left the room, trailing perfume, in cashmere, graduated pearls around her neck.

That was her way of saying I could stay. In my relief I wondered if I were in the Perigord, would I feel more than unfiltered anger at the loneliness and slowness of moments that came and went without relief.

The next morning I drove along the foothills to the Natural History Museum, a rambling adobe in oaks and boulders beside a stream bed, noisy, rushing with yesterday's rain.

Sarah Hoar, at her desk behind a heavy door, looked like my field hockey teacher, tall, rectangular body with downy, square cheeks. She remembered me and stood to give my hand a hearty shake. "How is your grandmother?"

"She suggested I come see you. She says you might know about a job."

"A job? There's too much else for me to keep straight. Look at the notices on the board down the hall."

"Any work at the museum?" I asked.

"No, except part-time in the shop. It's not for you."

"No?" I asked. I was desperate, wanted to consider anything. She didn't, and sat back down to her piles of paper.

As I thanked her at her door she remembered. "Alicia Lowell came in with something–that would be quite a task." Sarah rubbed her forehead. "If she's doing the family job, grab it. Before we do."

"Alicia Lowell?" That name again.

"Oh," Sarah paused to choose her information. "She's your grandmother's generation. She's on our Board. Lives on a ranch in Montecito." Sarah stopped there. She looked at me as if I surely knew more, but I didn't and she wasn't telling.

I found Alicia's notice, took it and left my card with my name engraved and my plea "Experienced scholar will catalogue your collection".

I stopped in to tell Mrs. Hoar. "Any advice for talking to Mrs. Lowell?'

She looked at me with a question on her transparent face. "Know the Chumash. She's Chumash and her project's bound to be all about them. "

The Chumash, what did I know then? Harry mentioned them in his journal. Pierre showed me treasures. They lived in Santa Barbara before the Europeans came. I had looked for their tools on the beach since I was a girl. I felt their enslavement, their annihilation was my white man's guilt.

I walked through the Museum's dark rooms, lit by dioramas of Chumash people living on the coastal bluffs of the Santa Barbara coast, half dressed in skins and furs and feathers, with reed houses and long canoes.

In a long room of shiny wood and glass cases filled with moths and butterflies, I imagined that I was a Chumash, sitting in the grass, watching them fly, velvety feathered wings, landing hairy bodies on the bushes beside me.

On my way out I called Alicia Lowell from the Museum pay phone set in a thick adobe alcove. I don't remember how I pictured her. Tall, long Mexican skirt, turquoise jewelry. She invited me over to talk.

I bought books on the Chumash to study. Could she pay me enough?

"You found a job?" Claudia asked me at dinner. The cook served in her dressy apron. Claudia seemed amazed. "Already?"

"I have an interview. To talk about it. A project about the Chumash, I think."

"The Chumash. When I was young we found their things in fields and on the beach. They lived here for thousands of years. We private collectors started the museum. Whose job is it?"

"Alicia Lowell" I said.

Claudia looked up slowly and stared into my face like I was hiding a ghost.

"You know her?" I asked seeing the answer in her face.

"I knew her when we were girls. Don't mention my name."

"Don't?"

"Not if you want the job." Claudia was not going to say much more, that was as plain on her face, as the regret in her eyes.

"Should I not want the job?" If my Gran knew something, surely she would tell me. I thought that when I was younger.

"It's up to you. There was trouble when we were girls. That's all. I don't see her."

I kept looking at my strong grandmother with questions.

"I was cruel." I thought Gran was embarrassed, as if she knew cruelty was impolite. "I don't know if she has forgiven me."

Only later would I learn how sorry she was. "She shouldn't take it out on you." Gran finished her water. "It must be her husband's notes. That will be amazing. Incredible." Gran seemed sent back into another self, a girl. "I went with him once. To town, to the adobes. He talked to the old ladies in black lace about their childhoods when the streets were dirt. And their mother's childhoods when the adobes' floors were dirt. He found the Chumash who survived."

"You knew Alicia's husband?" I asked, surprised.

"When I was a girl. Michael Lowell. I admired him – he lived with the Indians. It seemed they were all he cared about. He told me when Mr. Hope died the Anglos burned the Chumash village he was protecting. He wanted to save them. He had a son. Scott. Not a golfer like his cousin."

"Greg?"

"You know him?"

"We met at the Valley Club."

"Ah, yes. I remember."

"Yes." I had met his cousin. Who had Harry met?

CHAPTER 13

U p late, I left quickly for my interview with Alicia Lowell. It was raining so hard the day was dark. I sloshed in the old car across Montecito. The stone walls of the Lowell farm started miles before the entrance. I turned in their open ironwork gate between cactus and agave and drove slowly up the long drive, through orchards, into a courtyard at the house. Reluctant to arrive, I circled the stone fountain, felt like going around again, but parked in the gravel away from the front door. Not a guest. The fountain bubbled as the rain splatted around it.

From inside the door a woman motioned me to hurry through the solid buckets of rain. Alicia Lowell. She was round, round calves below a full skirt and then delicate shapely ankles that made her look so feminine, under her arched door. She was laughing at the ferocity of the storm.

I shook myself off in the entry, adding my tears to the water on my face because I cried easily in those days. I didn't want to be there alone. She looked me over.

"It's wonderful to have rain again," she said. She handed me a soft towel and I patted myself, too wet to dry. "That's why I laugh." We walked down the hall under red and gold painted beams. With determined steps she seemed taller than she was.

I followed her to a smaller room beyond the living room. She walked over to two chairs. Glass doors opened from the inside to a courtyard, a tile fountain, more rain and deepening puddles. Would they flow into the house along the shiny tiles to the Oriental carpets? We sat. Would we hold our feet up as the water took over the ancient stream beds?

She said. "Seven years of drought, this much is welcome. Springs were dried up."

"Will it flood?" I wanted to care about the weather.

"Streams flood already. Be careful. The underground rivers are starting to flow. The old falls." She didn't let on if this worried her.

"Waterfalls?"

"Down the face of the mountains."

"Do you know the story of the modern Montecito? My husband and I made this," she motioned to the rooms and garden, "out of a dirt dairy yard. We planted every tree and bush. Their size confounds me with my age and the swift passage of time," she sighed.

She rang a china bell and looked hard at me. "Are you from Santa Barbara, Mrs. Chase?"

"Not originally. I have family here. I visited often when I was a child." Off and on.

"Do you live here now?"

"Yes." For a while.

"Tell me your qualifications," she said and recrossed her ankles.

"I graduated in art history from Smith, did Sotheby's courses in furniture, painting and connoisseurship, did a <u>stage</u> at Druout in Paris. I have catalogued collections for private clients. I can give you a list -"

"Will that help you with my job?" So what was her job? My old self, escaped with Harry but rejoined in

Montecito thought it rude to ask outright. She'd tell me what I should know. I could feel Claudia's influence, back in her orbit. Alicia waited for me to answer, no smile on her face.

"I understand you have archives."

"Yes. Is that all you know? About my project."

"I have worked with archives."

"So?"

"I have experience and organizational skills." And I needed the work. Was I embarrassed to say that aloud? "Why don't you tell me what you need."

"My archives are California history," her hands in her lap she looked at me from her straight- backed leather chair. I was in a velour wing chair, sitting forward, both feet on the floor. "What do you know about our history?"

"A little." She was silent so I continued. "Named for Califia, golden haired warrior woman of Spanish myth."

"The Spanish. And before the Spanish? Before the Europeans?"

"Chumash lived here, along the Santa Barbara Coast and in the Santa Ynez Valley. They were great canoe builders. And traders. They were wealthy because they made the shell money on Santa Cruz Island and traded the wealth of the Channel. Their's was a hierarchical society of hereditary elites. When the Spanish came, they enslaved the Chumash to build the Mission. Most of the Indians died. Gold was found in the north, and the Americans came. Monterey fell, a Santa Barbara man led Fremont and his soldiers over the mountains to take this coast. The Californians made peace and California became American in 1850."

Her maid, in a white embroidered Mexican dress, arrived silently with a pitcher of lemonade on a paper mache tray. Alicia poured. Then she spoke.

"All right. That's a start. For this work you need to know the Chumash. Chumash lived here for thousands of years before the Spanish came." Alicia sipped her lemonade. "When Chumash built houses the arched doorway was a whale's rib bone, the walls and the ceiling were woven swamp rushes. My grandmother said if the Europeans knew what it was to bend under a whale bone, to have Jonah and the sweet cattails for a home they might not be as harsh or as lonely."

She seemed to recite. What was I to answer?

"Do you know Chumash myths?"

"I have read some, recently." I was never good at interviews.

"The gambling game that Sky Coyote and the Sun play at the end of the year?"

"No, not yet." I was coming up short. "Mrs. Lowell, it may serve you to have fresh eyes look at the material."

"That story's pretty basic. I hoped my notice at the Museum would find someone interested in the Chumash."

"I am interested, Mrs. Lowell. I don't know the stories." I didn't think I would tell her yet about the treasures I saw in Paris. I had that introduction to her world. Paris was far away and I wanted it out of my mind.

"Books will only have the outline of the stories. No one has seen my husband's notes. His is original research." I began to notice her art. Spanish Madonna with a tiger. Small Diego Rivera of calla lilies. "Do you know of my husband's work?" Alicia asked.

I shook my head. "No."

I lied, not to tell her about Claudia's girlhood story.

"I want it to be appreciated," Alicia said. "His dedication. As an anthropologist. He interviewed the last Chumash of the old era, as many people who knew as he could find. He took notes by hand. My task, your job, Mrs. Chase, is a warehouse full of his boxes. My husband's handwriting was small, and it is not clear."

"Did he publish?"

"No. He collected, what he could, and left us with it all. I need to see it. Before it goes into a museum back room with the other artifacts." She sounded bitter, looking at her hands as she spoke. "A waste. Work never shared. The lost knowledge still lost."

"What do you need done, Mrs. Lowell?"

Her bracelets were wood and silver. The wind blew the fountain. I wanted to know her better.

"The notes are there as my husband left them. They need to be found, to be put in order. The Museum wants the research, to turn its scholars loose, to digest it, classify it and publish it. But before I give it to them, I want you to tell me what is in there. And make a chart of where it is. Can you do it?"

"Mrs. Lowell, may I see the material?" I hadn't thought of Harry's murder since I'd walked into the house. I wanted this job. But I needed to see what I was getting myself into if she decided to hire me. Would I be carrying trash from one pile to another?

I also needed to be paid enough. Once I could work just to learn or to help. But I didn't live in that luxury anymore. No longer married to a star.

"I need to ask about the salary."

"Of course, Mrs. Chase."

I was silent.

She stood. "Can you come out now?" I had no idea what to expect.

I followed her. She looked so ladylike, balanced on little feet, her skirt swaying through a swinging door into a pantry then through a big kitchen and down a hall to a side door and out. She climbed into an old maroon convertible Cadillac parked under her huge trees. I sat next to her in the leather darkness under the fabric top. Her hair, braided and twisted against her neck, was white with black strands that looked like emissaries from her youth. I guessed she was in her seventies, near my grandmother's age.

"This is my grand old cart. I'm only allowed to drive it on the ranch. You'll be all right." We rolled away from the house and into the lemon orchards, as she took me up to the shed where I was to find my work. We drove past barns and corrals where dripping horses looked up from under wet lashes. I worried about the mud under the big car. She didn't and bounced ahead over the slanted meadow.

"We're lucky the shed is on this side of the stream. Flash floods. Never cross a flooding stream. You can be swept away, your car rolled with the boulders down the flood. Hear them?" Growling, a noise in the rushing water that I would have named animal, came from under the oaks behind the stone building where we stopped.

Hardly a shed. Did she expect me to find answers for her in there?

Alicia opened the door with an old key. Did I see her cross herself? She paused on the threshold of that darkness as if to brace herself or ask permission to enter.

Inside were green metal filing cabinets lined in close rows. The windows were covered with blinds so the darkness was almost complete. The open door set the dust of ages to dancing.

"Listen to the black widows plucking their webs-" Alicia said.

"Trying to scare me?" I couldn't hear anything but the rain on the metal roof, like rocks being flung in handfulls.

"You don't believe me?" She stomped her feet and clapped. "They'll hide from us. We'll check for them before we move you in." She screwed open the blinds. She knew I would take the job. She could see I was entranced.

I felt I could hide in that dusty warm warehouse forever, live with the dead, since the dead could not live with me.

"I need you to read all this and make a map so we know what is here," Alicia said. "I can afford to pay you up to five thousand dollars. Then we must stop and take stock and see how far you've gotten. Is that enough to start?"

Enough to find a lawyer to protect the Perigord property? Enough for a roof?

She no longer saw me as she walked through the rows of cabinets, touching the dusty tops, the metal handles.

I looked in the drawers of the desk under the window. Pencils, paperclips. She came back from that past and led me out of the musty stone building into the raining grey day. Her heavy Cadillac made it out in the even deeper mud. I was picturing the gluey brown soil seeping in the doors. I'd need boots to walk.

"Come in. You can scrape your shoes." Her manner was plain and warm. I was willing to follow this woman around.

In her bright kitchen with tall wood cabinets, she asked Magdalena, who read the newspaper at the square table, for hot chocolates.

Through the living room's tall windows the sun shone on the wet tiles and the burbling water threw rainbow bubbles into the fountain basin.

"Emma, I think you will be able to do this. We'll see. So you start as soon as you can."

"Thank you, Mrs. Lowell."

"Everyday–come here on your way out, and report to me. I'll give you lemonade or tea if you prefer."

"Report?"

"Tell me what you've found. You need to decifer the words of the very old. The last people who knew Chumash life outside the Mission and its death." Alicia sat in a leather armchair, looking like a Spanish lady, dark. "My people were slaves of my people–I have within myself the battle that this land has borne for two centuries."

She laughed at me. "Don't despair," she said. "No doubt Michael had a system in his filing. But he left no key. You need to make that for me. Read those notes. Discover what's there." She had hired me to face what she could not face. Acres of notes.

She seemed curious and, in retrospect, afraid.

I meant to sound businesslike. "Do you want written synopses? I'll keep a catalogue. I can mark for conservation –"

"You tell me here, over a drink. I don't want to read all that. And you don't have time." How did she know?

"Just a plan of where it all is. Work any hours you choose. I will tell Enrique at the gatehouse to look for you. The gate is usually open, he and his family keep an eye on it for me," Alicia said. I thought I could feel her relief at the task delegated. "You must promise that you leave all the research here, take nothing from the building. We will speak to no one else about the notes until we know what is there."

"Certainly," I said. I didn't ask why. Her request didn't seem unusual. Most of my clients wanted the contents of my work to be the family secret.

"Have you heard of a French explorer, Mrs. Lowell?" That name again. Harry, his journals had left my mind. She was a Lowell.

"French? Which one?"

"Leon de Cessac."

"De Cessac. Yes. Many of my people sold to him. And what he couldn't buy, he took."

"I just saw his collection in Paris. They were unpacking it for the first time."

"Good God, they found them. What objects he must have. Which museum has it?"

"The Museum of Man."

"In Paris? Us with the early Gauls? What did you see?"

I described what I could remember and she began to cry. "So much was lost."

"They told me his notebooks are still lost."

"The words, the European looks at my dying civilization. You will find our words in my Michaels' notes."

"Mrs. Lowell? Are you related to Greg Lowell?"

"Not close. From another branch of my husband's family." No more there. She seemed to hold it against me that I had asked.

Still she said to start work on Monday. I said goodbye in the hall and left her world. If I had known Alicia Lowell better I would have asked her about Mr. Skeffington. And about Harry.

Over sherry in the room colored like deep water, Claudia asked "What happened with Alicia's job?"

"She hired me. It's a mess of notes for sorting. There's enough material in those files to keep me busy for a long time. Alicia seemed friendly -"

"Did she?" Claudia paused. "I only knew her when we were girls, then briefly, during the war." Claudia seemed to see those years. And looked back at me with regret in her eyes. "We were never friends."

"How did you know her?"

"When my parents were building this house, Alicia with her mother brought lunch for the men. She looked like a Spanish angel with her basket. So beautiful, long brown braid, long eyelashes. Part Spanish and part Indian princess. Later one of the Chicago boys, a Lowell actually, fell for her and it was stifled. But she married his uncle – got a better man." This story, like much else, was as yet unclear to me.

"Were you and Alicia friends?"

Gran said. "My mother wouldn't allow it." Gran never talked about her mother, the heiress and socialite from Chicago. "When I told my mother I liked Alicia Ortega –" She mimicked an older voice. "'Laundry woman's daughter.' 'Mexican', with dismissal. 'Raise your sights.'" Gran shook herself.

"It wasn't your fault."

"I was unkind. And a coward. "

"Coward?"

"I could have disobeyed my mother. I wish I had. Alicia is Californian. Her mother Bernarda was Spanish and Chumash. Original." She had old pain on her face. "It's a shame. Skeff was her friend." Gran had a story in there beyond her embarrassment at family prejudices. But she wasn't telling me.

CHAPTER 14

Sunday, the clouds had left for the day. I had to get out on the water. I tried Maria to ask her to come sail. When we were young Maria got me out surfing, rare for girls in our day. She helped me feel less lazy, less depressed, those days that I wandered. Now I needed that and wanted her to tell me the truth.

"I can't sail. I'm at work. Beach walk?"

"Maria, you met Harry?" Why hadn't she told me she saw him? I was taught not to ask, wait to be told. Doesn't work.

"You know, I did meet your Harry, at Skeff's. I remembered. Let's walk. I'll tell you what I know, give you all the gossip." Spanish was evident in her voice, over the phone I could see her mouth shaped by the vowels. "I must go now. Soon, chiquita."

I'd see her that afternoon, before sunset at Miramar. I had a way forward.

On my own to go sailing, I drove my grandmother's convertible Chevy and let my hair blow. Off the highway at Bath Street I cruised past the old seamen's places, tiny houses with wood columns and porches.

At the harbor I parked beside a pickup, its truck bed filled with traps and buoys. I checked for wind on the water. Home, I met my girl self, the teenager, with the taste of hope that kept me up to foggy dawns. There was wind. The rental people could help me tie up when I came in, so I could manage the boat on my own.

On the walk along the water at the harbor I saw, his head down, pulling a cart, someone I knew. He looked at me.

"That's Emma Thorne? Scott Lowell." Same name. Related to Alicia? To Greg? To Harry's journal?

Scott stopped and peered, his eyes, dark blue, so dark as to masquerade as brown. His khakis were dirty, torn and his shirt untucked, his hair uncombed, short and wavy. "The archivist."

"Scott?" I used to see him at the country day school when I was dumped off with my grandmother and she thought I should go to school. One summer we raced at the sailing camp off West Beach. I'd forgotten he was a Lowell.

"Strange. You're here to sail?" His voice was a mixture of cowboy and banker. I thought a sister would be jealous of those eyelashes. Dark blond hair, pale skin, strong chin, tall and thin, too thin, with wide shoulders and big hands.

"Yes, I'll sail if they'll rent me a boat."

"I'm taking out my father's old sloop. Join me?" He looked at me, seemed sorry he'd asked. "We might get wet in this wind."

"I'd like that. Thanks. " I followed him down the gangplank onto the narrow dock, lined with boats. At the smell of the fishing boats I remembered trips to the islands with Maria and her family. Maria's uncles were fishermen, and I spent time with her along the slips where the men prepared their traps, hung out the thick wet suits with the piles of abalone shells, and coiled the air hoses for the sea urchin dive suits.

Tied in the slip like a calm horse, the wood boat was shiny with varnish, the sail covers splatted with droppings. Scott had the covers off and stowed quickly. "Herons, big birds," Scott said, as he held his hand for me. I took it reluctantly, never trusting a grip on a person as much as on a life line or metal stay. There were no life lines, the boat was simple and clean. His hold was strong and I stepped on without a rock.

"She's a beauty," I said.

"Love of my life," Scott said. "Looks like a day for a sprint out and in again," he said as he raised the main sail. He threw the lines onto the dock, flipped the bumpers into the cockpit and pushed off from the slip. He took the tiller. The wind was strong and from the north. The flag on the breakwater was blowing out straight.

The little boat caught the wind, tipped and sped out the harbor channel. Scott tacked and dodged a fishing boat, surfboards stacked, in from the islands piloted by sun- and saltwater- crusted young men.

"I wonder. Is that a better life," Scott said aloud to himself.

"What are you doing these days?" I asked.

"Lawyer in San Francisco. I come down here when I can." Scott reached around me and unfurled the jib sail and the boat heeled over to its rails. We passed the harbor bell. Seals lay on the rocking rim, and circled in the water, looking for a chance to leap on. Soon we were onto the open sea where the swells were higher than us. I sat stiff, feet braced just to keep the little boat on top of the water and me in it, hoping the grey whale migration was over and no sharks cruised. Sailing scared me. I liked that.

"Have you seen a whale out here?" I asked.

"Yes."

"Do they knock over boats?"

"Not them. It's the rogue wave," he said, not bothering to reassure me. "We're in luck, we have wind. This old boat has just the outboard and it doesn't work. There are days I can't go out, not sure to get back." A little engine hung from wood blocks.

We raced in silence. "These seas would be uncomfortable in light wind," he said.

His boat moved over the swells that tried to push it off course, sure in its cut through the water. The wind chopped the water into chunks that slapped the hull with the sound that I loved when I was a girl. We sailed beyond the oil derricks that stood off Summerland like black bugs, legs down in the blue water. Scott was silent. I pretended I was unafraid instead of uncaring. I could die.

"Let's keep going to the island," he said. I knew he was kidding. We had no food. "Here. You sail. I suggest we come about and head in before it gets too cold." He left the tiller and I moved over to take it. I needed that wave tossed silence. Time that I didn't think of Harry or my future.

"Ready about? Hard a lee," I found the terms and the daring to twist over the top of a swell and he winched in the jib sheet on the other side of the boat, cleated the line before it jerked in his hands. The sail filled to turn his boat like a little chariot and we were headed back to the harbor in the distance, hard to spot against the high mountains.

"You live in San Francisco? Come for the weekend?" I asked, braver as I piloted the craft over the roiling sea.

"Sometimes. To visit my mother."

"Have we met since seventh grade?" I asked.

"Sailing Camp."

"Is your mother Alicia?" I asked, dim to have just thought of it. He nodded. "You know I'm working for her, starting Monday?"

"Yep," he said. "I don't envy you."

"Why?"

"It's a big job," he said, noncommittal. What did he mean? "The Museum wanted the notes, as is. I think that's what's made her tackle them," Scott said. "We've all been avoiding the warehouse."

"First job I guess is to decipher your father's notation system."

"Good luck with the handwriting." He laughed and his face was transformed. I had seen that happen to Alicia's face when she spoke of her husband. Then the smile left Scott's face slowly and not completely. He seemed to relax a notch, his face smoothed out, the lips softened, cheeks flushed under his stubble of a new beard, businessman's weekend face.

"What's there?" I asked. He should know.

"Don't ask me."

"Why?" I asked before I thought better of the question. He was set to inherit them, whether he cared or not. I guessed he was bored with the Chumash, or took the world for granted. His mother looked part Indian, not he. He had escaped into white man.

"After my father died -" Scott paused for a long time, as you can on a sailboat. "When I was a boy I followed him everywhere I could. I met the old people. I saw ceremonies. "

"Like what?"

"The swordfish dance for whales. I thought it was a normal day's work. You'll read about it.""

"Can you read his handwriting?" My new most immediate concern.

"Sure -" his feet were up. The little boat was rocked steeply sideways by a swell passing under us. If I did not have the tiller I would be down, grabbing the deck.

The boat shuddered and righted itself.

He watched the pelicans fly beside us. "Their beaks end in a hook, like a claw, a nail. You'll get it."

"I'm there because your mother wants to know what's in all those files before she hands them over?" I was still trying to figure it out, the purpose of my task.

Scott was silent as if I had told him, not asked.

"Do you think I'll find what she wants?" The harbor, masts and the pier now showed ahead. "You think she's looking for something specific?"

"I don't know," Scott said.

I thought so, though I could not have said why. Something about the way Alicia looked at the cabinets, as if there was something, were words, in there that would jump out and bite her.

"She's never told me her secrets," Scott said. "Or my father's." Was he jealous? Had his mother kept him out on purpose? Didn't she trust him?

"I've got a head below, of sorts, I can tell you how to use it if you need it. You'll have to excuse me." That meant he pee'd off the boat behind me as I steered, quartering the swells trying not to knock him off.

"I used to watch you," he said. "You're still a sailor." That was not a question but a compliment. Scott checked the sails' trim and my course. He approved enough not to comment. I think I beat him in our childhood races.

"It's been years," I said, curious at the idea of his attention that long time ago.

"Why?" he asked.

"The boats I've been on had jealous captains. I never asked to take the helm. We were visitors. My husband didn't like to sail. My late husband. Harry Chase."

"Harry Chase was your husband?" Scott stared at me. "I'm sorry. I heard -. "

"I'm sorry too." What was the reply? He had heard of Harry's murder? "What did you hear?'

"That he was murdered. They found him." What could I ask? We were silent.

He took the tiller at the harbor entrance, between the wall of the breakwater and the high pier where people stood fishing. Scott pulled the jib onto the foredeck. As we reached the slip he dropped the main sail onto the deck and ran up to catch the dock. He was used to sailing alone.

"Thanks for coming Emma. I'll see you no doubt." He readied to clean the boat. I thanked him, but didn't want to stay around. We had sailed hard out into the Channel and back in. The clouds that had opened for the afternoon were gathering again. I was tired and wind blown and cold, wondering what more life could bring. Did Alicia know I was related to Harry before she hired me? She knew my last name.

I raised the canvas roof of the car, hooked it closed with the thick chrome handles. I changed clothes and cars to meet with Maria.

"There's a pretty car," Maria said as we met to walk to the beach. I was in a pale green Porche, she in a green pick up truck, parked in the dirt across the train tracks from the beach.

"My grandmother even has a car to race in the Memorial Day races." Everyday was a discovery.

"At the airport. I can get us onto the course. Have a go – see whose nerves are steely," Maria said as she sashayed beside me across the tracks, the water tower in the distance. "Remember James Dean in his banged up pale Porche? 1955, week before he died in that car. He didn't keep his curve on 133. Fatal road."

I remembered the day. I was 21, single, home for a visit before I went on and met Harry. "See him?" Maria had said to me in a loud whisper as we walked arm in arm through the racing pits.

"Yes?"

"He's the big movie star."

"Him? That's James Dean?" I saw a skinny man in blue jeans, unhappy but distracted from it by the races. Maria and I kept walking to the folding chairs near her friend's pit.

"He didn't seem like much back then did he?" Maria led the way past the road behind the beach houses. "Are you settling in?"

"I found a job."

"So that's a relief?"

"Yes, definitely." I hoped so – that was early.

We walked down the asphalt road onto the sand. The tide had cooperated and was out when we wanted to walk last time but now it was coming in, only a sliver of sand left in front of the houses on stilts. Was I ready to walk on the rocks? To get wet?

"Alicia Lowell hired me to organize her husband's files."

"Ah, yes. She had the husband who lived with the Indians. People thought him strange."

"I've just started. All I know is he has terrible handwriting." We took off our shoes and socks, hiked up our skirts for the walk between the rocks. "Maria, who are the Lowells?" The surf was too loud to ask once we started walking. She stopped to answer.

"It's a big family. Not lots of them. But they're very separate. And very rich. Michael Lowell and your boss Alicia Ortega married and shocked the town because he was Anglo and she Californio and Chumash. 'Mexican.' Their son is Scott. He fled to San Francisco."

"I just sailed with him."

"Oh yeah? Fun?"

"I guess. "

"Then there is George Lowell, the old man, Michael Lowell's nephew. So Alicia's nephew, by marriage. George's wife was from the East. She killed herself. Their son is Greg."

"Did they know Harry?"

"I don't know." She looked at me like I was asking a hard question.

"Well Skeffington did. And he's still in Europe." I should have stayed in London to waylay Mr. Skeffington. I could have easily gone from London to Rome or Venice or wherever he was. Now I needed to wait out on this shore. "How well do you know Mr. Skeffington?"

"I work for him. He entertains. Skeff, we call him. He's hired me to plan parties for the museum."

"I've not even seen Harry's plans for the museum."

She looked at me as we stood still to let the wave cover our feet, cold, and suck out again. Looked as if to say: Your marriage is not my concern.

"We'd better go back or we'll get very wet. Too cold for me." Maria was used to calling the steps, the more informed, the more local, the more practical of we two. I wished she could take over my life for me, decide, lead me from my confusion.

I followed her back toward the point. When the first waves of the higher tide splashed up my legs I let my bare feet take the shape of the rocks then leapt into the last of the sand.

"Maria, do you know Detective Garcia? "

"Yes, not well. He's a friend of my brothers. And of my parents and grandparents. Didn't he go to Hollywood?"

"Claudia said so. What have you heard about Harry? Anything?"

She paused, turned around on the rocks just above the water's reach. "He was a guest at parties, I know that. At Skeff's and others."

"Skeff again. What's the story on him?" Now I know I needed to ask about the others.

"Art collector, old Anglo family in town with an estate on Sycamore Canyon. Built a modern house up on the mountain, high. He's building a big place up there for – as you know–" she turned back to walk, saddened.

"Harry's museum for his collection. Why didn't we call you when Skeff first came to us?" Would she have warned Harry off? It had been so long since I'd said We and Us. "What else do they say?"

"He was a wild youth then settled down. They, the ladies on the porches, were mainly upset that he would never marry, Their way of saying he was homosexual. They don't countenance homosexuality."

Maria thought that was why the deep antipathy was in her aunts Until she learned the stories of Skeff's youth and of our present. The stories she skated between, ignorant enough to keep safe, outside the dangers of the plots. Until I came back.

"When I was supposed to be asleep I listened. Do you practice your Spanish?" She asked, fleeing the present into our history of trying to learn her family's language.

'More French now."

Maria dashed away to a bare spot of sand and I got wet above my knees stuck on a rock. Balance was still there but it was a winter ocean. And I had to wait too long to hear the stories.

"Harry met a Lowell here. Could it be Greg? "

"Probably not."

"Someone here–" The little beach houses were empty. We stood under one thick beam porch as a wave cleared off the last of the beach and rolled the rocks. Only when we were walking up to the railroad tracks could we see the trees and the blue mountains behind the beach. "Someone in Santa Barbara killed him."

"Or travelling through–"

How would my husband have been vulnerable to someone just going through, on the train, on the highway, stopped at the lights? I thought of the many ways strangers moved through this town. House guests.

"Workmen?" I asked. Maria knew the builders in the town – the stone masons, the carpenters. I didn't care she might be insulted.

"I know Skeff's crews. Nobody there."

"Could Mr. Skeffington be involved?"

"Skeff? No. He's an honorable man. He's old." Maria combed her hair back from her face with her fingers. "You have to let it go sometimes, Emma dear heart. I know it's so sad. Take a rest from it. This job, will it take your mind off your grief?"

"It will give me money to go back to France and heal. Here all I can think is who could it be. That took him away. The murderer." I was crying.

"Oh God, Emma. It's too horrible." She gave me a hug and a push to my car.

That night I skipped dinner and read a chapter in A.L. Kroeber on the Chumash.

CHAPTER 15

At drinks the telephone rang. Claudia went into the hall and walked back in with questions on her face. "A Mr. Miles?"

"Sorry, Gran. The private investigator."

The private detective sounded like he thought he had waited too long for me. "Well, about the locker?"

"I can't talk now." I didn't know what to say. I found a picture of a woman who might be drowned in front of a cave. Plans I hadn't faced. Lists. Maps

"Breakfast. Sambo's in Carpinteria tomorrow," he said. "We can talk then."

Garcia told me to stay away. I could have said no, but I was curious. I wanted to find out what he had discovered. I felt no fear, invulnerable in my grief and youth, and ignorant.

I wanted to see Detective Garcia again, not this man. I could report to Garcia on what he had to say. I hung up the phone to talk to Claudia.

As soon as I sat down with Mr. Miles, the private investigator, I was sorry to be in a booth. He was too big. Our knees almost touched. I wanted to be at a table, exposed. "Would you be more comfortable here?" I slid out, and walked toward a table, insisting, as if the seat in the middle of the room were safety from this man and his world that I felt dragging me under. He followed me with a look of dislike and rocked on the thin legs of the chair.

"Going for a ride?" He asked.

"I might." I was dressed in jeans and boots, my weekend uniform. "What did you find in the locker? Hand them over," he said darkly, matter-of-fact.

"What?" I asked, clear and truthful, unafraid yet. Only put off by his menace.

"The manager told me you were there. When did your husband rent the box?" Miles asked reaching for a toothpick in his pocket.

"When?" His seemed like a harmless question, but I still refused to answer. "I didn't ask," I said. "Stupid. That's why I'm not a detective, I guess." Claiming ignorance seemed easier than lying.

"You guess," he said, motioning to the waitress with his forefinger. He ordered hash browns and coffee, I asked for coffee and toast. I missed American diner buttered toast.

"So what was in the drawer I told you about?" He lay one fat hand on the formica table and tapped his fingers. The other was in his lap.

"Bulbs."

"Bulbs? Light bulbs?"

"No. Flower bulbs. In the freezer to keep them fresh."

"Why?"

"Harry planted bulbs on his sites. Early structure."

"Any photographs?"

"No," I answered. "Just the bulbs, and seeds frozen in ice cubes."

"Flowers? That's all?" I nodded. He didn't believe me, but he could tell I was sticking to my story.

What could I ask him? I couldn't say 'Do you know who the floating woman was?' I needed to ask him questions that didn't tell him what I found in the locker.

"Did you hear about Harry's last project?" I asked.

He was silent. His job was to ask the questions and to figure out what my real answers were. My job was to discern where his questions were probing, and where they came from.

"You've talked to the police detective?" He could see the answer in my face. "Of course you have. I know Detective Martin, we'll be cooperating." I nodded. There was Martin. I didn't tell him about Garcia. "Did the detective tell you not to speak to me? They always say that. They think what I can tell you will taint your memories of the facts."

"What can you tell me?" I asked.

"Not much more than you can tell me, Mrs. Chase." The beige man seemed weary and I was no longer spooked. Truckers leaned over their eggs beside us. He covered his hash browns with ketchup, chewed with his mouth open.

"You talked to the police?" I asked. I could try to parrot his questions. He was the professional who knew what to ask.

"Of course," he said. I didn't follow with a question, but he could see me searching. "Everything I learn is confidential, for me and my clients."

"Who hired you?" I asked.

"I told you before, your in-laws, the Chases in New York," I could see the food in his mouth. "My clients have the same goal as you in this matter. Find the murderer. Help me, help Lieutenant Martin."

It was hard to keep silent. I wanted to tell him what I'd learned, to share my early theories, to hear his

115

information. It was only the roots of the trust I'd seen for Detective Garcia in Gran and my belief in Garcia's strength that kept me as discrete as I was.

He finished the last of his potatoes and washed them down with coffee. "Who's been in touch since you've been in Santa Barbara?" he asked.

"No one. Except you. Not even my in-laws. "

"Was your husband having an affair?"

"No," I answered, though now I did suspect. Trying to sleep I tortured myself with that idea.

A look of disbelief. "Was he homosexual?" he asked again.

"No."

"There's danger for men who pick up men-"

"No, Mr. Miles, I don't want more questions. I have no information that can help you." I stood. He could pay for the coffee. It was his meeting.

"I decide. You owe me, Emma. Martin knows that. He'll know about the locker plant."

"He already does," I said foolishly.

"He'll remember more about the contents. He has it all?"

"Yes. The police have it all." I left Detective Garcia out of the discussion. "It's time for work. Let me know if you learn anything."

"You do the same, Mrs. Chase."

When I came out of the bathroom Miles was gone.

I called Detective Garcia from the pay phone across the parking lot.

"Detective Garcia, I've met with the private detective, Mr. Miles."

"Investigator. Listen, Mrs. Chase, -"

"He asked about Harry's locker. I told him there were bulbs and seeds in it. When I first saw him he asked about Harry's friends, about our marriage. Now he asked if Harry was homosexual."

"Was he?"

"I don't know." I should have known.

"Detective Garcia, I have found a job so I'll be here for a while."

"Good."

"I work for Alicia Lowell."

"I heard. I envy you. To finally see those notes."

"What have you found out? I might be able to help, if I knew more."

"Helping causes trouble," he said. And hung up.

I held the phone as if waiting for a goodbye. I was cold and alone in the parking lot along the Pacific and the coast highway.

CHAPTER 16

At dawn on Monday I drove the Porsche between the cactus and the open gates of Alicia's ranch. I stopped at the house for the key to the shed. Alicia's maid gave me a braided rope and a basket.

"Buenos dias, Senorita. Buena suerte," she said as I walked back down the hall to my car. Luck?

Past the gardens and into the meadow, I reached the edge of the orange groves and saw Alicia riding a palomino toward the barn. A dog ran behind her.

She dismounted, gave her horse to a boy and came over to the car. She wore a slicker over her riding clothes, a colorful scarf around her neck. She saw the braided rope with one big key and many little keys on the seat beside me.

"His lariat." she said. I thought she could see her husband holding those keys. "Thank god I haven't lost it." She sighed.

"Magdalena dusted your desk. That's all. I didn't want things moved before you got in. There will be some kind of order. Michael started -" Her lips softened and curled at the edges and the eyelids between her dark lashes turned red. I watched her, curious for myself at the threshold of the long grief of widowhood. I still thought Harry was away on a job—we'd be back together in a few weeks.

She pulled on her wet sombrero and tightened it under her chin. The hints of loneliness were gone. "Drive all the way over to the shed. Whistle for the black widows, when you go in. They'll hide."

Great. Another fear?

"We'll come up when you tell us where to clean. See you this afternoon." She waved goodbye and walked to her horse that was quivering under the little boy's brushes.

Past the barns the road ended so I crossed the field on an angle. Each sloppy roll of the tires tore out the new grass to the mud. I was swearing that if I didn't sink into pure mud, I'd walk next time, if I could only get out today. It wasn't raining, but it had been all night. I parked under a tree and hoped Alicia had a tractor to pull me out if it rained that day. The sky was deep blue, the clouds white and innocent looking, as if they were on their way somewhere else to join forces for rain. Spare us a bit I thought as one, speeding, its top falling, blocked the sun. I was jealous of the drought days, sun and more sun would be ok with me.

I opened the stiff metal door, whistled as loud as I could, and long, to the black widow spiders. I sat at the wide pine desk. I stared into the yellow darkness of the long shed until I thought I'd hypnotized myself.

In my daydream I heard paper falling, words crowding, dates, a jumble of lost languages that scared me, petrified. The door was open and the hard rain fell straight down, no wind driving it into my new musty domain. The stream roared through the trees behind me.

Where to begin? I unpacked the heavy basket; two thermos – one of lemonade, one of coffee, a glass and a mug, and a towel folded around sandwiches, biscuits and fruit. Sustenance. Company for the long day.

I walked through the rows of filing cabinets.

The drawers were dated. I carried a pad and started a map of the cabinets. Hours later I had a chart for myself. I walked back to my desk for a gulp of coffee, looking for labels on the keys on the lariat and on the locks. Numbers corresponded. I could unlock and open the rusted green metal drawers.

Inside were shoe boxes labeled with dates and names. I saw my ignorance in my surprise that the names were Spanish. The conquerors named the slaves, the Spanish named the Chumash. I took the boxes to my desk, and, delaying my plunge into this unknown, stared at the illegible, small handwriting on the tops of the boxes. Inside were cards, each scribbled with a date, and a heading. The writing on the cards was smaller than on the boxes, hurried, abbreviated, even more illegible to me. No wonder Scott laughed.

Work, into the files to find other boxes. I was in shabby, comfortable clothes. It was dirty work and felt like play, me an explorer, joining the French Foreign Legion to leave my troubles behind. In those green files I escaped from the deadly happenings in the real and present world.

I counted cabinets, drew and labeled a floor plan until the rain stopped.

I was at the desk, staring at my first box of cards when the door opened, fresh air and the afternoon sun slanted into my new world and Scott's shadow covered my desk.

"Here you are," Scott said.

I stood. A Lowell. The murderer or a friend? I didn't know enough to be scared.

"I've taken the week off," he said. "Have you found anything?"

"This is my first box. I made a list of the cabinets." Could I ask him for help? "Can you read the writing?"

"Show me."

I held up a card. Scott stood beside me and read: "'Inf.' means 'informant'. That's the person he is interviewing. Does the box have the name?"

"No, this symbol. And that symbol." I pointed to the designs that headed the card above the quotations in Spanish, English and what I guessed was Chumash.

I walked away from his side. "So does the box," I said looking at the front label on the box: a symbol that I came to know as that for Maria Solares.

'Festivals/Shell bead money/ headdresses, etc.' I took him to the filing cabinet where I found the box. The list on the front of the cold metal was long and inclusive with only a few etcetera's. Her symbol was there.

Scott flipped through the cards. "He was always in a hurry. He notes the central words, leaves out the transitions, the verbs, the English words for the Spanish. Only the salient words. Any thing he already had, he left out. And he let them talk. He only cared about the words."

"Oh no. Where does it say what he already knew, so left out?" I thought this a poor excuse for research. To leave your work incomprehensible. What did Scott think of his father?

"Check his library," he said. He sat on the edge of the desk.

"Did you think of doing this job?" I asked.

"Mother wouldn't let me," he said quickly. Then he looked at me. "So I assume. Well, she didn't forbid me to come in here, but I felt like she did."

"Why?"

"She shipped me out of here but fast. Off to boarding school. When my father died I was already in San

Francisco.-" Scott looked around at the rows of filing cabinets and cardboard boxes. "She told me I wouldn't be interested."

What a strange way to treat such a huge family chore. If he had been my son I would have had him in here doing school projects. That wasn't my business, those scribbled cards were.

"What does this say?" I gave him a card. He read it out loud to me, and the next, until I began to understand the lettering. As we kept working it was as if a veil was lifted from the notations and I could read. I showed him my early chart.

"So much work, so much time. We never had him – the work was more urgent," he said.

Scott and I wandered through the cabinets, opening drawers. "Where to start?" I said.

"Ask my mother – she'll say where to concentrate," Scott said. "We're riding later. Join us?"

I was dressed in a long skirt and looked at my loafer shod feet with a how could I look. "Not dressed. I'm sorry."

"Well. Next time." He left and shut the door softly. I wished I had worn jeans for the chance to be with Alicia. I needed to ask her about so much I was finding. Tomol canoes, Winter Solstice, the Paha and Antap, the Dream Helpers. The night before when I could not sleep I read the Museum bookstore offerings on the Chumash. Scanty and tantalizing, A.L. Kroeber's handbook asked for more research.

With desperate hopefulness, I searched for the crucial drawer containing the notebooks where Mr. Lowell clearly set down the keys to decipher his code. He gave only symbols for the names of his people. I wanted a list of who the scribbles represented. I wanted an index of the notes by subject matter. But I knew that was what I must create.

Hours later I heard horses shake their bridles and went to the door to peer into the sun. Scott and Alicia sat mounted under the tall oak tree.

"I'll see you at tea time?" Alicia called over.

"I'll be there," I answered, with questions. Could I ask about Harry and Mr. Skeffington and the Lowells? The Chumash world was so far a distraction and a way to keep the Perigord farm. I learned nothing about Harry without asking.

Alicia led me into her sunroom, sat and straightened her skirt over her legs like a nesting bird. I felt like a bird perched on a wire, ready to be blown upside down, gripping hard. She poured iced lemonade from the low table. "Tell me how you're doing."

I felt like telling Alicia to call in the movers to carry the files to the Smithsonian.

"Did you find a treasure today?" she asked with what became an opening line destined to make me forget what I'd been reading all afternoon. She smiled encouragement. "You'll be lost at first. But I can tell you some basic stories. If you know the 'myths'–" Did I hear disdain? "you may understand my anthropologist at work." She drank her lemonade, so I did. It was sour and sweet, delicious.

"This," she motioned around her, meaning outside. "This coast was an ancient grassland of mesas, and hills crossed by deep stream beds with falls of rocks, boulders rolled down and left by the fast winter water, like now. The fragrant sycamore trees grew where there was water and oaks in the fields. Under and in them lived birds and animals – coyote, lion, bear, squirrels, rabbits, quail, huge moths and butterflies and bats. Swamps and estuaries mixed the spring and rain water with the wide sea. A few trees grew tall, the brush grew denser and denser until fires came, popped the seeds and cleared the hills for more grasses and wildflowers.

"Santa Barbara Chumash traded the food of the mainland – acorns, wild cherries, sage seeds, pine nuts– to their cousins on Santa Cruz Island for money, hand-sized circlets of shells, holes ground with a sea lion whisker, strung on cord. This was the money for most of the Indians of Southern California so the Chumash were very rich.

"Chumash with their tomol, the long sea-going canoes, lived in villages on the ocean bluffs, harvested the sea and land and traded on the islands, up and down the coast and in the inland valleys.

"They died quickly when the narrow coast and bountiful channel were discovered by white traders and hunters. Murder, disease and the refusal to bear children into their changed lives finished the ancient civilization. White men's hunting, fishing and trapping almost finished the animals and fish that had fed the Chumash well for centuries.

"Steamships brought visitors and goods because the overland journey was hard – over sliding hills, long valleys, deep rocky streambeds, through ranchos, and the dry land of bandits, cattle, snakes, bobcats, bears and hawks. Now the highways make that passable, very quickly."

"What a history." As the rain fell heavily around us I asked "Did it flood then?"

"An evil sorcerer caused too much rain and was drowned by a mother and daughter in a sacred pool of frog urine," she laughed. "Do we think that's happening now? Tell me what you know."

I put down my wet glass and explained my preliminary chart of the files "May I add labels to the cabinets?"

"Of course." Stupid question

"I'll hang them on the handles so they're clearly mine," I said, businesslike.

"You'll find out what he's saved with what order." She stood to open a door so we could hear the rain. "I hope."

"What was your husband like?" At work I was allowed to ask questions.

"Michael. I'll show you a picture. Now I need a magnifier. He smiles back at me, and ahead of his truck is a dirt road into oak trees. He was a young man and he had been at work for years."

"How did you meet?"

"My brother knew his nephews. We heard stories from the women of his visits and his questions for the very old people."

Alicia gave me the photograph of her husband and sat down to watch me look at it. He wore a bandana tied like a cravat, tight around his neck, his fitted tweed jacket with two buttons done, his trousers loose except at the ankles and his feet in old lace up shoes. He was standing next to his Model- T or -A pickup truck. Its thin wheels had chains. Drums of extra fuel and water were strapped to the sides. He had a compartment open to show his equipment. A canvas canopy was up over the driver and passenger seat.

His hair was dark and his forehead went so far back it was as if his brain was exposed. His arms were long and slight but his hands were huge, one hooked on a post in the truck, the other pressed against his elegant jacket.

Alicia turned another silver frame my way. It was a photograph of him larger, standing against a rock his height. He looked handsome with a sense of humor. He had a big nose that shaded his mouth and a lower lip above his strong round chin and dimples that showed an inclination of a smile on his wide mouth. Lines between his eyes had begun to divide his forehead. Thought and squinting at the California sun will do that to a face.

"He took notes with all the California Indians he could find. Most of his work is at the Smithsonian. Chumash research he kept–we keep," Alicia said.

I had to ask her: "What are you looking for in there?" To me the storage building was a secret cave full of mysteries. Was it for her?

"I am Chumash, my husband was studying my people. I was young when so much was lost. I only knew what a child could pick up. I knew it was ending. Now, not earlier, now I feel I need to know what he recorded."

"How are you Chumash?" I asked. Claudia had called Alicia an Indian princess. I guess she meant it.

"Through my mother. Mixed with my Spanish father. With the conqueror. As my Scott is mixed with the Anglo subjugator," Alicia said, not smiling. "I was the first in my family to marry an Anglo."

"Do you speak Chumash?" I asked.

"Only a few words," she answered. "Michael's goal was to save the words. Don't worry, you'll discover the meanings. You have Spanish?" Alicia looked worried. "I forgot to ask."

I could see that Spanish was essential when I first looked into the files. Spanish, English and Chumash were used interchangeably. "I do know Spanish, a little. I'll need a better dictionary."

"Well, let's go into the library." She unfolded her legs and stood.

Scott had mentioned this treasure of his father's, the great library I was to come to know so well. She led me down the hall to a carved door that opened into a curtained room, air dim and dusty, high walls covered with books, globes in the corners and a telescope at the window.

Those books drew me with the promise of a journal that would hold Mr. Lowell's hidden codes to clarify his secrets. "May I look in here? Mr. Lowell refers to studies–"

"If you need to, dear. But don't take this room on. Scott promised me he'll deal with this library." She smiled with a mother's love. "At the rate he comes home, he'll get to it after I'm gone."

Did she know Scott and I had met and sailed? How much did he tell his mother? I must have looked confused.

"Courage, Emma. You'll figure it out," she said.

"I like this work, Mrs. Lowell."

"Alicia, please. Well, I'll see you tomorrow? You will learn about history, about tradition. Secrets."

"It's all secret to me."

She was silent. She watched the swallows fly from her eaves into the twilight as I left.

CHAPTER 17

U nable to sleep in the early morning I sped along the highway on the ocean to Summerland then over Ortega Hill back into the Montecito Valley. I took the road that cut into the orchard below Alicia's house to get to the storage shed to start the day's work. Up a left fork was a place I hadn't noticed, a farm house with wide steps to a porch between tall fat palms that waved and dripped water in the rain.

I parked in the mud. I drank sweet tea at the desk watching the rain out the small window, then went into more cabinets. No one came by, on horseback or otherwise.

An order began to show itself within the mess of the notes. Each note stuffed in the boxes was written on whatever piece of paper Mr. Lowell had at hand. Most had a name set off with colons, then Manuel, Josephina, or just, like Scott said, "Informant"- the most common name Lowell called the people who spoke to him, the old whose words he saved. The words were English, Spanish or strange hiccupping words with fanciful punctuation – the Chumash. Some notes had all three languages. I started a dictionary in my first notebook. To begin I had to trust that each scribbled word on random paper had something to do with the subject written in the three languages on the box label. I had hope. The language was revealing itself. I knew English and French enough to know their differences. Languages are the culture, embedded in the people. Language – thought and belief are contained there. A language lost is a culture lost. I began to feel the importance of the preserved words. "The sycamore provides the water for the soul for he whose Dream Helper is the sycamore. Without the sycamore– the tree, its breath or its idea – that person dies of thirst, as if from lack of water."

Would I find the intense pleasure of a scholar, discovery? I knew I worked to organize so others could find the messages left, the words preserved. These people were not assimilated, except for food and place names. They were erased. I knew that from other stories of Indians in America.

Culled from memories of the dead and the gone, there in the research of the dead anthropologist, lived the language. His notation for the sounds, funny jumping punctuation, was gibberish at first, then my eyes began to hear it, like Shakespeare after the second play. Words – cenhes he?isup is the wind; c?umas is Santa Cruz Island– jumped out and caught my ears. I heard the calls of the lost and wondered where to put them.

That afternoon when Magdalena took me into Alicia's sunroom I heard the sound of ice and saw the back of a man pouring Alicia lemonade. Scott was there. I wished I'd checked a mirror.

"Emma. My son Scott, home for the weekend. Scott, Emma, who has taken the task of mapping your father's notes."

"Emma, it has been a long time." Only then he looked at me and offered me a drink. He looked like he had been asleep all day, his eyes half shut, his hair wavy and uncombed. We were already a secret from his mother.

"Lemonade." He handed me the tall cold glass. "How's it going?" Scott asked. "Can you read Dad's handwriting?"

"Getting better. Thanks."

"You know Emma?" Alicia asked. Scott stood beside her with his hand on her shoulder.

"We were in school. And she beat me sailing, right?" He looked at me and smiled as if he wasn't telling her all. He didn't tell her I was from Montecito, Claudia's granddaughter. Did he know?

We sat with our drinks and watched the sun under a cloud light the trees into golden rooms of branches.

"You know my mother is a mestiza – Chumash princess with sangre azul of the Spanish –not a sea captain's bastard."

"Are you bragging?" Alicia said. "The senoritas of the sangre azul spared Santa Barbara war. The Americans were going to come and take it. So it's a good thing they married them first."

"Married?" I asked.

"My family never intermarried with the Anglo usurpers, until me."

"The Yankees married the local girls, Ortegas, de la Guerras, and got land. Lots of land," Scott said.

"The women's land?" I asked.

"Women could inherit –" Scott started.

"Chumash land. No one's land," Alicia interrupted. "Nature's, California's."

"The language?" Scott asked into the silence.

"I've started a list of the English and the Chumash and the Spanish."

"Can you translate Chumash?" Alicia asked.

Maybe, I thought. "Slowly. Are assistants in the budget? " I asked, joking.

"Too much for you?" Scott sounded sympathetic, but he acted as if I were about to spend his inheritance.

"You map it, then we'll decide," Alicia said.

"Those are my orders, solo forays," I said to Scott, thinking: I'd be jealous of me, so he must be. "I am making a dictionary."

He was looking out the window as drops of rain hit the pane and poured down. "Rain again. The moon is lying on its back, full of water -"

"Does it ruin your evening hike or were you going back to bed?" Alicia pinched Scott, teasing.

"How about a drive," Scott answered. "Let's go see the ocean, Mother, see it storm."

"Excellent. You drive. Emma, shall we take you home? Of course not, you have a car. Scott, we have a meeting to finish. You can stay and listen to what Emma has to report"

"I'm going to talk Magdalena into giving me some breakfast. Good luck," he said before he kissed his mother's head and ambled out, rubbing his unshaven chin. Something so male came and went with him. His mother looked blessed.

"This son of mine does nothing but sleep all day when he is here. What could he be doing at night?" Alicia laughed. "It's San Francisco, the city and his work and everything else. You know about that world?"

"A bit." Was I jealous of the city life, the busy life of light reflection? No, I just wanted my life back with Harry. What did Scott do in Montecito, besides sail? Did he know Harry?

Alicia was still thinking of her son. "I do love him to be in town. He stays in the old house. This was once a dairy farm, before my Michael transformed it into our home." She told me again.

"So, Emma, what did you find today?" Alicia asked.

"A box about the Winter Solstice." The references after the symbol mystified me for pages until I came upon 'Winter Solstice' with the same design in parentheses. A translation. I hoped the fog of ignorance might be lifting. Prematurely.

"Shall I tell you the story?" Alicia told me, "The Winter Solstice is the end of the year and the beginning of the year. Chumash people gather from the villages for days of festival. Chumash were gamblers, with bone pieces, in a game called, by the Spanish, 'peon'. So were the First People gamblers. The People who came before, who were animals and weather. Who became our Dream Helpers.

"On the first day of the Winter Solstice all debts of the year are tallied and paid. Sky Coyote gambles for the people against Sun, in game after game of Peon," Alicia said. Her glass dripped onto her lap and she ignored it. "If Sun wins over the Sky Coyote, there is drought and death the next year. Sun takes people up, tucks them in his headband and behind his belt and carries them to his castle of quartz crystal. Sun gives the people to his rattlesnake-aproned daughters to cook. Sun and his daughters feast on our dead. But when Sky Coyote wins, there is rain, and the earth is green and food grows to keep the people alive.

"Then, at the Winter Solstice, many things happen: dances, naming of the newborn. The dead are buried, their possessions burned and scattered. Sun is reminded by the ceremonies to come back to earth, to end the long nights. The Solstice makes the change. The people feast."

"And party," Scott opened the doors from the next room. "My mother's Christmas party is her modern version of the Solstice. She'll invite you next year." He had an old leather book in his hand. "I'm going up to the farm house, Mother. I'll come get you later." He kissed her forehead and pressed his cheek to hers. We shook hands. Was his house in the palm trees?

"You knew Scott before?" she asked.

"From school, parts of a few grades. I was in and out, depending on my mother."

"Perhaps we met?" Alicia seemed to look for the girl in the woman.

"I don't think so. I wasn't here for long, each year. " I would have remembered her. Did Alicia remember my grandmother, from their childhood? I guessed someday Claudia would tell me why they were enemies. For now I was glad the subject hadn't come up.

I wanted to talk about my family, but not the far past. About my part, my Harry. I could begin without preface.

"I miss having Scott here." Alicia looked lonely, ignorant of what I wanted to know, her face poignant with a beauty she had probably never seen in a mirror. She seemed oblivious of her looks. She must have been a beautiful young woman. "So I'm going to take advantage of his visit and cut our meeting short." She saw me look disappointed.

"Are you married, Emma? You wear a ring."

"I was married, until recently. My husband died." That wasn't true. Tell her the truth. "He was murdered."

"Oh my dear. Where?" Alicia asked.

"Here. In Santa Barbara. Harry Chase."

"Your husband was Harry Chase?"

"Yes, did you know him?"

"Ah, Good heavens, I am so sorry. I didn't think..." she stood and paced in the sunroom. The glass around us was streaked by the rain. She stayed standing, small and serious. "Manuel Garcia, the detective, he worked for me as a boy, and he's related–everyone is in this town-" She interrupted herself when she saw my face. "Detective Garcia came here, to speak to me about aspects of your husband's murder."

"What did he ask? Why you?" What did this lady in her refuge have to do with aspects of Harry's murder? A Lowell.

I wouldn't be able to escape here.

"Manuel said not to tell anyone." She smoothed her hair, sat and crossed her hands still on her lap. "I did not imagine you are the family."

I was shocked at this blunt fact of mystery. I was beginning to swirl. I thought I might vomit.

"What?" I sat and held onto the arms of the chair. "What do you know? Please tell me."

"Only, there were signs that suggested secret codes. We spoke of them. That's all I can tell you." She didn't mean to be heartless. She stood to say goodbye.

"Please tell me more. " I stayed in my chair. I didn't care about the job, what she thought of my stubborn attempt to make her answer.

"Ask Garcia. Emma, I don't want to upset you wrongly or mislead you. Manuel will tell you what you need to know."

I wanted to believe that.

"What did he ask you?"

"About history, a tradition."

Her elliptical answers angered me. "Mrs. Lowell, Alicia. Please."

She was silent. She watched the rain pour down the windows. I was still seated, staying.

"It haunts me. I need to know."

"He told me nothing. He showed me photos, sketches. You must talk to Garcia," Alicia said.

"Photos of what?" There was danger and knowledge anywhere. Could she help me? I began to see a ray through my anger.

"Emma, all I know, as I should not have said, is Manuel asked me about Chumash traditions."

"Chumash?" She had to have an answer.

"Detective Garcia thought I might know more about signs on your husband's body than they did. He knew they were Chumash. I did not have any answers for him."

"My husband's body." I was crying.

"I know there are secrets. But I don't know the secrets. Find those secrets in my husband's notes. Help look for answers."

I had my organizing principal. Alicia sent me wading uncertainly through the chaos, toward the Bear.

Garcia had photos of Harry, sketches of code, more code. I cried. What did Garcia see to ask Alicia about? Why did he talk to other people and not to me?

"I will go," I said, confused, alone.

"Tomorrow," Alicia said.

"Yes." With luck I thought. I had to get home to call Garcia and ask questions.

"Detective Garcia? You asked Alicia Lowell about Harry's murder?"

"For research."

"Into what?"

"Mrs. Chase, our investigations are not open, even to family."

"Alicia won't tell me what you asked her."

"Good."

"Tell me. This is my husband's life." My anger at being left alone overcame my tears.

"Mrs. Chase." He sounded stern, then even more serious. "Look for the Bear."

"Why?" I asked. Silence. He was finished with me. Was the Bear his hobby or did he have a plan.

"Copy the notes you find about the Bear."

CHAPTER 18

Early the next day in the warehouse, with new purpose, I cursed Michael Lowell, the amateur, for the mess he left, the man for laziness. Submerged between green metal filing cabinets I invoked whatever gods I was looking for and started the notes. What did these have to do with Harry's murder? Where was the Bear?

I slid open the files, lifted the stuck tops off the numbered boxes full of his undecipherable writing, some in notebooks, much scribbled on loose paper, crumpled and torn, notes taken in haste, on the road, in other's houses. He was in a hurry. It seemed to him the civilization was being eradicated. He must have counted on someone to do this, to find the stories in the shoe boxes in the drawers. I was working my way from box to box, noting cross references, mapping. Looking for Bear references.

In these notes Michael Lowell interviewed the few people in Santa Barbara who still remembered and had old tales to tell, the words of the old language still in their minds, with descriptions of what they had seen as children: the Chumash in the Mission era. Captive workers. Segregated.

'Informants' were those who would speak to him, who realized the Chicago man could save their language and their stories. They worked together to remember the almost-lost language, a lost culture. These early days they were only initials and numbers. I was sent from box to box by parenthetical references, Lowell interrupting the words of his informant to note other people who had remembered the same fact.

I found pictures of the people who spoke to him, later, and they were very dark, almost invisible, and beautiful.

Even that early day, I was beginning to love the puzzle that had been given me in that musty long barn. Once I could decipher the words, they called to me, like rocks to a beachcomber, to be picked up, taken home and saved, puzzled over.

In a box with a printed label– Chumash Hereditary Elites– were cards with names; antap, paha, wot.

I stopped myself from reading. That box was in order, my work already done, a prototype for the organization, calm and clarity lacking in much of the notes I'd seen so far. I left the file to read later about the ritual ceremonies and the power objects, the 'atswin, of these elites.

In a notebook I copied tantalizing messages that I felt were meant for me to read. I thought I could find my rope into and out of the depths of my life. I started then and everyday I put a quotation into a daily book. I thought it might amount to something. The rest of what happened went unnoted in that work journal.

"Frogs and rattlesnakes rained." Like it did then, that February 1962 when my Harry had just died.

"In the old days if a person didn't leave after doing something bad they would be killed." Coyote's wife Toad was killed in the land where the village gathered seeds, because Coyote had fooled Duck into marrying him with a great feast.

The wife was punished? Should I be afraid? Was Harry afraid?

"A pile of bones can be resurrected, revived. In the past they had medicine." I wanted that revival. Would it work with ashes? Harry was ashes.

Detective Garcia said to look for the Bear. I found:

"Bear sorcerers hung two bear paws and Bear teeth around their necks. These men wore their bearskin tied with cords and frightened women gathering seeds."

"At La Purisima they also killed another bear shaman. It was the first time he'd come out to experiment as a bear."

"Mateo also told Fernando that a bear-man hid his skin in a cave somewhere very secretly."

Bears could murder? And were murdered?

Alicia was dozing in the yellow afternoon light when I came into her sunroom. A sycamore leaf fell slowly onto the ground outside the open windows. A drying wind had relieved the damp for the afternoon but a new storm was predicted for the next day.

Magdalena followed me with a tray, green glass pitcher and glasses. The telephone rang. Alicia answered without a hello, as if she had walked into a room she knew well and continued a conversation. In the old times my grandmother and I spoke like that. When I heard Alicia talk to her son, I felt how that familiarity was gone between Gran and me. With Harry, I saw my own family in a clearer light. I felt how isolated we were each from the other. Maybe I could find my grandmother.

"We're here with lemonade. Are you coming?" Alicia spoke with her mouth far away from the telephone, loudly as if they were connected by string and paper cups. She listened and frowned. "He is? There?" She looked out toward Scott's house. "No I won't come up. Emma's here. I'll ask her. We're finished here.'" Alicia turned to me, held the phone on her shoulder like a pet, like a burping baby.

"May I send you, Emma?" Her voice said Please. "Scott can't come down and he has the meat for dinner."

I nodded. She went back to the phone.

"Emma will come. Why? Yes, sweetie. You can introduce them. Sure, she can." Alicia was reassuring Scott. I could guess he didn't want me up there. "She'll be all right," she said and smiled for me with what I guessed was a mother's delight. "You watch out for her. Bye."

I drove through the darkening orchards to the house wishing I had walked to delay my arrival. I stopped on the porch and I could hear the men through the windows.

"Your mother?"

"She's the same. She's sending up a new found friend, a young one."

"Good looking?" Greg asked.

"If you like the type. "

"A ball buster?"

"She's one of those cerebral girls. Visiting."

"Here to experience the Wild California West and find out what it is to get laid?"

I stood there as the stars appeared in the pale teal sky over the mountains. Scott opened the door before I rang the bell.

"Emma, you're here." He stared at me like I was an apparition. Then he looked annoyed to see me and stood aside. "Come in. I'll get the meat."

I walked in. He was close to me in the dark wood vestibule. Muddy boots, and walking sticks lined up against the wood walls and hats and jackets hung from hooks. "Where's the dog?" I asked and he looked at me rightly as if the question had sprung fully foolish from nowhere. Before he could find an answer the other man spoke from inside and we followed the voice into a big room furnished with long sofas and sagging arm chairs and fine tables.

"You didn't tell me she was beautiful, Scott," Greg said.

"Yeah?" Scott sounded unconvinced and looked at me to check for beauty.

"You didn't want to spoil the surprise." Greg smiled at me. He was the man in the dark at the Valley Club. Harry's Lowell? I was in the room with two Lowells. I had begun to ask everyone I met if they knew Harry. Did I dare ask these men?

Greg Lowell stood at the fireplace with a bottle of Scotch like an advertising photo of who he was, tan and tall in khakis, navy blue sweater, yellow polo shirt. He looked pleased to see me. Why was he flattering me?

"This is Greg Lowell, my cousin." Scott introduced us and Greg pressed my hand and looked into my eyes as if we had a secret. I remembered the turmoil I had felt when we first met and felt its return.

"We meet again. I knew we would. How well you look," Greg said. He had blond hair brushed back with water around his large head, behind his fine ears. "I picked the right day to come by and see you, Cousin," Greg said. "I would have run up. My route goes right by your driveway, but I thought arriving for drinks sweaty would be rude." He turned to me.

"Little did I know we'd have the privilege of such fair company. I'm lucky," Greg said. "I want to meet you and you turn up working for the family."

Scott looked at me to see if this stranger deserved such extravagance of courtesy. I was flattered and annoyed at myself for being so. I had no male attention in my life after so much in my marriage. This man paled, the two became the ghosts as I felt Harry alive, my husband.

Greg was grinning. Fit, his pressed pants tight, and his collar up, he seemed sure in his element. His eyes knew how light blue they were and stared into mine, the point of his eyes so dark, I didn't want to look into them long enough to see if there really was a blue ring around them. "So you're working for Aunt Alicia," he said.

Did Harry have a project with you? I didn't ask yet.

Scott walked between the two of us to the low cocktail table and broke the trance. Scott fell for the bait. "You know each other?" he asked. "Emma, we're drinking scotch. What will you have?"

I wished his mother had come up with me. Alicia would have been able better to protect me from Greg's snake- like focus of charm.

Hard to believe they were cousins. Scott was taller and could have been as handsome, but seemed have been cheated of the charm and energy of Greg. What was missing in his handsome face was obvious next to his cousin. An intensity.

"We saw each other at the golf club," I said. "My grandmother's award dinner."

"Not introduced," Greg smiled again. He intimated we'd met in passion on the grass links. I remembered my trip over a so-called branch in the dark and stars.

"Scotch?" Scott asked again across the low table. I accepted, though I had never liked it. My mother's boy-friends' choice. Scott took the bottle from the mantle beside Greg and poured for me. One of the boys, a role I could slip into and find comfortable.

"We were talking fish, Emma." Scott said. That's not what I heard from the porch. "Is anyone catching in the backcountry this spring?" Scott continued a conversation I interrupted.

Greg was still distracted by me so he just nodded to Scott. I felt bathed in the attention.

"Do you fish?" Greg asked me.

"A little." I loved to fly fish, to cast my hook and wait. Toss a piece of myself out into the water to wander in the currents, in a world I couldn't see, only feel, and couldn't otherwise ever know.

Scott sat in an armchair and seemed to reach for a dog to pet. He sipped his drink and watched Greg. I felt caught at their reunion, where I wasn't wanted. Scott was silent, giving the floor to his cousin. A few sips and I would ask for the meat Alicia had sent me here for.

Scott put his drink on the table that was piled with books and a dried bird's nest. "Excuse me a minute. In your honor Greg I'll check out my fishing gear. It's been in the closet for years, neglected."

"There's plenty of water in Los Padres," Greg said. Scott disappeared down a hall.

We were silent without him. Greg knew I was Harry's wife? Widow.

Greg sat on a sofa and put his tennis-shod feet on the low pine table. "That Scott. How can he stand to live in the city?"

"I ask myself that." Scott came back with a rod case, brushing off cobwebs. "Are you all right with your drinks?"

"Scotch is good. The real stuff. Our fathers drank Scotch." Greg leaned his head back into his crossed

143

hands, closed his eyes and breathed deep. "This house smells like old wood."

"That's what it is." He wound open the top of the khaki tube. "Father built the fire resistant one for Mother. This is the original farmhouse, still here. We've been lucky with fires so far," Scott said.

"The adobe builders burnt the first wood house. To stop change. Fires will never burn Montecito," Greg said as if he knew.

"This is my father's rod." Scott said as he took out the slender parts, twisted a delicate rod together and flicked it lightly. The tip whipped the air.

I wished for a dog to romp into the room and give us something to look at. It was not cold enough for a fire. If we stayed much longer Scott should build one, so we could stare into it.

"What do you do, what work for Alicia?" Greg asked.

I didn't look at Scott for the tack to take with his cousin, I opted for privacy.

"Curatorial work."

"How did you get into that field?" Scott asked me. Open season for questions. He deserved to ask. Those were his father's files.

"I had clients in England, and Europe, mainly with fine art to catalogue. My expertise is in the organizing."

"And you can find stuff, yes?" Greg asked. "Scott? We'd like that. Your father may have a map of Valerio's cave? Or better. I could help you, Emma," he said. "I know the subject."

Scott looked at him funny. "The luxury of having a professional to sort through the family stuff," was his reply. "I'd rather be a lawyer."

"What's in the collection? Emma, you don't know. Yet. Aunt Alicia has an offer for it, right?"

I treated the questions as if they were directed at Scott or rhetorical.

Greg sat with his legs apart, clenching his fists between them as he asked. Then he stood. "I have an offer, Emma. I'll explain it to Scott, and he can tell Aunt Alicia. My father's, our family's, collection needs Great Uncle Michael's work. The same buyer will be interested in both our family things. Those we're willing to part with."

Scott seemingly ignored us for the fly rod. I didn't want to say anything. I had no role in that level of the family business.

"Do you think that would be a good idea, Emma?" Greg asked.

"I wouldn't know."

"Only Mother knows." Scott pulled the rod apart. He wanted to get off the subject and seemed annoyed with his mother. "Greg and I were boys together. We played the Chumash. I was a canoe captain, and Greg, a grizzly bear hunter ready to do battle with only a knife."

"I'm still happiest in the brush. Of course, I take care of the family business, keep the trustees under control, the lawyers. I run the estate, the property, for Father. He's no help–I pretend to get his approval."

I remembered the Montecito standard of a productive life was not related to others' ideas. What the rest of the world would score as laziness, the Montecito people saw as privilege earned, by ancestors if not by themselves. Born to play in the beauty. Then there were those who fled. Scott? And those who struggled to hang on. Me, at this point.

Outside the day had finished darkening through lavender sunset colors to a deep grey twilight.

Scott said, "I'm going for wood. We need a fire. Can you stay, Emma?"

What else was I doing? I needed to talk to these men. Did they have plans with Harry?

Greg stared at the empty fireplace until Scott left, then zeroed in. "I've waited tor you." Greg turned the full force of his blue eyes on me. "Have you been into these mountains?"

"No." So?

"I can be your guide. Our mountains are part of the Los Padres forest that runs from the condor lands of the Sespe River to the Big Sur. With all this rain the springs are back. I can show you where they are, and the caves. We'll ride over. I keep horses at a friend's place."

I watched him talk. When was it my turn?

"I go back into the forest often. I know it as well as my father now."

When Scott returned, his arms loaded with logs, he came upon a silent Greg staring into my eyes. I held the front door knob as if it could anchor my dizzy feet. That man was trying to seduce me and it threw me. I'd ask about Harry another time, I didn't want to identify myself.

"I'll go now." I said.

"O.K. I've Mother's things out here." Scott dropped the logs in a tall basket.

Greg stood and took my hand. "Scott will give me your number." I could feel him watch me leave the room.

I felt my longing for the crush of flesh to flesh. Harry. To find another man? No search had been conceivable yet. How many people could I look for at once – the soul of my love and a murderer. Enough.

Scott walked me out onto the porch. The food was there in a cloth bag. "Bad to leave it out here, attract bears," he said. He lifted the bag and carried it to my car. "Fresh from the locker plant, for dear mother's dinner."

Locker plant? "What is Valerio's treasure?" I asked. I thought I'd heard something solid from Greg.

"A story of a bandit's booty hidden in a cave," Scott answered. "Gringo myth."

"Does Greg think your father has a map to the cave?" I asked. "Do you?"

"No, but I figure my father has the kitchen sink in there," Scott said. "Mother's told you to keep it secret?"

"Yes. I will, of course."

I felt for resentment against me in the tall man and found none yet.

I called to meet with Garcia the next day. I longed for Garcia. My Mexican protector. Was it because he was a policeman that I thought he had the answers? Or because he was so handsome? I thought he could find the answers and protect me from them.

"Ah, the guapo detective." I agreed. Word supplied by the old lady at the Mexican diner where we met on Haley Street with formica tables, padded metal chairs, a counter. Garcia picked Rosa's when I asked him to see me again. He was already there with a coffee when I came. The other customers had beers.

He stood. "Mrs. Chase?" Why was I there, a bother, his eyes asked. Right off he said, "What do you have for me?"

Bullfight posters behind him, Garcia looked like Zorro. I was captured by that image of him, felt glad to have Zorro on my side. What could I tell him?

I just wanted to see him.

"I found notes about the Bear."

"Did you copy them for me?"

147

"I will. I'm making notes. Tell me: The Lowells – Alicia, Scott, Greg. Harry met a Lowell and started using code in his journal. Why? Should I be afraid of them?"

"No need to fear Alicia. She is a good friend of my uncle. Like your grandmother. What that man doesn't know–" His smile was dazzling, foreign to me. "The others, I don't know. Always be careful."

Family love, I wish I'd known it. I only had my grandmother. Garcia, that Zorro, was the mustachioed embodiment of a male family love I'd never known. In my anger and grief I knew I was looking for a protective love. Too late for a father's love.

With Harry I found a husband's love. Now I was on my own again.

"Mr. Skeffington? Did you talk to him before he left town?"

"Martin did. He'll be back soon and I will talk to him." Garcia waved away the waitress. "I have to go home. Thank you for calling Mrs. Chase."

Detective Garcia, I couldn't help it, I watched myself follow, swoon to obey him. I wished he would ask me to do something. Now I knew only to find the Bear. What did he ask Alicia? What did he know? We want to assume the police know what they're doing. To feel safe. I no longer felt safe.

CHAPTER 19

I was just home when Gran called on the intercom to say the telephone was for me. I had a phone in my room but the ringer was off.

Greg Lowell, the voice I knew. "Emma, you're home."

"Mr. Lowell?" I asked.

"Please," He coughed an 'of course'. "Greg. Mr. Lowell is my father. Join me for dinner. Pete's, I'll drive. I know where you live."

Something was working for me. Greg called when I needed him to tell me if he knew Harry in Montecito. I felt like going out. I needed to remember there were still people, conversations, life. Try to find a distraction from my misery without Harry.

"I'll meet you there," I said. I'd pick one of Gran's cars for the drive into town.

"All right. Casa de Seville, lower Chapala Street, 6:30," he said. Good voice, deep.

A long shower, washing my hair, eyes closed, I had to force myself to turn off the water. I stood dripping and thin, a sad look on my ruined face. I exaggerate, I was young, but I saw what grief does to a face. I pretended, acting in the mirror, that my husband was alive, in the next room, or say in Europe. Emotional face lift.

I tried that in the red room of the restaurant. Pretended I was joining my husband, or we had not

149

yet met, this was his best friend and Harry would come later. My face fell as my mind brought him to Santa Barbara and to death. Gone. Greg stood at the old fashioned bar, foot on the rail, like a sea captain at rest.

"Emma," he called and made the people who weren't already staring look up. I was glad I'd combed my hair. It was cut well enough that I forgot about it, like my clothes. He walked behind me to follow the owner to the corner table. "How's the abalone?" Greg asked.

"Tender," the owner answered. Was he Pete? "Please give my regards to your grandmother," he said to me. Someone told him who I was? Who was my grandmother to these people?

"We're the new sensation, did you see how the place stopped?" Greg laughed. I like men who laugh. Greg watched me with his hands folded in front of his mouth.

We were the center of attention of the tables of white people, men in navy and women in bright colors. I felt again the inexorable push of society to couple up. I wasn't interested. I was a couple, though my man would not come back.

"Who's here?" I asked, to get my bearings. What did I expect to find, who could be there to brighten my life? It felt forever dark then. I guessed this was still our parents' restaurant. I didn't care. About anything, except Harry being gone, and my work, perhaps.

"The great Montecito estates have sent representatives to dinner. With us here the group is almost complete."

"This is the Montecito dining room?" I asked, caring only if anyone there saw my husband on his way to death.

"They probably know more about us than we do," Greg said.

I said. "Scary."

"Never mind them." Greg laughed. "You'll love Santa Barbara for the places outside," he said.

"Oh yes?" So far my grandmother's nursery, her garden, the shed at Alicia's and the car were my only places. And the water. I'd sail and swim again.

"I will show you the outside of this town," Greg said. "And the insides." His sureness almost captivated me.

"Take me where?" I asked.

"Santa Cruz Island. Have you been there?"

"Not since I was a girl." I'd motored over to Santa Cruz Island on fishing boats with Maria and her uncles and brothers. They dove for urchins and we looked for waves and swam.

"Come sail over with me." I doubted it and he saw. "We could go just for the day."

I knew the Channel Islands were too far for that. I watched Santa Cruz all my life, when the clouds cleared, the mountains beyond the water, bookending the Channel with the ranges behind us.

"Santa Cruz has everything – mountain peaks, canyons, valleys, coves, caves." He gazed into my eyes as if he thought he could see me understand the wild island. "Like this, before people ruined it.

"I'll tell you more after we order. Ignore the others around us." We ordered and Greg talked about the crossing, the island caves, the diving.

"When are you going?" I asked.

"When can you?" he asked.

"I'll look. I am tempted."

"Good," Greg said, smiling.

"I love to sail," I said in bad humor, explaining the temptation, lest he think he was the inducement. I wanted to get over again to those floating mountains I stared at so often as if they held an answer that was not here for me on the mainland.

"Your work goes well? Have you found the Brotherhood of the Bear?" he asked.

"Why?" I said, alert.

"Those men captained the canoes to the Islands. The tomol. They read the crossing weather in the stars. When the swells hid the low stars, the Channel was too rough." I found myself thinking of the stories in the files as I listened to Greg. I began to think he was a resource for my work – he knew the history and the tales.

He could tell the stories like a bard. Greg was the kind of man who pulled you in with his stories. I didn't really believe them, I just listened. The backcountry caves, the animal spirits. I took them for couched myths, entertainments he had concocted for the peasants.

I was alone, looking for stories, thrown out of mine, willing to listen to his.

The red room emptied around us. We both declined coffee and he paid the check with out any fanfare.

"Call me and say you'll go," Greg said as we went to our cars in the dark lot. We talked loud over the highway noise, 101 traffic rumbling by, stopped at red lights a few blocks below us.

"I'll check my schedule," I said as if there were things for me to do in this life. There was my work.

CHAPTER 20

I finished my coffee before Gran came to the table, left the toast and took the stairs two at a time to finish dressing.

Alicia's ranch gate was open. I wound through the trees' dawn shadows up to the warehouse without seeing anyone. No cars at Scott's house. Had he gone back to San Francisco? Was he coming to town for the next weekend?

The fields were an improbable bright green, fresh grasses high between the trees. It wasn't raining, though the radio said a front was just off the coast, hitting tonight. It would rain and I wouldn't have to go boating with Greg Lowell. I had decided over night that I should keep mourning for a year, follow the tradition that insulated widows before me from terrible mistakes. After we had been set too free.

I found a story about Vulture stones, buzzard stones: The frantic mother buzzard finds the rock that brings the hard boiled chick to life and then the person who stole and boiled the egg steals the rock for its magic. The powerful rock that can bring back the dead, revivify. Its owner can see distant secrets and into the future. In twelve years the owner will pay for the power and die.

I wanted a stone. To have Harry for twelve years I would trade my later days. But Harry was ash floating in trees, trampled in muddy grass, not a body I could place beside the stone to bring him back to me.

By second tea time I had found references to the Clan of the Bear. Why did Garcia want it? I found the Brotherhood of the Bear. The Clan of the Bear was a clan of men from the powerful guilds who owned the tomol, the ocean- going plank canoes. Great power attended those people with the Bear as their guide, the notes said. Canoe owners and chiefs were the highest clans of wealth and prestige. Hunters of sea lion, otter, swordfish, tuna, shark, they traded across the Channel for the shell bead money. Cash. They rowed to the place where the cash was gathered and strung.

They chanted as they ran into the Pacific Ocean, and rowed across the Channel between storms:

Give Room!
Give Room!
Give Room!

Do not get discouraged!
Do not get discouraged!
Do not get discouraged!

Help me to reach the place!
Help me to reach the place!
Help me to reach the place!

Hurrah!

Did the Bear paddle with them?
Did that matter to Harry?

The more I read the more I hoped somewhere in that work would be a consolation for me. Some words that could make me better. I read the Chumash believed in endless cycles of reincarnation. Will I pass a child one day, a new life, Harry's next chance? I laugh at myself. He may live again, but it won't be with me and that's my misery.

Alicia was curt at our afternoon meeting. I was to tell her another time what I had found. No questions for her about the Bear this day. She hoped there were more boxes already organized. I was ready to leave, my lemonade half finished, when I thought to ask her about sailing to Santa Cruz.

"It can get stormy between here and there. The winds and seas are the full Pacific winding around Point Conception. Be sure you have a good weather forecast." I didn't mention Greg. No reason to combine work with the little social life I found myself in. How close was she to Greg?

"Scott used to go over a lot. He has no time any more." Alicia said.

I waited for her to look at me to say goodbye. She looked up from her hands. "Scott is a mystery to me, almost like a lost love."

Alicia took a rosary from her pocket and began to finger the glistening beads as I took my leave.

From my cool room I called on the heavy black phone and got an answering service. I declined Greg's invitation to sail, and asked the lady to thank him. Greg called right back and I was unprepared. How much must I learn about him before I trusted him?

I remembered my husband here. Who did he see before he was murdered? Who were they that took him from me? I wouldn't meet them working in the Chumash warehouse and hanging out with my grandmother.

"Well, let's have dinner and talk about it. I know good Mexican food. I will take you, it's on Milpas." His voice suggested I'd need his strong shoulders in the Mexican part of town. That night? My grandmother was going out, bridge, and I wanted to eat dinner so I accepted, as much for the drive as the company, I told myself. I'd meet him there. I could ask him about Harry. What was Harry doing here that sent him into such danger? Inescapable? Not escaped.

My only pleasure in the day, except for the hard fought moments of understanding at work, was driving along the roads of Santa Barbara in one of my grandmother's cars. She had old sports cars in that barn of hers. To get over to Milpas Street I took a convertible MG on Alameda Padre Serra, the stone walled corniche along the foothills of the huge mountains.

We sat on a back patio. Ignoring his food after ordering mine, Greg asked about my grandmother, my health, as I looked over him to the stars above the street lights. He seemed to care only about me. Noisy cars cruised by. The food dripped on my hands, so I was slouched over, mouth to the side trying to eat the rolled tortilla. He picked up his fork and pushed the food into piles, separating out the onions. "How is the work going?" he asked. Changing tack.

"It's interesting so far. Eventually it may be illuminating."

"How's my cousin?" Greg asked.

His cousin? Called back, I must have looked blanker than usual.

"Scott."

Of course, I knew that. "I don't see him. How are you cousins?"

"Scott's father was my great uncle, my father's uncle. Scott's my father's cousin."

"When did his father die?" I asked.

"Last year," Greg said. "He wasn't much older than my father, my father's Uncle Michael, the almost-famous anthropologist. Is my cousin still in town?" Greg asked. "Scott the lawyer."

"I don't know. I'm buried in the shed."

"What have you found?" Greg asked.

"Illegible notes, so far. It's not easy going." I hadn't yet needed to test my promise to Alicia not to talk about her husband's research. Greg was the first to ask me about it. It was easy to plead ignorance.

Greg walked me to my car. "If you let me know early tomorrow we can still go to Santa Cruz this weekend."

"Honestly, Greg. I can't go to Santa Cruz. I'm busy on Sunday," I said, lying. He picked a hibiscus off an old bush, and put it behind my ear. A flower with no scent. Did it light my face on Valerio Street?

"Everyone's sniffing around I bet -" Greg said as he took my arm as if to promenade down the avenue.

"What?" I didn't think I heard right. "Sniff around?"

"Following close. You're in the place with all the information. There are secrets, hidden in caves. Some people've heard and they'd like to find them. What if you get a map—or a location? They'll want to know-"

There was a cave circled on Harry's map from the locker plant. Where? Who could I tell?

"What secrets? Valerio's?"

"Valerio's?" He laughed. "The loot of the highwayman Vincente Valerio is a treasure the gringos know of, cached in a cave," Greg answered. In the dark he looked less a gringo. "I know better."

"Secrets of treasure? Where?" I asked, brushing the shiny trunk of Gran's car as we reached it.

"You tell me, Emma. Be careful with the information. I know who's interested. Who to watch out for with your secrets. This is my town. I can help you." I believed him.

"Thank you." Anyway, I'd let Alicia be my guide.

"I'll show you a cave in the back country," Greg said. "We'll go riding. Back into the Los Padres," Greg said. The National Forest behind Santa Barbara reached to Big Sur.

"A cave?" I asked, sliding the old key into the silver lock.

"A painted cave," Greg said.

"Chumash?" I asked, opening the door, turning to him.

"Oh yes," Greg said. So I was interested. I'd read about the caves where the Chumash retreated to paint, seen sketches of the designs and color copies of the cave paintings.

I said, "That's tempting. I need to get outside." I'd let Greg show me his Santa Barbara. And learn his connections. So we made plans for a Saturday picnic horseback ride. I decided a ride was not as risky as a sail. I could walk home.

I drove home slowly through the little houses with flowering gardens, up to Alameda Padre Serra. I turned left, away from Montecito and drove under the stars into Santa Barbara, to the Mission, top down, the pink towers above me in the moonlight. Built by the Chumash for their Spanish masters. Rebuilt after earthquakes by the gringos.

Around the long fountain that was the Mission Chumash washing trough, around and around, staring up at the stars, wondering if they reflected in the water, I didn't want to stop, afraid of ghosts of the Chumash enslaved there. I gave up the thought that I had escaped to a forgotten place, a beautiful backwater where the landscape could assuage my pains.

In my room, with the lights off, I looked at my old toys, the books, their shadows, their darknesses. The nursery room still there for me. Its continuity kept me alive, but I was feeling sorry. It was not my own bed – I crawled into my grandmother's guest bed. My mother had never been around, nor my father, so I had only houses and servants to define my home. The houses were more reliable, but they were sold. I did not have a home until I found Harry. Then I lost him. My only home was with Harry and he was gone. My body knew it all the time and my brain repeated it like a mantra.

In the morning I called Garcia. 'You asked me to look for the Bear. I found the Clan of the Bear."

"Keep looking. I want symbols, images for body painting."

"Harry was painted?"

CHAPTER 21

An alarm clock got me up for work, not the watery dawn which made me want to sleep. I dressed without looking in a mirror. I headed for coffee and cinnamon toast in the yellow morning room. My grandmother was there, in a pale grey cashmere robe. Claudia sat with her tea, her white hair in a tight French roll– setting the curl for later. To show I appreciated the home she and her family had created, I said "The beauty of this place is a real blessing."

"Thank you darling. Turning religious?"

"Not Christian. I'm grateful for what is right for me, with so much so wrong."

I did not want to talk to her about the Chumash world I was wading into. Skeffington, Alicia, the Lowells – those were questions I could ask and did not, yet.

I made my toast. "I've been invited to sail to the islands, Gran. What do you think?" Though I'd already said no I did want to get across the Channel somehow.

"With a party?" she asked.

"You have hopes for my social life?"

She sipped her tea. "No, darling. What ever you want."

I asked, knowing her answer to my question. "A man I met offered to take me over to Santa Cruz."

"Certainly not. You don't go anywhere you can't take a cab home." I knew that rule. And always carry a dime for the phone.

"Saturday I'm meeting a new friend for a picnic." She looked at me, stifling her concern, her comments. I might have listened. "I may go riding, I miss that."

"You're a rider?"

"I like to go on a balade. Ride about —"

"With the Marquis through the villages – I know." Gran reminded me she had a life. "Makes sense. Your father and grandfather were big riders. Try Mr. Cathcart. I'll find you the number.

"Emma dear, how is your work going?"

"Still dealing with the papers Alicia's husband left her in total disorder."

"What an inheritance."

"Well, it's work for me."

"Inheritance. Those who marry an heir or -ess think of only cash. And properties – great places to go. They don't know, or they wouldn't marry us, that all they'll get is stuff. Physical stuff. And family stuff – old feelings, on-going problems."

"Was it hard, Gran, when your parents died?"

"No. It's all I had to do. My husband died young with nothing but ponies. So I was alone to deal with all this." She looked around the room.

"How did you meet my grandfather?"

"He was a polo player. A good one. That's how he got here – to die – that's how we met. Mother made me go to a party at the Coral Casino. Polo players were in town for a tournament. Such a night." I could see the young woman in her winsome expression. "I met your grandfather. We married soon. I followed him on the polo circuit. When I was pregnant with your mother we came back here and lived in a farm shed in Carpinteria. My mother bought him ponies and he trucked them around California to play. Until one of them killed him."

"Grandfather a polo player. Father a cowboy. No wonder I long to ride."

"Did you see your father?"

I shook my head. "He lived on a small ranch in Wyoming. He asked me out, but," I paused while I found an excuse. "I didn't know him."

"So you were afraid?"

"Was I?" I thought of my succession of stepfathers. "Maybe."

Gran said "I was lucky. My father – he did spoil me for other men –I felt his love all his life."

"You're better for it, right?" I said. "What's it like? A father's love?"

"With a father you learn what a man is like. You practice on him – see what pleases, what you can get away with. Useful knowledge, when you grow up."

"I hope I'm learning as I go." I thought of my love for my husband, a stranger to me.

"Was it hard for you, with so many stepfathers?" Gran asked me.

"Sometimes. Learned about creepy men. How to take care of myself."

"Oh dear, I was not much help there. You should have lived with me."

"Did you know my mother was fiddled with as a child here?"

Claudia looked so sad. "When I heard the stories about him, later, I guessed it must have happened here too. I was sick. He was her father's friend. I did not protect your mother. No wonder she left town and me."

Chapter 21

"Did she tell you it was happening?" What could my grandmother have done about a notorious member of the social set. Warn her never to open the door to him.

"No. It was my fault. We were never close. She didn't like me. So when she needed me – I stopped seeing him, once I knew. I would have screamed, slapped him, if I knew then. I don't care who his family is. I've heard he's an invalid, in bed. Good riddance."

"I didn't tell my mother on her husbands. She was oblivious."

"Oh darling. Are you all right?" I loved the way my grandmother's emotions showed on all her face. Her wrinkles moved, her eyes changed color, her mouth's involuntary reactions were true. But I wanted her to smile. Her angry face was scary,

"It was nothing serious. I got a lock for the doors."

"Good for you. No push-over, my granddaughter. My one and only– You'll have to deal with the stuff. Free rein, but all the responsibility. Not a cheery note to start the day." Gran looked apologetic. "I'll start giving things away."

"We don't have to worry." I could see the age in her back and gait. She could not leave me too.

At work I set down my thermos and sat to look around me. I gave up the search for a system and read what I found in each file in sequence and noted where I found it. I pretended I could create physical order.

Animals were once People, the First People. Then all People died in the Flood–except Woodpecker–and became plants and animals, and became Thunder, the Wind and the other forces. They became Dream Helpers who know human's life because they once lived it: the Eagle, the Beaver, Thunder, Whirlwind, Pelican, the

Bear, Datura Weed, Blackbird, Swordfish, Seaweed, Fox and Skunk. They came, the Dream Helpers, to help the plain people find and use the powers that the First People once wielded on earth.

"Power is energy scattered throughout the universe when it was created."

'Atswin gather power. Those are the things: the ritual, holy tools, and the personal talismans.

"Animals–serpents, bears, coyotes–can become human. People can become bear."

I felt I could immerse myself in those dusty cabinets and emerge in a different form – a form that didn't need Harry, a body that could carry on in my life. I would be willing to stay a woman, I didn't need to be a bear, except to chase down the murderer. Just as long as I didn't ache for Harry like this.

The Informant said and Lowell noted: "'Nunasis'– bears, serpents, malevolent–here since the First People, live in the world below, move among us at dark."

So there was reason to be afraid of the dark.

" 'Atiswin have more and less strength. Several 'atiswin have more power than one." 'Atswin were the tools for power, they were inherited. In a tale 'atswin take Coyote across the bridge to the nether world and they protect him in the Spirits' deadly games. The Spirits want Coyote to die so he will stay with them, so they try to kill him in sport.

Harry did not have the tool to protect him. Dare I look for a Dream Helper? For tools?

What were my tools to gather power? My great–grandmother's sapphire bracelet? My ring from Harry? My mother's diamonds? I've stared into these diamonds for years, watching the world. Distraction, not power. Can I find myself in their facets? But I'm not lost, Harry is. Where do I find him? Not in this sapphire. What power tools can bring him back to me?

A story stopped me then and now refracts into the past and the future:

"There were two men who had 'atswin of Thunder and were very 'atswinic. There were the father and his son. Even if they had once had good friends, now they were 'atswinic they had no friends at all and would kill anybody who came near where they lived." *??*

I guessed 'Atswinic meant captivated by their tools of power. Like me with my engagement ring? If these jewels were stolen from me what would protect me?

Home and clean I came into the room where my grandmother waited, my favorite room –high paneled with tall windows onto the sloping lawn, painted my favorite color, an antique blue green, that changed with the sun. Formal furniture, my friend the zebra rug.

"Hello darling. Come for a drink? Tea?" Hair down and wavy, a notebook in her velvet lap, my grandmother's feet were bare on the footstool. "Why is it called an 'ottoman'?" she asked laughing. She motioned to the bar on wheels. "Bring me a sherry, darling. My penmanship is going. I'm beginning to erase, like a child. Age. When I can't walk anymore, I'll move above the garage – that's a big flat apartment – and you can have this –"

I poured our drinks.

"If you want it. Not now. When you move back to town. After conquering the world."

I knew then I'd never want to move –'back?'– to Montecito. Ghosts, gardens of fear. There was one ghost I wanted to find and take with me. So I had to stay. Make the money for the roof. I could not face

another summer of moving pots around for the drips.
Alone in France.

"I've been thinking – You could go to our apartment
in New York. The heat works."

"Oh, Gran, New York alone in the winter. I have no
friends, no job. I have a job here. Am I a bother to you?"

"No dear. For now. You need this – the nursery;
family such as it is –" she pointed to her feet up, in the
living room as if I should be ashamed of her. Hair down.
"But Emma, there's more for you out there. You're
young. This is a backwater. What are you doing here?"

"Mapping stuff is my job. Not just stuff. Words on
stuff. Words in many boxes. I am learning from the
work Mr. Lowell did."

"The Indians' man. Is it all of his work?"

"Just his Chumash research – the rest is at the
Smithsonian."

"I imagine they want this too."

"That's my job really – to get it ready."

"So others can use it, make something of it?"

"I guess so."

"You've buried yourself in old papers. I have higher
hopes for you, Emma."

I steeled myself for a lecture about being disap-
pointing. "I'm sorry Gran. It's what I could find."
Ambition: mine was underdeveloped and now narrowly
focused on survival and my husband's mystery.

Claudia continued. "I see myself in you and want to
warn you. I was passive to compensate, no, to disguise
my strength. An American woman, bred too strong, not
skilled enough to hide it, not taught by the culture how
to use it."

"What about Southern women? They are skilled –"
She was not to be interrupted.

"I see that in you. Avoid it: the geisha, the cow-towing, the crossed arms, slumped shoulders – I know the times are very hard for you. But now, total change is possible. Recognize yourself soon so you can act. Be brave. Get out there."

"Can't I be brave here?"

"This town is small. It can't be your whole world anymore, unless you shut too much out. Then you end up either ignorant or bored and depraved."

"People have full lives here. They must."

"Maybe. What I know are missed chances."

"It's not too late for you, is it?"

"I'm old. I am beginning to meet myself as a baby. I feel my mind wandering. My life is set. Your life is ahead. Do something before it's too late."

"I'll call Maria and go out."

I dialed the black phone from my girl's desk, wishing for a photo of Harry. Maria answered. She was my Alicia, my local, my 'Mexican' friend. We were allowed to be together by our mothers' inattention. And by Gran who had learned her lesson, I now saw. "Meet me? I need to get out of the house."

"Even that house?"

We arrived at the same time at the Somerset, a bar and restaurant set back in a low brown building off the old coast highway in Montecito. Too early for dancing, the piano was empty, the drum set covered. We ordered drinks and dinner.

Maria's first question was about my new job.

"I'm organizing Chumash research an old man did. Lowell." I should have known that Maria would know.

"The Lowells?" She seemed shocked. "I didn't figure that."

"Alicia Lowell, her husband died. He was an amateur anthropologist. I'm hired to curate his notes on the Chumash." She stared at me. "I've only agreed to begin. Get them in some known shape."

"Alicia." She seemed relieved.

"Yes. In a big place on East Valley. With the orchards. You know them?"

"It's a big family. That one spent all his time with the Indians."

"I'm only in the Chumash files."

"Alicia has more than the local's passing interest. She is one of them. Greg Lowell is my friend. Her nephew I believe. He will want to meet you." I kept quiet. "He's a collector."

She said 'collector' like it was more than someone who buys and hoards things. I aspired to be a philanthropist. Though now I was poor. What did Maria want? Did she want a family? Or did she have enough?

"Your beau?" It occured to me.

"They're very private. Greg and his father, I set up their parties. They have themes, often Chumash actually. Greg, he was always handsome. Turned fascinating."

"What kind of parties?"

"I don't know as much as usual. He relies on my discretion. I set up the scene and leave. He doesn't use staff, so another crew cleans up, my cousin, who told me I don't want to know, when I asked. I don't ask Greg. I guess the mystery adds to his appeal." She looked dreamy, a little scared, then came back to me. "Have you met Scott Lowell?" she asked.

"At Alicia's. What's he like?"

"A little boring, for my taste. What did you think?"

"He's ok with me being there. That was my worry."

"You aren't thinking about men, so new a widow?" She smiled for me, looking for a spark I did not feel. "Me, I don't have time for men. I want a career. Don't tell my mother. She still pretends my father is the main tortilla winner of the family. We are women in the 1960's. We can be different than our mothers."

"I hope so," I answered, contemplating my mother's fate.

"When it warms up we'll borrow boards from my brothers and I'll take you out surfing."

"Can I still do it?"

"You can. You just need to remind the muscles. I go out when I can, to paddle. Good for the figure." It worked for her. "The cold water is good for your skin."

"Maria, can you get me to Mr. Skeffington?"

"He's coming back to town this week. You can call him."

"I'd rather be introduced."

"You do pick the private ones. I'll see what I can do."

"You met Harry."

"Yes, at Skeff's."

"How was he?"

"Handsome. Happy. Busy."

"Without me." I was still angry.

My bourbon cocktail tasted too good. I needed help in all parts of my life. Surrounded by papers with voices from the past, no contact with my old life, no new life.

I did not tell her I was going riding with Greg. It was too complicated and I was lost in the connections. And it meant nothing romantic, like her dinner with Harry.

"Please try to get me to Mr. Skeffington."

"You bet. Let's do this again," Maria said. "When there's dancing. Maybe we'll get lucky."

My luck was gone.

CHAPTER 22

Down a dirt road on Picacho Lane I found Greg on a fence in pressed jeans. "The lady's on time. You look French." I wore my riding kit that I brought back from France determined to find a way onto a horse in Montecito. I felt him look me over. He seemed to approve. "Let's go on. I'll drive." He held the door to his car, already running in the gravel. We drove in the old Mercedes, deep red leather seats, a clunk in the engine, to a dirt road through a meadow to a barn.

The horses were saddled and tied to a rail. Greg untied and led my horse to me. He handed me the reins, watched me say hello as I reached the leather braids over the buckskin horse's dark ears and grabbed them in the dark mane, ready to mount. He held my knee for me and watched me throw my leg over and settle in the western saddle. He checked my stirrups and took his handsome palomino. He mounted, flipped his reins, the silver bridle clanked and his horse shook its head. He kicked the horse with his rolling spurs, and pulled it back, showing off, making the horse jumpy. I felt my horse calm as I let him have his head to follow Greg's prancing horse. We left the corrals and rode a fast walk up a trail in the brush. Greg kicked his horse over and over to keep it climbing fast so it dug holes in the trail and heaved the big saddle. I told myself he knew the trail so I should not be afraid. At the muddy fire road, bulldozed up the side of the mountain and along the ridge top I rode beside Greg, paying attention to my seat as the horses slipped.

My first ride was on a broad and padded Western saddle, feet hanging in long stirrups, with my father. Very young, I held onto the horn and rode in the snow on a sheep ranch as we looked for orphan lambs to raise. Bottle feed, the sucking stronger than me. On the fall plains of Wyoming the horse knew more than I did. I figured this one did too. I wanted to trust the horse. He felt solid, a quarter horse, built for the sofa chair of the western saddle. And the view! I was entranced.

Greg talked and I listened and watched the birds fly out of the brush by the trail. "The horned toad rules the land animals, the swordfish rules the sea and the Eagle Sl'ow rules the sky. The Bear is the older sibling of all the animals. You know this now." He was naming my discoveries. What else did he know?

I liked the hint of the Wild West that this man wore like a bolo tie. My horse stepped high in the mud. I began to ache and stood in my stirrups to stretch my legs. Greg kept a few paces ahead, then as we passed beyond a cut in the hillside, he spun and flung his arms wide to the view as if he owned it. The mountainside trail opened to the coastal range of triangles of deep blue sloping into the sea that was shiny silver in the afternoon winter light. The sky was another blue. The day was suffused with blues.

"One day I'll bring you at sunset," Greg said. "We'll stay all night under the stars. Today we'll have a picnic."

That was enough for me. To be on a horse I felt almost like myself again.

We started down the back side of the mountain away from the sea into a thick forest of oak and brush. Finally we stopped and Greg unpacked his saddle bags.

He spread out a picnic and I tried to walk with stiff legs under the trees. Sandwiches, fruit, and candy bars, water, and wine and a thermos of tea. He told more stories, the Chumash myths, the life cycles of the moths.

After the lunch I should have felt it coming on, the edge the colors took, the bright at the seams. Greg was apprehensive beside me, not yet in motion, watching. I couldn't bear to look at him. I vomited behind a bush.

"Now I'll show you the cave. You're ready, aren't you, for the paintings." He had promised to show me paintings. Greg stood, and held out his big hand. He led me to a group of boulders. A cave, long and low, was carved into a curve in one big rock. I stooped to see in.

"Get in, then you can see them." His hand pushed me down.

I crawled in and lay flat on my back, like in a low headed bunk bed. Something flew by, furry, warning me. A huge moth? A bat? The horses were loud outside, animal, stirring. The trees reached down.

Greg's hand came in, aquiver. He patted me and it felt reassuring. I was lying in a rock, painted red, long enough to lie in, and too low to sit up in, a personal-sized cave, cold and hard. I tried to avoid the thought of a coffin and the claustrophobia that lurked in my mind. I felt like a hot dog in a bun. I remembered the Oscar Meyer Weiner car with its melodic horn and felt better and laughed at myself for getting into this.

Then I saw the paintings above me on the rough rock. I had entered the world of my days' work. Over my head and along my body, were the creatures, planets, serpents, demons, skies and sea of the Chumash cosmos.

Dark fishy, eel shapes swam in the dots and left wakes. Circles turned within circles, spinning me, and above my other eye circles pulsed out from a center star, radiating triangles like a child's sunbeams. Creatures were joined to creatures, sprang out and stood upon zigzag lines. A turtle of circles dragged its tail.

I turned over in the cave, arced back to see behind my head, the toboggan swirled, the earth sped with me, creatures waved to me, spirals spun.

Under a fish shaped shark's egg with marks inside like people with their hands over their heads, was a three eyed creature, outlined long in body, flattened with four hands and two little bent legs with a long tongue that became a manta ray sticking out from the darkness between the legs.

It looked like a map, of the sea, of events, of creation.

The cave was a present, my gift. I could stay in there and travel the world and the universe. It felt like Paris did once, I never wanted to leave.

The world lurched. Would an earthquake smash the rock onto me? Was I flipping out?

I stopped moving.

"Like it? Just wait," Greg said. Then it started to happen. In my imagination or not, I was switching with lurches into a sharper plane. It felt like drugs must feel, heightened colors, louder reality that was stronger than I, indifferent to my frailty.

"Come out before dark. Mountain lions," Greg said near my head. I heard his voice and it sounded reasonable, but too whispered. "What animal do you see?"

Did he do this to me? Dose me? Seemed unlikely. This was a lover of nature, a gentleman from a good family. A handsome man.

Not someone who would drug me and stuff me in a cave.

My fault. My brain was leaving me.

It fled into the paintings away from the man whose feet I saw, pacing. I lay still, I rode the earth's turn in that toboggan. Everything went faster and my mind whizzed in my rock space capsule to the places those paintings mapped. The sand dollars, the turtles, frogs, unknown creatures waved to me and I tried to wave back.

Then I must have fallen asleep. Later I rolled from under the low curved rock onto the damp ground below. I stood up. Greg was there and hugged me close, his wide shoulders covering me under his arms. He smelled of a wood fire.

"What did you see? Did you see an animal? I can interpret."

I said nothing. I wasn't going to tell him. Who was he?

"Can't talk about it can you." He started to kiss me and I pulled away, staggered into the bushes and took a pee. The relief did not bring back the ordinary life. I had been drugged or my madness was strong enough to color the day more brightly, to increase the sound.

"Don't tell me about it yet. Save your dream."

Did I dream? Did he trick me into the Chumash Datura drug ceremony? Pretending to be Antap, daring to give me tolache, the poison Datura, so I had visions to meet my Dream Helper? A turtle?

Greg gave me the tolache, he meant to control it, I see now. I was to find my Spirit Helper, the animal, the force to guide me. Once I knew how to find power – was I to join his world, or to be conquered in it?

I pretended I understood him, stayed silent, and waited for him to untie the horse and bring it to me. I hoped the horse was willing to carry me. I thought I would be free once I was mounted.

We rode back. I kept quiet and held onto the warm animal under me. Times the horse was jumpy, I listened for mountain lions. Only crickets, and then sometimes no crickets. What else passed? The brush was too wet to crumble under an animals' foot. The horses had to step around mud slides. Off above Santa Cruz Island were more clouds.

Greg rode ahead of me, ignoring me.

I sat in the dirt in the shade as he unsaddled and released the horses, asleep walking over to the water trough.

I pretended Greg wasn't scaring me. I believed it was strangeness in myself, not something he'd done to me. But I was silent in the face of his politeness. Had he drugged me? If I asked I would admit to him what had happened.

My work saved me. It had been illuminated for me. Good fortune put me in that cave and showed me those paintings. Now I had seen what my work in the field notes on the Chumash might mean. Could they talk to me? Would I see these people to be inspired? Or doodlers, drugged by the poison datura. They did not care what I thought.

For what I saw, was I to be grateful to Greg? I felt he had gambled with my mind. I was not prepared for the power of that cave.

I sat away from him as he drove me down to my car. We were silent. Too exhausted to say we were exhausted. "We'll save it for tomorrow," Greg said inside the car, a voice that didn't fit his face as I remembered it on my ride home. Then he was distant. Was it now thick with passion? "Now you must not fuck for 21 days. I know that, you're safe with me."

Fuck. I felt like I had just fucked the earth, the cosmos in my cave. But this man? Not if I could help it.

My own car. I was free. I shifted gears slowly, clutch heavy to push, along the Montecito country lanes, curves big and slow, trees drooping too low. Who could I tell? No one. I went to bed, to shield my mind from more, shivered with the loneliness of no one to talk to, then slept immersed in the nursery.

CHAPTER 23

Sunday morning I woke from a dream of color. I wanted to get into a cave again. What were those paintings, that color, that movement? What did Mr. Lowell's files say about the cave paintings? I wished I could start work right away, but I hadn't yet worked on a weekend–hadn't cleared it with Alicia. Monday I would search the notes for caves, now I knew what they could be.

I had my life before me. Did a turtle lead me out of the cave? I felt slow and careful, barely wanting to stick my head out, Cruising on levels of air like a sea turtle in water. The yellow silk walls suited my head – sunlight muted by civilization.

I needed to ride again. I couldn't depend on others. Alicia and Scott might invite me. Greg again? Too scary. Though my ride with Greg had given me, with all the rest, a taste for the distances and places a horse can take you. Also the interspecies communication I missed without my dogs. *Yet another incomplete sentence*

"Gran, is there a riding teacher in town?"

"Here? Mr. Cathcart. A White Russian who teaches. He has a small place down San Ysidro. Stables and a ring."

"I want to ride. Not that driving your cars isn't enough." She smiled back at me. "I could jump – I

177

haven't done that for years." I could fling myself over fences, disconsolate, brave. But I needed the horse and the ring.

"The National Horseshow is here, at Earl Warren Showgrounds. I have friends competing. Come with me? Have to see the horses rack on." Claudia smiled with excitement. "I'll drive." She seemed to guess I was not all there. I didn't know where the rest of me was.

She drove us on the highway to the other side of Santa Barbara. I followed her to her box on the big open dirt ring and watched men in khakis set up jumps.

Detective Garcia was by a truck at the entrance to the ring. In blue jeans and a worn hat he looked manly and at ease. Broad shoulders, big hands, his boot shod foot on a rail. I wanted him to look after me, to care about me and find my answers. He saw me and nodded. He stayed down on the dirt, near the gate and I stayed in my box. Neither of us waved. If he weren't so handsome I might not have noticed him, in his light hat among other men in hats and wide belts. Claudia looked over and saw him. She waved and he waved back.

"Adelino's granddaughter competes. I loan her my horse to ride."

"You have a horse?"

"Oh yes, she takes care of him and competes on him."

"Detective Garcia's daughter?"

"His niece."

As I was glad not to hear of a daughter of his, I suspected I had romantic notions for him. Hopes of a revival. Life and love. Deluded.

"I found the horse in Europe. She's doing well on him."

"Will you go say hello?"

"Not before her class. Don't want to make either of them nervous."

Chapter 23

I wanted to be closer to Garcia. To tell him about Greg and the cave? That would have to wait. Was it his business?

Something in me wanted to tell him everything. To ask him everything.

CHAPTER 24

Question marks, surmises of meaning, references to more folders, pencil drawings of the cave paintings' shapes; I was darting from drawer to drawer to find more and the day passed before I took time to look up at all the open drawers that blocked the way through the files.

"Emma?" A man's voice bounced through the metal maze. I jumped and didn't answer.

"Emma? It's Scott. Are you still here?"

I looked out the window. Black. It was late. It had been a grey rainy afternoon so I'd had the lights on all day. Now they shone only around the lamps and the interstices were dark.

"Yes, in here."

There was silence and then I jumped. He stood close behind me and sniffed my neck.

"Ah, like a librarian," he breathed deep as I twirled around. No point in clobbering him. The bosses' son. One thing I didn't expect on this job. He stepped closer to me so our thighs touched, my back against a cabinet. I leaned into him, gravity and then warmth and swelling. I wanted a man more than I admitted.

He whispered in my ear. "Have you found the lost treasure?"

"Which lost treasure?" I pulled myself away. He did not seem dangerous, just forward.

"The Yankee tale. Hidden in a cave, the robber Valerio's loot. Or the stolen Chumash treasure. You haven't heard the rumors?" Scott asked.

I went to my desk, sliding drawers shut. "Rumors?"

"You're rumor-proof? Good."

"Well, I have my own big story for rumors to attach to." I was not yet listening to other's stories.

He held my hand first like a boy his mother's, then in both hands, a man. "No one would know. Merry widow and the bosses' son. No one would suspect." He held out his arms. I was tempted to walk right into them. I would fit under his shoulders. I could see the bulge in his pants and felt flushed for the stirring of it. The intimation of sexual power. And possible pleasure.

"We were talking about treasure," I said. I wasn't ready for sex, I thought. Widowed and I barely knew the man.

He brushed my cheek with his fingers, "Don't say no."

I shook my head, the trace of his finger tips too warm.

"I'm instructed to ask you to come for tea." He backed up after a big whiff. Taller than his cousin, weirder. "You will come for tea," he said, more clearly.

"Yes." I had questions for Alicia.

"I'll wait for you. It's dark out there."

"Coyotes get me?"

"Maybe a pack but no, you're too big for a coyote. Bear maybe."

"Thank heaven no more grizzlies in Montecito." I closed the last boxes as he stood there, marked my places in the files.

"Do you see your cousin?" I asked as we stepped into the crisp cold.

"Greg? Last I saw him was at the farmhouse with you," Scott said.

"We went riding."

"Be careful there."

"Your cousin?"

"My father's nephew's son. His dad is more than the black sheep, he's a villain."

"Old?"

"Now."

"It there a stolen Chumash treasure?" I asked Scott who I could as much feel as see in the dark beside me. We walked through the blooming lemon orchards in the cold clear night. He held my hand and steadied me, the sky was so light with stars we had shadows.

"Which one?" He bumped into me softly. "Forget I said it. Don't tell my mother." He was serious. "She won't talk about it. Let me know what you find."

"You keep secrets from Alicia?" I was kidding.

"I'd keep us a secret, too. I'm here at the beach house." He took my arm and tucked it under his. "I could help you feel better -"

"An affair would help me?"

"Definitely."

"I'll keep it in mind."

Alicia was reading under a lamp in the dim room. She poured tea and Scott went into the next room and turned on a light.

"What new have you found?" Alicia asked.

"Caves," I said.

"Sea caves or land?"

"Land cave, painted."

"Ah yes. Where?"

"Behind these mountains. I want to find out what they are, find more."

"Roger's book will tell you," Scott said, a book in his hand. "I have it at the beach house."

"Where?" Alicia asked. She looked at only her son whenever he was in the room. Now he came and sat beside her.

"At the beach, in the library. Took it to read. Slow transfer of the California collection," he said to me. "She doesn't know."

"Verdad" Alicia said.

"I told you Mother."

"Return them," Alicia said. "Emma needs them."

"Follow me down to the beach. I'll hand it over now."

"What is Rogers' book?" I asked.

Alicia answered. "He mapped Chumash and earlier sites in the area for the Natural History Museum, published in the Twenties. So it's early Montecito too."

"Great." I wanted maps of caves.

"Follow me then," Scott said. He tucked the book under his arm.

"What are you taking now?" Alicia asked.

"Cervantes," he said. "You and Emma finish your debriefing?" he asked. "Mother, did you show her your writing?" He kissed her on both cheeks.

"No, corazon. You are dismissed." Alicia sat back in her night dark sunroom.

Scott's car led me in mine through the trees of Montecito to the ocean side of the railroad tracks. Down a gravel driveway was a Caribbean type house with low hanging eaves and paths bordered by banana plants.

He had the key. Inside, he left the house dark and pulled the curtains onto a long lawn that shone in the moon to the sea, bright silver and rough.

I was mesmerized–out of the hills and the tree covered valleys, down to sea level. Into light, motion. The waves were higher than us, breaking white against the berm at the end of the lawn.

His breath on my neck became a word, then turned into a tongue and back to a breath before I could answer the word.

"Outside." He opened the doors to my silence, the waves roared and the wind flew around us inside. He walked out and held out his hand to help me. He held my hand and we walked down the path toward the ocean liner-sized waves that shook the ground as they crashed over. It was raining with the spray and cold like a northern winter among the green grass and banana palms.

I walked close enough to the breaking waves to be scared of all that energy so near. The spray drenched us and we turned around and ran as it began to pour rain. We might as well have gone swimming.

Inside we shook and Scott left and came back with towels. "The shower," he said. He put his hand on my elbow and his arm around me. I walked, warmer, in step with him down the hall to a big dark bathroom. He left off the lights and turned on the shower.

He stripped, facing the other way and got in the big shower with two faucets and steam at foot and waist level. I stripped and went in, stood eyes closed, head under the hot water, hidden in the steam.

The bolting urge was warmed up, distracted, trusting. I leaned on the tiles. After a long time he got out and turned off the water. He handed me fresh towels, still in the dark, then an old terrycloth robe, too big for me.

"Now the library," he said. He had on another robe, even bigger. I hadn't seen him, hadn't looked except to notice his long pale back and young man's bottom.

The library was more a t.v. room, filled with long sofas and many books, on shelves, stacked on tables.

"I'll find it. Have a seat."

I settled into a sofa's deep corner, crossed my legs up under me inside the robe. He took his time looking, distracted by books he noticed in the search. I was curious what he had to show me and as curious about the room. Oil paintings, landscapes, dim but pretty, crooked on the walls between the bookshelves. California, New Mexico, the West made bluer and softer by its desert. The television was big and new dark wood. Beach rocks balanced on the top of piles of books on the floor.

He was gone long enough for me to settle into the sofa and bury my head in the pillows, dozing in the sound of the rain and the waves.

I jumped. He was behind me. He kissed the top of my head and held the book up. "Found it. But first." He kissed my ear and my neck in the back and then in the front under my chin. I slid deeper into the corner of the sofa.

His kisses touched my lips and knew them, moved with them and into them with such intimations of delight that I didn't laugh at the idea he might have to summersault over the sofa, and I didn't move as he came around, maroon book in hand, and kneeled on the floor in front of me. Then I laughed until he kissed my knees and held my ankles in the breadth of his fingers. I felt no control, no voice, no will to do anything but want to shiver some more, to open up to this man, whoever he was, his kisses–my body knew his kisses on a level where I didn't know my body.

He stood and pulled me up and to him. I took his hands, I wanted him now, to feel more and more. Pressed against him, my body felt it fit, owned to explore, if only for those moments. I didn't care who he was. I wished I didn't have to see him again but this night I was willing to do unforgettable things with him, whoever that man was who could kiss me places no one had ever touched so my closed eyes blurred then sparkled with the stabs of pleasure.

He held my hand and I walked with him, simple as that and we went down the long hall to a bedroom with windows on the sea.

The night was light outside. He pulled off my robe. He licked my nipples, so cold they stood up pressed into his rough cheek. Then he led me to the bed. I felt captive, wanting to feel what was next. Seduced into trust and longing that left me his creature, longing for more of that joy I felt shivering through me.

He lay me down and rolled me over so I pressed my cheek into the pillow, eyes out to the night, the palms and eucalyptus and the stars. He was gone. I closed my eyes to hear the surf and remembered my bare ass as he kissed it, startling me into fear of what was to come, of where I'd gone, past the point of a graceful exit line, into the realm of defenseless and naked and more afraid of myself than of him.

His kisses ringed my bottom and buried between my legs, then he rolled me over and kissed my belly. I held onto his shoulders as if they could do for the both of us and he pulled up and lay on top of me so I knew he was ready and teasing us both.

He kissed inside my arms and under my breasts and sucked on them, his hand between my legs and under my bottom, between and slowly into all parts of me, so I felt like passion was flowing from my nipples pulling for more from his fingers, to feel the circuit of current, to have more of those skillful knowing parts of him in more and more of me.

I panted, and swallowed screams with air to keep alive, to keep myself there as too much pleasure made me want even more, to know how much I could take and to go beyond it.

He forced aside and apart and pushed inside me, reminding me of him, a man thick with blood for me, for this, hot and big enough I had to stretch around him and felt him pound against the top of me.

Would it be over, this man was in no hurry, he held me up bottom resting in his hands so he knelt straight and held me to him, my back arching, head back to take.

Then slowly he stopped and pulled away and as I began breathing again, slowly, he turned me over and lifted me by the belly to find me again, fingers at work, himself deep inside and playing me like an instrument to his climax.

With that he shuddered and threw me down and lay beside me, asleep.

I wept. He slept. I stood and walked down the hall to the bathroom, found my clothes. Sore, dazed, my body new to me, I found the book.

Aftershocks on the drive home, memories of his fingers and tongue, determined to forget it happened. Ships pass in the night and signal from their loneliness.

I went to bed without bathing and remembered birth control, the reality of what I'd just done. It would have never have happened if I'd let myself know I wouldn't resist him. If I'd had to plan it, it would have been impossible. And, that night at least, I was glad to my bones that it had happened. Sex like that I'd never known.

The book he gave me had maps of the Chumash sites, the oak grove people sites, villages found and classified from their refuse piles. I read until I slept, deep sleep of fish swimming and bumping each other.

CHAPTER 25

The next morning I stopped by Alicia's back door, expecting Magdalena. Alicia was in her big kitchen, cooking.

"Emma?" she said, taking my unusual presence in stride. She was on her way to eggs, fresh and dirty in a bowl. She washed them and broke them into a thick iron frying pan. "Come for breakfast?"

"Ah." I was speechless in her presence. Her slow intensity of warmth and activity was mesmerizing.

"I have things to do, like you. But I am not going to rush. Cup of coffee with your eggs?"

"Yes, please." My boss. I obeyed. Alicia handed me a plate of eggs. A place was set at the thick bench table. She broke shells for more and kept talking. I sat at the table and stared at her.

Such things had happened to me since I saw her last. I'd been her nephew's captive in a cave, maybe. Then an eager, too-willing sex slave for her son. Scott. What did a mother think of a son? Alicia, could she see his tracks on me? Was she safe? A haven in the madness or a denizen of the delirium?

"Scott gave you the book?"

I said "Yes." Would she go any farther? "I started it. So much history in this place."

"Yes. Too much. My Scott is engaged, have I told you?" Alicia said as she passed me the mug of steaming coffee and a jug of milk.

"No, I didn't know." Understatement. I hadn't figured. Well, Scott wasn't available. He wasn't married, either. That was my surprise, really, I thought, not the other. But good. I was relieved. Scott didn't want people to know of our secret as badly as I didn't want them to know. We could ignore each other, even forget that one night our desire and our bodies had taken over, like succubae, ruling and leading us onto unknown charts. I had the book Scott loaned me in my briefcase and the marks of his teeth on my back.

"Dear patient Emma," Alicia said. Where did she get that idea? "May I complain to you. Can that be a part of your job? To hear a lady's complaints." Alicia spooned on fresh salsa and dipped sourdough bread in her eggs and I did the same.

"It's not the first engagement. He bolted before." She shook her head on cue. "This time I hope he does. It was embarrassing, his jilting the Brazilian. This one I'd like to see him leave well before the altar." Alicia soaked up the last of her eggs and the salsa with the crust of bread.

"It's my fault. I sent Scott away. Boarding school, Europe. He didn't want to go. He loved this town. But I wanted him to escape Santa Barbara. In a small town you live your life under the eyes of the other people caught in that one tale. There is only one story for you, and I wanted my son to be where he could invent his own life, without prejudice and the demands of ancestors." Alicia laughed sadly. "I am so unfree, I wanted to set him loose. He's a wonderful man because of it, but now I can't bear it, that I did this. He is a mystery to me, like a lost love."

Alicia fingered her pearls, big and pink, too short a strand for her to see.

"Marriage. I thank the God that accepts praise, the God of my Spanish fathers, for my husband Michael. I ask myself, is my son as lucky in his choice, this Missy from San Francisco? I fear for my sweet son, marrying a socialite." She finished her coffee and stood to wash the dishes, and handed me a linen towel to dry. She seemed to grieve. Secretly I was glad he was a bolter.

"This fiancée I've only met. He keeps her a good distance away. He's afraid I'll put her off. Thinks I don't like her."

I didn't want to think about it. I dried the plate. Those were not my plans, nor my people.

"Maybe he thinks who I am will turn her off," Alicia said as she poured tea into the thermos.

What image of herself was she conjuring up? As a potential mother-in-law she had everything – the estate, chic, an independent life.

"Indian, Mexican, Spanish, not a mixture that has much cache with the Nob Hill Brahmins."

"Oh, Boston?"

"No. Worse. San Francisco. Types feel superior to Southern California. Not that my mixture was acceptable to your Claudia and her mother, either."

"Well it's much more interesting," I said. So she knew about my grandmother.

She looked at me like I was a rank flatterer and poured more milk. "Exotic?"

Had I insulted her?

Alicia was ready for me to go up and start work. She took her coffee and nodded to Magdalena who was mending in the corner. Their day was about to move into action and mine was expected to do the same.

"You work, you learn, Emma." Alicia eyes lit the air between us and she whispered for me not to hear. "So I can forget."

I felt a sadness that made me cry on my drive through the beginning rain to my work shed. I so missed my husband. He had never made love to me like this stranger who belonged to another, who betrayed her with me. Not often, after the first few years, did Harry and I have sex together. He was travelling, I was travelling and when we were in bed, finally alone together we cared about other things.

When did it start that I hated my husband's kisses? They felt to me that he was kissing someone else, that his lips said nothing to me, lips that could talk so much, so well, said nothing I could feel. His tongue violated me, forced itself into my mouth without an introduction. I hated his kisses. I loved him, when we talked, when we walked and read, then we gardened and farmed. But I dreaded bed. I couldn't decipher his kisses and I thought that killed my desire for him. I needed myself for sex when I was with my husband.

Sometimes when I'd had too much to drink I'd seduce him, climb in the wrong side of the bed, lie on top of him and he'd play along or not. Always with affection.

I didn't know him, he was a stranger to me. Then he was gone.

Harry wrote me in London from Santa Barbara, but he did not ask me to come to him. I carried the letter with me and now kept it open on the painted desk at my grandmother's.

OK

"Pink fleshed trees line the roads. Eucalyptus trees strip naked, woody bark hangs around them in tendrils.

I understand you better, darling, here in your home.

Work is slow–always mid-project – Design is done. All I do now is pass on hiring. They're gathering workmen. I'm partial to the sons of the European masons who came here to build in the Teens and Twenties. The walls absorb me. They will affect my work. One site needs walls –

Sending photos.

I'll tell you all about it, next time.

Goodnight, Sweet dreams my love, kiss kiss, pats for the dogs -

I love you, Harry"

How I wished there were more for me to keep than his handwriting on airmail paper. How I wished he'd written "You must come now, forget your job, Dear Wife. I miss you and want you here."

My Harry had known me well and forgiven me my faults. With his clarity about people and their motives he led me through the minefields of desires and distrust. On my own I felt too vulnerable. Now I had to prove to myself that I was brave.

The storage room felt in its silence like it was full of noise. I went straight to the maps that were in the files so labeled. Looking for caves. The book Scott loaned me by Rogers had details and drawings of Chumash sites. Caves, some with paintings–one behind an oak tree on a farm, one beside a pool, all described with reference points that could have easily been torn down or built over. The road. The boulder and tree. I had to figure out where in modern Santa Barbara were those places. Where was the mountain cave? Harry's photo of the floating woman was at what cave?

With a magnifying glass I searched the maps I found, spread out on the floor. Above the pond on Henderson's Montecito farm–a road curved at the edge, was it there now? Where was Henderson's? I'd have to go to City Hall to make real sense of the names and details in the book from the Twenties. So until I could get to the old registries I put the maps back into the files and noted their location and returned to cataloguing, searching.

I pinned my hair off my face and started reading, moving through boxes quickly, inserting tabs with informants' names, with subjects: Coyote myth, winter solstice–and numbered references to the index I kept. No longer stopping to puzzle over the convergence of the myths, I read them quickly, let them seep into me to know them later.

The Chumash mermaid is mother of abalone, of all fish and coral snakes. She is the daughter of Sl'ow the eagle, and she disappeared fishing when she spurned and mocked Coyote's flirtation. She let him hang from her hook, slack so he had to swim to shore with her tackle. She repents.

What does she repent? Spurning Coyote? Or her wicked ways as a daughter of Sl'ow, cooking and eating people?

Coyote went under the Channel and saved the nephew of the village leader from the Swordfish by racing, eating, hunting and dancing with them.

The Swordfish come home heralded first with wind, then flying sticks and clubs, then a light fog and a dark fog.

"I was so disappointed when I woke and you were gone." Scott stood across the room, water dripping from his hat. "I didn't mean it to be like that."

"Like what?"

"Over so soon."

I looked at him, muddy boots and wrinkled pants, unshaven, more like a sorry intellectual cowboy than a city lawyer.

"Your mother tells me you're engaged," I said.

"So? That doesn't mean last night didn't happen," long pause, "or that it can't happen again. With variations." He smiled and I figured I was due to blush, if I ever had. I was in the dusky light, he couldn't see.

"Secretly?" I was tempted. I felt good. My body was grateful to this man and reached for him with its very chemistry.

"Just knock on my window," he said. "I'll be here for the rest of the week."

"And then you're gone."

"I'm gone." Then he was. And I was alone again with the spiders. I opened a box and read:

Hap, the leader of Santa Cruz Island, sucks in trees and mountains and the sea to capture his meal. He is usually after Coyote running away to the mainland. He formed the passes in the Santa Ynez Mountains trying to get one meal.

Now I fear the wind in the Channel. I hear Hap sucking.

This cold afternoon Alicia and I had tea.

"How do you know the stories, Alicia?"

"My family's stories. My husband told me. He told me stories to teach me the words. I'd not learned the Chumash language. Not even good Spanish. Only our local dialect mixed with English. Michael cared so much about the words, without him they would be lost."

"I've found a box labeled Shimilaqsha," I started my report, all questions.

"The Promised Land. Anything about the Western Gate?" She interrupted me. "Hollister Ranch?

"What?"

"Point Conception is the Western Gate, the place the dead wait before they go to the Promised Land. In the Journey of the Dead the Dead must cross over the ocean on the bridge to Shimilaqsha. First the ravens poke out their eyes."

I was already crying.

"The dead one must pick qupe, the orange poppies, to replace his eyes. When the soul of the dead one reaches Shimilaqsha, the Land of the Dead, the poppies are replaced by blue abalone eyes. To shimmer as he sees." Alicia saw me cry. "You already have blue abalone eyes. Your husband will be following mine."

"Do you think my Harry – Who goes to this Land of the Dead?" I wanted to think of him somewhere. On a bridge over a stormy sea? "Who makes the journey? Only Chumash? People who die in Chumash country? Die beside the sea, along the Channel that the bridge passes over? Who makes that trip?"

"I don't know Emma."

"What do you think?"

"Sometimes I think all of us go. Or maybe only the ones that believe."

"I suffer to think of Harry on that journey. His eyes poked out by ravens. He wouldn't know to take the poppies to be his eyes. He wouldn't know the rules of the games, nor have skills to win."

"He needs Coyote, right, Mother dear? We all need Coyote to help us play the games." Scott came into the room with a book and kissed his mother and left again.

Alicia glowed from the presence of her son. "I should just call in a moving van and send the boxes over to the Natural History Museum." Alicia drank her mint tea. Her hair was down in long braids. "But I feel they are first my responsibility, Michael's long hours, on paper and spool in there, trunks of conversations, memories. He recorded it so you could organize it for me? Clearly, dear."

"Has a lot changed here in your lifetime?" I asked Alicia.

"When I was a child there was real darkness over the sea, many stars in the sky, their reflection in our moving water. Now the ocean is lit by oil derricks. Soon towns and traffic will snake along the shore and dirty air will reflect the light all around us.

"Night will be banished to the horizon. To find darkness, you will need to look inland, over the mountains, for the star- filled sky, the comets."

"What's back in those mountains?" I asked.

"Brush, canyons, ridges, peaks. It's wildness all the way to the San Joaquin Valley. Now no grizzlies clear the paths, the inland chaparral is impassible."

"Bears?" I asked, prompting her story.

"Chumash believe the grizzly bear is our big brother, creature half of this world, half of the underworld, where he sleeps for months. Perhaps he dreams.

"Like a sleeping child does." Alicia seemed to see back to another scene, a mother's delight. I thought of my old dog, chasing and barking in his sleep. "Perhaps he dreams us," she said.

"I believe we need someone to dream us or we will disappear. Our mission from our ancestors will be failed."

What mission did my ancestors expect me to accomplish?

After some minutes Alicia continued. "I'm not sentimental. I don't want a grizzly sow and her cubs in my woods. But I know about the Bear." She looked at me quickly. "I wish I knew more. Michael knew from the old people who lived on, looking out from their yards in black skirts and shawls, silent until he came to visit. To record their memories." I knew that by now.

"In that shed you will find what the Chumash civilization dreamed to keep itself alive. Michael saved it for a reason. "

I felt she meant to inspire me, to make me become part of the mystic plan. I was willing.

"Why does Garcia want me to look for the Bear?" That kept me in there. Not the bosses' son, whose rustling in the library took too much of my attention. "Why the Bear with my husband? The murderer marked him with symbols?" I insisted to myself that it was with paint the symbols took Harry to his death.

"None that I could decifer."

"Oh god." This job was no respite. Rather than a distraction, the work was a path to find Harry. Better.

CHAPTER 26

On the drive home, I shifted gears, putting the Porsche through its paces. I forgot about the people in my life and gone from my life. The sun set on the cleansed day. The month continued rainy. The drenched trees were growing by the inch every hour, their leaves sparkling. In places the road was slippery with mud. Water seeped out the side of hills and dripped from under walls. The big mudslides, filled with trees and rocks, were plowed away over night like the snow in our driveway in New York.

Slowly, every day, I realized Harry was gone forever. Until and after I would be gone, he was gone. Harry liked me, then I think he loved me, at first he did. I amused him. Then I could feel a change – no rise to see me, but a fall, slight, but I felt it under his politeness and his duty as husband. A few months before I took my job in London I felt that again I irritated him, enervated him, as the French say. The feeling cut quick and deep and I pretended that I imagined it. It couldn't be true that my husband didn't love me anymore. I had taken on the curating projects to stem his disregard. I took work in another city, so he would miss me. We met on weekends at the house in France and it was like old times. From behind the huge vases of flowers I could see him lighten for my presence and I felt needed and loved.

Harry took me in, gave me a place to live, and a life, and I lived to return his favors. The first summer night my ride left Harry's party in East Hampton without me and I slept on his couch. Harry invited me to stay in the guest bedroom the next day. "That'll keep the guests away," Harry said.

When my father died, I was expected by strangers in Wyoming. My mother did not come. There was a new wife. When I fled back to Harry after the funeral he said "Welcome home" and I felt he meant it. He called me his housekeeper and I cooked. I thought from his base I could branch out. There I drove the roads for the views over fields and ponds to the ocean.

Sometimes I think it was because we liked each other so much that, to our surprises, we made love. With that, and with time, we did like so much more of each other that our friendship became love.

He asked me to marry him. "We'll get married in France–do say yes. "

So I did. And we decamped to France.

"I sent for the ring." Harry held my hand and told me over dinner on the terrace he built to face the moon-rise. "Made Father call the trustees. It was my grand-mother's engagement ring." The ring out of the safety deposit box, into a velvet pouch, onto the rough table in the wilds of France. Harry pulled up a candle. The ring– important, awesome, a stone as big as an eye, yet light, balanced, cabochon sapphire, white diamonds, marquis, point to point – thrummed and sparkled between us.

His mother died when he was twelve and gone at camp. Harry had a retired father who golfed and kept a traditional distance from his son, and a socialite stepmother who had more children. "You will have to meet the wicked stepmother," Harry said. "She is the type it's a tragedy to have in a family. The world revolves around her. Everyone in it is an agent of her desires."

"Oh dear. How do I behave?"

"She only thinks of herself, ever. That's all you have to know to understand her. And she's always been good looking and rich enough that others go along. I just got out as soon as I could." Harry leaned back to stretch his neck and I saw a motherless son and knew I could fill that love for him. Love is stupid enough to get what it wants. Harry wanted to marry me. I was immensely flattered. I put on the ring.

I wore it all the time until I started working. Then the family ring went into my box.

Harry took the project in Santa Barbara and I stayed in London. I wanted to finish my work before I joined him – Stupid.

I put the groceries in the kitchen for the cook and ran up to my bathroom. Then the phone rang.

"Emma?" it was Harry's voice. I sat down on the bed. For the first wild seconds I thought it was Harry. He had been hiding, it was all over, he was back, my Harry, my sweet, all my missing shifted to hope, to welcome.

"We've been out of touch, I know. We're here for my college roommate's birthday. Barbara is with me."

It was Harry's father, Lloyd Chase. Harry's father and the Bitch, as Harry called her whenever he had to be around his stepmother, and got away. I was not at all like the Bitch, he used to tell me. Harry loved me. I gave one sob on the phone. Mr. Chase harrumphed. "I don't mean to upset you. I know how you feel. I had to call."

I cried silent tears again. I had believed Harry was back, alive. That dream gone, I felt and knew deeper and more, the tragedy clear and endless that he was really gone. He knew me as I thought no one ever would and still he loved me so much I was encouraged and protected. How could I make my way without him?

I stopped crying as Barbara came on the line. I could hear her breathing, the clink of her glass and her bracelets.

"Well, we're all upset here. Lunch tomorrow? We're at the San Ysidro Ranch but I can tell you we've made a mistake here. Too run down for my taste. Meet at the Biltmore. 1? Great. See you Emma."

That was as warm as she ever got. What had their detective discovered? Would they tell me? He called and left a message I didn't answer. The week before he called again and said he would be in town this week. I supposed now it was to meet the Chases.

His parents were already seated behind big pots of palms on the patio of the seaside hotel. Outside across the lawn, the waves crashed soundlessly. In there, glass walls reflected the figure of me walking in a city suit from last year's collections, feeling like a waif in my mother's clothes, a shadow in the eucalyptus.

I thought of my mother as I went to meet Harry's stepmother. I don't think it had registered with my mother that I was a widow. To her husbands were left behind, like rental houses.

More from pictures than real time spent together, I recognized the senior Chases. Harry was like his father, with his long face, but Harry had a softer, kinder look that must have been his mother's. His stepmother looked like she had work done on her high cheekbones and pointy chin and still brunette hair.

Harry's father stood for me and she inclined a powdered cheek and pearl earring. We talked weather, old school reunions -I'd never gone, nor had she. He was a regular. Yale.

"Darling Emma, here we are without him. Our Harry, gone." She was downright emotional. I knew her orange juice was a screwdriver but I didn't think less of her for it. She probably started at breakfast. She and my mother could drink me under the table and maintain an elegant cool I will never have.

"Let us order," Barbara said and she did from the girl who ogled her jewels, the casual emerald, the diamond filigree cuff. "You know how much Harry cared about the family." Barbara started.

"His mother and I –"" Lloyd was next.

"He would have wanted the family to have his mother's ring – have it back."

"Where is it?" Lloyd looked like he hoped it was in Paris and we could be done with this topic.

"We will send a courier for it." Barbara knew I had it with me. Almost wore it for them to enjoy.

I was beginning to hate them. I was defeated by their avarice, the unkindness. They knew nothing about Harry's life, about what he wanted. The ring meant more to me with Harry gone. They did not care.

"Do they have clues about Harry's murder. Any evidence? A suspect?" Barbara was sure of her victory. The ring was hers. She assumed I was not willing to fight for it. I knew it came from his mother. And was mine.

"Emma, what have the police discovered? " Harry's father asked. "Or you, anything?"

Did they know I was playing sleuth in my early widowhood? I expected them to ask me about the farm in the Perigord, my plans for his property. I looked at them.

"I ask you the same. What did your detective find out?"

"Our detective? 'Our'?" they said together as if I was preposterous.

"Kurt Miles, your detective. He told me you hired him to investigate –" Their looks were so blank I didn't continue.

"He lied," I said out loud. Barbara looked like she was waiting for me to say something, as if she couldn't hear what didn't make sense to her cosmos.

"We've never hired anyone to look into this case for us," Mr. Chase said, puzzled, as was I. Deeply confused.

Who was that creep? How could I have believed him so readily? He knew the first police detective on the case, threw his name around. He knew about the locker. He asked all those questions about Harry. Garcia told me to stay away from him. I wanted Detective Garcia.

Lunch was a torture of seeing glimpses of Harry but older, diminished, in his father. Harry as he might have wrinkled around the eyes and under the chin. I saw Barbara in action, her every phrase meant to size up and exclude, to judge and to put herself in the center and in control. Harry's father talked about his dogs. She talked about the house in Florida. We played with our food and she ordered another drink.

"Will you go back to the house in France?" Barbara finally asked.

"I plan to. I have project here for now. I'll go back after it's finished."

I didn't want to tell them I needed the money from my work for the house. I didn't want to give them the satisfaction of not offering to help.

"If you ever want to sell it Emma, give us first refusal. Can you promise us that?" Harry's father asked.

"Whatever for?" Barbara said, querulously to her husband as if he was springing a surprise on her.

"I'll do that, Mr. Chase," I said.

"You know he left you everything in it as well," Mr. Chase said. "We read the will last week. I have a copy of it for you."

The library was mine. I took the manila envelope.

"His brothers have no problem with that–he had none of the family things with him there," Barbara said, no doubt thinking of her sons, Harry's imaginary half brothers, he called them.

"It came furnished, didn't it?" John Chase said.

"Barely," I said. Harry had filled it with treasures from his searching. I saw him unpacking boxes from distant lands, placing the new buys.

"I need to go now. Get back to work. It has been good to see you." I stood, kissed their cheeks goodbye and left.

Detective Garcia, where was Garcia? I stopped at one of the little wood and glass rooms in a row that were the hotel phone booths and called Garcia's number. I knew it now and kept his card in my wallet.

"Garcia," he said.

"It's Emma Chase."

"Yes?"

"Harry's parents didn't hire the detective -"

"That guy about the locker plant?" Silence while he thought. "You have his information?"

"Yes."

"Okay, his name?"

"Kurt Miles."

"Number?"

"I have it at home. I'll call you."

"Who else did this guy know?"

"Martin. Your predecessor on the case," I said, remembering back.

"What did he ask you?"

"If I thought Harry was homosexual. If I knew his friends in town."

"How often have you met him? "

"Not since I did not give him the envelopes from the locker. I told him I'd given them to the police. I lied then but it's true now. When will you give them back?" I didn't want them.

CHAPTER 27

At the end of the next confusing day in the safety of the shed I found my boss in the garden. "Remember you asked me if I spoke Spanish?" I asked Alicia, draped in a soft shawl, as she picked the last roses off the winter bushes, low, beginning new deep purple growth.

"Yes, so you could read the files. Spanish first replaced Chumash. I have a question, Emma. How can there be so many notes?" Alicia asked, looking sideways at me to see if I was still up to the task.

"There are many versions. Versions of the English translations of the Spanish versions of the Chumash. I've found a vocabulary list, thank god, annotated with the names of the informants who told him. I've decided to read the Chumash first. I pretend I'll begin to understand it, like Shakespeare."

Alicia was sizing up the last roses, counting down to five leaves and a bud, and clipping down the flowers past their prime. The winter bloom of California roses, color in the rain, was such a luxe. Alicia gave me roses every day for the shed.

"I've found plants, dried in newspaper, with tags. Labels. One named 'frogs eye'–"

"A fern. Any recipes?"

"There may be –"

"Let me know." We sat silent. "They were all old, his informants. They knew age and its remedies. I can use that now." She smoothed her skirt, drying her hands, roses in her basket. "You're not talking to anyone about what you find?"

"No ma'am. Only you and my notebook." I no longer wore a skirt to work. It was too cold in there. I stayed out of the warmth of the space heater working in the metal cabinets until I was too chilled and returned to warm my hands like at a fire.

"My dear. You must be cold in the hut."

"Better than too hot –" Scott came up behind us. "No help for that."

"Emma has found dried plants."

"It's a wonder those plants survive."

"You're the first person to spend time in there since Michael." Alicia lifted her face for Scott's kiss.

"He left for months, then holed up in there when he came home," Scott said.

"I was busy with the farm – and you –"

"We didn't see much of him." Scott watched his mother as he spoke.

"He was on a mission, his whole life. The Indians –"

"We were incidental."

"No, Scott. I don't want to hear that."

"It didn't hurt my feelings. I knew we were less important than saving civilizations." Scott kissed Alicia again and walked out to the fountain that was full in the rain.

"Alicia, I found a note about a concoction of whisky and yerba santa – holy grass?"

"A herb. Chumash wishap'. Liniment for soreness and a tea for chest colds and fever."

"Do you grow the plants that are in the files?"

"Possibly. Most. My second herb garden is only the old plants. Some I've brought from inland and from the desert. They may not be surviving in this rain. You're going to find me the recipes, right? "

"Tell me more about what to look for," I asked.

"Datura, Jimsonweed, Toloache is mo'moy. In the coma caused by mo'moy the child found its Dream Helper, who truly helped."

"Did you take the datura?" I asked Alicia.

"No, it was too dangerous. The ones who knew the plant – where to collect it, how to make the potion and how much to give, they were gone, or too old."

"I may find a recipe–" How did Greg make his tea?

"Any new mystery?"

"I found a box, many boxes perhaps, of notes in French."

"What did you say?" Alicia turned to hear me better and pressed the clippers against her heart, flicking the safety catch.

"I've found French notes, in a different hand than your husband's," I said. Alicia leaned into a bush and poked her arm on a big thorn and cried out.

"Oh dear. Are you all right?

"God, the Frenchman," Alicia said squeezing blood from her tissue skin. She cut a rose that was above her head into her bag and, with the clippers, threw its tough stalk, dangerous with thorns, into the center of the horseshoe garden.

"'The Frenchman'?" I asked. "French notes?" I thought of the find at the Museum of Man.

"de Cessac." Alicia said, ruffling her bag of flowers. "Spiders, climb out," she said as she inclined it for them to drop to the ground.

De Cessac's notes. Could I tell Gerard? "A friend in Paris told me about him."

"You remember our agreement? You will not tell your friends in Paris. What you find."

"Tell me what it's about." Would she tell me more?

"Leon de Cessac." She looked at me as if I were not there, only the memories I had brought her. "He was here for possessions and stories of the Chumash. Back when there were more people alive who remembered. In my grandmother's time."

"So he was here earlier than Mr. Lowell?"

"My husband Michael started his work in 1918. De Cessac was here in the 1870's. California had been American for twenty years. The Missions were sold off and Chumash dispersed forty years before that."

"De Cessac took artifacts?" I asked. Had I told her what I saw in Paris with Gerard?

"He took everything he could find," she said.

"My friend, they found objects in Paris, recently. Sun sticks, flutes, stone bowls, baskets and skirts, head-dresses, wands, 'atswin. I saw them, before I came back." She looked at me like I was a spy. "Could these French notes be his?"

"Find out," Alicia said with a dismissal that was a challenge. "Do not tell anyone."

Home at my grandmother's, I took a cup of milky tea up in the elevator and called on the black phone. Garcia was gone. I sat at the nursery table with a skirt and avoided my eyes in the mirror.

CHAPTER 28

Claudia was out for dinner so I took a bath and went straight to bed and slept until the next morning. The pink dawn sun lit the tree trunks and the sea was so rough I could hear the surf in my bathroom, half-imaginary like in a shell. At 8:00 I called Garcia, the scholar cop.

"What is it, Mrs. Chase?" I heard concern that belied his abruptness. I felt it, there or not.

"Detective Garcia, I need to ask you about something I've found in the files. Alicia says the Chumash are your hobby." What else did he like to do in his spare time?

"Yes."

"Who is de Cessac?" I asked him. Had the Frenchman left local traces?

"Leon de Cessac, explorer, collector. Why?"

Should I have to tell him? What stopped me? This was a man I wanted to know everything. Garcia was on my side, right.

"Why, Mrs. Chase?"

"De Cessac. The deeper I read, he's there. I saw his collection in Paris, when I was back, crates brought out of the basement after being lost for a hundred years."

I couldn't tell him Alicia's secret, that in Mr. Lowell's files, I'd found drawers of French notebooks. I wanted to know about this Frenchman who kept intersecting my life. What did the notebooks have to do with Harry's murder? When Mr. Skeffington came back to town, I thought then I would find my Harry's last days.

"What have you found out, Detective Garcia, about Harry?"

"Let's meet, Mrs. Chase. El Paseo for coffee in forty-five minutes?"

"O.K." I'd be later than usual for Alicia. She demanded no certain hours, I'd established my own and she had not commented except to insist on our daily lemon tea.

The shopkeepers at the old Spanish style market-place had baskets full of paper garlands and flowers under the shelves in the bay windows. I walked quickly, bending under the low roof of the interior adobe walkway that curved like a tunnel, lit by star lamps. The old de la Guerra adobe.

Detective Garcia wore khakis and a tan tweed jacket. He let me go first in the cafeteria line and took out his money for his own coffee behind me. We sat on the patio in the sun at a metal table.

"Tell me about Harry's case." I cried, eyes over-flowing, my mind back on its one subject.

"Nothing to report," Garcia said. "How are you?"

I could have told him about the ride to the cave that haunted my sleep. Or my night with Scott. One didn't talk about sex. And those adventures were secondary.

He stood to shake the hand of a man in a suit with a fat hard-sided briefcase who had stopped in mid-rush to say "Manuel, they let you out". The two men had the regard for each other of old friends – checking each other's stomachs and eyes, a condition size-up, a comparison, some concern. The man looked at me with the beginning of curiosity and then away quickly. He did not need my grief. Leave that to the cops.

"See you in the water," he said to Garcia as he resumed his rush.

"In the water?" I asked as Garcia sat back down with me.

"Surf," Garcia seemed to shake off the sense memory of riding waves and came back to me. "Mrs. Chase, I am concentrated on your husband's murder. That's not a consolation but let it be one. I'm determined to stop his murderer."

Why did he say 'stop' and not 'catch'? He looked at me. Eyes locked on mine, he was onto something serious.

"Keep your work private. If de Cessac's name comes up, tell no one about it."

"I tell Alicia what I find, every day but she's the only one. We have that agreement. Unless she says otherwise."

"Leon de Cessac was a French student of the Chumash and prodigious collector of things Chumash back when the getting was good, in the 1870's."

"And?" I wanted a lecture.

"And his collection was lost. Everything- until a few months ago students found the objects in Paris. A huge collection I've heard." I could see it, the treasures, the feather capes, in the diesel air of Paris. "That may be what you saw. Probably we've seen similar pieces. Looted by other 'explorers'. His 'collection'. I heard sacasm in the earnest policeman, "the things, the artifacts, are only a part of his work. De Cessac was different. He did more, like Michael Lowell but with different motives."

"Why different?"

"He took notes. With a focus on potions, instructions, recipes. Supposed to be extensive."

"More than Mr. Lowell's?" I couldn't believe that. I was still drowned in the papers.

"De Cessac asked questions forty, fifty years earlier than Michael Lowell, that much. He had Informants who were alive Pre-Mission. Closer to the pure Chumash culture? The hardships and the power."

Detective Garcia nodded to more people who cut through the patio of the Spanish style marketplace on their way to work. His focus came back to me slowly like a sleepy brown-eyed snake. "Where are the de Cessac notes, you might ask. They're lost, Mrs. Chase. They're a rumor, a mystery."

"A rumor?" I now believed rumors, like myths, could be as true as anything. "Tell me."

"Police detectives don't pass on rumors."

"But Detective Garcia, this is not police work, this is history, scholarship. Not about murder–"

"With luck you'll find the notebooks and we'll learn what's in them, Mrs. Chase."

"Do police detectives believe in luck?" I thought of the boxes of French writing.

"Yes, and you can. Despite your circumstances."

"We may be in luck," I said. "Tell me more."

Garcia knew the import of my brag and began to talk to his hands. "The Frenchman asked and he asked the elders who still had the knowledge."

You couldn't tell from looking at him but his voice had dropped so only I could hear it. "We believe de Cessac's notes recorded the secrets of the Chumash, the antap and 'atswinic mysteries. Described the rituals of Acquired Power. The uses of Acquired Power." Garcia watched my reaction.

I sat silent to absorb the news. "People believe in that?"

"Mrs. Chase, the Frenchman's notes have secrets people want. If you learn where to find them, keep the secret. They've caused treasure hunts before–don't start a new one."

"Graduate students beating down adobe doors?"

"You know better. People kill for power, ruin lives." he said, buttoning his jacket as the clouds took over the sky and ended the late-winter warmth. "What if your husband was murdered by a fanatic cult, and their marching orders are Chumash? It's possible.'"

He held my eyes as I shook. I put on my sweater, pretending the trembling was from the cold. "I'll look. For the Frenchman and the Bear. But I can't tell you unless you ask Alicia."

"Mrs. Chase, who do you socialize with?" Garcia asked, a frightening non-sequitur. He stared at me, brown eyes deep and ringed with blue.

"Do you mean, have the files made me new friends? No."

Garcia waited as if he knew my flippancy was defensive. I answered, "Alicia and Scott Lowell, Greg Lowell and my grandmother. Maria Ortega, an old friend from the beach."

"The Lowells. Be careful," he said. "Don't work too hard." Did he mean too hard or too late?

"Are you too thin, Mrs. Chase?" Detective Garcia stood.

"Thanks." Would I ever be Emma?

"Mrs. Chase, the dirt on his shoes, on the boots from the trunk, in his pockets. It wasn't the same dirt he was found in. It was lighter, dusty, mountain dirt. Cave dirt. Stay out of caves." Now he tells me, I thought. "And, Mrs. Chase, we think someone local may have hired that private investigator. We want you to be careful, Mrs. Chase. I want you to take precautions."

"What?"

"Lock your doors, don't open for strangers, Don't be out at night by yourself. Don't pick up strange men in bars. Don't hike alone. The usual."

"Would you have told me about this if I hadn't called?"

"You did, Mrs. Chase. Have a safe weekend. I'll walk you to your car." He stayed close to me as I stood from the heavy iron chair and gave me his arm when I stumbled at first over the cobblestones into the adobe tunnel of the mercado.

"Fear makes me weak?"

"Or stronger."

CHAPTER 29

Garcia walked to his office and I passed him, straight back, long strides, on my way to work. I worried about the future to distract myself from the past and the present. Would I ever get back to the Perigord? Would I be alone all my life, climbing into stranger's windows for their touch? What were the answers? What were the questions?

That evening I stayed in the nursery at my Gran's, safe enough. I had just put my feet onto the bed, with mint tea, when the telephone rang.

"Hummph?" Greg Lowell on the line, loud. "The rains will open for the weekend. So come fly with me, over in the Santa Ynez Valley?" Greg Lowell began his sentences with a harumph rather than a pronoun, and was almost French in the way he used expressions to keep the conversation in his control. There was no need to make small talk. He was always talking or about to talk. "Humm, I can fly you over, show you the back country."

Greg felt so local to me. He had deep roots and still lived here. I felt his connection to Montecito and it pulled me. He had not called since our ride. I was sick of mistrust, suspicion, fear. Harry didn't have enough of it to save himself but my having too much wasn't going to make up for that nor bring him back.

I flew with Harry and I loved the feeling. I missed that change of perspective and weight. Harry became a pilot when he was a boy and, when I met him he romanced me by taking me flying to see his project sites.

Did Harry fly over these mountains?

"Meet me here and I'll drive," Greg said.

"I'll only insist that I drive," I said and could feel his displeasure. I knew that was not etiquette but I believed my excuse. "There's a car here that I am dying to drive over that pass."

"A car lover?" Doubtful.

"My grandmother has a 1952 Ferrari Princess." I hadn't asked her yet for the key to that silver curved beauty but I was ready.

"That's a car to love," Greg said. "I'm game. Pick me up, Saturday at 8."

I hung up the phone relieved that, as the driver, I didn't need to make excuses about having to be home at a decent hour to take my grandmother to a party. I couldn't resist Greg's invitation but I wanted to avoid any romantic advances.

At work, for two days I led a reluctant Alicia through the files, showing her the categories, the boxes and the cards. What she had control over was too much, daunting for both of us.

Saturday morning I took a leather jacket and a scarf, expecting an open cockpit, I suppose, romantic notions, not far from the truth, as I roasted under the rear glass bubble of a Navy trainer. Half nauseous from the heat I was flown in swoops like in a glider over the meadows of the valley.

Greg piloted in the front bubble. He flew the plane over a windmill, a small wooden town, then banked behind a wild ridge that was the start of a pleated land of brush and trees and piles of rocks with clearings.

"Inland Chumash painted caves below us," Greg said through the intercom that came into my ears from thick padded leather muffs. He didn't say anything else. The space was hot and noisy with the air rushing outside.

After our flight, I helped Greg push the plane back into its hangar. I drove the Ferrari up the pass to a stone tavern, a stagecoach-stop turned cafe in dripping redwood trees next to a waterfall. I was still taken with the day's visuals and the physical disorientation of flying in the hot sun and I began to shiver from the cold. I bet the rain never stopped in that patch of forest curved into the wet hillside. We sat inside, in the dark wood room.

"How's Alicia?"

"Do you know her?" I asked him.

"Not well. Scott I know better," Greg said. "Poor Scott suffered with no father," he said.

"He did?" I didn't see it in the hale man. Overwork, yes.

"Hard times," Greg said. "A breakdown."

"Really?" I was surprised. Scott seemed reserved, secretive, not fragile.

"Scott didn't wash or cut his hair or his fingernails for a year. He wouldn't talk. Then, he came to see me, filthy on my doorstep. Months, I was the only one he talked to."

"Good God."

"His father, that's what I think."

So many ways a parent can harm a child. Though "father" made me long for a moment to know what the word meant.

"Rumors." Greg seemed reluctant to go into the family story. He looked at me, silent to force a response. To set me imagining.

"It must have been hard on Alicia," I said.

"I worked with Scott and he got better," Greg said. "Now he's doing well in San Francisco." He was congratulating himself.

"He gives up a lot by leaving here," I said, thinking of Alicia sitting alone on her beautiful ranch.

"I don't think he could handle the responsibility," Greg said. "His life down here, his family, there are burdens some people cannot take on." He paused. "His father and his mother. Practically incest."

"Really?" What in the world? He wanted to talk about it. No story is simple. Is this what Alicia wanted Scott to escape?

"Alicia was my uncle's lover during the war. My father's brother. He jilted her and she went after their uncle."

"Who?" I was confused.

Greg watched my eyes as if testing me with his revelations. Would I be shocked? I was relieved other people's families had quirks. My mother married many times. Those were a string of stepfathers.

"Uncle Charles' never came back for Alicia so she married Great-Uncle Michael," Greg said as if it was a scandal.

"That's the incest?" I said.

"Fortune hunting, more likely." He looked away. "She may be a Chumash princess but she had no money. Or land."

I guessed then it was prejudice and family jealousy I heard when he talked about Alicia. I was surprised to hear Scott had secret, subsurface disturbances. You never know. That could explain his hiding out in his farm house. Was Scott cured? I'd just stay out of his way. Hate to set him off. Though he had gone a long way, law school, well-employed. He seemed sure of himself, of his touch.

"Been flying before, Emma. Seemed game for it. Didn't hear any screams over the earphones. You covered the mouth up for the screaming?"

"I've flown before," I said. "With my husband."

"Of course, your husband?" Greg said. "We haven't talked about him. We can."

"I flew with him over his sites. He was an architect."

We drank our beers and were silent for a few minutes. Then Greg took my hand and held it between his. "Do you know who I think you are, Emma?" He asked.

"No," I answered, unsure where he was leading me in this shift of attention.

"Coyote, in disguise as a beautiful woman."

I laughed. Flattery made me uneasy.

"Coyote, he must be in those Lowell files," Greg said.

Coyote is an ever present, changeable character in the Chumash stories, lustful, hungry, thieving, wise, skillful. I didn't feel a bit like Coyote yet knew enough to be only slightly insulted.

"Why Coyote?" I asked.

"The beautiful woman part. Coyote could make anyone fall for him – man or woman – by changing his shape to please," Greg said and finally let go of my hand.

I never relaxed in his grip. My mind was on Harry, the past. I couldn't look forward. Greg seemed too serious, not like his cousin who got me by his lightness. Greg's future was dim, dark, though he looked so fair and straight-forward. Small town boy.

"I've fallen for you. So you must be using sorcery, humm?" Greg said.

I didn't care enough to be flattered. Figured he was exaggerating. "Come now," I said and took a drink.

"Tell me more about the Chumash." Why didn't I say about my husband?

"Transformation. Chumash elite could change form if they collected enough Power with the sacred tools. The Initiated passed on the tools and the secrets of the rituals. As they were killed off by the white man someone recorded the secret knowledge. Great Uncle Michael Lowell? You will find out. Keep your eyes open. That knowledge is worth many chateaux in France." How did he know I had a crumbling big house in France?

"Transformation? Changing form? You think they could really do it?" I asked. Did he believe that? "Transform into what?"

"Into Bear, for one," Greg said as he cut his steak and stared into the fire. I ate my trout.

Greg said "I was born to this. I know how to behave. I was initiated. I acquire power, you will learn. By action, we invoke power. We have our ways. One day you may join us." I listened, ready for a tale. Where was he going?

"Sapaquay, the last Chumash leader, who left for the Tejon, said:" Greg recited, "'All has ended now–all the practices in which we indulged for our salvation or diversion, for there are few now who believe in them, and the next generation will not endure the hardship and suffering that is necessary to maintain them." Greg spoke with underlined words. He paused for attention. "I, I maintain the Chumash practices with suffering and hardship." Pause. "But I need more perfect knowledge. The old ways."

He looked at me as if I understood. Was that where I came in, I thought, suspicious. The knowledge in the files. Everyone wanted something out of the lost Chumash world. I was beginning just to want out. Too much.

"I have vulture stones–you know them? Chumash raised the dead with their vulture stones," Greg said.

I didn't believe him and felt I was humoring him. Greg was silent. I said "You would use the stones? What about the payback? The Snake will come to claim your soul in twelve years as payment for the power."

"Why don't I lend them to you," Greg said. "For your husband. Maybe you'll see into the distance and find your husband took a cruise and is just returning."

"My husband?" What did he know about Harry?

"You're a widow." A word I rebelled against.

I smiled at Greg to thank him for sympathy I was not sure was there.

"My cousin Scott has a grizzly skin," he said. "I want it."

Again I didn't believe him. "From Alaska?"

"No, from here. Montecito was overrun by grizzlies. His pelt is a cape and ties by cord wound with feathers. You want to see it –" He looked at me, "Do you want to see our Chumash collection? For a price... "

"Oh yes?" It was unfamiliar ground, this sparring for favors. Did I want to play the game?

"For a kiss."

"Seems a small price." Ready to give over a peck to see his treasures, I thought.

"A kiss is never small." He took my hand again. His were a strange combination of soft and hard and were very warm.

"You don't think a kiss can be in friendship?" I asked.

"Not the kind I want."

"Greg, I am in mourning. I don't think about other kinds of kisses now," I lied, feeling still swollen from

Scott's kisses. "Have you shown Mr. Skeffington your collection, for his museum?"

"You'll get to see it first." Greg pushed his bench back and leaned forward. "A kiss."

"Maybe," I said.

"I knew your husband, Emma," Greg said, taking my hand again.

That was a shock. I pulled my hand back to push hair out of my face. "Harry?"

"Yes. You didn't know? My father and I were deep into Harry about a project. We spent -"

"You did?" Was this the garden in his envelopes? Was he going to send for me? "How did you meet my Harry?" I asked.

"Through friends. We shared interests. He came out flying with me too."

I was so surprised, I couldn't picture it, my Harry the intellectual aesthete with this athlete, this local braggart. Greg took my hand again and held it hard so I had to leave it there or make a scene. I guessed then that his civility was a thin crust over his sensuality. And he knew my Harry.

"What kind of project?" I asked, unwilling to think through the implications without more information.

"A chapel you could say, in the garden."

"For Harry to do next?" How could this man know more than I did? And now he tells me.

I wanted every word. "Did he tell you anything that could be a clue?"

"Clue to what?" Greg asked. Didn't he know about the murder?

"To his death." I said as Greg stared at me. "I need to know what he was doing before he was killed."

"Let's not talk about Harry, I want us -"

"Shall we go?" I pulled my hand away and took the car keys off the table. I had to think.

"What about our collection? When do I get that kiss?" Greg asked.

I think I just stared at Greg.

"You're thinking about our kiss?" he asked.

"Do you see my friend Maria Ortega?"

"Why her? Let her join your husband, we won't waste our time together on them." He put his arm around my shoulder. I wondered if his was the arrogance of the living or was he callous and unkind.

A big motorcyclist and his padded rider walked out, their boots clanking and I pulled away from Greg and got into the car. Greg was quickly in after me and silent on the curving ride home, his window down to the rushing air.

I stayed in the low car in his courtyard. Greg bent down to look in my window. "I'll take that kiss later."

Maria and I met at the Somerset. We sat at the bar with drinks, our backs to the piano player and the tables. There were only couples there – we would not be dancing that night.

"How are you? What has Manuel learned about the crime? "

"The crime, the mortal sin. Razor blade to the fabric of my life."

"That one."

Maria looked around and focused on a table of two men, one older and the other European, both in suits and colored socks. "That's Skeffington." She stood and straightened her skirt. "I'll introduce you."

She walked over to their table, arms and hips swinging naturally, feminine.

The younger man kept talking, he did not even see her there. His eyes were hooded and lazy, his mouth alive with the pouts of a Frenchman's. I thought of M. deVlamnick in Paris.

Mr. Skeffington stood for the waiting Maria and kissed her cheek. Then his dinner companion looked up. He looked more interested as Skeff introduced her – like he could see a way to use her. Skeff excused himself and came over to me as the man looked at me.

"Mrs. Chase, I am Walter Skeffington. What a tragedy – for me too, especially for you. My condolences. I am sorry I have been gone. You must come by. I am in the telephone book."

He must have known I'd been calling.

Maria sat down pleased. "Finally."

CHAPTER 30

The telephone rang and I jumped. The long shed had a quiet buzz when it was not raining. "Emma, I need you to go to Walter Skeffington's." Alicia asked.

"Mr. Skeffington?" I did not have to call him out of the blue.

"I'll give you directions. You'll like him. Skeff. He wants to talk about my husband's files. You may speak freely to him. Let him know what we're up against. Come for tea now."

I sat with her, so much unsaid. "The notes just wander," I began, ready to listen.

"My husband didn't ask questions, except about grammar or how to say a word. He let the old people talk about what they wanted. For the vocabulary.

"For him I wore bangs plastered to my forehead. He loved that I am Chumash, from a high family. 'Antap. From the only tribe with a hereditary elite.

"Chumash did not make alcohol. I drank at first with my Yankee husband, but women then knew not to. Now it's lemonade. Would you rather have tea? It is more tea weather."

"Yes, tea please. I'm finding more dried plant specimens. I need to look at the growing plants." I wanted to see them alive.

"In that mud out there? We'll find tok, Indian hemp, in the oaks, it's so wet. Coyote twisted the tok into fish lines for the important people of the village."

"That would be your family?"

"We had them." She looked so sad. The windows were open to the cold clear day. We sat next to the fire. "Scott is here. He did not have a Chumash baby cradle made of dogwood."

"Do you have dogwood?"

"These floods will have scoured it along the creek."

"Let's go look?"

"It's no time to be hiking, Senorita." Alicia slipped into Spanish as Magdalena came in with a tray. She set down lemons, a knife and board, a silver faceted cone to extract the juice, cups and saucers and, in a silver pitcher with a wood handle, hot water for our lemon tea. I had reduced to one lump of sugar. Alicia took none.

"There's my baby boy." Scott had come up behind me.

"Skeff wants to see you Mother–"

"I'm sending Emma."

"You know him?" Scott asked me.

"No. My husband was here to work for him, until he died. We met last night at a restaurant."

"He is Scott's godfather." Alicia took his hand. "Does Skeff take care of your religious and moral education?"

Scott laughed and kissed his mother. "I'll be down for dinner. Bye Emma."

"Alicia, I'll follow Scott out. I'll report tomorrow."

"Darling, she'll go on to Skeff. There's no harm in it. He'll like her."

At the doorway Scott said "Did Mother tell you? Skeff wants to buy my father's notes." He kissed the top of my head.

Mr. Skeffington's butler met me at the door of the modern white house, in uniform. We walked down a hallway of black and white diamond tiles, long glass windows interspersed with dark furniture under paintings.

The stark open living room floored me. I was dazzled in place by the beauty and steepness of the fall into the view. My eyes flew down purple hills to the ocean and out to the islands covered in high clouds. Over the fireplace and the chests, more paintings, Degas of race-horses, a small Rembrandt, a Matisse cutout, two Van Goghs. I saw two Modiglianis in the next room, the dining room.

I gasped, involuntarily. "Spectacular."

Walter Skeffington came up behind me from a room in the long hallway. "Isn't it?"

Here was the man Harry came to work for.

"Mrs. Chase, it is a pleasure to meet you again." He shook my hand and bowed. "I am so sorry, I can not say."

"Yes."

"What can we do? We must carry on." Skeff's voice had a deep, East Coast American accent, so distinct it was almost foreign. With his hand in his pocket like Fred Astaire, he was an elegant old man now backlit by the view.

"Harry came here often. I gave him a key. He liked to sit in my house."

"I can see why." What light, what art!

"I built it to liberate the paintings. Grabbed them and fled my father's house down there." He looked into the view. "Dark hallways in the shadows of oaks. Now, I worry about sun damage. My father died young. Years younger than I am today. That's hard to reconcile."

I felt young and didn't know then that it would not last.

"How old was Harry? May I ask?""

"Thirty-seven. In December."

"I want you to know his work here was important. We were building a sacred library. A library of the sacred." He looked into my eyes, searching deep with a fond gaze, then he left to straighten a painting. "Would you like to walk the site?"

Of course.

I followed him down another windowed hallway, outside into a Japanese rock garden. A fluted stone and steel Brancusi cast shadows over desert plants, beside a long pool. Mr. Skeffington took my arm on the narrow path. Among the boulders were sculptures of ancient Greek men, here set free to look out over the sea.

"I hear you are a great collector."

"You don't approve?" How could he tell?

"Why amass things? Participate in a system that values only with money?"

"Is that what you think? Collectors take things from the people who need them and lock them in cabinets?"

"Those were my thoughts."

"Collectors protect too–"

"So they're not blown up in Athens by the Turks?" I was rude in my widowhood.

"Exactly. Nor looted and discarded. Civilizations can be saved by collectors."

"You're building a 'sacred library'? " I asked. What project brought Harry to his death?

"A safe home for Ritual tools. Chumash artifacts. This library will lend the tools– the sacred tools– for people to use them. Let them hold them, see them. Perhaps rescue the culture. Gather the sacred that is on the auction blocks, for sale in the windows of galleries in Paris. If I collect them here, for the Chumash, I can keep them from being lost."

The Chumash. Did Mr. Skeffington take Harry into the Chumash world–into the far past of this place? My Harry, lost in the near past, forever.

"When did you see Harry last?" I asked.

"The day he was killed. He was here. Together we interviewed builders on the site."

"Builders?"

"Yes. People I've worked with for years."

"No clue there?"

"None. And now I meet you, the granddaughter of my old friend." Mr. Skeffington kept my arm as we walked and talked above the birds. "We watched Isadora Duncan dance, scarves flying under the full moon. Hid in the bushes. Your grandmother was the true friend of my youth. We spied on your great-grandparents' parties, when the world's performers came to Montecito to entertain our parents. When the estates were young."

Mr. Skeffington led me into his amphitheater at the stage level. Below us the ocean was deep blues. "That is the site, above my amphitheater."

"The walls look familiar."

"Your grandmother's mason built it for me, a few years ago, not back in the Thirties when everyone needed work."

We sat on the wall of the stage, legs dangling and looked up to the arcs of stone between dirt terraces. "We sat like this, your grandmother and I for hours on her mother's stage, talking, looking at the empty audience. Now I imagine we would sit in the audience and look for ourselves back then. Before these many years." He looked at me while I searched for questions in my confusion.

"How did you know my grandmother?"

"You mean to tell me she never told you?" He feigned a glancing hurt vanity, but I thought I saw regret in his mouth, I guessed for lost youth. He was still handsome. He looked like a cliché, blue shining eyes and a strong nose, hair silver, strong chin, high forehead, warm mouth. I could not take my eyes off him. I wanted to see him young, what was behind the man, the years, the taste. His clothes were old and soft. Now I'd met the man I could understand why Harry wanted to work for him. I was already charmed and glimpsed Harry's fun in a project with him.

I was ready to ask about Harry.

Shadows darkened in the pink and yellow- brown stones of the walls. We both looked up as the planets appeared in the cool teal sky.

"Why did you hire my husband?"

"He was recommended by friends in Paris."

"Who?"

"The Doncourts, the de Vlamnicks, and more- he is the best for a small museum such as I envision."

"Was." I tried to get accustomed to the past tense. With tears. We sat silent. "What happened?" I asked. "You were with him in his last days." De Vlamnick, how did he know that man? "What happened?"

"I don't know, Mrs. Chase. Detective Garcia has asked me," he said. "That's really what this visit is about, isn't it." What else, I thought.

"On my part. Alicia Lowell sent me up to see you too."

"About her precious files. I want them for my library. Mine and Harry's."

"Who did Harry meet here?" I asked. I should take notes.

"Me," Skeff stood beside the stage. "Through me; contractors, engineers, stone masons. I don't know who he saw socially. We worked long hours here. He came to every meeting with ideas. This library will be his. And it will be beautiful. And important"

"You try to reassure me that my husband did not leave me for nothing?"

He peered into my eyes. "He did not leave you. He was taken from you, stolen, from us all." He put his big hand on top of mine, his skin thin vellum parchment, warm. I was crying so he kept talking. The breeze cooled my cheeks.

"He was an artist. I never was. I collect. By inheritance, and from love. It's a disease. Harry knew that." Mr. Skeffington took my hand for the jump down from the stage.

"You are a lovely woman–lucky to have your grandmother's bones." He brushed my cheek with his fingers. "You have her sweetness of expression. Your grandmother and I were lonely together." He took my arm. "I was an only child, with no mother. She was an only child of an absent father and a mother who was no mother, like many those days." He walked close to me as if we were found friends.

"May I see Harry's drawings?" I didn't want to leave this man and wasn't sure I'd be asked back.

"Let me show you." We were soon at the house. The scent of the mountain sage was strong and I was cold. Mr. Skeffington took me into a small room of blond cabinets, walls filled with drawings in gilt frames. He poured us mint ice tea from a small refrigerator.

In his study, as he lay out Harry's sketches on a table, I looked around, once again flabbergasted by the art. Singer Sargent portrait of a seated woman in a paisley shawl, a painting of a small man on a dog sled on a field of snow in front of a huge blue glacier. "Rockwell Kent'" he said. An asymmetrical Ben Nicholson abstract framed the door to a room with more paintings and books.

In Harry's sketches, his quick hand of site plans, elevations, interiors, I could feel Harry, discovering his client's wishes. I wanted to caress the paper, trace the pencil marks. Underneath were the more detailed drawings.

"We will continue with the work, " Skeff said. "I will pay all on-going monies due for Harry's work to you."

"That's kind of you."

"Fair," Skeff said.

We're worried about fairness? I thought. His courtesy felt disarming but out of place.

"Come by again, Mrs. Chase. Could you finish your husband's brilliant plans?"

"No." Did he think I was an architect by osmosis?

"We can go from here with what we have. I've found a local man to do the working drawings. Then we will proceed. We mustn't lose each other. To Harry." We drank our cold tea.

What else did he and Harry do?

"Please come tomorrow and we will talk about Alicia's project."

CHAPTER 31

Again I was led down the windowed gallery to the living room by the old Chinese man. This time I dressed as I had known I would be at Mr. Skeffington's. Why didn't I face my grandmother over breakfast with the questions I had been saving? Who was this Skeffington? What world had he brought Harry into?

"My, you're elegant," I said to him, unable these days to hold my tongue. Mr. Skeffington was dressed like his father, I bet, velvet slippers, flannel trousers, cashmere sweater over his linen shirt, and a silk cravat. He stood next to the fire in the shiny black fireplace beside a Van Gogh of swirling trees. With Skeffington was a young woman in a light blue suit and flats. Her full face, hair slicked back, dark beauty and her voice, laughter, beamed through the room. Looking at her, I could remember how it felt to be so alive, happy.

"Emma, let me introduce Susan, my new colleague from the art museum," Skeff took my hand. "Susan, this is Emma, granddaughter of my oldest friend." We said our hellos. I looked to Skeff to start the conversation.

Susan continued, her voice low. "I have to go so I'll be brief. I'll send my opera list for the opening. Skeff, you'll get the museum, the Casino, the Valley Club -" She noticed me. My face must have looked blank. "The party lists." She turned back to Skeff. "Why is she here?" Meaning me.

The glass room was warm, bright. Harry's plans for Skeffington's museum were open on the central table.

"Were you a journalist, Susan?" Skeff asked. As if : Why the questions?

"No. Hollywood," Susan said. "I move things along–T.V." Susan said to me. "I'm sure you don't watch."

"We are talking about my library. Fundraising. And publicity, I suppose," Skeff said looking Susan up and down, as if appraising her efficiency.

I took a seat and a glass of water from the butler and waited to be filled in on the reason I was at this meeting. I wanted to ask more questions about Harry. Skeff knew more than I did, more than anyone about Harry's last days.

"You can help us, Emma, I'm sure," Skeff said. "And I want you to tell Alicia our plans–she could make this all possible."

"Alicia Ortega Lowell? She must have a good guest list. Even I've heard of her Christmas parties." Susan asked and drank her water, ice clinking.

"Yes. Also. She has the collection." Skeff looked at me. "Come and see the model? It just arrived."

He took me into the blonde octagonal room with the model on a table in the center. Skeff said "Stay and we'll talk privately. I want to hear about your work."

"Emma is living with her grandmother in Santa Barbara on one of the grand old estates," Skeff said as we emerged. "Susan has taken a weekend house up here."

"So I'm available for tennis. I've even got a court," Susan said without looking up from her bag.

"Great," I said to the top of her head.

"Sunday morning?" She stood, bag on her shoulder.

"Yes, thanks." A plan.

"Well, that's accomplished." Skeff said, watching us with an old man's appreciation. "Now will you join our committee, Emma?"

"What to do?" I asked, wary.

"To start the creation of the library. To have a party. An opera party," he said to Susan. "We'll have a second party the next night for my birthday," Skeff said to me. "The opera company will be here so why not have another performance?"

"Do we sell tickets for both nights?" Skeff shook his head. "What are you up to here, Emma?" Susan asked.

"Emma's husband designed my building," Skeff said.

"I'm an archivist," I answered.

"A full time job up here." Susan looked out at the view. A clear winter day, the islands looked like they were only a few miles away across the water. "I bet there are a lot of moldering treasures in these hills."

"You think?" I said. What had she heard? Me, next to nothing.

"Why do you guys call it Santa Barbara when it's Montecito?"

"Not to be snobs," Skeff said.

"Hiding where you're really from?" Skeff and I looked at each other. We knew we never called our town Montecito, but Santa Barbara. Except to each other. "So Emma, for work, you organize, you balance between pleasing clients and solitary research?" Susan said.

"Exactly."

"We'll sell tickets to both nights. Two operas, al fresco," Skeff said. He'd decided. "Use my amphitheater."

"OK, Boss. New boss. Will you help us with Skeff's project?" Susan asked me.

"I have the time."

"Good. I need a local." Was I a local? "I'm new up here and don't know people. I've just gone on the Art Museum Board, out of town member – Skeff enlisted me from there. Your husband? He could help."

"No," I said.

"I should have said 'Emma's late husband'," Skeff said.

"I'm sorry." Susan said and was silent briefly. "Was this his last job?"

"Yes," I answered.

The butler brought us high tea, an export Chinese tea set, the ballast of the tea ships, crust less sandwiches, finger size, and cakes and tea with a pitcher of milk and plate of lemons.

I was hungry after a hard day in the files and understood the British custom.

"Please," Skeff passed me a plate. I was on the loveseat facing the sea view, small and comfortable in the aerie with the coastline below us. Skeff sat next to me. We were silent. I drank tea and ate a cucumber sandwich. The sun set into primary colors as the black of night waited at the edges.

"I drove up this afternoon – heard on the radio about a murder up here," Susan said.

"Murder?" The word grabbed itself out of my head with a jolt.

"A young woman, found under the train trestle north of here," Susan said.

Not my murder, it wasn't news any longer.

"How?" I asked.

"How what?" Susan asked back.

"How was she killed?"

"Didn't say."

"I'm surprised there was a report at all," Skeff said. "Usually there isn't."

"Was there news when Harry was found?" I asked Skeff.

"No. I heard through friends."

"Did M. de Vlamnick know?" Skeff looked puzzled at my question.

"I told him. He said he had heard and had met you in Paris."

"What happened?" Susan asked.

"My architect was found stabbed to death."

Susan looked shocked, her worldly brashness breached. She left soon after.

"Tell me, what do you think of Susan?" Skeff asked me after she left with promises to meet on the weekend if it wasn't raining. "She's new on the museum board. I spotted that energy and immediately enlisted her." He poured a whiskey for himself and poured me more tea, as I watched him.

"Lively." I would be glad to have a friend.

"Has Alicia told you what is in the files?" Skeff asked after a silence.

"She doesn't know. That's my job. I tell her what I find. She tells me old stories."

"Emma, if Alicia agrees, her husband's research will be the core of my new museum. Do you know why I'm doing this?" To pull Harry into the Chumash world? To amass more?

"My White man's guilt. Most of Chumash culture was lost with the speed of their death. Michael Lowell was one of a few people who tried to preserve the old knowledge. Most people who studied the Chumash culture took it away into storage, what hadn't been erased by the Spanish. So the objects of Chumash culture were lost or collected and sent away with Vancouver to the British Museum, with the Mallaspina expedition to Spain, to the Smithsonian, to the Museum of Man in Paris." We sipped our tea and whiskey and watched the sunset through the storm clouds.

"I want to talk to Alicia," Skeff said. "– but she told me you were her person to deal with about the files. She said she's staying out of it for now."

With all her questions to me, Alicia was very much in those files – I was the spy, she the controller. I emerged every day as if from underground to report.

"Michael Lowell saved a lot, I'm sure, the tales, the words. The information. We want to make a Chumash culture center to work like a lending library, so the people can use the information. Chumash used words and their tools to control power, to order the world. There's a benefit in the knowledge, in the words, even without the tools. To buy Alicia's notes and put them in this library for others to study, that's what I want.

"Look hard in there. For clues. We need the tools–" Skeff said. "The artifacts. I have a few–"

"You need them to make the magic?" I said face-tiously, to make light of it. But I had seen them. Did I feel their buried power?

"Someone does. We stole them, all of it. Alicia hasn't agreed to sell to me yet. She tells me she wants to know what is there first. "

"That's why she hired me." I guessed she sent me to meet with Skeff because I knew so little, I could reveal nothing.

"What are you finding?" Skeff asked.

"Random notes. Sometimes they add to or contradict stories and customs mentioned in earlier notes. I read them, mark where they are. It sounds easy but you haven't seen the handwriting."

"Have you found any objects? Maps?"

Objects, the artifacts, that's what he wanted. Was Skeff interested as a collector? To fill his shelves with the last articles in the wild.

"No artifacts," I answered. But I hadn't yet looked in all the cabinets. "What kind of objects?" I asked, though I began to know what could be there–sun sticks; 'atshwin', the charms that held a person's power; head-dresses. "Will I find anything?" I asked.

"I'm curious," he said. "I hope you do. If Michael Lowell managed to save some of Alicia's family things, we will have a collection that matters."

"Alicia's family?" I asked. What did he mean?

"Alicia's mother was part Chumash. A chiefs' or priests' family, I was told." Skeff poured himself more Scotch. "In the Thirties, a few Chumash objects came on the market–my father noted it–then they disappeared. Rumor was that the pieces were from Alicia's family. I've never asked Alicia about it–I doubt if it's a good story for her, whatever it is. My father never said who might be selling them. Maybe her husband bought those and you'll come on them as you catalogue the files."

"I'll look." Unopened cabinets awaited me. "Were you and Alicia friends when you were children?" I asked.

"No, not really. In those days we didn't mix. Your grandmother and I were allowed to play." He paused. "Your grandmother was my first love," Skeff said. "We were children. I thought such love would come again."

His telling me surprised me more than the fact. Would Gran have told me?

"Did she know?" I asked.

"We were best friends. We spent months together in silence, exploring, comfortable."

"What happened?" I asked.

"What do you mean?" he asked.

"Are you still friends?" I felt like I knew nothing about my grandmother.

"Oh, I'm sure we are. Montecito has changed a lot since we were children. The hills were bare then with a few oaks and now a forest blocks the view of the sea." He was avoiding me.

But not from there, where raining fog had come in to fill the canyons up to the house and make the coast and ocean below a pool of thick white cloud. As if the sea rose to the house on the mountain.

"My godson told me you met."

"Who?"

"Scott Lowell is my godson. I keep an eye on that young man. He's hard working, intelligent, a bit conventional socially, especially in his taste for women." I had no response.

"Emma, you have your grandmother's figure but hide it. Too early for that. Though who can tell the young how to dress." He smiled tolerantly at me. Was I young? "Who can tell the young anything?" He looked so far away.

"What did you try to tell Harry?" I asked. Skeff gazed at the cheek of the Modigliani woman.

"Harry?" He seemed reluctant, I bristled, but refused to stop. My mind was a geiger counter for intentions. From the years of moving and solitude, for self-protection I had learned to read what others were thinking, to calculate where they came from, so I could guess how to behave, how to smooth the waters, whether I needed flee to avoid harm. Now I had to change, to attack, not flee.

"Mr. Skeffington, please help me. Who did he see? Who were the mutual friends? The Parisians who recommended Harry to you, did they have friends here?"

"I don't know his friends. Nor at all what he did with his time." Skeff looked at me, his reluctance now sadness. I glared at him as if he had betrayed a friendship. Impertinent of me. He saw my desperation. "He may have had secrets that he did not want others to delve into. We all have parts of our life which are secret. That's privacy. I do." Skeff said. "Do you want to go there? For what purpose?""

"I must. I'm asking about Harry. Not your secrets."

"Oh no?" Did he start to challenge me then drop it? "I'll ask around. We'll meet again soon. You bring Alicia and I'll bring information." So he had some?

Skeff was of another generation, his perspective refracted through his memories. What was true?

CHAPTER 32

"**Y**ou will use my horse, Mrs. Chase. The horse knows the commands but that's all right at first. I'll switch to another language when you become more advanced."

"It will be good to ride again. I haven't taken lessons since I was a girl."

"You are still but a girl–" Mr. Cathcart stood, bandy legs in jodpers, clean scuffed high boots. "Come, I'll show you." Crop in hand, he held the door for me. From his lawn we could see the ring and stables. The ring was muddy and churned by hoofs. I was not the kind of horse lover who spent my time grooming my horse. I liked to get on a horse and go places, and run for the thrill, wind against my face, staying with the rhythm of the horse's gait. Throwing myself over fences on a leaping horse could come close. So I was there for paid lessons. I wouldn't have to be polite or get in caves.

"Mrs. Chase, will you start this week? Saturday?"

"I think so. Let me call to be sure."

"Are you the widow of the murdered man? I don't mean to intrude but I need to know you will be careful with my horse."

"I am not suicidal."

"I am sorry for your loss. Do they know what happened?"

"Not yet."

"I heard he was in with a bad crowd – then he was gone."

"What crowd?" This random man knew more than I did?

"You don't know?"

"No." I was trying to stay calm. "Who?"

"I don't know them. It's from the exercise riders and the polo players I hear about these things."

"What things, sir."

"Men with men. Violence. There were old stories, but they stopped. This is new stuff, stranger."

"Please tell me who–" I was crying but calm, tears flowing down my cheeks.

"I don't know them. I don't want to know them." He hit his boot top with his leather crop. "You don't want to know them."

"But I must. It was my husband."

"Tell the police to talk to the polo exercise boys. They know about everything in this town."

Detective Garcia –

I shook the riding instructor's hard hand though I didn't want to because he would not tell me any more.

"Why was your husband here?"

"Designing a building for Walter Skeffington."

"He's one to ask." He saw my face. "Maybe you should wait before you get on a horse. Grief can make one foolhardy."

That's what I was. And foolish.

To get to work I dodged rocks fallen into the road with the rains over night. Storms continued to pound onto the coast and drench the town.

I called from the phone on my desk in the long shed. "Mr. Skeffington, it's Emma Chase. May I ask you some questions?" I must have been yelling over the noise as the trees blew beside me and dropped their store of the night's storm onto the tin roof. With a half startled warm voice, calming, as if to say No need to scream he answered.

"Why Emma of course. Come before lunch?"

"Yes, thank you. I'm at work, not far."

"I can see new waterfalls behind Alicia's." White stripes cut the deep blue green of the mountains

"Look for waterfalls above me when you come over. Don't cross if the creek is over the road." He hung up and I put the phone down to turn back to the files.

I read Chumash could travel on shouts – ride the shout to be with the echo on a distant hill. Then ride the echo to the next hill. I had to drive.

Skeff was dressed to go out, cashmere scarf tucked in his jacket, gloves hanging out of his pocket. With a welcoming unhurried air he twirled my wet umbrella and put it in his plexiglass stand at the door.

"Will you stop for a tea?" Skeff asked. "I have a few minutes."

We sat next to the fire, away from the windows that showed the mountain world under the fog and rain. The green of winter was deepening to show new lime grasses, the grey plants green again, pale lavender buds on wild lilac bushes, stalks of flame white yucca. Skeffington waited with his legs crossed and arms folded as I came back to him from the view.

"It does catch one, doesn't it, even when the sea is hidden," Skeff said. "You had a question, Emma?"

"Mr. Skeffington, you know Harry was murdered here?"

"Yes, Emma." Skeffington seemed to change gears. The change registered in his mouth. His lips were not set, but wary, ready to smile but not feeling like it. His eyes watched me.

"What do you know about it?" i asked

"Manuel Garcia is on the case."

"Nothing seems to be happening."

"Trust Garcia. Don't think he's only a born-again movie star. Garcia knows this city deeply. He's also a skilled amateur of the Chumash and the Mission period in Santa Barbara." He paused. "I expected your questions to be about Alicia or the Chumash."

"Why the Chumash? What do the Chumash have to do with Harry's murder?"

He just looked at me. Skeff wasn't going to say anything except to answer. Out of habit, or for self protection, I wondered.

"Detective Garcia sends his regards. He suggested I show you this." I gave Mr. Skeffington the private detective's card. I lied. I wanted to know.

"'Private detective'?" Skeff asked.

"That's what he told me. And his card says so."

"You met this man?" Skeff asked.

"Miles asked questions about my husband in Santa Barbara." Feeling dense in retrospect, it occurred to me Skeff hired Miles. The envelopes from the locker plant–there were notes about Skeff's project. Did Skeff want to know what else was there?

"If it's the same man," Mr. Skeffington stood and looked out his glass walls. "I knew Miles a long time ago. He wasn't Private Detective Miles. We were acquaintances when he was working his way through town," Skeff said, his fingertips against his lips. "He was a sexy guy. When he started going to clubs I had to give him up."

He was telling me this? A homosexual. "Clubs?" I asked. I knew he didn't mean golf or tennis clubs. De Vlamnick's club? Harry's?

"Sex clubs," Skeff said as he put his hands in his pockets and walked over to a sculpture. He looked back at me. "I never liked much to share."

I got very quiet, inside and out."Sex clubs? Here? What for?"

"For sex, private, public, whatever you choose and the club allows. There are few rules."

I tried to imagine. The energy must be incredible, the many orgasms and the strivings.

"The concept is orgiastic. The reality, I fear, less so," Skeff said, reading my mind.

"I quail at the thoughts of hygiene," I thought out loud.

"Passion can be a great cleanser, don't you find," Skeff said.

"Or a distracter," I said, feeling no lust in my body nor romance in my soul. "Why go to sex clubs?"

"To get some. Secretly." Skeff moved on to a small Van Gogh painting and followed the brush strokes with his eyes as if they were his fingertips. "Men. And some people need more than normality, something different to get them going. For adults, why not, as long as you can opt out. I opted out."

He spoke of these things with me as if we were discussing a Dutch painter he collected, or sailing.

"This Miles," I pointed to the card on the glass table where he had dropped it. "said my in-laws hired him. They didn't hire him. I'm trying to find out why he was asking me questions about Harry."

"What does Garcia say?"

"He thought you might know Miles." I didn't say Did you hire him?

"Tell him what I say. Miles was a player. He liked to swing, both ways and in public. I haven't known him for years, and I wouldn't open the door to him."

"In what crowd?" Was Harry part of it?

"It's not for ladies. I'm out of that world."

"Who is in that world now? Was Harry?" There I asked the haunting question.

"I hope not. Tell Garcia. I could only tell you about the past." He gazed off into the view. "Here I feel the past reach into the present and future."

"My Harry is in the near past. I want to catch him, follow his last days."

"Be careful, Emma."

I cried as I drove with one hand down the winding road from the high mountain to East Valley Road and across to Alicia's ranch. I called Garcia and left a message. "Please tell Detective Garcia, it's Emma Chase. Will he meet me for coffee at El Paseo at the end of the day? I'll see him at 5."

I went back to work.

Garcia leaned back in his chair with his coffee when I arrived. There were puddles but no rain. I wondered why he had given up the movies. He was still handsome, probably more attractive now in middle age than he would have been as a wiry youth.

"Why did you quit the movies?" I asked Garcia

"The jobs were harder to get and I thought I'd do it for real. And in real life I get to be the good guy, even as a Mexican."

He was a perfect dashing Robin Hood-for-the-Californios type. I liked to see him behind his desk – then I could really look at him. When we met out for coffee we sat side by side. He never asked me what I saw, but he made me feel like we looked out together onto the world that swallowed up my Harry.

"Did you know Michael Lowell? " I asked. Did he have a connection with Alicia's husband?

"Some. He was a focused guy. If you were not part of his obsession he didn't see you. When I went down to Hollywood we lost touch."

"And before?"

"We went fishing."

"Did he talk about his work?"

"No. I was a kid and he had finished his research. I think it was too painful for him. All the old people were gone and no one cared. I cared, but he didn't want to talk about it or answer my questions. He kept reworking his notes as if they could reverse the people's decline."

"Why are you interested in the Chumash?" I asked Garcia.

"Like everybody," he said, from modesty I assumed. I didn't think many other people cared about the Chumash.

"After storms I found Chumash things on the beach – bowls, arrowheads. Do you know the idea of a 'calling'? Catholic. I felt the Chumash called me to know them. I saw how little survived so I searched for what did come down to us."

"Because you were a lucky beachcomber?" I said, daring him to go deeper.

"Right. That and the family myth that some ancestors were Chumash. I wanted to know what that meant," Garcia said.

"Why do you want to know about Bear?" This time Garcia was not going to answer me, either to confirm or deny, I could see that on his face. He could have been a silent screen actor for the skill in which he communicated by expression and bearing.

"Mrs. Chase, I have to go back to work. Was this all?"

"Why the Bear?"

"Look in those boxes of Lowell's. See what you find."

"What about the symbols in Harry's journals?" I asked, thinking his desire to find import in the gathered knowledge of the past was crazier than mine. He wasn't going to answer.

"Alicia said you asked about symbols on Harry's body."

"She did?" Was Harry painted with cave paintings? "Did you ask Mr. Skeffington if he knew Kurt Miles?" Changed the subject.

"Skeff said he was a social climber, worked his way through town, at sex clubs." I paused to see if Garcia was shocked.

"Miles asked you if Harry was homosexual?" Garcia asked.

"Yes. Why would he?"

"I don't know." No answer.

"What does Skeff mean by 'sex clubs'?" I asked.

"Clubs, gathering places, social, but for sex, not conversation or darts." Garcia looked at me as if I was being disingenuous.

"In Harry's and my world there were house parties. And they were about flirting and infidelity, I thought."

"Did your husband frequent sex clubs?"

"I don't know." I thought of de Vlamnick in Paris.

"Some people like to show off." Garcia sipped his coffee while that image soaked in. "What I distrust are the clubs of ambition and domination. And sex. Those people think they not only show their power, they create their power, gather it to their worthiness by buttfucking and beating, razor slices and pikes."

"Jesus. How do you know?"

"I know these things. Maybe I wish I didn't."

"Why tell me?" What did this have to do with Harry?

"You asked, Mrs. Chase."

"Mr. Cathcart said the exercise riders for the polo ponies know all about everything."

"I talk to them. Some are my nephews."

"Who killed Harry?"

"I can't answer that. When I can I will, to the prosecutor."

"The widow's the last to know?"

"Usually."

CHAPTER 33

I talked myself out of bed for tennis with Susan. A clear day, the sun over the ocean, I drove the Porsche top down. Susan was standing at a big wrought iron gate, and rode with me up side roads to her cottage. She wore long white sweatpants and a hooded sweatshirt. That morning, before Susan became my friend, I saw her as a possible refuge. She was young, self- concerned and a new acquaintance. She wouldn't notice a difference in me. I could invent myself anew, act as if nothing had happened. She knew about Harry, but she didn't know me before. What else had happened? Something was different since I'd been in that cave. My mind had left me for unfamiliar climes and had not come back the same. I was excited.

I'd gone through Gran's sportswear closets to find tennis clothes to borrow. Feeling sorry for myself, in her old elegant life without mine. I didn't want to remember where I had jettisoned my old clothes. Into the Atlantic. Welcome to the Pacific.

I found white linen slacks and a v-necked sweater and I bought shoes and socks in the village on the way to the game.

I followed her fast pace around her tile roof cottage, and through the aisles of a formal hedged rose garden to the tennis court.

"I'm lucky. Guest houses for rent aren't easy to find. Saving them for guests. What a place to grow up," Susan said. "To wander around secret gardens. You're living with your grandmother? Got to be different. I couldn't take it."

"It's fine. I'm used to it. I came when I was a child. And I like her."

"Do you like tennis?" Susan asked me as she warmed up, pulling her foot to her bottom.

I had loved it, games in white on green grass. "I haven't played for a while. I did before I was married," I said. Susan twisted and put her elbow behind her head. I reached down and touched my toes, tight and stiff.

"God, I am sore," Susan said "Have a great masseuse, I'll give you her number if you get down to Los Angeles." She pulled her arms across her chest. "Ready?"

I straightened the strings on my racquet, pulling the round gut with the tender tips of my fingers. As I looked into the grid and onto the red clay beyond, my eyes fuzzed and the strings and court became other courts and then no court at all and then all courts I had stood on, waiting for the ball, the serve, the game and its ritual social words and crossings, handing over the balls, praising shots, shaking hands. I stared into the racquet and panicked deep inside. Where was I, what tennis court, who was I playing with? Had I escaped the danger?

"Rally first?" I heard Susan from the other side of the bordered rectangle in the greenery. I had a home here, my Gran remembered me.

Play tennis with a new friend. Luckily the ball came over the net and hung in the air ready to be sent back here in the depths of Montecito, just as it had at the Vanderbilt in London, the Racing in Paris, in the potato fields in the Hamptons. I did not have to know where I was to hit the ball. I did not have to know who I was hitting it to. My ball landed hard at Susan's feet at the net and Susan missed the return.

I watched the ball passing between our strokes; my reason for being for those minutes of comfort. I could hit it well, so could this go-getter of a young woman.

"We'll play? First ball in," Susan called through the damp silence. The sun was hot on the court. Clouds rose over the mountains.

I crouched in second position and watched for the serve and answered with a tough shot to Susan's back-hand corner.

"Great! You're a good player," Susan said, smiling. She bounced two balls and put them in her front pocket, getting lumpy.

She latched on, radar fixed and shots came hard and direct. Then Susan served a high soft one that I had to run off balance to lob back. So much for radar. She wanted to win, and she would with those squirrely serves.

I let the game take my mind away from the scary days. I was losing but not badly. We played even tennis, trading games.

Susan smashed a second serve at my feet and said "There's an old estate next door. An over grown fantasy land. No one pays attention. Want to see? I'll show you. I climb over the wall to spook around. There's a pool. With a cave."

A shudder of excitement. I was thrown back into the memory of that mountain cave. I wanted to get into a cave again. Those paintings, their color and move-ment, I felt as I had never felt, outside myself, insignif-icant but vibrant and exquisite. Flying. Those paintings didn't have answers for me, they erased my questions, pulled me into their dance.

Harry's photo of Ophelia drowned was in a pond in front of a cave. What pond? What cave?

Susan won the match. We drank from paper cups and a thermos she brought from the house. White clouds filled the sky and set off the deep blue. "More rain," we both said.

"There's a cave?" I asked. "Is it have painted?" I whispered. *? half*

"I've only been as far as the pond. I saw a cave mouth, I think, in the rocks above it. Do you want to see?"

"Yes." I was ready to follow this adventurous girl. Susan led me through a thick pittisporum hedge to a high wall of the local creek stones placed without mortar. We climbed, easy enough foot holds up and down into the far woods of another estate.

"Is the cave a new one, like a garden folly?" I asked, reaching for a landscape design to explain this cave before I saw it. I wanted to tell her about the photos, the journals, my search for Harry's murderer. But I didn't, not trusting an ambitious stranger. "Chumash?"

"You mean the local Indians? Looks old to me," Susan said. We were speaking softly, good girls trespassing for fun. We could be out for garden cuttings.

The path she took me on was open at first but overgrown. We could walk standing, then had to crawl at the end, up the steep slope. Stooped we looked out at the cave in the boulders above a pond that began to erupt with the first raindrops. Frogs croaked.

"Sacred frogs' urine," I said, recalled from my research.

Susan laughed. "Is that what it is. Frogs?"

"So I've read," a few references. "Chumash say the water in the springs and streams of earth is the urine of the many frogs who live in it."

The cave opened in huge boulders, and it looked deep, like it got bigger inside. There was room to walk around the pond and climb up the rocks to the cave opening and there was another pond below. Ponds. I thought of Harry's photo of the woman floating. I'd given all the envelopes to Garcia. He was silent about them.

The rain fell, so hard we felt it through the brush above us and, without speaking, we started back down the hill. I cut my face. Wet and running we dashed along the path. We climbed back over the gleaming rock wall, into the pittosporum forest, to the tennis court and into Susan's cottage. She put water on for tea and lit a fire as I stood at the window and watched the wind blow the rain.

Susan sat down. "Now you, what do you do? Do you read all day? Or file?"

"Both. I chart. I read documents and note where they are, make a map for my boss. I read about caves. And bears."

"No bears here, right?" Susan asked. "What about that cave next door? Would you call it a garden folly? A fake or real?" Susan asked.

"A landscape architect's idea of a Chumash cave. Or a Chumash cave. Have you been inside?" I asked her.

"No, but I'd like to. Will you come with me?" Susan asked, planning the next adventure.

"Do you know that it's abandoned?"

"No one seems to care for the place. But I'm only up for weekends. There could be a weekday sect that meets there and leaves little trace. " We thought she was joking.

"Who owns the property?" I asked.

"I don't know. I'm counting on an absentee," Susan said.

"How about here? Who is your landlord?" I asked.

"Dreamy guy, Greg Lowell. His dad actually." That was a surprise. "Do you know him?"

"At work. He's related to my boss."

I didn't want to mention I had been into the wild with him in case she had romantic aspirations. Did that mean I had them? He'd shown me so much already, I knew then that I had secret hopes he'd show me more. Did I imagine the two of us in a cave, moving gently, piercing each other, feeling for the interior spaces. Ironic.

Susan asked again "How do you know him?"

"We met at Alicia's–at her son's house on the ranch. He's her nephew."

"Owns a lot of properties I understand–or his father does. My real estate agent said his father owns this little place, and I dealt with Greg about using the tennis court."

"What did you think?"

"He was a bit of an old lady–didn't want any changes, worried about noise. But I thought he was attractive."

"Yes?" Was I ready to back off my nascent erotic thoughts of the outdoorsman? I wanted to keep them. It felt like life then. My world was limited, yet I had men in my life. Now that my one man was gone. Did I notice them more because I was single? Widow. Garcia was the handsomest, Scott the tallest and Greg the most dynamic. I wanted my Harry, medium size, goofy looking and kind.

"Not really my type. But I could see myself Mrs. Estate Owner," Susan said.

"Trade your glamour life for that?" I asked.

"No, not yet." So she was reserving the right.

Well, I knew it was all women out for themselves. We'd only met, Susan and I. What about Maria?

"Lucky we got some tennis in. What a year -" she started the rain talk.

"Do you ride?" I asked. Did Greg take everyone on the cave tour?

"No, I don't trust a horse. Brain as big as your thumb."

"I'd like to get closer to the cave, see what's in there," I said.

"I'll go back in with you," she said. "Wait for me. Next weekend I'll be up." I'd content myself until then with work, looking for caves and paintings, bears and sex in the miles of files.

CHAPTER 34

Home in the nursery of Gran's big house with only the attic between me and the rain, I washed my face and tried to shake off the paranoia that made me feel the world too small in its cast and too big with its secrets. I wandered downstairs in my robe and found a message from my grandmother. Mr. Skeffington asked me for drinks, to meet a friend from Paris. M. de Vlamnick? Could it be the strands of Harry's noose were to come together at Mr. Skeffington's? So easily?

A rich man's private museum–what a feeble reason for Harry to die, I thought. It brought him here, alone. Must I care that it would be a library as well? For a culture.Who wants to check out a sunstick? Was it just an excuse to bring my husband and kill him?

I lay in my bed with Conrad, bound in old leather. The English words treasured by the Pole.

I let myself ask what Harry did here alone. The so-called detective and I had been over those questions, though I had resisted clear answers then refused to think of where they led. The obvious: women, sex. Drugs, though I didn't believe that. Drugs bored him. Harry thought they dimmed his mind and dulled those already dim around him. He wasn't alone here. He flew with Greg. What else? Garcia had the journals except the one. I needed to see his Black Journal.

"Good, Emma, you will come at 7? One never knows, last minute plans often work the best."

His gentleman's voice soothed me. I felt that through him I would find the answers and face them as a lady.

Saturday at home in rooms lightly used, light filtered. I spent the day reading my grandmother's books on the Chumash – museum monographs, and editions of the local historical society she saved in a chronological row. It was not raining that evening, a break in the steady flow of storms from the sea. My grandmother's garden was shaking its water off in the wind, nasturtiums blooming orange on the sliding hillsides. Sand bags kept the water from filling the kitchen garden like a pond. I walked the high spots to the back garage and drove out bouncing in pothole puddles.

My first cocktail party in Santa Barbara, first since Harry had died. Wear pearls, call it tea and relax, that's what the old ladies do, I told myself, as I searched for the road left off East Valley Road and up into the mountains. Skeff told me his drive was passable so I took it on faith that a creek would not wash me away as I wove between boulders and through rivulets up to his house on the mountain ridge.

It started to rain. The butler met me with an umbrella and took me inside. He asked for my drink order and motioned me down the windowed, black and white tiled hall to the end room, where I heard male voices.

The Degas ballerina statue tiptoed at the entrance, her tutu and hair ribbon dowdy, her posture ageless. I stood up straighter.

Outside the door, I waited silent to have a chance to observe. Mr. Skeffington, in smoking jacket and cravat, saw me and the other men turned. I could feel the shock of my arrival in the room. I had interrupted something. I had interrupted them so completely that I felt an intense glare and could not look up. I took a champagne from a tray and watched the bubbles. Confident women flirt, I thought, then felt the shift away from me. How did I insert myself into the silence to ask questions? What questions?

Skeff moved away from the table covered with papers to take my hand and hold it in both of his. "Emma, thank you for coming."

Skeff gestured to a stranger, very handsome, older, hair darkened, nose broken. "Emma Chase, Thierry DeLotte, the great interior designer here from Paris." Thierry stood and mock-kissed my hand.

Scott Lowell was there. He nodded from the bookshelves across the room.

"You know my godson?" Skeff asked quietly.

"Yes," I said, noncommittal. How secret were we?

"Of course," Skeff said. Skeff began to explain me to the others. "Emma's husband was my architect for the museum. You see his drawings here," Skeff said.

Skeff led me to a comfortable chair, Chippendale with an embroidered seat, among the sofas. Skeff sat in the matching chair at the other end of the low table covered with blueprints. I could see Harry's designs. I lingered with the belief that he would come in from the outer room to care for them.

Thierry spoke, a tall thin man with a red scarf around his neck tied in one of the mysterious French knots that seem too intricate for an American to do. "I know his work, of course. I have worked on a few Chase houses." He had the accented English of a Frenchman that made his voice rise at the end of his sentences. "Always a pleasure."

"Thierry is here from Paris to help with the museum interiors." The Frenchman sat back in the sofa with a nod. Could be a good sign, a Frenchman who didn't pretend to smile because an American expected him too. Or did he look hostile?

"Scott, come join us," Skeff raised his voice so Scott could hear him. He was looking at the books. "Scott, my godson, local boy moved to the city. San Francisco. I dragged him down to help me with the library, the opening's guest list and all other crucial decisions. So no wandering," he said. Scott leaned back on the shelves of art books. "Maria Ortega will join us. She is our liaison with the local Chumash for the library, also my construction coordinator. She will make Harry's and Thierry's designs happen here on the mountain side." Skeff stood and raised his drink. "Together you are the third generation of my Montecito, complete when Maria comes." He gestured toward me as he put his drink on the low black enamel table. "Emma Chase, granddaughter of my first best friend. Scott Lowell, son of Alicia, the Spanish Indian girl we loved from afar, too grand for us."

I could feel Scott in the room and wanted to lean against him. How did Scott feel to meet me there, together once more, outside his mother's realm, and outside his bed? Strangers again. Scott looked like he had been caught in a noose. Very still, listening for footsteps.

"Scott's father Michael Lowell was my sailing friend. Only because of that did Alicia take me in when we were adults. Maria who you'll soon meet," Skeff looked to his man at the door who shook his head. "She is the granddaughter of Bernarda Ortega, the lady who arranged all fiestas for our parents." Skeff sat down, the subject made general.

Skeff was ordering the room and the relations within it. I wish he could. I wanted to take him into his blonde wood bar and force him to tell me his secrets.

"For a party you may have to tent the whole place, look at this rain," Thierry said with as much wonderment as disgust. "Where is the lovely Emma's handsome husband?" Thierry asked. "The architect to the chic and elegant."

"He was the best," Skeff said sadly.

The dapper man's hand immediately went under his chin, his eyebrows up, surprise then curiosity, listening to the tension and waiting for an answer.

"'Was' the best? "

"Il est mort, murdered," I said, understatement of bitterness. Here, sitting in front of his last work, with people who saw him later than I did, with the man who brought him here.

"You're kidding." Americanism from the Frenchman. He looked at Skeff who shook his head. "Oh zut. Dead? You must be very brave. " He paused and looked at all our faces. At Skeff's for hints, at mine for suspicions.

Scott stared at me—was he looking for widow's tears? Then he gazed out the window like he wanted to be somewhere else. It rained even harder.

Was I projecting, or was there a conspiracy blowing in the undercurrents? Thierry, brightened with news of tragedy, was sitting almost off his chair he was so full of questions. Skeff crossed his arms and patted them with sadness. The men were silent. No one would ask or answer. I was under inspection. I wanted to know what was behind it and where Harry fit in.

"Let me ask." Each man turned to his drink then back to me. "How did you know Harry? Were you friends? " I asked.

"I didn't meet him, Emma. I started coming down recently," Scott said. I could feel him not looking me over. I believed him.

"My condolences, Mme. Chase. It is a small world. There are only the mutual friends in Paris." Thierry looked into my eyes, his thoughts opaque behind the social politeness of his answer. de Vlamnick? "Life has many weavings, loose and tight," Thierry said. His stretched handsome face looked tired. He pulled amber beads with a tassel from his pocket.

"Too tight," Scott said.

"We don't know what happened to him, Emma. It's horrible that it happened, and here," Skeff said.

Scott watched it rain. The night and the long views had disappeared in darkness, the thick rain drops lit from inside made a silver curtain of closeness.

First the sound of clicking heels then Maria Ortega walked in with a quick sashay. She was in a dark purple suit and high heels, business wear, and makeup. Did she thicken or thin the soup we were in?

"Mr. Skeffington, I'm so sorry to be late." She shook Skeff's hand. "Scott Lowell, it has been too long."

Scott kissed her cheek. "How are those brothers of yours?" he said.

I remembered her brothers. Three of them, almost the same age. Inseparable, wide and silent, they seemed a quiet wall behind her. More like a high wall around her, she told me one day when we talked in the surf about the brothers waiting for her on the beach.

"Fancy meeting you here," Maria said blowing me a kiss. She saw the men without jackets and took hers off. Maria's arms were shapely bare and her dress was tight. She carried a notebook and opened it as she nestled her bottom into the sofa. I found her entrancing, grown up so female.

"Maria, you've met Emma?" Skeff said.

"We spent years together trying to catch waves," Maria smiled to me as she took a lemonade or a marguerita from the butler.

"Thierry deLotte," Skeff said. "Maria Ortega-Gutierrez."

Thierry stood and walked to her and bent over her hand.

She nodded a hello. "Charmed." She focused on Skeff and began the business meeting. "The crews are ready to break ground when it stops raining."

"The national Museum called with a new offer. Skeff, they want your collection in DC and they have an offer for my father's files," Scott said, interrupting.

"Will your mother sell to them?"

Scott shrugged. "Conservation, preservation. Capital."

"That's one option." Skeff looked at Scott. "I can also provide capital. If we send the material to Washington, it is a continent apart, a long ride or a plane ticket away from the people who need it. Locked away from the ones who can use it. Ask your mother to wait."

"Your museum is too beautiful not to build," Thierry said.

"To Emma's husband, " Skeff said. "Our architect." This time he drank after he raised his glass.

Maria set her manicured hands flat on her file folders and looked into my eyes with a sadness I felt too strong. Then she shifted away. "Well, do you want the parties anyway? Chief?"

"Yes. We want celebrations so people will understand the library's mission and will support it." Skeff said as he motioned the butler to come in with Chinese dumplings.

It was obvious that Maria was more to Mr. Skeffington and to Scott than the contractor and the caterer. I could multiply the few months over the years that I'd known Montecito by many fold and imagine the skeins that connected them. Crashing came the familiar loneliness of a stranger, the separation from all around me that my husband had briefly saved me from.

We took lacquered trays and dumplings with antique chopsticks. Skeff stood. "I asked you all here to toast the venture. Also to brainstorm on some of my last minute plans," Skeff said. "We'll take turns."

Thierry stood. "I begin with credit to Harry Chase. His concept, his drawings, guide us. My vision for the interior celebrates both Mr. Skeffington's ideas and Harry Chase's building, the exterior." He showed us Skeff's preliminary choices for the floors, the colors, the furnishings. I drifted off watching the silent rain drops and imagining myself on the French street at night that Van Gogh painted and Skeff hung beside the window.

When Thierry finished describing the plans, Maria reported on the contractors. All those years of bossing her brothers around were major career preparation. She was a general with long eyelashes and braided hair.

"The party, Maria?" Skeff said. Maria described her forces of staff, the food, the drink, the music, the accommodations for the opera company.

My body sat there, listening to Maria's description of the flowers for the tables, flag garlands for the tent and rush for the walkway from the amphitheater to the tent. Opera in the amphitheater, masks, dancing. Maria took notes. I felt dizzy and wondered how it could matter.

"Now, the guest list. You put a few San Francisco names on that list, Scott. We expect to meet your fiancée, before the date, dear boy." Skeff was baring all secrets. Did I want to meet Scott's fiancée?

I stood and left the room. Directed by the butler who walked with me, reflections in the night mirrored hall, to a mirrored door, I pushed in to the silver powder room and lost myself in my images.

When I came back, silent in flat shoes, I heard Skeff say "So it is a mystery, our architect's fate."

"Another secret?" Maria's screech was a whisper, her modern composure gone, her back slumped.

What other secrets in this mystery? In the cold hall between the paintings and antiques I staggered with a surge of dizzy fear. Then I knew I wanted more than escape. Stabilizing hatred stiffened me. I wanted revenge.

I walked in.

"Emma," Maria said. "- how hard it must be for you to sit here and listen to us plan a party when your husband has died on this project." She knew.

"Yes," I said and looked for my friend Maria. She was gone, back into herself. I wanted to take Maria and leave, distrusting the room full of men. She would talk to me alone. What were her secrets? Did I have to shake it out of her? Did she, or they, know who killed my husband? What could I do?

The rain had moved on. Skeff's view through the mountains to the sea opened up so the plain of the sea shone in a path under the moon.

"Harry collected when he was here." I watched Skeff. "Photographs, plans. Objects." I was trying to tempt Maria or Skeff or Scott to know of the photos in the freezer box, the Miramar box, the journal, the missing journal. "There's a journal I can't find. Did he give it to you?"

No one spoke. Yet I felt I had put myself in danger. They looked at each other as if asking old friends How do we respond to this stranger?

"What did your husband photograph?" Thierry asked.

"Landscapes, people," I answered. How well did the Frenchman know Harry?

"I keep asking myself what was he doing when it happened?" I asked, desperate for someone to answer my focus. Tears fell down my cheek and I watched their faces gather round me.

"Who did you introduce him to?" I asked Skeff.

"Vendors of wares, mysterious and nefarious?" Thierry asked, posing like a silent movie actor. He saw Skeff's disapproval.

"Workmen mainly. Garcia knows."

"Do you know M. de Valmnick in Paris?"

"No," Tierry answered. Did I see Skeff startle?

Maria looked around for relief.

Scott had come to our side of the room. "What do the police say? Any closer to finding the killer?" he asked me.

"No."

"Have we finished business here?" Skeff asked and all nodded. "I know Maria is in a hurry. We reconvene soon to finalize the plans." Everyone stood.

Maria gathered papers and walked close to me. "I have a secret for you, Emma. Come out with me." It occurred to me I was set, on my way to the truth. We went to the powder room together and I watched her in the mirror, her shadow on the foil wall. Her brown eyes had dark circles, sunken in the dim light. "Emma, my big secret. I'm pregnant–embarazada." She looked so pleased, I knew the tack to take. Not: unmarried, a baby! I needed to go sailing.

"Wonderful Maria!" I gave her a hug meant for the baby. "Wonderful news," I said. Who's the father? I did not say. Was she secretly married? What did her mother think? Her brothers?

"I have much to tell you, darling. Let's meet tomorrow, lunch?"

I held out for that promise.

In the hall she clicked ahead, her notebook out, to catch Thierry who talked, head close with Scott.

Skeff walked up beside me. "Emma, thank you for joining us. I know it's not easy."

I felt I'd joined the conspiracy against my husband. Somewhere in this world he'd found his death. Was it Skeff's world?

"Emma. You must join us –." Skeff motioned for his butler to bring our coats. "I'll plan on it."

Maria looked at me delighted with her news as the butler helped her into her raincoat. She spoke to Skeff as they waited at the front of the modern white house. Maria touched her warm cheek to mine outside and hurried away from me. The last I saw of her she waved from the car and sped up the hill in a spurt of little rocks. The sky was dark black with the clouds of stars in the Milky Way over us on the wet gravel drive.

CHAPTER 35

When we were there, in that floating room, those men and Maria could have spoken, shared the parts they'd seen, what they'd heard and done to make a whole story. But no one told me. Instead the stories were different for each of us, as different as what we cared about. I wanted to know the whole story, to join it together in myself, to bear witness and so to judge, and to punish, if only by wishing hell and damnation on the man. I guess now, that only Maria knew or could have guessed. Skeff knew the fringes of the world that reached out of its vileness to destroy my Harry. It took me dangerous days to learn what went unsaid that evening of fog and rain.

Scott came out behind me. He kissed my cheek. "I leave for San Francisco tomorrow. Come over tonight." I ached, electrical chemistry of his touch mixed now with the feelings pulled up by that night – hatred, anguish and lost love.

I wanted Scott's bed, his big hands and his desire.

"Come to my window," he said.

"Maybe," I said.

"Now. It's late," Scott said.

Skeffington came out into the moonlit night and was surprised at Scott's lean into me. I could see it on his face. Thierry walked toward the guest house and distracted Skeff.

I drove after Scott, pretended with each turn that I might stop following and go home to bed. But he was irresistible, his car pulled mine through the curves, right at the intersection of the two country roads and down to the beach. I rode, windows down, the heat blasting on my legs as the cold wind shivered my shoulders. I didn't think of what I was looking forward to.

We were silent. He waited for me outside in the dark and took my hand. The front door was unlocked. He locked it behind us and left the lights off.

"What do you see," he whispered in my ear, his body light, warm on my back, coming in again, heavier, warmer, my skins' synapses quivering. Abandoning myself to him, with him, I didn't want to talk, I wanted to groan and quiver some more, to relax and go beyond and let the pain of such conquest merge into stronger pleasure.

I didn't know who he was.

He pushed hard, I slipped down, in farther, his hands lifted me up, we were kneeling my head back on his shoulder. He pushed me down onto him, hard.

"What do you see?"

"Paintings. Cave."

"Let's go underwater." He bit my ear softly, pulling me with him back off balance, onto our sides and he turned me over, stretched above my stomach then came down and up, gently then hard. I held on and found a vein of pleasure that I'd only glimpsed before as I rode, breathing with him, until my body startled and let the pleasure go away in waves of answer to him.

Scott lay his head beside mine and held my shoulders with his arm under them so my body curves met the indents of his side. In an old movie we would have smoked but we lay there awake. I began to wish I was already gone, instead of having to take my leave, withdraw from this intimacy and look the man in the face.

I started to pull away and he held me tight.

"Wait. Talk to me," Scott said. "You saw Chumash paintings?"

"In a cave, back in the hills." I wasn't sure about this talking in bed. That mixed our roles. "I knew they were Chumash from your father's notes, and the drawings."

"You were in a cave?" Scott asked. "Where? With who? "

I was thirsty. Scott sat up and poured us glasses of water from the tray on his bedside table. All set up, in silver. I stayed on my stomach.

"Your cousin Greg. We rode back into the national forest to a cave."

"Greg?"

"Yes."

"As I recall he's big on 'The 'Antap's Way'," Scott said, pouring more water.

'Antap' I knew from the notes. The Antap controlled the ritual objects, the 'atswin, and used them to maintain cosmic balance, to cure illness, and more. I was coming back to myself, still unable to talk. Where were the covers?

"Chumash used caves," Scott said. "Greg had a club, a joke version of the Chumash way. Not a good joke."

I reached with my feet for a blanket.

"The Chumash painted the caves," he said.

"Yes, this much I know." No blanket.

"Some say the paintings were about sex," Scott looked at me, my naked backside. "Initiations. I never fell for that."

Found a sheet and covered myself, my cheek on the pillow, I didn't want to roll over. "Fell for what?" I asked.

"Greg's club, I never made the trip to the cave to be 'initiated'. You?" Did he look at me suspiciously? Me? He had a fiancée.

"I got in a small cave alone to see paintings," I said. "It felt magical. Or like I'd been dosed with drugs."

"Could be. Never know with Greg." Scott smoothed my back and pulled my ear lobe. "I doubt if it was vibrations left from the old Indians that got you high."

"Your cousin wouldn't dose me, right?" I sat up and clutched the sheet.

"If that's all he did, you got out lucky, as I hear it," Scott said, stroking my head. "A father raped his son in a painted cave, to join him to the cult."

"God." Was it Scott? The research made his father crazy?

"The son had to go camping with his father every weekend." Scott shuddered. "Some bullshit about a Chumash bear cult. More like a modern whack-o's excuse for buggery, I say. Buggery of boys." Scott kissed my head. "I like girls."

I shivered with fear and dread and desire as he looked at me like we had unfinished business, more exploring to do. Then he pulled his gaze away.

"Was it you?"

"No!" Scott said. It was still dark, but very late. The sea seemed louder. A morning train hooted and birds began to call.

"Did you have a nervous breakdown and go to Greg for help?"

'Hardly. What in the world? Is Greg lying again?"

"Does he lie?"

"Yeah. He came to me like a hermit out of a cave."

273

Change the subject and think about who was lying later. "When your mother has a full catalogue will she sell the files to Skeff?"

"I don't know." He kissed my arm. "I have to leave tomorrow. Today. And you, what next?" Scott asked me. I reminded myself that I didn't need to ask the same of this soon to-be-married man with a legal practice in the city.

"I will get back to France, to my house there. But first I need this work. For a new roof. After your mother's, Skeff may have a job for me. And the other Lowells. Greg –"

"Greg? And his father?" He seemed incredulous. "His father's dangerous. " Scott was far away.

"Still? "

"He's alive." Scott's attention returned. He kissed my shoulder.

"I thought the old man Lowell was always in bed now?"

"Could we do that for a few weeks? Bed," Scott said sliding down beside me.

"In another world."

"We're there now. Stay for dawn. I don't know when I'll be back."

"After the honeymoon?" I didn't want to care. But my body hurt at the thought of his leaving. The more I had with him, the more I wanted.

"Stay. Sleep." Scott said, reaching along my sides. "Be careful if you go to work for George and Greg Lowell."

"Someone should have warned me about you," I said arching over to him.

As Scott and I lay tired again, my cheek on his chest, feeling too comfortable, he said "Maria told me your husband was homosexual."

"What?" I sat up and stood out of bed.

"She saw him go to parties here, she said. If he took part in things, found out about practices? We know he found danger."

"Tell me."

"Ask Maria. Soon. She'll not last long if she keeps up her talking."

Scott watched me as I looked for my clothes and dressed.

I had to find Maria. What kind of whore was I to be in another man's bed?

He spoke as I opened the tall window to go out into the wet dirt between banana plants. "I won't see you. Be careful."

I felt I'd torn myself apart from him, ripped the fragile membrane and left sore flesh. And I was afraid.

CHAPTER 36

Too early to call Maria, I went to church, to see the old Mission and sit in the dark. Let my body melt into the hardwood pew, my brain one with the dust flying toward the dawn light in the windows.

As they set up for Mass I left and drove slowly home along the corniche.

My grandmother met me with a kiss. "Breakfast in the sun room," she said. "Let's talk, Emma."

"Let me wash up." Did she wonder where I spent the night? Was she evicting me for bad behavior? There I was in the mirror and felt more like myself with a clean face. Quick change into a skirt and I was ready to face Claudia, I thought. We met in the yellow room, now so familiar somedays I did not notice the adventurers on the wallpaper.

"I'm glad to see you're having a social life." She smiled and I looked for disapproval. "Who are you seeing of the Lowells? Alicia at work of course, but?" She waited briefly. "Who, Emma?" An urgent questionand I began to be afraid.

"Why, Gran?"

"There are stories about other Lowells that I don't want you to be part of."

"Like what?" Too rude. "I've met Scott Lowell and Greg, his cousin."

"Greg called here for you."

"What stories?"

"I wouldn't trust either one alone with you."

"O.K. Gran, I can avoid them." Not really. Too late. "What have you heard?"

"Rumors about Greg's father: dirty collecting."

"Oh." Cardinal sin of rich people.

"His son is too quick with a laugh." Claudia's intuition was firm in its judgement. "They say his father is a sex maniac."

"What do they say about Scott?"

"He keeps getting engaged."

"Is that so bad?"

"If you're the one he's leaving." She passed the coffee. "It shows instability."

"Lawyer in San Francisco." She shrugged as if that was no recommendation. "What does Greg's father collect?"

"Chumash artifacts, maybe more. The great, and honest, collector is Walter Skeffington. How is his collection now?"

"Beautiful paintings, Greek statues..."

"I hear he is buying all the time, adding to his father's collection. His father was in Europe with Duncan Phillips, in the studios of the best."

"What do you mean by 'Dirty collecting'? Thievery, forgery, bad sportsmanship?"

"I don't know Emma, there's just a swirl of bad words around the family. It must mean something."

"He collects Chumash things?"

"That's what I hear."

"Does Skeff know? Or Alicia?"

"Ask them."

"Have you seen that collection?"

"No. I am not friendly with George Lowell. Supposedly no one has seen his collection. He even keeps the Museum out. Don't you be friendly either.

"Will Alicia donate her files?"

"She hasn't decided, as far as I know"

"Is your work still interesting?"

"More so, the more I learn." The cave came to my mind, vivid.

How could I see the secret collection without giving in to Greg's demand for a 'kiss'? The son was not the father.

I reached Maria at work. We planned lunch at the Pharmacy the next day. I held the heavy black phone, like a big baby rattle and thought she sounded fine, business-like, surrounded by people. I hung it onto the cradle above the dial and tried to feel reassured by the click of the fit.

The telephone rang and I jumped. "Where were you last night?" Greg's voice sounded like it was in some-one's pocket, released after a long silence. "I called and Claudia said you weren't in."

"I came in late." I didn't like his asking, but, sur-prised, I didn't protest. So what is it to you, I thought. Or was this a man to protect me? First name basis with my grandmother was my third thought. It did feel like Greg was chasing me and I could feel his attraction. I thought of Maria. How small was Santa Barbara that this was the man for her? I would stay away from his romanctic plans. And go in the window to Scott in the secret intervals, my mind scared me with a wicked turn of temptation. Were the cousins rivals? I didn't think I was in danger. They operated in different spheres. And Greg was Maria's.

"Where were you?" Greg sounded as if he had been worried about me.

"Did you need something?"

"You." He laughed as I waited. "You, Emma Chase. We, my father and I, need your expert services. I told him about you and he'd like to meet you." Don't tell Claudia. My grandmother had her own stories and I mine.

"Expert services?" How was he touting me to the father?

"You are an expert with collections. Right? My father has a collection. Come over for a drink. I'll show you our things. See if it suits you. We'll go on to dinner."

The collection? See it for Alicia and Skeff was my first thought. What job would they have for me?

What job did they have for Harry? God, I might have collaborated with Harry, my dream, a floor pulled away, flipped like a bed spread out from under me.

What did the rumor-mongers know? Did my grandmother's warning mean I had to refuse dinner? Or a job? Alicia's job would end. With a second project I could work to pay for more than the house repairs in France. The more I earned now, the sooner I would be free to find my new life.

Gran was to be out and I was hungry and in no mood to cook. I wished I'd asked Maria for dinner.

"Emma, say yes."

Greg's intensity made me nervous but the collection and the connection to Harry tantalized. I needed to know why and how Greg was in Harry's journal. Could I find traces of the murder? At least live with Harry those last days through Greg's stories of him. Revenge was less on my mind. I would go on, whoever killed him.

Tell me about Harry, I could ask. Would he answer?

"Should I dress? Where do I go?" I asked, excited to see his house – whichever one was his. Was it where he met me to ride? I was confused by their land holdings, places here and there reputed to be George Lowell's and his son. I'd seen their name on the old maps and the new. Now I knew the orchard land of Alicia and her barns and house. But I only knew this Lowell's property from the the periphery of Susan's tennis court.

"Take East Valley to Sycamore, go right, and look for the eagles on the gate posts." An invitation to the big house. Above Susan's. Would his father be there? Was his father's collection there? "At 7, Emma. Not formal."

Gran's stories did not scare me, they piqued my interest in his father's collection so I looked forward to our evening. I took a long bath and thought just once of Scott. Had my body forgotten my husband? His awkward kisses. Was it hard for him because I was a woman he kissed? Harry was more lost to me, unknown alive, to my blind eyes.

I ran to the garages through the big rain drops. Gran's roof did not leak, she kept checking the sweet dusty attic, so I was cheered by the hard rain, the sound of the creeks, musical with water flowing between the boulders. I felt energized, glad to be there, plumped by all that water. The cars looked sleek and still, the light film of dust invisible in the watery light. I took the Jaguar.

The gate to the Lowell estate was open and I rolled into the drive through wet trees that dripped with the wind. In a square courtyard with a square fountain, Greg stood on the steps at the front door. He held my arm and led me in. He put my coat into a big closet under the stairs.

The house seemed half used. Greg took me down a long hallway toward a bar and pool room with green lamps. Dark rooms with half closed doors led off the hall. I could spy large furniture like cabinets in the chilly rooms.

As Greg poured me wine, I asked him "What did we pass in those rooms? May we go see – I saw out here -" and I was out the door, ostensibly to show him what I was asking about, actually to lead him where I wondered if he wanted to go. Greg probably had other things in mind than a collection tour, I thought on arriving. I should have known to find him so dapper, expectant and polite, romance in his eyes. But I was determined. Secret or not.

"Shhsh! Don't wake my father!" Greg followed me with a hiss. I stopped.

Where was his father? Did he sleep in one of the dark rooms we passed?

"I'll show you, but we must be quiet. He's just above – " He looked up, as if to the heavens.

He turned on the light in the first room – and the glass shined – long and high cases of it, in polished dark wood. When I saw what was in them, my urge to know and see it all right then, made me very still, waiting for Greg's cue. My wonderment. In front of me was the finest, richest collection of Chumash culture I'd ever imagined. Even after Paris.

"Do you know want you're looking at?" Greg asked.

Why was I hiding my excitement? I acted mildly curious.

"The feather headdresses look Chumash." Could he feel my gut turning under my false deep calm? I walked closer, nonchalant. Looking. 'Atshwin, the personal power tools of the Chumash- rocks shaped as animals, shells poked in for eyes; whale, seal, otter, bird, in row after row. Shell inlaid miniature boats, basket hopper mortars and sandstone pestles, donut shaped serpentine rocks, digging sticks, and baskets. I stopped agape, so fine were the baskets.

"Your father collected all this? How -?"

"Ah, this is only a portion," Greg boasted. "If you play your cards right, I'll show you the important stuff." He laughed and handed me my drink.

"Where -?" I started to ask. "You must have to go to the auctions in Europe for this quality."

"A lot, my father was lucky." Greg said. "An important cache."

"I say so."

I was looking at the sacred objects as I talked, pretending polite indifference still, a defensive posture I felt I needed. "Why did your father choose the Chumash to collect?" I asked, wowed by an otter cape.

"He grew up here. He was chosen to find this and more. He learned. He believes what the ancients believed. He added pieces. He initiated me. I became a collector."

"You too?" Keep him talking so I could keep seeing the relics of a cluture.

Greg said. "Collecting is a responsibility. Collections are alive, you know," Greg said. "They need to be fed."

I ignore that weird idea. "You've followed your father's lead?"

Greg seemed insulted. "I will always come after my father. But I play my part. I collect."

"How did you become interested?" I asked. The feathers on the cape were still iridescent.

"My father passed me his belief, like a religion. But this is a total religion, physical and spiritual. I believe." He was looking at me, for something. An acolyte?

"You believe these objects are sacred?" I wanted to be intellectual about this. "That's unusual. For collectors I've known, one culture's religion becomes another culture's art." In farther cabinets I saw Chumash whistles of bone, rattles of snakes, a feather tufted hat and feather skirts. Pinned to the wall was a shawl made of a Mexican flag.

"We are not art collectors. These objects do not represent. They embody, they contain power. My father collected these objects for their power."

"Idols?"

"Chumash believed power was scattered in the universe. My father and I believe in Chumash power. Chumash used these tools to gather the power. We use these, and others. We practice the power. We know ceremonies."

I thought of the swordfish dance I read about at work. Many other references to dances, secrets. What did Greg mean? "What kind of ritual?" I asked to be polite, bent closer to the glass, still looking at the art embedded in the everyday objects of the Chumash elite.

"Dances. Some we must create. I create dances, 'rituals' to you." He took my arm and put his hand on my back. "You have the access. You will find secret rituals in those notes."

He spoke to my eyes. I looked away, wanted to see more of the treasure around me. I didn't want to think about his theories, or his rituals.

I went to the last case in the room and found a sharks' tooth belt, a crystal-topped wooden wand, and then a sunstick beyond any I'd read of.

The sunstick was the tool the Chumash priest, the paha, used at solstice ceremonies. With the sunstick he called the sun back to the people. The paha did the astrological calculations and performed the rituals that Chumash believed kept the skies and the earth and the waters in balance. But this sunstick was not the usual circle of wood or stone, its pointed rays not shells stuck into their pattern with tar but a big carved jewel, jade or emerald with pearls marking the rays. A jeweled sunstick.

"Is it a modern copy?" I asked Greg who followed me close behind taking advantage of my focus elsewhere to be so near.

He whispered in my ear. "Do you want to see the best of it?"

"There's better?"

"Remember the cave. Riding?"

He kissed me, a brush of a kiss behind my ear, seductive. I didn't want to like it.

I turned around. "Did you put something in my drink there or was that cave mind blowing?" I was jocular until I looked at the drink in my hand.

"Both," he said. His smile got bigger when he saw me looking at my wine.

"We'll come back after dinner to see more," Greg said as he led me to my coat and outside. I thought it was all right to follow him.

But I felt the need to keep my own wheels with me, for the freedom. "I don't want to leave my Gran's car."

"I lock the gate," Greg said. "You don't have to worry about your car." Fingertips brushing my cheek, a hint of more to come. I ignored it. My body still ached from his cousin's touch. I got in his car. He drove fast on both sides of the road, with a local's confidence. "Do not talk about the collection, in the restaurant, what you've been chosen to see."

Greg ducked under the stone arch and I followed him into the Plow and Angel, the bar under the San Ysidro Ranch restaurant

In the silence after we were seated I asked, "Have you read <u>Catch 22</u> yet?"

"No." Greg motioned for the waiter and ordered cocktails. "You've heard Michael Rockefeller has gone missing."

I hadn't. It was only a family name to me. I sipped my drink, sweet bourbon, and shook my head.

"He was a collector. Like I'm a collector. It is not the objects we want." He slurped his drink, thirsty. "He went in too far."

"Where was he?"

"New Guinea. Those natives are still alive."

"Was it a plane crash?"

"That would be civilized." He sounded snide. "Head hunters, I'd bet money."

"Maybe he just escaped the family." My abalone was delicious. Made up for the horrible American salad.

"You think a man can escape his family?" He gave a laugh. The piano player started his jazz and it hummed off the rock walls.

"Have you been to Paris?" I asked

"Only as a tourist." He finished his drink. "I prefer it here. More sun. Usually."

"The jazz in Paris is great."

"I don't like jazz."

"How well did you know Harry?"

"Let's not talk about the past. We only need the past to use for the future."

"I'm trying to figure out what happened to him."

"Why?"

"I feel I need to know."

"I'll help you find out. I have connections."

"Do you know Mr. Skeffington?"

"In passing. We have mutual interests." What was I to think of that? Dread as the Paris club came into my mind.

"I've just met him."

"Watch out there."

"For what?"

"We'll talk about it later. I'm ready to go home."

He drove me to his house. I kissed his cheek and looked for my keys in my purse.

"Leaving? You stay for a nightcap," Greg said.

"I can't." Ready to make for my car. The car knew the way to my grandmother's house, just over the hill. And there would be no cars on the road.

"Stay." He saw my face. "Or, say you'll come tomorrow. Then I'll unlock the gate for you."

"Tomorrow I can't, I've promised my grandmother." I wanted to put him off. I needed the gate unlocked.

"We have unfinished business," Greg said. "Your work for us. My father will be clearer, he will decide. Plus, I have family secrets to show you." He put his arm firmly around me. "I'll let you play with them."

I looked at him for the cue to laugh. My laugh ended in my throat before it started. From his mouth and his grip on my shoulder, I feared I would have to struggle to get away. There was no one to call out to and the gate was locked. I made ready to run and climb if I had to, something in me was not willing to take my chances of his being polite and serving me a brandy with no complications.

Talk my way out. "I hope I can work with you. I do want to see what you have, another time. My old friend Maria Ortega said you are good friends." I know you have another girlfriend I was saying, so let me go. "We've known each other forever. I so admire her."

"She cooks for me." He dismissed her to me.

How to free myself from his embrace. I had watched him drink too much at dinner and wished then that I had my own car. I felt inept and foolish, like a teenager on a bad date.

I turned my shoulder to look at him and said "Maria speaks highly of you."

He let me go. "What's she doing, speaking of me? " His anger was buried in coldness. "Good night."

Poor Maria, had I ruined her chances with him? Whatever, I was free to go home and sleep alone, reclaim my childhood bed, my solitude. Safe. Had I really been in danger? I felt danger, but needed to continue with him. That collection – did Alicia know? Skeff? I had an excuse to call Garcia.

CHAPTER 37

Late night had turned into early morning. Had I just escaped Greg? More to worry about.

I found Claudia in the cool watery living room, her pale skin and the air infused with the blue green color of the walls.

"Maria called to cancel lunch," she told me.

I went to the phone in the kitchen and tried Maria at all numbers to no avail. "Gran, what did she say?"

"She isn't feeling well and she'll call." Morning sickness? So where was she?

I poured myself tea. "Gran, tell me more about Mr. Skeffington?"

Gran stood with her back to the strong winter light. She pulled a long curtain to shade a watercolor from the low sun, unveiled by a break in the storms.

"You've seen more of him?" she asked. "Skeff?" I didn't tell her much at our daily drink as she didn't ask.

"Yes. We talk about Harry and their project. He told me you were his first love."

"He says that?" Gran smiled and walked across to the fireplace. "He told me once he did not believe in love. I believed him. His father loved his mother so much he suffered too much when she died." Claudia began to pull all the curtains. The sun would shine straight into the room later. "We were best friends. I thought."

"What happened?"

"We were young – everything changes."

"Yes? Tell me?" I wanted to know more about Skeff. And I knew nothing about my grandmother's childhood.

Claudia sat beside me and poured herself tea. "At Christmastime, 1938, I was home from Europe, here in Montecito for the holiday with my parents. They could see the trouble coming in Europe and brought me back. They made me stay. I was young and did not want to see the War coming. I had had my year of finishing school, came out in Chicago and moved to Paris. I felt sophisticated, pretty. I wanted to show off for Skeff. I invited myself over. He warned me he had a guest. The sun was low, like now. I sat alone on the sofa, Skeff on the chair across from me. His 'guest' stood behind Skeff with his hand on his shoulder. He left his hand there and whispered to Skeff and they laughed together. Skeff wore pale yellow socks unlike any I'd ever seen on an American man. His friend wore baby blue. We talked stiffly. Then his friend sat beside him and left his hand on Skeff's thigh. I understood the message."

"The message?"

"I used to picture myself the mistress of his father's house. I thought I could lighten it, fill it with flowers, and children. When I saw Skeff with that man I knew. I imagined then that I would spend my life in hotels. My father gave me this house and saved me from the itinerant life. Thank God. What would I do without my garden?"

I looked confused and she imagined why.

"Skeff is homosexual," she said, as if we were both understanding but ignorant.

289

"Ah, yes." That was not news to me. But how it affected my Gran was. How sad for her. I bet he left a generation of disappointed women.

Was Harry homosexual? He loved me. Could he?

"Skeff has asked for my help. With the opening of his museum-library."

"Well, good. He's a charming companion. He ruined me for all the rest." She patted the top of my head as she stood to leave.

"Harry did that for me," I said though I thought of my body with Scott. Gran's look showed me there was no comparison. I had a life, though short, with Harry.

"Something happened between you two?" Claudia asked as we left the big blue-green room for the entry way and the stairs up to our gear for our days.

"The same things Harry married me for pushed him away. He found me lost and alone, gathered me up and gave me a home." My grandmother clucked. "I kept up with him, traveled in an hour's notice. I amused myself in strange cities, blended into house parties without a fuss." I loved to give him blowjobs, I didn't say to Claudia. "I took messages, arranged travel, unpacked bags and entertained clients, happy to be with him.

"He started to stay out. To say 'Don't you have plans?','Don't you care about your work?'

"I hated his disapproval. He encouraged me to be serious about my work even if it meant time apart. So I was not here with him soon enough."

"Let's go walk in the garden," she said. Like ice cream that was her answer to all turmoil.

"I have to go to work, Gran. Later?"

Before I left I tried Maria again at her office, her house and at her mother's. No answer anywhere.

I wanted to think only of work. What could I find to explain anything?

Stopping at the big house, I found Alicia at the table in the kitchen. "Alicia, Have you seen your brother-in-law's collection? George Lowell's -"

"Not my brother-in-law. His collection?"

"Greg showed me cabinets full at his house on Sycamore Canyon," I said. "Incredible Chumash work, baskets of such quality–, miniature canoes. A shawl made of a Mexican flag."

Alicia was shocked out of her chair. She paced, looking out the window at the new rain that fell between the sun in patches. "There is a rainbow somewhere." she turned toward me. "Let's go look" She crossed the house to her front door. As we searched the sky for a rainbow she told me.

"The shawl, the Mexican flag is the flag that was lowered in Santa Barbara in 1850 in the face of the conquering Americans. " Alicia said. "The Mexican commandante's wife took the flag and gave it to her children's Chumash nursemaid, who made it into a shawl. I saw the flag shawl at dances when I was a girl. The family brought it out on important occasions– christenings, the last dance under the Parra Grande, before the grapevine was cut down and sent East to the Exposition." Alicia stopped herself from storytelling, as if that were a part of her she had to stifle.

"What else about the collection? What was there?" Alicia asked. Alicia sounded fatalistic, deep voice, hearing of a tragedy, inevitable in retrospect, knowledge forced on her that she already knew.

"How did those Lowells get such a collection?" I asked. I assumed it must have come up for sale and

Alicia and her husband didn't buy it before the acquisitive other Lowell, Greg's father, did.

"George Lowell," She said, looking alone, frantic. "What else did you see?" Alicia became very still, focused on me as if she could change my answer.

I tried to list all that I could remember. "Stones carved into animals, feather skirts and feather capes. Headdresses, all still bright. Most amazing was a sunstick, unusual in the materials – Jewels, I think, -"

"Was there a large wooden bowl, ringed with abalone shell in this pattern?" She cried tears as she handed me a little bowl, like a child's.

"I didn't see one." Why would she cry?

"I have to look for myself," she said.

"Haven't you?" I asked. "You're related?"

"By marriage. By events. My foolishness, his thievery."

What did she mean with her intensity?

"Hidden treasure?" I remembered Scott's phrase.

"Who said that?" She was ready to direct her anger at me, brown eyes narrowed.

"No one. Just a saying. That collection is a treasure, and seems to be a secret. Most collectors would have given it to a museum. Or donated a few pieces for the fame."

"Not George. Not that collection."

"Where did it come from?" I asked.

"A cave," she answered, looking inward or back, to somewhere I could not go. How could I learn? I decided to keep talking.

"Greg Lowell showed me a cave, back in the brush. The cave walls were covered with paintings. I didn't know how exciting they could be. "

"What else?" She stared at me with a new look. Did she see the tracks of sex and attribute them to Greg?

"I saw another cave, with pools," I bragged to her. "In Montecito. I didn't go into it."

Her look at me was one of extreme impatience. How foolish I sounded to myself, how little I belonged in her world, and how little I knew of it for all my studying.

"Where?" she asked.

"Next to a new friend's rented cottage. We went over a wall from her garden."

"Tell me exactly where it is."

I tried.

She said. "That's part of George Lowell's place."

More fear, I could feel it in my arms, my heart. I thought of the photos in Harry's envelopes. They could be of that garden. She could be dead floating in that pond.

"What did Greg say when he showed you the things?" Alicia asked me.

"He said it wasn't the best. He said the 'most powerful' objects were somewhere else, he might show me later."

"Sounds like a seduction."

I was surprised. "That's what I thought. I didn't believe him."

Then Alicia asked "Did you see a jaguar?"

"A jaguar?" I ran through my memory of the small atshwin, pondering the carving and believing in a jaguar. Mountain lion, perhaps.

"A stone chair, jade jaguar with emerald eyes," Alicia prompted me.

"Good god, nothing like that, " I answered remembering the collection.

"Just feathers, sticks and bones?" Alicia said sarcastically. Just what I had been thinking. Jewels were still my idea of treasure.

"And the sunstick," I said. "It was pearl and gems."

"The jaguar chair will tell us," Alicia said.

"What?"

"Whether or not this collection is mine."

"Yours?" I asked, shocked.

"My family's"

"How?" I asked.

"How to him? Theft, as usual," Alicia said.

"Theft?"

"The 'hidden treasure'. Was Greg so arrogant to call it that?" she asked. "Stolen."

I was tempted to say Scott gave me the idea, but didn't, not a rat. So Scott knew, or was he bantering with me?

"Why 'theft, as usual'?" I asked.

"You know. Museums financed 'gathering expeditions'. Explorers came and took what they found. To Paris, to Berlin, to Washington." Alicia was looking at her hands, fingers entwined. "George Lowell stole from me. I believe the 'objects' you describe are my family's. My family's responsibility." We sat silent. "Now I may no longer suspect, I must know."

"What can I do?" I asked, emboldened by the tragedy in her voice.

"Can you get to the 'better' cache Greg talked about? Find out where it is?"

"I don't know," I answered, picturing what I could do to see it. Offer to buy it? Kiss Greg?

"How do I get into the house?" Alicia asked.

"Can't we ask to go over?" I said. "For my research project. They will-"

"George Lowell will never let me in there," she spoke with hatred.

"Why not?" I was ignorant, and didn't want to be. There was too much I didn't know and I was sick of it. "I can tell Skeff–he can ask to go see it, take you. It's natural. He's funding a Chumash museum -" I said.

"You can try Skeff," she said. "But I bet he won't go near George Lowell. There's a story there." Alicia looked so far back, I was left in the wrong century, I thought. I was for certain the wrong generation. Fingers to her pearls, back in her room Alicia saw me again.

"Your grandmother may still know him, George Lowell," Alicia said. "They were the Chicago kids. Out on their private trains together." My Gran was the right generation. She might know more than she said about the George Lowell story. This was the first time Alicia mentioned Claudia. "She might still speak to him."

"I don't think so from what she said. But I'll ask her. And Skeff. He'll have an idea about how to get to that collection." I was trying to sound active, as if I could help her. I did not want to call Greg. "George Lowell may be sick. He may want to sell the collection?"

"And I must buy it back?" She was angry. "Pay more for what was stolen."

"Where did you lose it?"

"Stolen from a cave, an island cave. A cave in the rocks against the sea. We thought we needed the Lowell brothers' boat to move everything to safety."

Another cave. Another Lowell.

"The cave in Montecito, with the ponds. Maybe it's all there."

"Where?" Alicia asked. I had lost her.

"My tennis friend, Susan, said she'd take me into a cave she found next to her cottage. I'll take my camera.

If it's George Lowell's property, maybe that cave has what was stolen."

"What I lost." Alicia said, looking at me with angry, sad eyes. "What if it's there?" She seemed like an old lady again. "What do I do now?"

"Skeff buys the collection back. He puts it in his library with your husband's notes." I wanted to provide a solution. She seemed to admit no such possibility.

"You don't know the Lowells." What could that mean? She was one, so was her son.

How could I console her? "I'll take photographs of what's there, you see for yourself and decide what to do," I said, ready to spend the weekend skulking around the estates of Montecito. What else did I have to do? Find my husband's murderer and exact revenge. Had I given up that thought? I was a modern widow, ready to leave revenge to the State of California. I could search to know and curse.

"Be careful," Alicia said.

"I will. For now, I'm going to work."

"Come by for tea," Alicia ordered.

I restarted a box labeled 'Bear Clan'.

"Fernando says the last member of the bear clan was forced to sell his bearskin, his 'atshwin, his pouch to a white man. 'Stolen by a white man.'"

Another theft. My life was thrown into a nether world by Harry's death and, now, I was drawn more and more into the Chumash world. Thefts. By osmosis, I was believing I had to track this Bear power taken by a white man. Harry was clawed.

After my lemonade, Alicia handed me a leather notebook. "I will show you what I wrote about this story, one that I have not told. Except to my husband— he knew it all, the only one."

I began to read. Her handwriting was clear.

"1925. I see the days as separate days and feel myself there in that year in this town.

Charles and George Lowell, boys, had a new sailboat, come by train from Chicago. Their uncle Michael, my Michael who I had not yet met, sailed it up from Los Angeles and anchored it off the city piers. Two piers then, one at the foot of State Street, one at the bottom of Chapala.

Charles, eldest, was captain, George the first mate and my brother Manuel was their sailing companion. I watched them from my favorite perch on soft pine needles on the bluff above Butterfly Beach where the monarch butterflies came in the winter and hung from the trees.

I sailed with those brothers and my Manuel one day, afraid of the swells that rose high behind us and lifted under us.

One night that summer my mother called me onto the porch in the dark. Crickets and frogs were loud and there were many stars. My mother told me family secrets I had never heard.

Why tell me now? I asked her.

'You must take care of them, you must become their keeper, the secrets and the treasure. You are old enough. I will teach you before it is too late. You ask all the questions. Now you shall know the answers.'

Mother told me: 'We are caretakers of a religion older than the Christian. This religion balanced the world. Its civilization lasted for thousands of generations. This religion is based on ceremony.

'To perform the ceremonies that maintain balance on this earth the people must use the tools. The ceremonies live in the objects. The feathers, the bundles,

the sunsticks, they live. They have power from the generations of prayer and belief given to them. Our ancestors held them, they gave them to us to give to our children. You and I, because of our family, we must guard these objects." Mother scared me. I did not want that seriousness. She told me, fatally:

"Our family has to care for these treasures. At the end our mothers collected the 'atshwin. When people went to the Mission, believing in Christ's power, they left them behind. 'Atshwin were thrown out by the friars, or smuggled out before the priests found them. Our people gathered and hid the sunsticks, shell decorated headdresses, feather and fur robes, crystals for safety in a cave so the Dream Helpers and the sun would not forever desert the people.

'When the times came for celebrations and rituals and they needed the families' atshwin and the ritual sticks, they sent a bearer after them. The 'antap, those who controlled the celebrations, knew where they were hidden. Our family is 'antap. Our sunstick is precious jade and pearl brought here by a long ago marriage.

We hid Chumash treasures from the Mexicans. Greedy American thieves thought the tiny war of Fremont gave them the right to take our Californios' land. They did not even know what they were stealing with the land.

When the gold seekers swarmed through the interior, the Chumash elders of our coastal village, of our family, decided to move the treasure to the caves of the Channel Island. They added the personal 'atshwin of those who had died or were lost.

'We survivors must guard our religious tools because we believe with them we have survived. If *we lose them we are cursed. And, worse, our culture will die.*

'This is a secret that you must keep. No one who would steal them must know they exist. Be careful Alicia. The number of thieves have grown.'

Mother told me about the treasure in a sea cave deep under Santa Cruz Island, and exactly how to find it. The remains of our tribal cache was there: baskets full of shell money; woven trunks; cloths full of their ancestors' 'atshwin; robes; crystals; the jade jaguar stool.

'She told me now we must move them again, carefully. Pieces were stolen when they moved the treasure last time, in 1857, and the terrible earthquake of Tejon Pass happened, when they were passing through. Disrespect or dishonesty will bring chaos.'

Mother's words stay in my ears and haunt me.

'The treasure has been safe in the island for years. Now the foreign fishermen are setting nets in the caves for the sea lions and the film makers are using the caves. Both are coming close to our cave's secrets.' Mother's cousins, fishermen's' wives, had told her of the danger.

Mother admitted to me that she was tempted to let the responsibility go, to forget her promises to the Chumash girls before her, to forfeit her role as guardian. She was busy in the changing Santa Barbara, in the Church, so now I, the earnest and curious student of our Chumash past, was to join her as a keeper.

I knew that I could not move the cache without my brother's help. Mother allowed me to include Manuel in the task. Manuel had the plan to move the treasure into the interior to a deep cave in the brush, where it would be safe from people and fire. Manuel knew we needed a boat so he told Charles Lowell who had the yacht we could use to sail over to Santa Cruz.

Charles wanted the adventure and offered to help. But he brought his brother, George.

Perhaps we could have found another boat, a fisherman or diver, a cousin would have taken us out. Things would have been different, but both my brother and I felt tied to the version of the story that was unfolding in our plans. To choose another plan would have taken older, calmer minds. We would have been spared sadness if we had envisioned another way."

Alicia looked pale and tired as she watched me read. "I never knew if George told someone else, bragged, or took it himself. He must have followed us into the back country."

She was the embodiment of all I studied, daughter of the Chumash elite. Her hair was white with dark streaks, thick in a braid above her neck. She saw me looking at her. "The old stories are dark screens that keep me from my Chumash past. I lost that family, so here I am, thanks to my husband, a Montecito lady."

With her chin angled forward below her full lips and strong nose and short forehead, her face had the curves of an ancient head – Olmec or Mayan. She was exotic, more exciting than the ladies who lived around her. I went back to the leather bound book. There was another marker, velvet ribbon. Alicia nodded when I found it.

"In the winter of 1940 and 1941, 45.21 inches of rain fell. Rain and the War, in my mind they came together and everything changed. My cousin lost her house and her dog in the flood. I lost my brother for years when he enlisted. We helped my cousin rebuild, set the house between the boulders that had washed

out of the mountain. I cooked for the crews and made her curtains, and she was happy with the new home. I knew nothing would be the same.

"*That spring Charles Lowell came back, a soldier on rest leave, and my calm was ruined forever. We danced and kissed and behaved like war torn lovers with a spell of home. I found true love and worried how long it would last. I shouldn't have worried. I should have loved all I could and forgotten the future. I loved and I think he loved, but only when I was in his arms or in his eyes did I stop worrying about the time that he would leave. He thought he would come back and I pretended to believe him. Perhaps if I had really believed, he would have come back for me.*

"*He gave me a sapling to plant in my father's yard. He told me when we married we would move the tree to our house and it would grow to shelter our family and friends like Dona Marcelina's Big Vine, the Parra Grande that grew on our street until they cut it down for the World's Fair. Dona Marcelina's young man came back, after he proved himself worthy to her father, to find the vine that she had nurtured and they married.*

"*I knew I didn't have that chance–picture me going to Chicago to show his mother I was a lady worthy of her son. With him, I could have. But he went home to Chicago first and stayed there. Santa Barbara became a vacation place.*

"*The fantasy land of War was over. The soldiers who knew the Coral Casino heated the beach with pipes were gone.*

"*Love is like a prickly pear cactus fruit–the deep red oval. The sweet may be in there–if the time is ripe– but if you touch it little thorns go into your fingers.*

*Invisible thorns that sting when you brush by them
and give you gooseflesh still when you think they're
gone or you've forgotten them.*

"Those years ago, when I was very young I had
loved Charles Lowell, I loved him on the adventure of
our sail to the island cave, when he was so wrong to
bring his brother, then again, during the War, when
he was here to recover.

"After the theft of my family's cache was discovered I moved to Santa Ynez to live with relatives. I told
my mother I would not act with the servility demanded
by the new people of Montecito of anyone with dark
hair and an Indian face. But truly I wanted never to
see the Lowell brothers again. My brother was their
friend. My brother did not suspect."

"What in Charles was quiescent and confused in
the young man, was strong and clear in his uncle, my
Michael. When we first met I was afraid of it, I loved
it so much. It was more than kindness, it was a pur-
posefulness that I wanted to be a part of.

"Michael and I, we met in Santa Ynez, when it was
hot and dry. We courted at night. He sat on the steps,
I sat on a carved bench hung by chains and peeled
corn, swinging and catching the silken hairs in my lap.
I asked him 'What shall I do after we are married?'"

"'You can do whatever you want.'

"'In the old days the women caught grasshoppers
and clammed with the children.'

"He answered me, 'And the men, disguised with
herbs from the sweat house, deer heads over their
heads, stalked. You and I do not need to scavenge nor
kill for our living. We have piles of money, gathered
by my fathers when the gathering was good.'

"He found a farm for us in Montecito. And we kept a place in Santa Ynez for the days we tired of the fog.

"He was a Yankee, the respect for work bred deep. The worship of work was still an uncertain hybrid in the people of this land of long ranch days and plenty of Indians and Mexicans to do the hard labor."

I looked up, ready to read on until I finished the notebook. Lives becoming real.

"That's enough," Alicia said and took her book. She held it close, as if it were the embodiment of the past it contained. "Get me into that collection."

CHAPTER 38

My grandmother and I were dressed to go out, pausing for dry sherry and nuts from old silver. "Gran, when I was first home we talked about police detectives– Martin, Garcia -" My straight backed grandmother smiled when I said 'home'. "What did you mean when you said 'Martin is too accustomed to ways of doing business in this town'?"

"Martin is from the old school -"

"Old school of what?"

"Old hands-off policies."

"What?"

"In his time there were certain people for whom certain behaviors were not criminal."

"Such as?" I asked.

"Rape," Claudia stood and walked to the tall glass door. Inside the deep green of her hedges, the bright green of the lawn plus the borders and forest made a jungle of greens. She turned to me, pink against the greened window. "Hunting accidents. Gun accidents. Others should not know–suicide. Murder. Desertion. People disappeared and no one cared except their family. And they might have been relieved. Martin knew when not to make trouble."

"And now? Who is involved? Who didn't Martin make trouble for? God." I was physically ill, nauseous.

"You have Garcia. We will find out."

"I just talked to him."

"And?"

"He says to be patient." No. I wanted at least a theory of what happened to Harry. "Who are the same families?"

Claudia straightened the gold frame of the black and white photograph of her father on the glass table.

Was Harry in with the wrong crowd of rich boys? Jesus, Mary, Joseph. I wished I had Maria's religion. Was it helping her now? "Who are these families?"

"Emma? Have you stopped to think what you will do if you find out who murdered your husband?"

"No." I saw the worry in her face. "I'll tell Garcia.'"

"Leave it to him. You're alive, you're young, you must live on. Pay attention to yourself, not to the dead. "

"It's hard." Honest with my grandmother.

"Well, you have your work."

"I'm having dinner with Walter Skeffington."

"You're lucky, he is charming company."

Did she want to come? See the art and her old friend? "Do you want to come?"

"No dear." She looked at me as if I knew better.

A flock of white-breasted birds flew above me as I drove across the valley and up the mountain to Skeff's house. The birds kept going down the coast, and I crunched over the sparkling driveway gravel to Skeff's door.

We ate alone with no ostensible purpose to our evening. I waited with my news. We spoke of Europe, New York, favorite museums. The butler served the meal at the dining table flanked by Modigliani paintings. I stared at the long-necked women and thought of mistresses and poverty, suicide.

"She jumped, pregnant with his baby. I almost didn't buy it." Skeff said when he saw me gazing at the painting in reds. "I'm watching a man showing in Los Angeles just now. Big soup cans, Campbell. A girl from town is working with the artist in New York. There's a local girl who escaped."

"My grandmother uses the same term. She says I have to 'escape' Montecito."

"Emma, why didn't you bring Claudia with you? I should have asked. Next time. Have you decided to join our committee? Just for the parties – later I'll presume to ask you for the board."

I ate the petrale sole as he talked. Was he nervous? Avoiding questions about Harry?

"How are you doing with your work, Emma?"

"It's beginning to get organized. I have a map of almost all the files, an index to the contents. I've resisted changing how Mr. Lowell organized his boxes. There is an internal order to them that will interest the graduate students."

"Have you read through all the boxes?"

"No, I've some to go." Four filing cabinets in the back of the room, so full I closed the drawers quickly every time I opened them. Plus more French files which I was afraid to delve into. New language, new unknowns.

"Have you found any mention of hidden artifacts? A forgotten cache?"

"Mr. Lowell has notes about theft of artifacts but not discovery, not locations," I answered. "But, I need to tell you, I saw Greg Lowell's family collection. Incredible. There's a cache for you. Beautiful things. Baskets, shawls, bowls–amazing." Skeff's collecting bug could get into those darkened rooms.

"Oh, God. It's good? George Lowell, he's one to avoid. But I may have to go over there."

"Alicia wants to see it too. His stuff would be brilliant for your library -"

"Only Harry called it the Library. That was the vision we shared."

After an apple tart he offered a tisane and we sat in the living room, sipping our herbal infusions as the butler cleared behind closed doors.

I stared out at the rainy winter night. It was black, the clouds were too high to reflect the town's lights, yet they covered the stars and any moon. I turned around to face the windows that reflected to me, darkly separate, the scene inside the room. Skeff, tall in grey, took a telephone from the butler in black and white, a match with the floors as if he grew from them and descended into them. Skeff listened for a moment, the phone away from his ear and motioned for me to come back.

"Raoul, yes, now I'm free. Do tell," Skeff said. Skeff sounded wary. Not wary enough to save us from the journey we were about to be sent on. I was sure he would move to another phone. "It's me, Raoul. You called me." He listened.

"Raoul, let me interrupt." He looked at me as if to see if I was the girl he thought I was.

"I've just dined with the young wife of the architect your friends sent to me for my museum."

He looked at me, with a painful question. Whispered "Will you listen?"

I nodded and took the extension from the butler. The Spanish voice spoke from far away into that room of reflected light, bright oils and shadowed sculptures. He whispered.

"In Paris darling. It's late. I am so tired. But do I have a story for you, dear one. I was in a party, well, when I heard Montecito, I listened. I thought of you–you know I don't forget our time -"

"Yes," Skeff said.

"I knew I had to tell you. It might matter to someone there. The party was at our club–you can imagine. S&M and more. That night, after things started going, getting hot, an American bragged about Montecito. The things that men will say as they come on themselves under the whip. You never went in for that, did you dear?"

"I haven't changed Raoul." Skeff was cold and without a look at me was silent for the man to continue.

"Well, old man, you said to call back. This fellow. Sometimes people just brag, they talk murder to impress and raise the —"

"Murder, Raoul?" He looked at me. "Murder where?"

"There, mon cher. Montecito."

Ask, he asked. "Who was it, Raoul?" I felt he was asking for me, but he wanted to protect us both from the answers.

"A buttoned down, strong chin, macho type."

"That could be a lot of men in this town. Could be me."

"He was younger. Familiar. He said Montecito. He would have been just a boy at our evenings, my soirees in your pool house," he laughed. Skeff cringed. "I thought I should tell you."

"Who did he kill?"

"A woman. Maybe more than one, if we can believe a man in such a state." Did I hear Raoul breathe harder. "But he bragged about a man. Killing a man, recently."

"Describe him."

"He was that Western six-gun type, probably started in cowboy boots." Pause. "But with an East Coast voice,

you know the inflection, the rich man's cruelty. That
twisted type that gives it to everybody, and then comes
to a city where he is unknown and takes it with more
passion and lust for the memories of how he has dished
it out to others. S and M switch hitters. Dangerous.

"How are you doing, my Skeffington? Did you like
the gorgeous man I sent you?" Silence. "Did you get to
find out for yourself, handsome?"

"He was murdered."

"Jesus." He panted. "You don't think he met
this cowboy?"

"I'll talk to the police."

"Oh god, all I need." The voice was fading. The
drugs must have been wearing off. Bed time. "Well,
come to Paris if you're bored. Or scared. Ciao."

Skeff hung up the telephone. He stood at the
window so I was the reflection and he was blacked out
to a shape of a man.

"Raoul. One night I paced in my garden, up wind to
keep away the screams. I saw a stretcher carried out to
the service gate and came to my senses. The next day
Raoul's trunks were packed, an apartment rented in Los
Angeles, and I learned to exercise the self control my
father gave me"

Jesus. This elegant, distinguished man?

"Before I sent him away I stayed alone in my father's
library, one cognac after another. I'd pretend to read,
wonder what was happening in the pool house. I did not
want to be that. I can still feel my shock, the revulsion
and, of course, the pain at the whip wielded by my lover.
Not for me, never again. But at first I was willing to sit
in the house, behind the reflecting pools, the badminton
courts, the swimming pool, alone, jealous, if he came
home to my bed, replete, with enough of his desire for

violence, that I could not comprehend, worked out of him so he would love me like a lover should."

Skeff talked to me as if now I needed to know everything. I was in shock.

"I'm no longer so needy. Such hungers cannot be satisfied. The longing for love and affection is never ending and unanswerable, except perhaps by a mother for a child before the emptiness arises."

"Was my husband the gorgeous young man?" I asked.

"Raoul and de Valmnick – Harry was recommended by many –"

"Was Harry homosexual?"

"Not with me, sadly." He sighed, and laughed, I assume, before he remembered who I was. "I would not know. No harm intended."

"That's the trouble, Mr. Skeffington. Harm was -." I wanted him to take blame.

"Forgive me, Emma. I don't mean to be flippant. I will back you up on this call. You report it. Let Garcia know he can call me."

After I left the fear kicked in. I drove and I thought of every man I knew who wore cowboy boots – Scott, Greg, Adelino and his nephews. Garcia. Not Skeff. The girl murdered and left by the train. Harry murdered and found on the tracks. I swerved, almost pushed off the road and wanted to think that it was the wind.

CHAPTER 39

At dawn I started calling Garcia. He answered at 7:00. "Detective, I, last night Mr. Skeffington had a call, I was on it – I need to tell you–"

"Be calm. Let's have coffee at El Camino pharmacy, on Old Coast. See you there in fifteen minutes."

He was on a round red stool at the counter with two coffees. "I'm glad to see you," I said as I stepped up to sit. "It is scary out here in the wilds of Montecito–" I made him smile. This longing for his regard was so strong even I noticed it.

"I was at Mr. Skeffington's. A man called from Paris–" The man's exact words rushed out of me like projectile vomit.

"You believed him?"

Was I gullible? "Skeff believed him. He'll tell you. Me? I'm looking for some story, an idea of what and why. The story could be Harry's –" I was crying.

"Or not. What have you found about Bear?"

I gave him my notebook to read.

If a man wants to be a bear shaman he kills a bear and pulls the skin off over the head in one piece, cutting the paws and the skin from the head carefully and fills it with grass to dry.

Bear shamans–some whose body becomes a bear, some others own the tools that are the power.

311

Some are born Bear, some have the device for bear power.

The Bear Shaman carried shell bead money in the stomach of the bearskin to pay anyone who discovered them to keep the Bear Man's secret."

Bear shaman have no socially acceptable purpose, no use for the village.

"Those are the rumors still," Garcia said, handing back the book. "Anything else?"

"A white man stole the atshwin of the last Bear shaman."

"And most else."

"Greg Lowell showed me his father's Chumash collection." There I surprised the calm detective. His eyes opened wide and he waited for me to say more. "Alicia thinks it's her family's cache, stolen forty years ago."

"You are full of news, Emma." Garcia turned to put his boots on the ground and stood. "What makes Alicia think it's her family's things?"

"A shawl of a Mexican flag. She says there are other pieces that will tell–" Should I tell this man about my private life? "Greg Lowell told me he would show me more of his collection– better pieces–"

"He'll show you?"

"Probably. Alicia wants me to see."

"Can I persuade you to stay away from all this?"

"How can I?"

"Stay with the research." He put dollars on the counter. "Do you see Maria Ortega?" He answered my expression. "Her brothers are friends."

"Yes. We're waiting for a clear day, and me for warmer days, to surf." I was not going to tell him Maria's secret, just most of mine. Did he need to know about Scott? I thought not.

I feel we walk along an edge. I have lived in fear of falling off that edge into a life of worsening chaos, a spiral down into unalterable misfortune and misery, worsening with every attempt to better it, unforgiving life that catches to drag me down.

Harry fell over the edge and I saw, in losing him, I saw into the abyss that waits for the unwary.

But now I had a routine, I felt like I had some control.

At Alicia's ranch I rolled to a silent stop by the kitchen, planning to sneak by Alicia, bolt up to work for an early start. I wanted to look for more on the artifacts in the collection Greg showed me. Stolen from Alicia?

I guessed Scott was back in San Francisco, engaged, but I didn't want to chance an encounter. I could still make myself buzz with the memories of our nights together. I did not want to suspect him.

I called Maria again the night before and then early this day and left messages with her family when I could. I was worried and hoped Maria was avoiding me.

I let myself into the back door of the ranch house.

Magdalena sat at the kitchen table, her head and a rosary in her hands. She told me without looking up that Alicia wanted to see me.

Barefoot, Alicia was kneeling on a red velvet cushion below the statue of Mary and baby Jesus that stood in the alcove, ancient, carved and colored by Chumash neophytes, still aghast at the new myths.

Alicia stood and came across the cool tiles and motioned for me to sit next to her. She forced her hands to be still, bringing the right hand that wandered to her pearls back into the left.

"Maria Ortega has been attacked. Stabbed, " Her voice broke and she cried. "She may live."

I felt that sucking chaos, that spiral never to be re-ascended. The baby.

"Where?"

"They found her in the hills. Mountain Drive."

"Dumped," Adelino said. I jumped at his deep voice. "Senora?" Adelino, my grandmother's mason, the wall-maker, stood in the doorway, his hat behind his back.

"Adelino, what can we do?"

"Senora, I am here to ask you to come with me to pray."

"Of course Adelino." She moved toward her jacket. "How can this have happened?"

"Stabbed? Killed?" I asked, aghast, ashamed, afraid.

"They found her in time," Alicia said. She put her hand on Adelino's shoulder. He looked into her eyes. "Another stabbing, too close this time, always too close to someone."

"She was clawed and left in the trees," Adelino said. Oh God, the maw of the beast opened wider.

"She will live," Alicia said.

"I need you to come with me to pray," Adelino said. Alicia took Adelino's arm and they walked slowly into the hallway, older from the news. Alicia took a black mantilla and mother of pearl Book of the Mass from the front chest.

I followed them unbidden, unwilling. I could not have guessed. I was there for Maria.

Alicia's maroon Cadillac convertible sat with the top down in the sun. Adelino opened the door for Alicia, his sad eyes staring at her.

Alicia slid in on the leather back seat and I fol-lowed her. Would I be able to talk to Maria about what she knew?

Clawed, stabbed. What she knew? Did that put her in the way of the knifer, the one who killed Harry?

Adelino put on his cowboy hat with a thin snake band. Through the cool morning, Alicia cried, her shoulders shaking, and Adelino drove, up past the stables and tack barn, the hay barn, between the muddy upper corrals, and up the noisy full creek. He drove the heavy car through the open meadows still climbing. Adelino said nothing, nor did we. Adelino's kind lips and strong nose were in shadow under the big hat. His hair was black, straight and thick like Alicia's hair, rolled this early morning on her neck. She stared over her side of the car.

A line of quail trotted into the trees.

Adelino parked near the top of the ridge at the far reach of the ranch and opened Alicia's door. They stood in the shade of an ancient oak tree next to a shed.

"Here, Adelino?"

They were both more serious than I had ever seen anyone.

Alicia ignored me. She had told me one afternoon that she'd known this old man since they were both children, distant cousins through her mother's family, the Chumash side.

"You know the old ways." Adelino gave her a look that told her not to argue falsely. "Chumash ways. Your family are 'antap. You must preside over the ceremony for the people."

Alicia saw the pole, painted black, with shells and pine cones and seeds at its base.

"He reminded me of my mother, stern, unforgiving." Alicia told me later. "He didn't know my past was in fragments, unclaimable."

Then Alicia was crying, just tears. "Those are lost stories you want me to remember, old friend. What can I do?"

"I have a death gift." Adelino looked at the pole. "We can have Shihuch."

"What are you asking? Alicia stopped crying, shocked and seemed so stern to me I thought Adelino had asked her to kill. "Shihuch for the dead? Maria is <u>not</u> dead." Alicia paced across the damp dirt amid wildflowers and grasses. "Yet we must try. Can two old diluted Chumash, without our tools, bring back a young flower, call her back from the Western Gate and the journey away. "

Adelino opened the stone shed with a big key. "This I can do."

Inside was a covered cage, a Gothic arch under a saddle blanket on a strong table. The door closed behind us. In the near dark Adelino raised the blanket. There, looking sullen and dazed, stood a young Golden eagle. Its eyes were fierce and yellow brown, stronger than imaginable yet captured. The golden eagle Slo'w, who played with Sun in the gambling game against Coyote. Against the people.

Adelino said "I pay you a death visit for my niece. Shihuch."

"Not yet," Alicia said. "She will live. She has modern medicine. Thank God."

The Golden eagle clenched and unclenched his talons on the scarred perch. Alicia dusted her fingers over feathers on the table below the young Golden eagle. "Condor feathers," she said.

Adelino had complied with the tradition to make a pole. Now to tie the feathers, precious feathers, and make headbands.

"You have been planning." Alicia looked dizzy and leaned on the dusty table near enough to the eagle for him to look at her from under his hooded eyes. Adelino seemed shorter and squarer, more Indian, his skin dark, lined deep.

"Why the Peoples' way Adelino? Why not a Mass?" Alicia asked him with the eyes and respect of one who knew that he was an uncle, her friend and her family, that his family lived with hers in this village for centuries. "I've known you, your work with the stone walls, since I was a girl too proud of my riches, too greedy for experience. We went to Mass."

Did he know Alicia's story? What did he know of mine?

Adelino's voice was low. His eyes black brown and fierce, like the eagle, but big and deep. "The family will be at Mass. We two must perform the ceremony. Balance. You, Senora, of the 'antap. You may talk to the golden eagle. You must. 'Shihuch'."

"Listen to me. I say this is not Shihuch. Not a mourning ceremony, Adelino."

After a death, until the mourning ceremony, relatives could not bathe, could not marry. Life could not resume its normal routines. At Shihuch, offerings and the belongings of the dead were burned. Shihuch was the swordfish dancer. Alicia told me she saw as a child the twirling sword at night, the egret feathers, the shell inlaid mask. The circle of the swordfish who could drive ashore the whales.

"You are 'antap. You can do this," Adelino said.

"Maria has a long life for the Sun's Eagle and the People's Coyote to play peon over. We must harness the forces you have faith in to save her. To defeat this evil sorcerer." Alicia stared at the eagle.

Was Alicia humoring the old man? He had brought her the tools, and she would have to face up to much, she told me later.

"We go to the eagle."

Alicia said a low word to the bird, furious in the hands of man, a whispered command, and it seemed to calm. Alicia opened the cage, spoke again to the eagle and took the big bird onto her arm where it gripped down to blood. She softly asked it for its feathers, reassured the creature its feathers were necessary, in case they must call on the Eagle emissary to guide the lost woman to her next home. She ran her hand over the strong quivering wings and found three feathers that came with her fingers. She let them fall onto the floor and sang softly to thank the eagle for its sacrifice.

At her nod Adelino opened the door. Alicia walked out into the sun with the weight of the bird bending her and raised her bloody arm. The eagle held on tighter until she spoke to it once again. "Go play for the soul of the world. Let us have our niece." The eagle spread its wings, hitting her face and flew. A few wing strokes and it was up and glided across the field above the trees and toward the top of the mountain.

In the meadow Alicia tied two of the feathers onto the square pole painted with a black circle. She looked for Adelino. He brought a bundle to the pole and hung a baby's shoes from it. Adelino lit a torch wand of sage.

The bundle burned damp fragrant smoke. Alicia waved the condor feathers in the last of the smoke and Adelino tied them to the pole, the feathers pointing to the sky, their tips showing a breeze. Alicia prayed, her eyes on the feathers, and cried.

Adelino opened the Cadillac door for Alicia and then sat behind the red steering wheel and drove along the edge of the clouds, down the slanted mountain. The sun flashed through the small curled leaves of the live oak trees, dizzying me.

Adelino left us at the back door and Alicia washed her arm in the kitchen sink, bandages in the lower cabinet. We sat together in the formal living room, silent as Magdalena brought bitter hot chocolate.

"Where is my son?" Alicia said. "I need my son."

After minutes of listening to the rain and the fire across from us, Alicia spoke again. I knew nothing to say. Yet couldn't leave.

"Eagle who is Sun and Sky Coyote play gambling games. When Sky Coyote loses, Sun carries people away to his snake-aproned daughters to cook. Sun eats the people and piles the bones outside his door.

"In years of drought Sky Coyote has bad chance in the gambling game, Sun wins and Coyote's yips announce the losses. The people die, the plants die. When the Sky Coyote wins we have rain. He wins too much these days. Our land is melting," she said. "Floods, droughts and fires. And when the great serpent tires of holding up the world and shifts, the earth quakes."

Alicia began to stare at me, but I think only because I was in front of her eyes, not really seeing me at all.

"Catholicism has been our refuge. Father O'Brien and the Brothers at the Mission will say Masses for Maria." Alicia cried tears without sobs. "When I was a child I adored the Madonna, Mary, the Mother, her head bent down to the side, who showed under her scarf that she knew and suffered so for the misery of the world that she sent us her divine motherly love. It was a comfort. I knew she spoke to her Son, Jesus Christ, for us, brought to his busy attention our small stories of woe. I have lost her.

"Emma. You are here to work?"

"Yes, ma'am." She was like a stranger to me, this Chumash.

"Not today. Tomorrow bring me notes on the Bear and any you have found on my theft," Alicia told me.

"I saw Greg this weekend. He told me Scott has a bear skin, sounds like a shaman's cape," I blurted to the already disturbed Alicia.

"It's not true," Alicia said. "I would know."

"Greg said it is a grizzly skin that ties with cord intertwined with feather." Alicia looked as if old thoughts were dawning in her eyes.

"Greg knows about the capes."

"He offered me vulture stones," I said. Wants something from me as payment, I didn't tell her.

"See if he tells the truth. Look," she said. "Go home, Emma."

On my way out I asked Magdalena the news of Maria. She was in the hospital, no visitors allowed. I had to call Greg, obeyAlicia.

What made Garcia say Harry was 'clawed'? Now Maria, and Adelino's word was the same.

The Bear, the cult, the caves–the collection drew me as if those ancient tools had use for me.

CHAPTER 40

The door was open to the grey day. I was so accustomed to rain that winter that a drizzle felt like clearing.

"How early can I call Skeff?" Gran and I ate our eggs.

"I would not know darling. You know him better than I do these days." She seemed sorry. I needed to reintroduce them. "He used to be an early riser."

"I promenade in my paintings" Mr. Skeffington walked me around a white room hung with landscapes. "They teach me why art has become religion. It grabs you and takes you into it at a level you don't control."

I longed to go back to the France of his Cezanne. To the hillsides of the Monet. To leave the drama in the landscape below us.

"Maria –" I could see from his stricken expression." You heard?"

"Yes. And?"

"She's alive. I'll go see her today. Mr. Skeffington–"

"Please, call me Skeff."

"Skeff, Alicia needs to see George Lowell's collection. Can you help her get in there?"

"I don't know." Mr. Skeffington took his hands out of his pockets and sat down. He leaned forward, intertwined his fingers and clenched them. "I stay away from them. But they know I collect. Maybe the old man is ready to sell. We can put his name on a bench." Mr.

Skeffington's distaste was palpable. He stood and paced before the view.

The butler appeared in the door.

"Are you sure you won't stay for breakfast?" Skeff stood to dismiss me.

"Thank you, no. Claudia and I ate before I called." His eyes smiled at her name. "I need to visit Maria before work – so I have to hurry."

"How is she?" he asked as we paused to watch a bird cruise the sculptures and settle on a curve of iron.

"I don't know. I'll see."

"Give her my love. Don't upset her. You must not let your will be too strong."

Will? I felt my only willed action was to hang on. To what? To myself. Trust that someone might care about me.

I drove to the hospital and, armed with the number from the volunteer lady at the front desk I found Maria and sat by her bed.

She opened her eyes, saw it was me and closed them again.

"Chumash princess and the Bear. I thought he would be proud. But when I told him -" She cried. "He killed the baby."

"The Bear? Who, Maria?" That was the question. The father of her baby?

"You know."

"No, I don't!"

Her nurse walked in. "Are you her family? Detective Martin was here."

"Who!"

The nurse shushed me and hummed as she wrapped Maria's round arm with a grey belt, pumped and watched the gauge. I leaned against the wall and worried about my fallen friend, so wounded, and suspected Scott. Why did he ignore Maria at Skeff's? I didn't want to feel it possible that the Scott I knew would stab her, try to kill her. Engaged, afraid to ruin a good thing, her pregnant with his child. He with the bear skin.

"Maria, who?" I whispered.

"You have to leave now," the nurse said.

She started to answer. "The Bear, the white shaman's son, you know–"

"Scott?" Was Michael Lowell more than the recorder, the repository? Did Michael Lowell keep the notes for himself so he could practice the secret rites? Did he figure himself the inheritor? And Scott his monster? Was that why Alicia wanted Scott to stay out of town?

"Ma'am, you must leave my patient to rest," the nurse was insisting.

"Who? Who Maria?"

She shook her head and didn't open her eyes.

"We have to stop him, Maria."

Maria cried with pain, such a scream I recoiled and the nurse pushed me out of the room in front of her as she charged down the hall and said "Morphine drip, 22" into the telephone.

White shaman? Who in the world? Son of the white shaman? Greg? So drawn by the Chumash, jealous of the bear skin. I was furious, unsympathetic. How dare Maria leave me, descend into her own suffering with such an abstruse clue.

"Detective Garcia, I saw Maria. She said I know the man who stabbed her. She said the Bear -"

"Who?" he asked.

"'Son of the white shaman' is all she said. 'The Bear.'" I looked at myself in the window of the phone booth. "She screamed and I was hustled out for pain medication. I think they have to keep her sedated so she doesn't hurt herself by moving. She lost her baby. She said 'he killed the baby'."

"She was pregnant?" Garcia asked.

"She wouldn't say who the father was. Today she said he wasn't happy about the child. She said he was the Bear."

"Oh, God." I could picture Garcia, taking careful notes, on cards so he could shuffle them. He and my bosses' husband. "Meet me later. El Paseo."

From the hospital I drove down the street that was a tunnel of trees to the highway, the fastest route away. I let the semi, cruising through from distant places, pass me, then I sped, hair wild in Gran's convertible, around the dawdling cars. I wanted clear road to press the accelerator and go to Montecito as fast as I could to get away from the ideas in my head. Maria's attack was related to Harry's murder by more than me and my misery.

I knew Scott. Was he perverted by the family knowledge, the family business? Greg? His pull into that world was very strong. His father was a bedridden hermit, not a white shaman. Who else? Adelino? Garcia?

What to do? Greg's story of Scott, Scott's story of Greg–who to believe? I had to get out of their world– those tales even partially true were enough to send me fleeing. Harry's ghost couldn't protect me. Did Harry cross this world alone? I admitted then the vision of Harry in a sex club, a ring, and killed. Was that why? Someone's kicks, for God's sake. But what was this bear, clawing?

I went straight up to the shed to work. The sun was bright. The ruts in the meadow were almost dry, the grasses as tall as the car's doors. Spring was pulling the green and flowers from the puddles and marshes of sodden earth. The mud was blooming.

I opened the doors a desk covered in boxes of Bear notes. I'd been through all of them. Suddenly I thought to look under 'Ours' in the French research. There was a card, in English, in Michael Lowell's writing :

'Bear Cult:

'Tradition: Cult of Canoe captains, elite, antap, leaders

'Costume: Bear skin with head and paws for dancing

'Grizzly Bear: recent developments, frightening: 'White-man driven. Strange practices, see later"

'Rumors: White man with bear skin. Cult of power seekers.

Perhaps: Pedophiles, mutilation.'

I froze there and reread the cards in order. 'See later'? I was in almost the last boxes. What else did he know?

Over hot chocolate I showed Garcia the notes I'd taken from what I found on the Bear. I asked him "What was Harry like when they found him?"

"Fingers were missing."

"You told me that. What else?" I asked.

"OK. Details. No one outside my department knows. Look for more hints in your work," Garcia said. He used me to see if his theory proved out, this coordination of myth and history into a murderer.

"And Harry?" I asked.

"His skin was flayed as if he was clawed by a bear."

"Oh God." What was his theory? Who was guilty? What was the danger?

"Mrs. Chase. Do you want to know the rest?"

I nodded, but I didn't mean it.

"Your husband was disemboweled," Garcia said.

"God," I retched, ready to vomit and my eyes cried.

"He had semen in his body." By then I felt I was crumpled in a heap on my chair sobbing.

"Why?" I asked God but watched Garcia.

"That was how they killed bears and Bear Shaman."

"Harry?"

"Most victims are killed by knifings, one could say clawings. We see this -"

"Maria," I gasped.

"Did Maria say the man didn't want her baby?" Garcia asked.

"Yes. How can we be chasing a bear?" I asked.

"It's not a bear, Mrs. Chase. Someone uses that guise to murder. The bear doesn't matter."

I no longer believed that, so immersed in the Chumash was I, so under the spell of the lost civilization in the shed. Alicia, Scott, Greg. I believed somewhere here the Bear existed.

"Someone has claws and uses them. We have to find him," Garcia said.

"Him?"

"Whoever kills, or tries to kill is very strong. Not a woman."

"Maria?"

"She'll live, then we'll know," Garcia said.

CHAPTER 41

The sun was shining – I couldn't believe the brightness of it and the colors – so many blues and greens. The mountains were purple. The storms had cleared. I could see spring in the lightening days. The sun lit the high trees' branches into yellow chambers, halls and ballrooms for the birds, too quick for me to see.

I called the hospital. Maria was asleep. No visitors allowed. I turned on the radio on the way to work: "Eagles were stolen from the Natural History Museum, speculate they were killed and taken: Two golden eagles and one bald, the one-winged bald saved from an earlier gun shot. Shell casings, blood and feathers found in the eagle enclosure. Experts ask: What were the eagles taken for?"

Maria saved, clinging to life by modern medicine, I thought, and by Alicia's prayers. Her eagle was alive. Adelino's eagle was not stolen.

"They may have been stolen for their feathers," I heard as I turned off the radio to listen to the sounds of the ranch, to leave the rest outside. The sun shined on the rocks, the leaves. The birds were loud.

The old Chumash must have had a trained eagle–the priest a falconer too.

I needed to keep so much in my head. All that might be purposeful or causal — the bear clawing, secret projects, the museum, Harry's mysteries. And the Chumash — the mystery of all that disappeared, the enigmas of the collectors. What coincidence, what fate had brought me into a world that spoke so much of my husband's death? Back to my small town.

I came into this world and it was showing me the answers, whether I wanted or not. The direction of discovery — what was pulling me there? Curiosity? Harry's ghost? Maria's pain. I would find out where the answers were then send Garcia, not go myself. But I was tempted. What else was I living for?

Scott was back in San Francisco, I supposed. Middle of the week. Maria was stabbed Saturday or Sunday. Scott was here then. I felt fear. I looked around at the dusky files, rows of shadows and sun. The sun was still out.

The bear clawed Informant's father's horse, left strips of flesh. Informant's father disemboweled the bear with his knife and released it to die.

A bear cannot stand to see a pregnant woman without killing her.

Maria! I wanted to escape the Bear, I wanted out of this shed

When I got home the phone rang. I jumped at the bell. It was Greg. "It's my birthday, Emma. Come out for dinner, yes? I'll pick you up in my new car." No mention of Maria.

"Greg?" Automatically and, I hope, from fear, I began to make excuses. "No. I'm sorry. Rather late notice–"

"Come on. Emma, I've found something you want to see."

I was greedy to see more art and to help Alicia. I felt apart, too different from Maria to be in danger. So I agreed to see Greg.

I called Garcia.

"For Detective Garcia? Please tell me slowly."

"Emma Chase will be with Greg Lowell tonight at his house. At his father's house." I wondered if the message would ever reach him.

I wanted Garcia to know about me, to know enough about me to care about me. So I would be all right. His caring was so strong it was a respite and a beacon, even a widow on a case could feel it. I knew that was all I was, but I had fantasies of an uncle, a brother in him. I laughed at my face in the mirror, make-up on, as it softened at the thought of Garcia. "Dada." I mocked my smile with a doll's words, told with the pull of a string. Was I looking for a murderer or a family?

I felt safe going to see Greg – out in a restaurant. I would ask about the collection, praise it. It rivaled the de Cessac trove in Paris.

I felt better to have told Detective Garcia, even through the answering service.

Greg picked me up at my grandmother's. He waited outside in his same car and drove to a bar on the pier over the sea. From a table in an alcove the restaurant was dark, parties of couples, laughing loudly. The waiter took our orders and left us with drinks. Greg opened a ring box.

"I said before – you have great power. I can see it. Objects have power too. The sensitive can feel it. " He pulled the candle over to shine on the big ring in his palm. "Believe me, I know."

Greg put the ring, a large domed green stone with pointed diamonds on its two sides, in my hand. So much like Harry's mother's ring.

"Oh, my. What a gorgeous ring," I said and looked through the green. An emerald. Like Burmese cave air inside.

"Wear it," he said.

"Try it on to feel its power?" I put the ring on and it was heavy but well balanced. "I believe in the power of jewels. The yogis say big ones can cure you." I joked. He watched me.

"Whose ring is it?" I asked.

"Mine," Greg said.

"Birthday present?" I said as I took it off and reached across the table to give it to him. He wouldn't take it.

"This ring was my mother's engagement ring."

"Lucky lady," I said, not sure where this was leading. I held the ring open in my palm like a cube of sugar for a horse.

"I want you to wear it."

"Your mother's ring?"

"True. She didn't last long. She knew too much, couldn't do anything with it and went head first into the bottle. No help for a son, no stamina. I found my own, had to.

"It's for you," he said.

"Me? " I was shocked. Was he asking me to marry him? Out of the blue.

"No, I'm not proposing." He laughed so I felt better. "I just want you to wear the ring."

"For dinner? You want to share the power?" Why in the world would he give me his mother's ring? Squandering his inheritance? Stealing from his father? "I can't, Greg. I'm afraid I'll break it." He wouldn't hold out his hand.

"Wear it," he said. "Feel the future, our future when you wear this ring. This ring tells you more than your conscious mind knows now. Objects carry their own power and they can give it to the person who knows how to use them. My father used this ring to woo my mother, it can work again."

"Are you wooing me, Greg?" I asked gently, not wanting to trample toes, holding the ring like a frog about to leap.

"Of course I am, Emma," he said and put his hand on mine.

"Oh my," I said. Again I considered a proposal for a second before I found my excuse, which I believed so he would believe. "Greg, I'm a widow. Recently widowed. I'm observing the one year of mourning."

"Why? Old-fashioned idea -" he said. "Wastes time."

"Based on truth. Widows are too sad, too crazed to think straight about men. Right now, you don't interest me, as a man. I can't think that way," I said the words as I thought them and reached out to touch his arm. "I don't want to insult you. I can't think beyond my days and my work." And finding Harry's murderer so I can leave town, I thought but didn't say, hesitant to show the demons that drove me.

"So I must find cupid's bow," he said, picking up the light snaring ring. The anger I saw in him didn't scare me. I told him the truth. More than that I couldn't do. I thought he would realize that and forgive me. He wouldn't know about Scott, our nights together.

I toasted his happy birthday with wine and we finished dinner in near silence. Greg didn't drink, I did. Greg played with the round box that held the ring, and put it in his jacket pocket as we rose to leave.

Greg drove back to Montecito along the water and up the foothill roads. He said. "One day we will go up to the Camino Cielo, the road along the top of this ridge.

331

But we're in a hurry, aren't we? You want to see the cave? I have much more to show you."

Did he say cave? "Not tonight Greg. I've had enough of work, enough and I'm exhausted. This has been an emotional evening." I was an uneasy flatterer.

"No, Emma, you must. You need to see what I will show you. Trust me." He put his hand on my knee, then back on the gear shift, and drove faster.

"What do you want to show me?"

"You want to see the best pieces of my father's and my collection? Now's the time. Father is gone, so I can show you now."

"Will you tell me about it?" Talking he seemed less dangerous.

"No. I'll show you." I wanted to take the chance while his father was gone — find out for Alicia what was there and where it was. So I did not object. But he did not take me inside to the cabinets.

Greg parked behind the main house and we walked away from it into the clear and star-filled night. The Milky Way flowed and twisted and made it look like the Earth whirled fast in the night.

Greg stood very close beside me, his arm around me, too attentive. "Now we'll do what you've wanted." He guided me the way we were to go. Up a hilly lawn, into oak trees, tangled black branches. I saw the wall and I knew we walked toward the cave that Susan and I had seen from across the pond. Suddenly I was afraid, as if all the rules had changed, the world shifted on its axis.

"Not tonight. I have to go now, I'm not feeling well." I pulled away and Greg said "No." He took a knife from his boot and pointed it at my heart. He pushed me and I walked ahead of him, through the paths in the ivy and high hedge, following his directions – "Right, left, straight," trying to memorize the way. Trapped in a maze, disguised as a formal estate garden, I longed for people, for safety. The low stone walls and planting ended. I looked for the perimeter wall, for the chance of an escape from this garden. I could run. Did he have a gun? What part of me would he shoot? Head? Brain? Liver? Calf?

We entered a meadow, bounded by a tall stone wall. Above the field was a lighted grotto with statues of boys and lions. The stone work was so weird, sinister in its purposeful disorder – as if the builders, the stonemason and his master, had wanted to create a savage place and had done so by making it insanely off, jagged and confused. A waterfall fell beside the grotto into a pond.

"You feel the excitement don't you?" Greg was beside me, staring into my eyes, his fingers light on my back, the others on the knife.

"Tell me what you've found at Aunt Alicia's." Greg waited silent.

"A mystery. I'm puzzling out a civilization. Daunting."

"Animal references?"

"Can't we talk without the knife, Greg?"

"Can we?" Greg asked. "You have me confused."

You! I thought. I was swirling in chaos. He stopped us by the pool and I gazed into the water, moss outlined by stars.

"Many animal references." I felt I should keep talking.

"Bear?" He kept the knife out.

"No." I lied. "No bear, not yet. I've almost gotten to those boxes."

"So you don't know," Greg said. "Miles was right." The private investigator. His private investigator. Greg put away the knife and held me close. "Let's go."

333

He pushed me up the steps in the jagged rocks next to the waterfall to the level where Susan and I had crawled through the bushes to see the cave. The pond at this level was bigger, the cave a grotto, unreal. A concrete pathway ringed the water.

"You see my cousin Scott?"

"You were right, Greg. You warned me. He told me the story about his father," I said, panting at the top of the hill. The crickets and frogs were silent around us. Would Scott be there? Did Scott use Greg? Another bear?

"His father?" Greg snarled and grabbed me to walk around the pond next to him.

"Raping him, camping."

"He claims that?" Greg mocked, and tightened his grip. "That was my father, my initiation," Greg said. "My story, his loss." Jesus, I thought. Who was I to believe and why any of them?

"Your father?"

"My father's hands were so big. Mine could never be that big. Because of my mother."

The cave was dark in front of us, a hole in a huge rock face. Greg pulled me into the deep grotto that made an entrance and I saw it hid the real cave. The cave had bars at its mouth. Greg pushed a button under a rock ledge and a metal curtain rolled open so I could see beyond the bars. I could see objects on shelves, crowded shapes. It felt like something was captive behind those bars. The objects were practically humming. I thought there could be live things in there. Greg smiled at me and pushed another button. The bars rose, clanged, pulling up into the rock.

Greg pushed me in, lit a lantern that made a twilight. Jade jaguar stool with emerald eyes looked at me. Teeth

334

barred, tail curved under. I stayed still. The grate was still open.

He moved closer, I tried to twirl away and could not.

Greg faced me in the alcove, very close, as if to whisper tendernesses. "Go in, I'll show you."

Arm around me roughly, he pulled me sideways. My feet followed sideways so I didn't fall. Then he held me close to him.

In his arms, I felt an insistence more like violence than sex demanding me to let him take me to a place I didn't know. He pulled my shirt up, above my breasts cold in the night air. His fingers squeezed my nipples hard then unbuttoned my skirt and let it drop.

"Miles said you found your husband's photos," Greg said. His hands found every hole and hurt me.

Shit, I thought. Where was I?

"We will join our powers.

"Harry's power was facile, too bred-in, couldn't join with him. Fuck him, yeah, but not a dynasty. You...you just trick me like Maria did, we will have children. I will raise them." Horrible thought.

"He only pretended interest in the Bear, to be with me. Isn't that pathetic. Before him was the spectacle, the proof of supernatural power, the ritual of acquired power, my family's power, and he was willing to be a part of it because he wanted to fuck me."

I flinched.

"Or be fucked by me. He was in love with me. I have that effect on people, don't I, Emma?"

"You do."

"You want to fuck me too."

"Let me see what you have first, it will excite me, Greg, I admire how you've collected, Greg," Flattery.

"My father found, I hunted." He jerked me with him.

"Have you been initiated?" I asked. Silence from him.

"Does the Bear bring you power?" I asked.

He looked sexy, lowered eyes, slow voice. "You laugh," he flexed his fingers.

"I've found the notes. The old Chumash knew of it, the soaring, the visions–" I stared at him, my peripheral vision peeled for an escape. Chumash treasures on shelves all along the walls. "Have you? The feeling must be amazing." I tried for admiration in the voice that sounded rushed, squeaky. Naked. "You know the rituals?"

Greg nodded, staring at me close in profile, like a snake. "You know the recipes for the datura?" I said. The poison plant they used for visions. "For 'ayip?"

"Alum and rattlesnake. There she is–" A rattlesnake dozed in a big cage. "Rattlesnake tail. She lets me harvest her tail for my potion."

"Do you purify yourself to use it safely?"

"I don't purify."

He still held me like a rough date as if we were going someplace and had to stay together. I kept talking.

"I've found another.'Both the ritual and the recipe must stay apart and secret, until an antap with enough power comes.' That's what I read." Now he heard.

"The recipe is the key to the power and only for an antap worthy and ready." I saw him covet, the face was transparent with longing. How badly did he want the recipe for the potion and the incantation? Where was the knife? Was there a gun?

"Might you be the one to use the power?" My language tried to ice him.

"Bull shit." He turned away for a second to light a candle on the wall. "You have more to see."

336

He pushed me in front of him. "Go first, I'll be sure you don't get lost."

I stumbled along beside him toward the back of the cave. His arm hurt my shoulders. I had no skirt. I had to get out alive. Who was going to rescue me? Or was this it? Where I met Harry, in the final moments. I could not afford resignation.

Greg whispered, "You know I want to marry you and you see the wisdom of saying yes, now. But I warn you, I get carried away in here."

Greg pushed me down and lit a hanging lantern. A grizzly bear head and thick long fur rested on a woven reed bear, like ancient Japanese armor. On the table before it was a bear paw with human fingers making the claws. I barely looked. I didn't think about them. Escape! was all I could feel. Later I remembered, felt how my stomach turned, how my heart screamed, muscles sore from panic. I was almost naked and freezing from terror.

He kept talking, first like he was telling me a sexy story, then incantatory. "I can sit inside the bear. I can walk as the Bear. My father's bearskin. Now it is mine. I killed my father tonight. The tough son of a bitch." Greg put on a net shirt of cane, took off his pants and came over to me, erect.

"We rode into the mountains. My father drank. An owl hooted. Silence. You are the last Grizzly. At his command I stood, and roared, a grizzly."

"'Son of the grizzly bear, Son of the grizzly bear!' Greg yelled, he shook me, hatred coloring the handsome face to ugliness. Then he dropped me. Greg's inner focus was so strong, I thought he had forgotten about me.

In my dream I ran ahead of him across the field into the brush. I tripped on torn bark, ignored the pain of the thorns and sharp sticks. Behind me I could hear him grunting to catch me.

Greg staggered over to me.

"Then, Father finished his bottle, broke it, the man. He crawled, crawled over to me and rose the bear.

Greg made me rise up. "Father whispered," Greg whispered into my ear, his hands on my bottom. "I listened to the words. I was a boy, I knew I had to learn, to grow up and be a man."

"'I am the bear. You must have my power. You will be the last grizzly bear, fierce and alone,'

"Then my father poked my ass." Greg stuck his finger, no longer caressing, roughly into me and I cried out, "with his penis." He turned me, ripped away my underwear, crushed my back to him and hooked me with a hard thrust. "plunged it up into me" he pushed, he pushed and grunted. "I was a child, I screamed." He panted, and pounded. "Last grizzly bear, stabbed but not dead."

God, how did I get into this. I was terrified and hurt. "Not dead. Not dead. Not dead, grizzly bear. Ahhh." He moved his hips to his words, in and out.

I was writhing in pain and mortified. I had to get away and I couldn't. He was hurting me. I cried.

"My father fucked me and ranted."

Greg dropped me with a laugh and paced below the lantern. "I only give it in the ass, except to Maria, she guided me wrong, thinks I'll be happy about a baby."

I lay still and listened for an escape. Clean air, night sounds, frogs, crickets, rain. Greg's voice got lower and louder, that other voice: "'You are the last Grizzly. You must defend the treasure.'"

I tried to close myself, pull into a safe ball.

Greg looked over at me and I froze trying to be invisible.

"After the first time, it didn't hurt me. Then he began to burn me, so he got hard, but I learned not to hurt there anymore. You'll like it too." He looked at me to show me I was not forgotten. "Some women like to be spiked. They have orgasms as we push it in. "

"Datura? You take datura first?" I asked. Drug save me.

"No," Greg said. "I have better."

"I found the Chumash recipe. The one that sends you to an edge beyond the edges humans can reach. "

"I find edges," he said. He took a long thick knife with a small curved point from the table with the bear paws. I pretended not to see it. See no evil. I was desperate. And could not beg.

"I'll kill Alicia then I'll take the notes I want."

Greg poked the tips of his fingers with the tip of the knife. "People like edges. They volunteer." He looked up at me staring at him. "They do. Harry found out, he volunteered. He wanted to be tied up. I had my boys sucking and poking him to his distraction, then I cut, then he saw what he had volunteered for. The penultimate voyage of discovery. Gone. Launched into the ultimate. As you will be."

"I do not volunteer," I said.

"Doesn't matter," he said.

"You see," he said calmly. "Maria didn't die, so now you must—she will tell you. She loves you."

Oh God.

"I'll take you away from here. They'll never connect my cave to you. You can derail a train."

339

"I never do it in here, not even the final rites, not any. You know I can fuck you before and after, you'll still be warm. Feel you off to Hell."

And I ran. Jumped up and ran to the mouth of the cave, swimming for speed with my arms crashing baskets around me. I was running for my life.

Greg caught me and threw me to the ground. I crawled.

We were almost to the cave door. Tables, shelves, feathered poles. Could I hide?

"I have a question for you." I crawled. I could still speak. "Does a wife share in the power?"

"You're the expert," he flipped his thumb on the blade. We were in the cave mouth, on the soft dirt of the cave's open ledge above the pond.

I was ready to do anything to live. In my dream I heard the shot and saw him fall. Garcia knew I was with Greg. Would he rescue me?

"A wife with the recipe and the old knowledge might share in the power, right?" I said and sat down. I couldn't run faster than him. "You offered me your mother's ring. Am I too late to accept? Think of the family ties–a merger of fortunes and breeding." I leaned back on my elbows opening my heart – Could it escape? What lived on? – pushing out my breasts, curving my pelvis to receive.

"You flatter yourself," Greg said. He walked over to the bearskin. He bowed to the bear's head, hanging like a helmet on its stand. He slipped under the bear's fur, hung the arms over his chest. He slipped his arms under the heavy bearskin arms. He reached to pull the bear head over his.

Then he put on the bear head. "The dance of the bear. Owls watch him. Crickets shut up when he passes. Deer scramble away. I will show you the dance of the bear. I warn: If you speak I will bite you. The others never knew that rule, so you, who may be my bride, know more than anyone, you know how to behave to live."

Greg panted, he stooped and his head waved as if light. His eyes were calm as if his purpose was sure. Greg's boot crushed a rock into the cave dirt, so heavy he was as a bear. He sweated under the skin. Under the fur Greg began to dance. Gourd rattles hung over his chest, I heard them as he moved.

Suddenly I noticed the wall, like an amphibian rising up beside the pond. I could find an escape, hidden foot holds over and out of this man's hell.

Again I ran, out of the cave. He came toward me roaring in anger. I grabbed for the wall. A rock was loose, sized to grip and long. I whirled with it against his head. When I heard the crack I knew I was saved. He fell sideways, pulled off balance by the bearskin. His eyes open, his head bleeding, he stayed down, the bearskin under him. I pushed him with my hands and with my feet and he rolled into the pond. The moss on the water opened up, the bearskin sunk after him and then the moss closed again. I saw no bubbles. A frog jumped away.

The wall, I had to get over the wall and away. I guessed on what side of the blackness it rose and I stumbled toward it. I crawled along the outer wall, my hair ripped and my hands bloody, gulping the air like water. I found the escape in the old stones and climbed, scratched, blood dripping down my face. Vines caught my feet. Broken glass along the top of the wall was cleared at the escape. I pulled myself up and crawled over, with a thanks to the workmen who built the wall and those who kept the old knowledge of the place and left the exit open.

I walked the miles down the road to my grand-mother's, hiding in the bushes when cars passed. If one was Garcia I did not see it. I went in the back gate and sat on a bench crying. I survived the nightmare. The money, the privilege, the isolation, people without boundaries, allowed, twisted, with no rules that applied to them.

CHAPTER 42

Spider webs. In the day light I ducked spider webs, lace of waterdrops across the paths, shining in the rare sun. Dark, after running home I was covered in spider webs across my face, over my head, my neck, my chest. I broke through the strong silk this night. Did the spiders come with the webs? Stay with me?

In a blanket from the closet, wrapped up, I waited for dawn. I paced on the slippery grass up and down the terraces. How could I have let myself be in that cave, be taken there? Was it my fault? Harry's path was too dangerous yet I searched for it, and followed when I found it. I survived the man at the bottom of the pond. I was left alive to wonder. Was it my fault? Harry's fault to lead me there? Did I need to atone?

Birds told me the pale-ing of the dark was real. I buttoned a wool dress over what was left of my torn clothes and drove to Alicia's ranch to tell her what I'd seen and done.

Magdalena came in drowsy when I called from the kitchen. She went upstairs to get Alicia after only a look at me. I waited in the sunroom in a cold panic. I felt in waves the calmness of revenge exacted, justice done. I didn't matter.

When Alicia sat to listen to me, it was as if I described another myth, as if I were relating to her a symbolic pattern, the shape of an inevitable tale. My mind was adrift in déjà vu. I felt the walls and glances and words reverberate between the past and present as I tried to tell Alicia with plain words what I had seen and done, words that were already there, already said before and again. I found the story for her as I paced from door to door. I was in shock.

"I saw the jaguar, Alicia -"

"You got in -"

"A grizzly bear skin and human fingers. Greg was there, with his knife. He showed me. Fingers."

"You escaped?" Alicia asked.

"I hit his head with a rock. The bear skin pulled him down. Then I pushed him. I left him there in the pond. Under the water.

"I had to. He was going to kill me." I walked back and forth, glad for a big room, the wood floors squeaking with my steps. "He told me he killed his father." I looked at her for her shock. Did she looked pleased, relieved? "He said now the power was all his. Since Maria didn't die, he said, I must." I sat down and stared at my hands. "Fingers." I hiccupped over and over. "What if they find the father and think I did it all."

"I'll call my brother. Manuel knows the policemen from high school. He'll know who to call." She sat at her desk and dialed the telephone. "Manuel, come here, will you? I need to talk to you, for your advice. Now, my heart. Yes. Good. Soon." She hung up and sighed. I had stopped hiccupping and rocked in the deep corner of the sofa.

Alicia rang and Magdalena brought hot coffee.

"You keep warm, Emma." Alicia took a soft blanket from a carved chest and put it over my shoulders and my knees. Alicia brushed my hair off my forehead and smoothed the back of my head.

"I ran home for a car and came here. I haven't told anyone. In the cave, those must have been your treasures. Greg is in the pond."

What shall I do? I asked her with my eyes, I felt she knew so I should stay there.

"We need advice. I'll call Scott." She took up the black phone again. "Please tell my son to come home now. I need him. It's an emergency." She hung up. "That'll get him. He worries about me."

Alicia called again and spoke Spanish, "Adelino, ven con hombres, por favor." Would she send in her men to get the treasures? The body? Greg.

"Skeff, I need you over here. Now, yes." Alicia hung up and looked at me watching her. "He's the best connected of us."

"What about Garcia?"

Adelino came first. "My nephews are outside with the truck, Senora," he said.

"Ask Juan to get my car and be ready to take Emma home. Ask Magdalena to give the others coffee and have them wait." She led him across the room to the other side of her desk and they spoke where I could not hear them.

I held my face in my hands, hiding. Any calm was leaving me. I heaved and gasped for air. Skeff walked in, looked at Alicia and came over to me. He sat beside me with his thin arm along my shoulders and his big hand clasped me so hard I was startled into breathing.

Alicia and Adelino returned to the light around the sofas.

Frogs croaked in the grey dawn and the wind blew with the fragrance of sage and wild lilac, a wind off the mountains. A wind shift.

"Skeff, it's Emma's story. She can tell the details. Greg Lowell, George's son, tried to kill Emma. Emma says he's dead, drowned in the pool at his father's. He has a cave on that land. Emma said inside the cave were terrible things. And treasures. My families' cache, stolen years ago." Alicia's voice died and the tree frogs squeaked.

"Your watch?" Skeff asked. Alicia nodded.

"I'm sending Adelino to retrieve my treasures. I want my pieces out before the law descends." Alicia stood and looked like the rancher she was. Determined, ready to face it and at home with disaster and danger.

"Alicia, dear heart, Greg who?" Skeff asked. "Who are we talking about?"

"Greg Lowell."

"Good God." Skeff's answer was a long thought. Then to me: "He tried to kill you?"

"Yes. He showed me human fingers. It's all there. In the cave."

"I'm going in to get my family's treasure," Alicia said.

"Alicia, hold your horses." Skeff was deceptively light, elegant. "Sit down, Alicia. Think. Don't compound an old mistake. Family, Alicia. Scott, your son, is the only living Lowell heir. It will all be yours anyway, or Scott's. Legal heirs."

Alicia paused to listen. "You see disbelief. Why should I believe in this law that has cheated my people so often? He could have a will. They both have wills."

"Alicia, dear, If there's a bequest elsewhere, we'll sue and prove it's yours. Or I'll buy the collection for my library and it will all be available. You can take it out. You can be responsible for its care." Alicia sat disquieted. Adelino stood behind her chair and stared at me. Open dark eyes staring to see who I was.

"I hit his head with a long rock, like a pinata. I pushed him into the water. He didn't come up."

"Why?" Skeff put his arm around me, solid, like a coach. I breathed deep the tweed and leather smell of an older man and wondered again for a fleet instant if that was what a father felt like.

"Why, Emma?" Skeff asked again, his face close to mine, his eyes looking for me inside my shock.

"He had people's fingers on a bear claw. He told me he killed Harry. He raped me. He was taking me away to use his knife on me. I had to." Angry. No tears. I wanted Skeff to understand the inevitability, my justification. Skeff looked to Alicia for comment and held me tighter. "Sounds like you were a lucky one." I heaved and cried my first tears.

"You got him." Skeff kissed my head, gave me his soft handkerchief. "Who do we call first?" He stood to pace. "Have you told Claudia?" he asked, stopping suddenly.

"No. I came here," I said, feeling myself back in the tall bushes, panting, running, afraid to ask anyone for help.

Alicia came over to me and held her hand on my head, so I had to hold very still and began to feel my exhaustion.

"Adelino's nephew is ready to take her home. I think it's best. Emma? You must be tired. Skeff?"

"I'll take Emma. Warn Claudia I'm coming," Skeff said to Alicia and roused me from my rest under her touch.

347

"Now?" I did not want to tell my grandmother the story. She wasn't a part of this world. She didn't want me to suffer. I wanted her to be where I could go and be free of this burden. I thought there might be such a place, foolish.

Alicia handed me her telephone and I dialed, picturing my Gran in her cream and nightgown unaware of the nightmare I was to bring to her.

"Gran, it's Emma. Mr. Skeffington is here -" I couldn't go on. Skeff took the phone. "Claudia, it's me. I'm bringing Emma home. Yes. No, she's all right. Upset, but she'll be all right. We'll be there in a few minutes."

"The police?" Skeff asked.

"Manuel will call," Alicia said. "My brother is an old friend of Detective Garcia."

I knew better. I took the phone from Skeff and dialed my cop's number.

"Garcia, it's Emma Chase. I found the cave. And the fingers. He was going to kill me too, and I hit him. Greg Lowell. He's in the pond. He said he killed his father."

Alicia looked at me. I saw her curse. This was no longer her secret. Would she have to battle in public for her treasure?

"I'll be at home," I said to the policeman. I wanted the law to forgive me. I needed to tell my story early and clearly. Not to run and hide.

The ride home was cold. I shivered in my whole body. Skeff covered me with the two lap blankets from the leather pouch along the back of the front seat and sat close to me as his driver drove us across the valley to my grandmother's. The day was dawning clear.

Claudia was at the front door in a long robe dress from a Forties movie, her hair loose down her back.

Chapter 42

"My Claudia," Skeff said. "I'll tell her, Emma." He took my arm and walked me up to the front door and handed me to a confused and worried Gran. "Is there someone to draw Emma a bath?"

"I'll do it. Skeff. Come in. You remember the library? Down the hall on the left. There's coffee. I'll meet you there. Come dear. Let me put you in a warm bath."

I followed Gran up the curved stairs, my hand waving along the railing, a child, losing my mind, relieved to be following.

Whatever might happen, what nightmares might come, and guilt and sin, I had killed Harry's murderer. Harry would not come back for it, but I was free of that obligation. I had the unknowable future to deny the cost.

Clothed in the webs and not much else, I tried to undress and the webs clung to me, strong, invisible. For days I found raveling web on me.

In the bath I was hidden in thick bubbles from myself and the cold air. As I sank down, the bubbles cleared around my body, reminding me of moss. I wanted to disappear, to forget about life, the reality that danced around me with menace and somebody else's purpose. I went under the too hot water until my nose rested in the steam. I saved myself. Like the brass lock on my bedroom door when I was a child I escaped, and this time, he paid. The man paid. Did that mean I felt like a victor instead of a victim?

The water got cold before it swallowed me up. I fell asleep, head nodded forward until the bath took on the day's chill and woke me. I dressed over-warm, as if I were in the snow and in slippers went downstairs for a drink.

First I checked the library. Skeff was there, his arm around Claudia as it had been around me at Alicia's. Her

349

head fit on his shoulder with a comfort that made her look like a girl and she stared off and did not hear me.

I took a glass of water and an apple from the empty kitchen and went out onto the round porch with the columns and high sky blue roof. I heard frogs and birds and a car.

What would the world do with me? What would God do with me, what would Life do with me now that I'd caused a death? I hit him, I pushed him in. I could have tried to pull him up. I stood there and watched the stagnant pool still itself around him. I began to imagine him somewhere on the bottom as the life left him.

Skeff scared me at my elbow. "The telephone is for you," he said. "Claudia's all right. I've called home for my man to bring me a case. Claudia has given me the lilac room," he said as I listened to the telephone and heard Scott say,

"Emma, you're OK?"

I couldn't answer yes.

"Emma are you there? It's Scott. I spoke to Mother."

His voice was so close I could feel him. I was afraid I would fear him. Another man, what did he do in private?

But his voice reminded me that I knew.

"Emma?" I hadn't spoken. "Say something."

"Scott."

"Emma, go to bed and stay there. Let Skeff and Alicia take care of you. Go to sleep, no dreams. Let me talk to Skeff again."

"I'll have to find him."

"Please."

Who was Scott? What did he know of his cousin's collection?

"Scott? "

"Don't talk. Go to sleep."

"Once I find Skeff."

He was in the library, holding Claudia's hands. She looked at me as if I had come from another time, then with concern and pity. I felt the sucking fear that no one would ever see just me, without my tragedies as definition.

"Emma, dear, I'm so sorry." She came over to me and held my hand.

"I'm going to bed, Gran. Don't worry." I kissed Claudia's cheek. Skeff nodded with the telephone and stood against the curtain. I wished I could kiss him, but raised my hand to say goodbye and stumbled up the stairs. Fatigue rose up and grabbed me and I barely made it to the bed.

CHAPTER 43

The afternoon sun was low in the window–I opened an eye to see it shine onto me then slept on in its warmth. I felt drugged, ready to sleep for days, certainly the rest of that day.

My dreams were that I was awake, doing what I should have been doing that day, but slower and to another purpose.

France, I could go to France where the stories weren't mine, those were my first thoughts when I awoke and remembered. Escape, another flight to flee.

I had my life. I followed Harry as far as I could, and I learned I wanted my life. More life. I escaped, not yet bound, like Harry in trust or in a game. I saved myself and got my revenge by my desperation. Now for the consequences. I wanted them all to go away, to release me from this story.

"Emma," Scott's voice and his body next to mine. I thought the dream, then woke, startled away then held close and steady by the real man so I fell in and relaxed and pressed into the parts between us where the pieces fit, we fit and I was hidden and not alone.

The next time I woke he was there patting my back. When I woke again he was gone and I got up.

Was he a dream? I knew the horrors of the night before were real, all else thrown into question. Today's warmth, the holding on, the breaths, it could have been a dream. I'd met secret lovers in my dreams before. I wanted to fall back to sleep, Rip Van Winkle, let the time pass over me and away, but I was curious.

I stared at my childhood pillow, the needlework deeply familiar, the threads of the designs gone, the needle marks barely there, worn away by my baby affection. I was a child and had been shocked into adulthood. I almost lost my life. I saved my life. I felt strong.

Dressed in slacks and a sweater and loafers, not the demure hose and skirt of a murder suspect, God, what was I to do? All I knew was to tell the truth. I'd seen enough movies where the story only got worse with delay and evasion. It was self-defense. I had to count on justice and powerful friends to keep me out of jail and court. Would I have to go to court?

Scott was in the breakfast room. "Your grandmother is in the garden with Skeff. She doesn't seem too worried about you. I am," Scott said as he pulled out my chair.

I trembled as my body began to remember the day before. I sat down on the yellow damask cushion, my eyes on the Chinese wallpaper. I could tell from Scott's expression how bad I looked.

"Eat. You need your strength." He put his hand over mine then took it away to let me eat.

"Is Garcia coming? Will he take me to jail?" I asked Scott. Who could tell me? Was he in the next room? Was this my last meal? A croissant and coffee didn't France make.

"I don't think they'll take you in," Scott said. "Mother has my uncle on the case-"

"Another uncle?"

"Her brother. The California side. His connections in this town are legendary. But he didn't know about Greg. He's in touch with lawyers to be sure the Chumash pieces come back."

"I need a lawyer."

The doorbell rang and Gran's maid came to the breakfast room.

"The detective is here to see you, Miss Emma."

"Tell him you need to talk to your lawyer first," Scott said. He stood quickly and held my arm as I rose. "I'll come with you?" he asked.

"No. I know Garcia. I'll be OK."

"Listen to what he has to say and admit nothing,"

"I know what I did."

"Don't tell them."

Scott was adamant. He came with me to the study, lined with old books and wood boxes. Garcia stood in the door at the far end looking out on the pool and the rose garden.

"Mrs. Chase. And Mr.?"

"Lowell, Scott."

"Oh?"

"Emma works for my mother. Perhaps you know my Uncle Manuel."

"Perhaps. And you."

"Well, I'm a friend of Mrs. Chase and I'm a lawyer -"

"Mrs. Chase's lawyer?"

"No."

"Well, if you'll excuse us, I have a few questions and some news for Mrs. Chase that she may or may not want to share with you."

"Scott can stay," I said.

"No he may not," Garcia said.

"I'm OK, Scott. I'll be right out."

He left after a kiss on my cheek.

"What's your news?" Garcia asked.

"You tell me," I asked. "Please."

"We found Greg Lowell drowned with a blow to his head. Probably hit his head falling and lost consciousness and drowned," Detective Garcia told me. "We've pulled the body out. His father was dead in the house."

"He said that. He said he'd killed his father -"

"Greg did?" Garcia wasn't believing me yet.

"He said it. Go look at his cave, his gruesome souvenirs-"

"You were there?" Garcia said.

"Yes," I answered. "I left a message."

"Last night?"

"Yes."

"What happened?"

"Greg took me there to show me his Chumash collection. Then he talked about Harry, fucking him, murdering him. And he said, 'Since Maria didn't die' he said, he was going to kill me. Maria would tell me."

"We found a collection of fingers—We haven't I.D.'ed them yet."

Then I let myself admit that when I saw the fingers, I looked for something that looked like Harry and saw only sausages with nails.

"The photo of the dead girl in the pond. Looks like the same pond."

"Yes."

"What happened, Mrs. Chase."

"He took me there with a knife. He raped me. Sodomized. He was going to kill me. I hit him with a rock and pushed him into the pond. He said he killed his father -"

"We found him too, smothered and cut up. You didn't see the father?"

"No. Greg told me he was dead. An obstacle was cleared from his path."

"Where was this path supposed to lead him?" Garcia asked.

"I don't know."

Garcia stayed silent.

"Greg believed in the Chumash powers. He had the stolen tools. He thought he knew how to use them," I said. "But what he wanted the powers for I don't know," I said.

"Why did you kill him?"

"To save my life. Didn't you find the knife?"

"Yes."

"It was for me this time- I had to get away -so I found a loose rock, hit him and he fell."

"Greg Lowell fell as he was chasing you."

"Yes. With the goddamn knife."

"That should take care of it." His eyes were so beautiful brown as his face smiled around them. "You have made Montecito safer." Garcia looked at me and squeezed my shoulder kindly as he shook my hand. "No need for you to come down for testing." I'd bathed, tried to wash everything away.

Garcia left. He knew I would call him if I needed him.

Scott came back into the dark library. The afternoon outside was so bright the windows seemed to look out on only light. "What did he say?" Scott asked after waiting a few seconds for me to volunteer.

"He'll take care of it."

"How?"

"With the truth. Greg was chasing me with the knife he used on his father, on Harry – I hit his head and he fell into the pond."

"Shit. You're O.K.?"

"I am alive, totally gratefully alive." I realized the truth as I said it.

I wanted to spend weeks in bed with him.

Scott stood right next to me, arm a warm fit over my shoulders. We looked out the dark room and stared across the lawns and trees to the ocean.

Scott asked me "Come up to the city, stay with me. You can hide out. Play house. I have the room." I looked at him. Young, earnest eyes willing to take me in.

"Your fiancée?" I asked to his mouth. I couldn't say no if I looked at his eyes again.

"She's out of the picture," he said. He reached for me with his chin, calling for a kiss.

"I don't believe you," I ducked.

With his back to the light he was a shape, dark on one side, rimmed by sun. Scott brought me out of the shadows.

"She can be gone. She has many suitors," he said.

He kissed my cheek. I ached but waited for him to stop, arms down. He was a magnet puzzle where all my pieces fit.

I could stay, live on with Gran in her beautiful place. Alicia's work could go deeper and deeper. I could watch Skeff and Gran find each other again. The longing I felt for Scott was for the most fun, the most life. Was Scott a future?

"You need someone with you now," he said, husky as I was beginning to swell with desire for him. My body wanted him more than my mind, my will. He put

357

his face in my neck. He had one hand in the pocket of my back, debonair.

My work in the files was almost done. I dug out the first steps up the mountain to the puzzle of all that Michael Harrington saved. The mysteries in that trove I left to others. "I have another week to finish your mother's job and then I'll go to France."

Scott seemed jolted. "Paris?"

I lost Harry and my Montecito. What was I to do with my favorite places become dangerous? Could I walk down a Paris street again? Over a bridge? Could I go to the cherry orchard, breathe in my lost life? My dear one.

Scott held me, ribs crushing, sad, as if we had to grab the chance.

"How can you leave me? We've found each other" He spoke into my hair. "This whole world and we met —"

"I'm the girl next door, not counting orchards." I didn't want to move my face off his arm.

"You need comfort and safety" Scott pulled away and stood beside me. He had let go.

I lived alone until I found Harry. I could protect myself. I had the bravery of youth, though I felt older then than I ever would.

"I'm planning a long engagement." Scott held his hand on the top of my head until it was warm, then held my hand. "It all may change —"

"I'll go back to the country. I can come back when I am more of me. Scott, may I borrow your boat? I'll take good care of her. Keep the lines supple.""

He didn't want to say yes and give over his fine sea chariot. "O.K." I guess he felt sorry for me. And was relieved I wouldn't be moving in on his life. I trusted we would meet again out in the world.

To love myself enough to forgive and keep going. That was the modest power I could take from Montecito. That and vigilance. I knew the world was not safe, no matter how beautiful.

I was the victor, not the victim: Did I learn victory is power? Not carved animals. But I'm afraid. I left there afraid and I'm still afraid. I might be afraid all my life.

What do I let that do to me?

****

ACKNOWLEDGEMENTS

The scholars whose books and periodicals are listed below also informed and inspired me.

Anderson, Eugene N., Jr., The Chumash Indians of Southern California, Banning, California, Malki Museum Press, 1968. Print.

Blackburn, Thomas C., ed. December's Child, A book of Chumash Oral Narratives Collected by J.P. Harrington, Berkeley and Los Angeles, California, University of California Press, 1975. Print.

Gibson, Robert O., The Chumash, New York, Philadelphia, Chelsea House Publishers, 1991. Print.

Hudson, Travis, Janice Timbrook and Melissa Rempe, ed. Tomol: Chumash Watercraft as Described in the Ethnographic Notes of John P. Harrington, Santa Barbara, California, Ballena Press. Anthropological Papers 10, as quoted in California's Chumash Indians, Santa Barbara Museum of Natural History, San Luis Obispo, California, EZ Nature Books, 1986. Print.

Hudson, Travis, Guide to Painted Cave, Santa Barbara, California, McNally & Loftin, 1982. Print.

Hudson, Travis, Underhay, Ernest, <u>Crystals in the Sky: An Intellectual Odyssey Involving Chumash Astronomy, Cosmology and Rock Art</u>, Santa Barbara, California, Ballena Press, 1978. Print.

Laird, Carobeth, <u>Encounter with an Angry God, Recollections of My Life with John Peabody Harrington</u>, Banning, California, Malki Museum Press, 1975. Print.

Lee, Georgia, Ph. D., <u>The Chumash Cosmos, Effigies, Ornaments, Incised Stones and Rock Paintings of the Chumash Indians</u>, Arroyo Grande, California, Bear Flag Books, 1981, 1997. Print.

Miller, Bruce W., <u>Chumash, A Picture of Their World</u>, Los Osos, California, Sand River Press, 1988. Print.

Rogers, David Banks, <u>Prehistoric Man of the Santa Barbara Coast</u>, Santa Barbara, California, Santa Barbara Museum of Natural History, 1929. Print.

Timbrook, Jan, <u>Chumash Ethnobotany, Plant Knowledge Among the Chumash People of Southern California</u>, Santa Barbara, California, Santa Barbara Museum of Natural History, Berkeley, California, Heyday, 2007. Print.

Tompkins, Walker A., <u>Old Spanish Santa Barbara</u>, Santa Barbara, California, McNally and Loftin, 1967. Print.

Tompkins, Walker A., <u>Santa Barbara Past and Present</u>, Santa Barbara, California, Tecolote Books, 1975. Print.

Tompkins, Walker A., <u>Santa Barbara History Makers</u>, Santa Barbara, California, McNally & Loftin, 1983. Print.

The quotations of the myths on my pages 129, 138, 139, 154, 164, 165, 221, 296, 311, 312, 325 and 328 are from:

Blackburn, Thomas C., ed. <u>December's Child, A Book of Chumash Oral Narratives collected by J. P. Harrington</u>, Berkeley and Los Angeles California, University of California Press, 1975. Print.

The song on p.154, sung to launch the Tomol canoe is from: Hudson, Travis, Janice Timbrook and Melissa Rempe, ed. Tomol: Chumash Watercraft as Described in the Ethnographic Notes of John P. Harrington. Santa Barbara, California, Ballena Press. Anthropological Papers 10, as quoted in <u>California's Chumash Indians</u>, Santa Barbara Museum of Natural History, San Luis Obispo, California, EZ Nature Books, 1986. Print.

CPSIA information can be obtained
at www.ICGtesting.com
Printed in the USA
FSHW011055170119
55052FS